I DON'T WANT YOU BACK

BY:
CHENELL PARKER

Prologue I

"**R**edd is out here looking for you Candy Girl!" one of the other dancers walked into the dressing room and yelled.

"Okay, tell him I'll be out in a minute," Faryn replied with a sigh.

Candy Girl, the name that Faryn had grown to hate, was given to her by the owner of the strip club that she'd worked at for the past four years. The same name that all the customers knew her by. Thankfully, Faryn was working her last and final shift at the smoke-infested hole in the wall. In one more week, she would be walking across the stage and receiving the master's degree that she'd worked so hard to obtain. She'd already received her bachelor's degree two years before, but she wanted to take it a step further. Financial aid and her job as a waitress helped her out a lot, until the restaurant where she worked started cutting her hours. Faryn was already living in a rundown apartment where she paid weekly rent, but there was no way that she could afford a roof over her head and school too. That was until one of her customers slipped her a card about making some extra cash on the side by dancing a few nights a week at a popular strip club in the uptown area of New Orleans. It was a no brainer for Faryn and she showed up to audition the very same night. Not only was she given the job, but the owner made her one of the opening acts.

"Girl, you made a killing out there for your final show. I'm gonna miss you, boo," Slim, one of the other dancers, walked in and said.

"I'm gonna miss y'all too, but I damn sure won't miss this place," Faryn admitted.

"Redd is gonna lose his mind when you leave. That nigga been coming in here for a whole year, just to see you. He doesn't give anybody else the time of day," Slim replied.

"I know, but he better find himself another favorite," Faryn said.

"Girl, you must be crazy. That nigga be breaking too much bread for you to just walk away like that. You should keep in contact with him," Slim advised.

"You know the rules, Slim. No real names and no personal relationships. I already fucked up by messing with him outside of the club. JB would have fired my ass if he ever found out about that," Faryn noted.

"Yeah, you're right about that," Slim said as she sat down at the vanity right next to Faryn.

Faryn looked in the mirror at the light coat of makeup that she'd just applied to her face and was satisfied with the outcome. Most of the girls wore pounds of cosmetics on their faces, but Faryn didn't need it. She had a natural beauty, even though she didn't always feel like it. Life hadn't always been kind to Faryn, but she was thankful anyhow. She'd come far and beat some of the odds that were stacked against her.

At only twenty-six years old, Faryn had seen her fair share of heartbreak and tragedy. Being raised by a drug-addicted mother and grandmother was only one of many things that she had to endure and overcome. A generation of curses was what she called it and she made it a point to break it. Her grandmother, Eunice, had introduced her mother to drugs at a young age, but Faryn was stronger than that. Eunice had died of a drug overdose and her one and only daughter had met the same fate only five years later.

Faryn didn't have anyone, but she'd learned to take care of herself when she was only twelve years old. Their house had become the local whore house with different men coming and going to support her mother, Alisha's, crack addiction. Faryn hated to hear her mother's moans of pleasure all throughout the night, but she was thankful that Alisha used her own body instead of hers. Some of Faryn's friends hadn't been so lucky and their innocence was taken from them at no fault of their own. She still had to fend for herself because Alisha spent every dime that she had to support her out of control habit. There was never any food in the house and all the electronics that they'd ever owned had been pawned a long time ago. Thankfully, rental assistance took care of the rent and lights, or they would have been homeless as well. Some of the men that Alisha entertained had a heart and would sometimes bring fast food for Faryn to eat whenever they came over. Some of the others just didn't give a damn about Alisha and they cared even less about her child.

Faryn was cool either way. She had her own thing going and she kept a few dollars in her pockets. Taking a page from her mother's book, Faryn did her thing with a few boys at school to ensure that she always had a backup plan. She never went as far as having sex with any of them, but she gave hand jobs behind the bleachers every day during her lunch and gym times. The boys would be looking for her early in the mornings and all throughout the day. She started staying after school late, just to service her rapidly growing list of clients. For five dollars, Faryn gave them five minutes of her services. Sometimes, she serviced two boys at the same time if they agreed to it. She never made less than fifty dollars a day and that was a lot to her. She could buy herself some decent clothes and she never went hungry. She was young and dumb, so she saw nothing wrong with it.

Faryn quickly earned the reputation of being a slut, but she didn't care what anyone said about her. She did what she did for survival and not many girls her age understood that. The girls at her school hated her, which was why she got into so many fights. Either they were jealous of her or pissed that their boyfriends were one of her satisfied customers. She kept that up for a while, until one of the local dope boys, Jo-Jo, decided that he wanted to keep her for himself. He wanted more than a hand job and he told her that from the first day they met. He pissed a lot of boys at her school off when he started giving Faryn money and taking her shopping. She didn't have to do hand jobs anymore and he dared her to even try.

Because of his generosity, Faryn gave him her virginity at only fifteen years old and she thought she was in love with him. Since he was nineteen years old, she started staying the night at his house and no one ever missed her presence. That went on for months, until he went to jail one day during a drug bust while Faryn was in school. It was the talk of the block, but Faryn was used to being let down. She felt bad for Jo-Jo, but she went on with her miserable life just like always.

Two months after Jo-Jo got locked up, Faryn caught the eye of another local corner boy. Barry was considered an up and coming hood legend and he wanted a girl like Faryn by his side. Unlike Jo-Jo, who was sweet and down to earth, Barry treated Faryn more like his property than his girlfriend. He had no problem raising his hands to her. Faryn had more busted lips and black eyes than a girl her age probably ever had to endure. Thankfully, that relationship only lasted for a few months before Barry was shot and killed in front of the same corner store where Faryn had met him. Faryn was done with trying to have a boyfriend by then. Several other boys in the neighborhood tried, but she turned them all down.

Six months after that, Faryn went home from school, only to find her mother's cold, lifeless body in the hallway, dead from a drug overdose. She was only sixteen years old, but she didn't even cry as she called the police to tell them what had happened. One of Faryn's brothers, who she hadn't seen in a while, picked her up a few days after hearing of his mother's passing and moved her in with him and his girlfriend. Faryn was the youngest of her siblings, but she hadn't seen them in almost five years. Once they were old enough to fend for themselves, Faryn's siblings left and made their own way in life. Last she'd heard before their mother died, her brothers were locked up and her twenty-year-old sister was living with a fifty-year-old man. She must have been looking for a father figure because older men were what she preferred. They were all fucked up and couldn't do anything to help each other. They loved each other, but they had to survive any way they could. They didn't know how to love because they were never given any.

By the time Faryn graduated high school and started college, her brother had gone back to jail and was given a three-year sentence. Her brother's girlfriend, Syria, let her stay there for a while, and Faryn had no problem helping with the bills. That was, until Syria got a new man and he started looking at Faryn with lust in his eyes. She quickly gave Faryn the boot, but that was nothing new. Pain and suffering had become the norm and didn't even bother Faryn anymore. She rented a small apartment soon after and focused on her studies. She enjoyed the company of two male companions occasionally, but she never got into a serious relationship. It was basically sex for money and nothing more. Faryn hated to feel like she was a replica of her mother, but she was no better. The only difference was that she was paying for tuition and bills instead of drugs.

"Girl, bring your ass out here and stop keeping my best customer waiting. Redd has been waiting on you for almost thirty minutes," JB argued when he saw that Faryn was still sitting at her vanity.

"I'm coming," Faryn said as she stood up and smoothed out her knee-length fitted dress.

She had already finished her show for the night, but she usually worked the crowd and gave lap dances if she had to. Since Redd was there, she knew that she wouldn't be doing that tonight. He paid well for Faryn's time and he didn't want her attention on anyone else. He also tipped JB well for letting him have Faryn all to himself. JB loved when he came there, and he made sure that Faryn kept his favorite customer happy.

"It's about damn time. What took you so long?" Redd asked as he flashed a beautiful smile when Faryn walked over to his table.

"I had to shower and change clothes and stuff," Faryn replied, as he pulled her down on his lap.

"You smell so good. I'm trying to spend some time with you tonight," Redd said as he buried his face in Faryn's neck.

"Okay," Faryn happily agreed.

She and Redd had grown close over the past year that he'd been a customer at JB's Gentlemen's Club. Redd saw her giving a lap dance to another customer and he called her over to his table. He was there with some of his boys, but he dared one of them to touch her. Faryn had him gone with the way she moved her hips and grinded her plump ass on him. Redd pulled out a knot of money and paid her to entertain him all night until the club closed. He didn't come every time she worked, but he paid her to stay with him the entire time when he did.

Two months after becoming her regular customer, Redd had propositioned her for a little more than a lap dance. Faryn knew all about the other girls in the club doing more than just dancing in the private rooms. JB knew it too, but he didn't care, just as long as they continued to bring in the customers. Faryn had been in the private rooms more times that she could count, but she never went too far. Besides a lot of grinding and touching, she had never been intimate with any of her customers. Faryn was a nervous wreck, but she really could have used the money at the time.

School and bills were killing her pockets and every little bit helped.

When she agreed to take it there with Redd, she had no idea what he had in mind. He didn't take her to one of the private rooms like she thought he would. He rented a suite at a fancy hotel and treated Faryn like a queen. That was only the first of many times and, before long, Faryn didn't have to entertain anyone else once she did her thing on stage. Redd lavished her with gifts and money, and she appreciated him more than he knew. Faryn knew that he had to have a girl because he couldn't always get away. That was cool with her because she wasn't expecting too much from him anyway.

"I got something for you. I'm so proud of you, baby," Redd said as he smiled at her.

"Thanks Redd. I appreciate it," Faryn replied.

"Your education is important and I'm happy that you know that. Some of these hoes will do this until the day they die, but you're smarter than that. I'm happy that this is your last day here, but this is not our last day together. I still want to see you. We can still meet up at the room just like we do now," Redd noted.

He would never admit it out loud, but he had fallen hard for the caramel colored beauty. Faryn was a breath of fresh air for him and he looked forward to their times together. He had a family at home, but Faryn helped him to forget about all that for a little while. Being a family man got boring at times and he needed her to add some spice into his life. Sex with Faryn was amazing and a nice switch up from the norm that he experienced at home. Faryn wasn't like the rest of the girls at the club. She was smart, and she proved that by getting her degree. She didn't like to get too personal, but that was cool with him. The less she knew, the better for them both.

"That's cool with me," Faryn agreed, even though it would never happen.

She was quitting the club and quitting her arrangement with Redd too. He was cool, but Faryn didn't want to live that life anymore. She no longer wanted to use her body to earn money. She wanted her degree to do that for her. That was her purpose for getting it.

"Go get your stuff and let's go. I'm free all night, so I hope you're ready," Redd said as he kissed her hand.

"I'm always ready. I'll be right back," Faryn said as she got up and walked away.

She was happy to be walking away from her past and into a better future. She just prayed that things in her life were normal for once. She had been through enough hell to last her a lifetime. The statement 'been there, done that', sounded like the story of her life after all that she'd been through. For once, she needed some peace and normalcy. Having a boring life sounded so good to her and she couldn't wait to finally experience it.

Prologue II

Landon sat on the sofa in a daze, trying to process what he was hearing. Malia, his girlfriend of eleven years and wife of eight, had to be speaking a foreign language. There was no way that the love of his life and mother of his two sons was sitting there asking him for a divorce. She had even taken the liberty of having the paperwork prepared and ready for him to sign. The fact that she'd gone so far let him know that she'd really put some thought into it.

"Wait! What?" Landon said as he snapped back to reality and tried to grasp what his wife was saying.

He didn't see that coming at all. He and Malia were doing fine, as far as he knew. If anything was wrong, she never called it to his attention.

"Did you hear anything that I said Landon? I'm sorry, but I just can't do this anymore," Malia said with tears in her eyes.

"Exactly what is it that you can't do Malia? Be a wife? A mother? What exactly are you saying?" Landon asked.

"I'll always be a mother, but being a wife is what I have a problem with. I'm not happy Landon. I'm tired of pretending, when I'm dying inside," Malia replied.

"When did you come to this conclusion Malia? We just finalized our plans to build our dream home. They're scheduled to break ground on the lot in less than a month," Landon reminded her.

"I know and that's why I'm telling you before that even happens. I don't think it's fair for me to have my input on a house that I have no intentions on moving into," Malia confessed.

"The fuck?" Landon asked aloud, stunned by everything that his wife was saying.

He was hoping, no, praying that it was all a joke or maybe even a bad dream. He and Malia met when she was fifteen and he was sixteen. They started out as friends, but decided that they wanted to be more soon after. By the time Malia was seventeen and Landon was eighteen, they had already welcome their first son, Lance, into the world. They were married a year later and the following year, their second son, Lennox, entered the picture.

Landon, being the smart man that he was, had a solid plan in place for his family. He was offered an internship with NASA for their Aerospace Engineer's program. He was guaranteed a starting salary of six figures and they were paying for his entire education. Landon jumped at the chance and he excelled in the program. He originally wanted to go to school for accounting and business management, so he took a few extra courses at their local community college for that as well. His mother's ex-husband, Clarence, was a pro at investing and Landon had learned a lot from him.

With Clarence's help, Landon had learned to turn his little money into a lot in no time at all. He'd always dreamed of having his own business and his dream became a reality when he saved up enough money to buy a commercial office building in the central business district of New Orleans. There were fourteen offices in the building that Landon rented out to various businesses. Not even a year later, Landon had made enough money to purchase two more buildings and the money was rolling in. Malia had been his support system through it all and he loved and appreciated her for her patience. He had to put in some long hours to finally see their dream become a reality. Malia didn't work, so she took care of the kids and the house while Landon stacked their chips. Their bank accounts were better than ever, and they were both still under thirty years old. They still lived in a three-bedroom townhouse, but Landon promised Malia a brand-new dream home and he finally had enough money to make it happen. Now, she was telling him some bullshit about not even wanting it anymore.

"I'm sorry Landon, but we're on different pages now. I'm only twenty-six years old and I've been a mother and wife since I was eighteen. I have no life outside of you and the kids, and I feel like I'm suffocating," Malia said as she tried to produce some tears that never came.

"That's bullshit Malia. We were fine, and you seemed happy when we were meeting with the contractors a few months ago. What happened between then and now?" Landon questioned.

"I just told you what happened," Malia said as she lowered her head.

"So, who is it? It's must be another nigga in the picture for you to have a change of heart so suddenly. I'm not buying that bullshit story that you're telling, so just keep it real with me. Who have you been messing around with?" Landon asked as he turned her face around and made her look at him.

"His name is Roman, but it's not what you think it is. We're only friends," Malia hurriedly answered.

"Wow," Landon chuckled. "You're sitting here telling me that you want a divorce and, yet, you want me to believe that you and this nigga are just friends. How long has this been going on?"

"We met six months ago, when me and my sisters went out with my cousin for her birthday," Malia admitted.

Landon remembered that day like it was yesterday. Malia's cousin had just turned thirty and she begged her to go out with her. Malia kept turning her down, but Landon encouraged her to go. Malia never really went anywhere, and he wanted her to have fun. He had no idea that he was pushing her up to go out and meet another man. That shit was really one for the books.

"Okay, so you met him six months ago, and now you want a divorce to be with him? Do you even know this nigga like that Malia?" Landon asked.

"I know that he makes me feel young like I'm supposed to and not like an old maid. I know that I'm happier when I sneak out to be with him, instead of being here, cooking and cleaning all the time like a personal chef and maid," Malia replied.

Now, that hurt. Landon always tried to consider his wife's feelings, but he couldn't fix what he didn't know was broken. He asked her if she wanted to further her education, but she always insisted that she was fine. He would have never held her back while he pursued his dreams, and she knew that. He and Malia were each other's first everything. He would have never dreamed of being with another woman, but the feelings obviously weren't mutual. To know that his wife had given her body to another man was unforgiveable, especially since he had never dreamed of doing the same. He didn't know many men his age who could say that they'd only been with one woman. Hell, if he was being honest, he didn't know any at all.

"Oh okay, so that explains your frequent trips to your mama's house during the past few months. Does Cora know about this too?" Landon asked, referring to Malia's mother.

"Of course not. You know she would never condone anything like that," Malia replied.

And that was true. Her mother always complimented Landon on being one of the only young men that she knew with his head on straight. He was a great husband and father and she loved the way that he took care of her daughter and grandsons. Her other daughters weren't as fortunate. They ended up with deadbeat dads for their kids and cheaters for themselves. Malia didn't have that to worry about.

"What about your sisters? You tell them just about everything. Do they know that you've been cheating on me for six months and want a divorce?" Landon questioned.

"Why does that even matter Landon?" Malia asked.

Unbeknownst to her, she had answered his question without doing so. It was no secret that Malia's two sisters, Felicia and Monica, were jealous of her. She didn't see it, but it was plain as day. They both lived in the projects with their kids and they were envious of their younger sister and her accomplishments. They looked up to her in a way, but that didn't stop them from hating. Malia only had a high school diploma, but that was more than they ever had. She had married well, and they weren't as fortunate. They always threw shade her way and it always seemed to go right over her head. They were probably happy to help her do him dirty and ruin her marriage.

"Please Landon, just sign the papers and let's not make this harder than it has to be," Malia begged.

"This is crazy Malia. I never even knew that you had these feelings until now. We could have tried to figure a way out of this mess or at least talked to somebody. We're in the process of living our dream and you wanna hit me with this shit now. You wanna tear our family apart over a nigga that you've only known for six months," Landon snapped irritably.

"I don't expect you to understand Landon. You were out seeing the world, while I was stuck inside with two babies on my hip," Malia replied.

"That was your choice though, Malia. I asked if you wanted to go back to school and you said no. You could have had an entry-level receptionist job at my company and worked your way up, but you declined that offer too. I was out there busting my ass to make sure you and my boys didn't want for nothing. We had a plan and I stuck with it!" Landon yelled.

"I'm sorry Landon, but my mind is made up," Malia replied.

"I love you, but I can't make you stay. You barely know this man and you're trying to move out to be with him. My main concern is my sons. I need to know that they're safe and in a decent environment," Landon informed her.

"They will be because they're staying here with you," Malia said.

"What!" Landon yelled angrily.

A feeling of déja vu hit him as he zoned out and thought back to his own childhood. Landon's mother, Robin, had been a single parent for most of her life when he was growing up. He and his sister, Makena, never knew their father, but Robin made sure that they were well taken care of. When she married Clarence, things seemed to only get better. He treated her kids well and they loved and respected their stepfather. Things were going well, until Robin met an older man named Leroy and decided that Clarence was no longer what she wanted. Leroy lived across the street from her mother, Ella, and the two of them used to flirt with each other all the time.

It didn't take long before Robin left Clarence and moved her two children into the house with her and her new man. That, unfortunately, didn't last very long. Leroy was an older man with grown kids and grandkids. He didn't want to start all over again with eight-year-old Landon and ten-year-old Makena. He tried to break things off with Robin, but she wasn't having it. Instead of getting her kids and moving out, she packed them up and paid her mother to keep them across the street with her. Landon and his sister never even visited, but they watched from the front porch of their grandmother's house as their mother welcomed Leroy's grandkids with opened arms. They were even younger than her own kids, but Leroy didn't mind them spending the summer with them. Landon's grandmother Ella treated them well, but it wasn't the same as having their mother there. He and his sister developed an unbreakable bond, but they never felt the same about their mother again. They had no love for her and they didn't even try to hide it. Robin's ex-husband kept in contact with him and they loved him like a father. Clarence never remarried and he had no kids, so Landon and Makena made sure that he was straight. He was a smart man and he'd taught them a lot over the years that they'd known him. Landon prayed that Malia didn't make the same mistake with their kids. He didn't want his sons to experience that kind of hurt from their own mother.

"They're boys, Landon. They need their father. I can't teach them how to be men like you can," Malia said after a long, uncomfortable silence.

"And what am I supposed to tell them Malia? Am I supposed to say that their mother decided that a six-month affair was more important than them?" Landon asked.

"No, because that's not true. I love my kids more than anything and that's why I'm leaving them with you. You're a great father, Landon, and that's the only reason why I feel comfortable with my decision. I don't want anything from you but a divorce. You can keep all the money and everything else since the boys will be with you. I've already made that clear in the divorce decree," Malia replied.

"You seemed to have had this all planned out for a while now," Landon said as he thought over everything that he was hearing.

His hurt was developing into hate and the sight of Malia was starting to disgust him. He couldn't believe how he'd known her for so many years, yet, he really didn't know her at all.

"You put in all the work and you deserve to keep it all. It's the least I can do after springing this on you so suddenly," Malia said with her head held high, like she'd done nothing wrong.

Landon noticed that she'd never let go of the divorce papers that she'd presented to him. There were a lot of papers to look through and he wasn't signing anything until he did.

"I'll have my lawyer look over these and get back with you. Since your mind seems to be made up, you can get your stuff and leave. I'd prefer if you'd leave before they get home from school. I'll sit down and talk to them later," Landon said as he snatched the papers from her hand.

Malia didn't even try to put up a fight. She nodded her head and went upstairs to start gathering her belongings. Landon dropped his head in defeat as his heart damn near beat out of his chest. He didn't know how he was going to do it, but he prayed for God to give him the strength to be a single father. The entire situation was embarrassing, and he wasn't looking forward to having to tell anyone what happened. He knew that his family would have his back, but it was still going to be hard. His kids were looking forward to moving into their huge house with the built-in pool, but Landon was ready to throw in the towel. It made no sense to him to have a family home if he had no family to move into it.

Chapter 1

"Yes ma'am, I'm on my way now," Landon said before he disconnected the call.

He blew out a breath of frustration as he made a detour and headed to his oldest son's school. Lance was only ten years old, but he was becoming a handful already. He had never given Landon any problems, but that all changed once Malia left. It had been a little over a year since she'd been gone, and she and Landon were officially divorced. The first few months were hard on them all, but Landon had to be strong for his sons. He was severely depressed, and he halted the plans on getting their house built. His grandmother had to talk him off the ledge a few times, but he bounced back like it was nothing.

Malia was worse than he thought she'd be and the kids barely saw her. She always made promises that she didn't keep and that was the worst part of it all. Their oldest son, Lance, had started acting out because of their family problems and he was always fighting with someone. He was transferring his hatred towards his mother onto other students and he had major anger issues. Lennox, their youngest son, was the total opposite. He loved his mother and he believed every word that she said. There were many nights that he refused to go to sleep because he was waiting for her to pick him up like she promised. It got to a point where Landon wouldn't even tell them anything that Malia said. He was tired of her lying to them and leaving him to clean up the mess.

"I'm Landon Reynolds. I'm here to get my son, Lance," Landon said to the secretary when he walked into the front office of the school.

Lance had gotten into so many fights the year before, that the private school that he and Lennox attended didn't allow him to come back the following year. He was sent to a school for troubled children, even though he was the smartest one in his class. His behavior was the thing that did it.

"Thanks for coming Mr. Reynolds. Lance is across the hall speaking with the disciplinarian, but Mrs. Jennings is waiting for you in her office," she said, referring to the principal.

Landon followed, as she led him to an office that he had become very familiar with. School had only been in session for three months and he'd lost count of how many times he'd been called down there. The receptionist knocked on the door before opening it and ushering him inside. She pointed to a chair for him to sit down before she left him and the principal alone.

"I'm sorry that I have to keep calling you down here Mr. Reynolds, but I'm really concerned with Lance's behavior," Mrs. Jennings said once he was seated.

"That makes two of us. This is all new to me too, Mrs. Jennings. Lance has never given me these kinds of problems before," Landon honestly replied.

He wanted to say before his mother left, but he kept that part of the story to himself. Mrs. Jennings knew all about their family issues because Landon was very forthcoming with her from the beginning. Her heart went out to the troubled child and she wanted to do everything she could to help him.

"I honestly think he needs to speak with someone," Mrs. Jennings replied.

"Speak to someone like who?" Landon questioned.

"A professional counselor. Someone outside of the school. Usually, with children Lance's age, we would refer them to our local boys and girls club. I don't think that would work for him though. You're a very active part of his life, so a mentoring program isn't the answer. I think he needs an unbiased adult who he can open up to and vent if necessary," Ms. Jennings suggested.

"I'm willing to do whatever I have to do to get him back on track. I really want to pull off my belt and beat his ass, but I'm trying to be patient. This behavior didn't start until Malia left. He's hurting, and I guess this is his way of acting out," Landon replied.

"I agree, but we're going to do everything that we can to get him right. Lance is one of the smartest boys in this school and I know that he comes from a good background. He's in fifth grade, but functioning on a seventh-grade level. I don't want those kinds of smarts to go to waste. We might be looking at the next black president." Mrs. Jennings smiled.

"How many days is he suspended for?" Landon asked.

"I'm not suspending him this time. I've made him an appointment to see a behavioral specialist next Saturday. I've heard nothing but great things about this counselor and I think it would be good for Lance. Here is the address and time of his appointment," Mrs. Jennings said while handing him the information.

"Thank you, Mrs. Jennings, for everything. I really appreciate all the support you've given me since Lance started here," Landon replied.

"You're a good man Landon and a great father. I wish we had more like you in the world. You let me know if there is anything else that I can do to help. You can bring Lance back tomorrow, but have a talk with him about that temper. He told me that he gets it from you, but I find that hard to believe." Mrs. Jennings smiled.

"Looks are deceiving Mrs. Jennings. I grew up faster than I wanted to when my boys came, but I had anger issues worse than his," Landon admitted as he stood to his feet.

He sympathized with his son because he understood his frustrations. He was around Lance's age when he was abandoned by his mother and that shit hurt, especially because no child deserved it. Landon walked across the hall to get his son before going outside to his car.

"I'm sorry dad. I tried to walk away, but the other boy kept talking," Lance said as soon as he and his father were alone.

"This shit is getting old bruh. I'm trying to be patient, but that's wearing thin too. I'm out here busting my ass to make sure that you and your brother are straight, and this is the thanks I get. I had to leave work to come down here for this bullshit," Landon fussed.

His son didn't know, but he left from work all the time just because. Their work was mostly done by a computer and Landon checked his emails right from his phone. He remembered when he worked nights. He would be home in bed with Malia and his kids while he was still on the clock. He and his co-workers had an understanding and they all did the same thing. They were salaried, and they did their jobs properly. Landon was making so much money with his commercial office rentals that he'd been thinking about resigning. That would have been a stupid move, considering he was making six figures for basically doing nothing.

"I'm sorry dad. I promise it won't happen again," Lance swore.

"You say that shit every time I have to come here Lance. Do you want to go live with Cora? You know she's been asking and I'm thinking about taking her up on her offer," Landon threatened.

"Dad, no! Please, don't make me go live with my grandma. Her entire house smells like coffee and peppermints!" Lance yelled, making his father laugh.

Landon would die before he let his boys go live with anyone else. Malia's mother helped him out a lot, but she always offered to take them in to live with her. She didn't condone what her daughter had done, and she made sure to let her know it.

"You and Lennox begged me to go through with getting our house built and I did that. Everything that y'all wanted me to put in it is there. I don't know what else I can do to satisfy you, bruh," Landon replied.

His sons were ready for a new start after their mother left and so was he. Landon scrapped the old plans that he and Malia had for the house and redesigned the entire thing to his liking. His sons got their pool and he hired an interior decorator to make their new house look like a home. They hadn't been living there very long, but Landon loved his Barkley Estates mini mansion.

"I am satisfied dad," Lance said after a long pause.

"Okay, so what's the problem?" Landon questioned.

"I don't know. I just get so mad sometimes and I want everybody to leave me alone," Lance noted as he looked out of the window.

"You told me that once before, but what makes you that angry Lance?" Landon questioned.

"I don't know," Lance whispered sadly.

"I can't help if you won't talk to me, son," Landon said.

He knew why his son was behaving the way he did. Landon was the same way when he was younger. Every time he thought about his mother and how she'd treated him and his sister, he got angry and needed someone to take his anger out on.

"I do talk to you," Lance replied.

"Are you still angry about your mother leaving?" Landon asked.

"No," Lance quickly answered. "I don't care nothing about her."

"I think you do. I think you're upset and you take your frustrations out on other people," Landon said, calling him out.

"Can we go by GG until Lennox gets out of class?" Lance asked, referring to his great-grandma Ella, who they nicknamed GG.

"Mrs. Jennings wants you to see a behavioral specialist. She made you an appointment for next Saturday. I suggest you open up and tell somebody how you really feel. You're gonna be sleeping on Cora's plastic covered couch if this doesn't work. I'm not doing this with you no more," Landon threatened.

"I'll talk to the counselor, I promise," Lance swore.

He would do anything he had to do as long as he didn't have to live with his mother's mother. She was nice and all, but her house was old fashioned and boring. Lance and his brother loved going by their father's grandmother, Ella. She always had lots of food and she let them do whatever they wanted to do. She was also funny and kept everybody laughing. He was all smiles when his father pulled up to the house and he saw his auntie Makena's car. Lance and her son, Ross, were the same age and he loved hanging with his cousin. He was sure that Ross was still in school, but he wanted to see his auntie anyway.

"Hey, my baby. Why are you not in school?" Makena asked Lance when he and his father walked into their grandmother's house.

"Fighting at school, just like always," Landon replied.

"I hope he won," Ella replied as she inspected her great-grandson's face for scratches or marks.

"Yo, are you serious right now grandma?" Landon inquired with a smirk.

"You damn right I am. I didn't take no shit back in the day and I raised you and Makena to be the same way. Did you beat his ass Lance?" Ella asked.

"Yes GG," Lance replied with a smile.

"Good, now go in the freezer and get you some ice cream," Ella replied.

"Don't reward his bad behavior with ice cream grandma," Landon argued once his son was out of the room.

"My baby is not bad. That bitch leaving is the only reason he's acting out the way he is. Her sad ass abandoned her kids over a nigga. At least Robin threw us a few dollars occasionally. That bitch Malia barely visits," Makena snapped.

"Robin is a dumb bitch, but karma is real. I regret the day I ruined my figure and pushed her out. I knew I shouldn't have been drinking while I was pregnant with her ass," Ella fussed.

"This lady don't care what comes out of her mouth," Makena laughed.

"I'm serious and Malia is gon' get hers too. You just wait and see. I've been praying for God to send you a good woman and I know He will. She ain't have no business abandoning you and them babies like that. No wonder Lance is so angry all the time," Ella replied.

"Yeah, but that doesn't excuse his behavior though, grandma. His principal made him an appointment to see somebody. Hopefully, that helps," Landon noted.

"My grandbaby ain't crazy. He don't need to see no damn shrink," Ella argued.

"It's not a shrink, it's a behavior specialist," Landon replied.

"Same difference to me," Ella said right as her front door opened and her daughter, Ava, walked in with her husband, Kane.

"Hey everybody," Ava spoke when she walked into the room and kissed her mother on the cheek.

Ava and her twin brother, Aiden, were what Ella always referred to as her surprise babies. They were a year older than Landon and a year younger than Makena. Landon, Makena, and their other cousin, Raheem, grew up in the house with them, but Ava made them all sick at times. Raheem and Landon were the same age and his father was Ella's oldest son. He wasn't the best father and the streets were his first love.

When Raheem's mother died when he was ten, his father dropped him off to Ella and never looked back. She loved her grandson, so she never gave it a second thought when she had to raise him. Thankfully, Aiden hadn't corrupted Landon or Raheem and they both walked a straight path. Raheem didn't graduate from college like Landon did, but he still had a great job and a place of his own. He lived in the clubs, just like his father, but he never got into any trouble.

Ava, on the other hand, was spoiled rotten and she thought the universe revolved around her. She was Ella's youngest daughter and she was mostly to blame for that. Her husband, Kane, was no better. He catered to his wife and she wouldn't have it any other way. Aiden couldn't stand his brother-in-law, but he let him make it on the strength of his mother. Ava was never that bad until she got with Kane. His money turned her into someone that she never was before.

Aiden had been in and out of jail since he was twelve years old, and Ella was happy that he'd managed to stay out of trouble for the past year. Her son was a hot head with a bad temper that he had a hard time controlling. He, Landon, and Raheem were tight, but he hated when Landon invited Kane to come along. Landon went to college with Kane and they worked together at NASA. Hanging with Landon was how Kane had met and married Ava. They had a four-year-old daughter and had been married for five years.

"The hell you doing home from work so early?" Kane asked as he gave Landon dap.

"Nigga, I should be asking you the same thing. I thought you were working a double," Landon replied.

"I'm working it right now," Kane said as he and Landon laughed. Kane didn't really have to work, but what he did was easy and it paid well.

"I had to leave early to go get Lance from school. His ass got into another fight," Landon informed him.

"Damn, Tyson be knocking niggas out," Kane laughed.

"You need to whip his ass Landon. He can't keep using Malia leaving as an excuse to act up all the time. He knows you won't do him anything and that's why he does it. He gon' be just like Aiden, in and out of jail all his life," Ava butted in.

"He better not lay a finger on that child. You need to stop being so insensitive Ava. You don't know how it feels to be abandoned by your mother. You had me here with you your entire life until you got married and moved out on your own," Ella argued.

"I know that it had to hurt, but that was over a year ago. He should be over that by now." Ava shrugged uncaringly.

"Man, let me get out of here grandma. With the way I'm feeling, I'll have to slap a bitch for playing with mine," Makena said as she stood to her feet.

"Let me get my son and I'm right behind you, sis," Landon replied.

"You can leave Lance here for a little while since you have to come back to pick up Lennox," Ella said.

Landon's youngest son's bus dropped him off right in front of his grandmother's house. He never rushed to get him because he knew that he was in good hands. Landon followed Makena out the front door, with Kane walking out with them.

"That bitch gon' make me knock her stupid ass the fuck out," Makena fumed as they stood on the porch.

"Fuck that bitch. That's exactly why I don't fuck with her stupid ass now," Landon replied.

"Excuse me, but that is my wife that y'all are talking about," Kane said as he lit up a cigarette and took a puff.

"I don't give a fuck! Behind my brother and nephews, that hoe can catch these hands," Makena warned.

"Calm down sis. Her stupid ass ain't even worth it," Landon said, waving her off.

"Let me go home and cook before my husband and child gets there. I'll bring some food to y'all as soon as I'm done," Makena said as she kissed Landon's cheek and walked away.

If their grandma didn't do it, Makena made sure that her brother and nephews always had a hot meal. Landon could barely boil water, but he never worried about going hungry. He'd just learned how to do their laundry properly because Malia used to do everything.

"Aye bruh, I know that Ava is a piece of work, but that's still y'all auntie," Kane said, defending his wife just like he always did.

"I'm sure you already know this, but I really don't give a fuck. I've been keeping Makena off her ass for years, but it is what it is now. She needs to watch that slick ass mouth of hers before she gets slapped in it," Landon replied.

"Man, I know that y'all are family, but I'm not letting nobody put their hands on my wife," Kane said, sounding like the weak pussy ass nigga that he was.

"That's cool with me too. You can get the business just like your wife. You already know what's up with me." Landon shrugged.

Landon was always the smartest one of the crew, but he also had the worst temper, aside from Aiden. There were plenty of times when they'd hang out and Kane had to help their other friends pull Landon off someone. He had major anger issues and he was like a wild animal whenever he attacked. He was known to knock niggas out with one punch and he had witnessed it more than once. Kane was nothing more than a college frat boy who threw his money around to get noticed. He and his sister came from money and that's what drew Ava to his lame ass. He didn't want no problems with Landon and he knew it.

"We're family bruh. It don't even have to be all that," Kane said, trying to diffuse a potentially bad situation.

"I don't give a fuck about that either. Sometimes, your family will treat you worse than a stranger would. She's living proof of that," Landon said as he pointed across the street at Robin.

He and Kane observed his mother walking out of the house and up to Leroy's brand-new Cadillac. She smiled at them and waved, but Landon didn't bother waving back. Robin was dressed in designer labels from head toe, with a fresh weave flowing down her back. She didn't feel the least bit of guilt for how she treated her children and that was obvious. Not only was she a horrible mother, but she was a horrible grandmother as well. Robin had three grandsons, but they barely knew her. They had never set foot in her house and she didn't see anything wrong with it. Just like Landon was cool not having her in his life, he was cool with her not being in his sons' lives as well.

Chapter 2

"Come on Faryn. You never go anywhere with me. I'll even drive, since I know you hate to," Faryn's neighbor, Harley, said.

She and Faryn had gotten close over the past year that they'd lived across the hall from each other. Faryn was a beautiful girl with a figure to die for, but she was too much of a homebody in Harley's opinion. Men would fall at her feet, but she never gave them a chance to get close to her. Faryn was sorry when she got on the elevator and saw Harley running to catch up. She wanted the doors to close, but Harley made it before that could happen. They both lived on the fourth floor of their luxury apartment building and they'd moved in during the same week. Faryn had a lot of things that needed to be hooked up and Harley's husband, Kyron, lent her a helping hand. Kyron was cool and he looked out for Faryn whenever he could. She was a single woman, so he didn't mind. Harley liked her and that was good enough for him. Kyron and Harley had just finished the first-time home buyers program and they were in the process of looking for a house. Harley hated that she would be leaving Faryn all alone, but she was okay with being a loner.

"I keep telling you that I have to work tomorrow Harley. Besides, you know that your girl hates me.

Why would you want me to go anywhere with her?" Faryn questioned.

"Monica is cool in her own way. She's just intimidated when she sees another woman who's doing better than she is," Harley replied.

"That sounds stupid as hell. She doesn't even know me. It's not my fault that she lives in the hood and has multiple baby daddies. I've always tried to be nice, but fuck her," Faryn argued.

Harley's cousin, Patrice, used to come with them all the time, but she was pregnant now. Patrice was cool and she and Faryn got along great.

"Forget her Faryn. Are you gonna come out with me or not?" Harley asked.

"Not," Faryn said as she fell out laughing.

"Ugh. You make me sick. You don't do shit but sit inside and look up Pinterest recipes all day," Harley fussed.

"Bitch, I don't hear you complaining when it's time to eat it though," Faryn replied, right as the elevator stopped on their floor.

"I'm no fool honey. That shit be good as hell," Harley laughed.

"Bye Harley. Not all of us are off every Saturday. I need to get ready for work tomorrow," Faryn said as she pulled her keys from her purse.

"Seriously Faryn? It's only six o'clock. Will you at least think about going out with me tomorrow night?" Harley asked.

"Yes Harley, I'll think about it," Faryn replied.

"I know your ass is lying. You have no life outside of work and home. You might as well become a nun," Harley said, right as Faryn entered her apartment and closed the door in her face.

Harley was always saying that Faryn had no life and was probably a virgin, but she just didn't know. The saying, 'been there, done that', truly applied to her life, but Faryn didn't feel the need to disclose that information to anyone. She had seen enough drama to last her a lifetime and she welcomed the peace and quiet that she now had. Although she'd danced in the club for years, clubbing was never her thing. Faryn was happy watching a movie or curling up with a good book. She didn't care what anyone said about her and she never did.

Faryn let out a breath of relief, happy to be back in her comfort zone. She looked around her modernly decorated apartment and smiled in appreciation. Faryn had moved in with only a few pieces of furniture, clothing, and electronics. During the first few months of her stay, she managed to fully furnish her two-bedroom apartment and purchase a car. The apartment that she lived in was pricey, but it was worth it. All her utilities were included, as well as a washer and dryer. She didn't try to live above her means, so rent, car note, and insurance were really the only bills that she had. Faryn kicked off her black leather red bottoms and went to her spare bedroom to put them back in their box.

Faryn was never the type to care about labels, but her red bottom shoe collection had become her babies. It was Faryn's guilty pleasure and she purchased a pair every time she got paid, as a special treat to herself. She had quite a few pairs of red bottom heels, high tops, and a few other styles that she had fallen in love with. Aside from bills, it was the only thing that she'd ever spent money on. Redd had purchased her first pair for her as a graduation gift and she had been hooked ever since. A few of the girls in her graduating class wore a pair and, for the first time ever, Faryn felt like she fit in. She smiled at the shoe boxes, happy that she'd purchased them the honest way. When Faryn's phone rang, she looked down at the screen and shook her head in disgust.

"What's up Redd?" Faryn said as she answered the phone and made her way to her bathroom.

"Stop asking me what's up like you don't already know," Redd replied.

Faryn didn't know if he was dumb or stupid, but something had to be wrong. An entire year had passed since she left the strip club and last saw him. He called her just about every week trying to hook up, but

Faryn's answer was always the same. They still hadn't exchanged real names, so he should have taken the hint.

"I have to work in the morning Redd," Faryn said as she took off her work clothes and tossed them into the hamper.

"What about when you get off? I miss you, baby. I miss the way you smell, the way you taste. I just miss everything about you," Redd confessed.

"I know Redd, but I be so busy all the time," Faryn lied.

"Do you even still live in New Orleans? I don't understand how I never ran into you nowhere for an entire year. This city is too damn small for that," Redd replied.

"Of course, I still live here. I've never been out of New Orleans before in my life," Faryn admitted.

"I can change that too. Just meet up with me and let's talk. You got me feigning like a damn crack head," Redd laughed.

"I'll see Redd," Faryn replied.

"You must have another nigga or something. You ain't never used to turn me down before. This tongue used to have your ass climbing the walls at one time. I guess that new nigga must be hitting it right," Redd speculated.

"There is no new nigga," Faryn replied.

And that was true. The last night that she'd spent with Redd was the last night that she'd spent with any man. It had been over a year since Faryn had sex and that was fine with her too. She got the urges from time to time, but the feelings always passed eventually. She swore that the next time she had sex would be because she wanted to, not because she had to. She wanted to be intimate for pleasure, not profit.

"What's the problem then?" Redd asked after a short pause.

"I just told you, Redd. I be busy with work and stuff," Faryn said, trying to let him down easy.

"Just tell a nigga the truth. If you ain't fucking with me like that, just say that shit," Redd snapped angrily.

"Seriously Redd? You've been calling me asking to hook up for a year now and I've never agreed once. I mean, let's keep it real, I never even told you my real name. I thought you would have gotten the hint by now," Faryn argued.

"You should have just been real and said that shit. You kept stringing a nigga along like you were thinking about it, when you know you weren't. All y'all hoes play the same games. I don't know what made me think you were different," Redd barked.

"If I'm a hoe, then stop begging to eat me out and fuck me. Get a fucking life and lose my number!" Faryn yelled as she hung up the phone and blocked his number.

He had her heated, and she needed a drink. Faryn didn't do hard liquor, but she grabbed a bottle of wine and poured her a big glass. She was worked up, so she threw on her gym clothes and headed on the first floor to the twenty-four-hour gym in her apartment complex.

***

"What kind of stuff are we going to talk about?" Lance asked his father as they pulled up to the office building.

"I don't know bruh, but you better get it off your chest. I understand if you don't want to say anything to me, but you need to talk to somebody," Landon replied.

"Okay," Lance said as he and his father got out of the car and walked into the building.

"Good morning. Can I help you?" the secretary asked when they walked up to her desk.

"Yes ma'am, my son has an appointment with Ms. Clark," Landon replied.

"Okay. What's your son's name?" she questioned.

"Lance Reynolds," Landon replied.

"I need to see his insurance card and your identification," she requested.

Landon watched as she made copies and handed everything back to him. "Thanks," he said while putting the documents back in his wallet.

"You can have a seat and I'll go let her know that he's here. You're in for a treat Lance. Ms. Clark is the best counselor that we have here. All the kids just love talking to her," the lady said as she looked at Lance and smiled before walking away.

Landon sat next to his son and gave him some encouraging words. Lance was a smart boy, like his father, and he wanted him to do great things. Getting suspended every other week and fighting all the time wasn't going to cut it.

"Good morning Lance," a young lady walked up to them and said.

"Damn," Landon mumbled when he looked up into her beautiful smiling face. He was so busy talking to his son, he didn't even see when she approached.

"Good morning," Lance replied.

"I'm Faryn Clark and I'm the behavior specialist who's been assigned to your case." Faryn smiled as she reached her hand out for Lance to shake.

"Okay." Lance smiled, feeling better already. He was happy that his counselor was a woman because all the male counselors at his school were mean and yelled a lot.

"Are you his father?" Faryn asked as she tried not to stare at the handsome specimen that sat before her. Her breath caught in her throat when Landon stood up and she saw how tall and fine he was. His hair was cut low with a part on the side and one of his arms was completely covered with tribal tattoos. His beard was cut low with a thin mustache connected to it. Chocolate was her new favorite flavor as she studied the milk chocolate Adonis in all his magnificent glory.

Faryn had to pull her eyes away from him and focus on the floor instead.

"Yeah, I'm Landon Reynolds," he replied as he extended his hand for her to shake.

Unlike her, Landon didn't look away as he openly admired her beauty. Faryn's skin looked like it had been kissed by the sun. Her nude colored lips were full and pouty. Her hair was long and curly like she'd rolled it or applied chemicals to make it that way. Her perfectly arched brows sat atop the prettiest set of eyes that Landon had ever seen. She was dressed down in jeans and a black t-shirt that bared the name of her agency on front, but she was the sexiest thing that he had ever seen.

"Okay, well, we have a waiting area across the hall where you can relax until we're done. Help yourself to the coffee and snacks and we'll be done in about an hour," Faryn said as she grabbed Lance's hand and walked away.

Landon watched her like a hawk until she was out of sight, before he went to the room that she had pointed out. There was no one else inside, so he grabbed a bottle of water from the cooler and sat down in one of the plush chairs. He grabbed a book that talked about different behaviors that problem children exhibited and the main causes. Landon felt bad when he read a section that spoke on the lack of parental involvement being the number one cause of most of the issues. He knew that Malia leaving affected his sons in a negative way and he tried to do everything that he could to make them feel better. He had one son who'd started acting out and another who just wanted her to embrace him. Lennox was crazy about his mother and he looked forward to her coming to get him. Lance, on the other hand, didn't want anything to do with her. Landon's mind was all over the place as he sat there for over an hour and read up on different things.

"Hey dad, I'm done," Lance ran into the room and said to his father. He had a huge smile covering his face and Landon hadn't see that in a while.

"How did you do?" Landon asked as he stood to his feet.

"He did great," Faryn said with a smile as she walked into the room.

"Ms. Clark wants to talk to you," Lance said while looking up at his father.

"Yeah, I just wanted to go over a few things with you and I'll set up his next appointment," Faryn interjected.

"Okay, sit down until I come back," Landon instructed his son as he followed Faryn back to her office.

The entire room was decorated in pink, black, and white and smelled like tropical fruit. Faryn had her degree on the wall, along with a picture of her graduating college right next to it. Landon looked for pictures of kids or a man, but he was pleased to see that there was none.

"I just want to start by saying that Lance is a sweetheart. I can tell that he comes from a good home and he's being taught well," Faryn said as soon as they took a seat in her office.

"Thanks, I appreciate that." Landon smiled.

"I was happy that he opened up to me on the first day. That doesn't usually happen too often. He told me about the fights that he's been getting into at school and we discussed his home life and things like that," Faryn spoke up.

"How did that go? I've been trying to get him to talk to me, but I guess he doesn't feel comfortable enough yet," Landon replied.

"Yeah, we talked about that too. He told me about his mom leaving and stuff and that seems to be what bothers him the most," Faryn noted.

"I figured as much," Landon replied.

"That's why he started acting up in school. He was trying to get his mother's attention. He thought that she would come back if she saw what he was doing. After a while, he started acting out because she didn't," Faryn said.

"I wish he would have just said something, but he won't open up to me," Landon confessed.

"Yeah and he told me why. He feels like you're making him have a relationship with his mother and he doesn't want one. He said you make him talk to her when she calls and you make him go with her when she comes to pick them up," Faryn said, making Landon feel even worse.

He really thought he was doing the right thing when he encouraged his boys to spend time with their mother. Malia didn't come around very often and that was his reasoning behind it. He thought that making Lance spend time with his mother would help, but it appeared to have made things worse. Malia called a lot, but Lance hated when he had to talk to her.

"Damn man," Landon said as he ran his hand over his face.

"Don't feel bad Mr. Reynolds. You're doing everything right and Lance seems to think so. He speaks very highly of you and your sister. I just don't want him to think that his mother leaving has anything to do with him. I told him that it's not his fault and I need you to remind him of that when y'all are at home. Overall, I think we made a lot of progress for our first session. He has a card with my number if he ever needs to talk," Faryn replied.

"Are you allowed to give him your personal number?" Landon asked skeptically.

"It's not my personal number. The agency gave us a phone for the children to have twenty-four-hour access to the counselors," Faryn answered.

"When does he come back to see you?" Landon inquired.

"In two weeks. I'm here every other Saturday," Faryn replied.

"Okay, cool," Landon said as he stood up and prepared to leave.

"Have a good day Mr. Reynolds!" Faryn called out to him.

"Landon." He smiled and winked, right before he walked out and closed the door behind him.

"Jesus," Faryn murmured as she took a folder from her desk and fanned her face.

She hadn't had sex in over a year, but Landon had her kitty jumping. Faryn had never had a real boyfriend in her adult life and getting intimate with one of her patient's parents was against company rules. A one-night stand wouldn't hurt anybody, but Faryn knew that it was wishful thinking. She was sure that Landon had gotten a girlfriend since his divorce, but she would never approach him if he didn't. Lance had told her a little about his father and she had to admit that she was impressed. His appearance screamed dope boy but, when he opened his mouth, another side of him was revealed. Landon spoke with intelligence and his son confirmed that when he told Faryn where he worked. She didn't know who his ex-wife was, but she had to be a damn fool to leave a man who apparently had it all.

Chapter 3

Malia bit her lip hard enough to draw blood, as the sweat from Roman's body dripped and mixed with her own. Her feet touched the headboard, as Roman pounded into her swollen middle. The pleasure was mixed with pain, but it wasn't anything that she wasn't used to. Sex with Roman was always animalistic and sometimes lasted for hours. He had the stamina of three men and Malia quickly learned to adjust. Landon made love to her, but it was straight fucking with Roman. Still, she would never trade her exciting life with him for the mediocre one that she had with Landon. Admittedly, she still loved her ex-husband, but she wanted more.

Landon was all work and no play, which was how he'd acquired a few million dollars in his bank accounts. He was a pro at investing and it didn't take long for his investments to pay off. Malia wanted to live life in the fast lane, and Landon was moving too slow for her. He promised her so many things, but Malia had met Roman and left him before he could make good on any of them. Even though she was entitled to half of everything that Landon had, she didn't feel right taking anything. He was taking care of their sons, so that was the least that she could do. Besides, Roman took very good care of her, so she didn't need it anyway.

"Oh shit! Roman, wait!" Malia yelled as she tried to push him away.

"The fuck you mean wait?" Roman questioned as he looked down at her and frowned.

"Stop trying to man handle me all the time. I already don't like that anal shit. The least you can do is use the oil before you try to do it," Malia argued.

Malia had only tried anal sex once before with Landon and she swore that she was never going to do it again. Her ass felt like it was on fire for days after and she hated that feeling. Landon didn't care one way or the other, but Roman didn't give her a choice. A few weeks after she moved in with him, he was oiling her ass down and forcing his way inside. Malia told him that she didn't like it, but he told her that she would get used to it. A year later and that proved to be a lie.

"Fuck!" Roman hissed as he slowly guided himself into Malia's asshole.

He was never a big fan of anal sex until one of his side bitches turned him on to it a while ago. She was a straight freak and, now, he was addicted. He felt Malia tense up when he started moving inside of her, but she would be okay. She was boring as fuck in the bedroom, so that was the least she could do. Roman was ready to go buck wild, but she kept putting her hand up to make him slow down. The shit was getting frustrating, so he pulled out and slipped back into her kitty. She had him fucked up if she thought he was about to be on some love making shit. Roman flipped her over on her stomach and went straight savage in the pussy.

"Oh shit! Fuck! Roman, baby wait. Slow down," Malia begged, as he pulled her hair and fucked her like a dog. The position had the right name because Roman was dogging her.

"Stop bitching and throw that ass back!" Roman barked as he slapped her ass and continued to stroke her.

Malia was starting to piss him off with all that complaining and that was exactly why he was doing him. Things started out fine with them in the beginning and Roman loved her innocence. He was used to dealing with hood rats, so Malia was a breath of fresh air. Malia had a cute baby face with a nice, slender body to match. She was slimmer than he liked, but she was still sexy with it. Malia was a little old fashioned in the beginning, but he turned her out in no time at all. She ditched the jeans and sweats for sexy dresses and heels. The boring ponytails were replaced with weave down to her ass, along with a collection of expensive makeup. She had to step her game up to be with him and she caught on fast. She saw the kind of women that he liked, and she quickly became one of them. Roman was never into the relationship thing, but Malia made him change his mind about that for the second time in his life. He didn't care that she was married. He wanted her, and he got her. Now, after more than a year of being with her, he realized that he didn't want her anymore.

For as long as he could remember, it had only been Roman and his brother, Chad. He didn't have much of a family and he never did. The ones that he did have, he hadn't seen in a while. He never had much of a mother when he was growing up, so his relationships with women were never the best. Having kids were out of the question because of the fast-paced lifestyle that he and his brother lived. It wasn't fair for him to bring kids into the world knowing that his only outcome in life was probably jail or the grave. He was realistic if nothing else.

"Ooh shit," Malia moaned as she came for the third time in a row.

Roman was still going strong, but she could tell by his short, labored breathing that he was almost done. He was grunting like a wild animal as he slammed into her slender frame. He let out a loud roar right before he pulled out of her and released all over her back and ass. Malia hated when he did that, but he didn't see the problem.

"Damn, I needed that shit," Roman panted as he collapsed in the bed right next to her.

Malia snuggled up behind him and wrapped her arm around his waist, listening to the rapid beating of his heart. Roman let her stay like that for a while, but it didn't last long. He pushed her away and sat up on the side of the bed.

"Can we just lay here and cuddle for a while? Why do you always have to rush to get up right after we have sex?" Malia nagged.

"I keep telling you that I'm not the cuddling type. You need to get a teddy bear to sleep with for all that," Roman replied as he lit his blunt.

"We used to cuddle all the time before I moved in with you," Malia whined as she tried to pull him back in the bed.

Roman was so much more affectionate before they started living together. Having Malia around all the time was starting to get to him and his actions showed it. He never had a mother around, so he wasn't very affectionate towards the opposite sex. All that cuddling shit just wasn't his thing.

"Chill out Malia. I need to hop in the shower. I got some moves to make," Roman replied.

"You told me that you were staying inside today. You just got home at eight this morning," she reminded him.

They'd just had make-up sex after arguing about it all morning. Roman hadn't even gone to sleep yet and he was trying to leave out of the house again.

"Man, I'm out there making money. I don't have time to be sitting in here up under you all day. You don't complain when it's time to shop or go somewhere," Roman noted.

"I know baby, but when are we gonna do something together? You've been promising me a vacation for months. When are we gonna go somewhere?" Malia asked.

She was damn near thirty years old and had only been out of New Orleans once. Landon took her on a cruise for their first anniversary and that was it. He traveled a lot with his job in the beginning, so he got to see the world while she was stuck at home with two babies. Roman promised to take her somewhere, but he never made good on it.

"I told you to give me some time Malia. I need to get my money up some more before I can take a vacation. We just had this conversation a few days ago. Don't stat nagging me and shit," Roman warned.

"How is me wanting to spend time with my man nagging?" Malia questioned.

"Just give a few months baby and I'll take you wherever you want to go," Roman swore.

"You promise?" Malia asked him.

"Yes, I promise," he replied as he kissed her lips and headed to the bathroom that connected to their bedroom.

He made the same promise all the time, but that was good enough for Malia. She smiled as she got comfortable in the bed, preparing to take a nap. She barely got any sleep because she was up calling Roman's phone all night. It wasn't his first time sleeping out, but it had started to happen more frequently. Malia hated to be on his back so much, but that was just disrespectful. She had never stayed out all night since they had been together, and she wanted the same respect.

"Roman!" Malia yelled after trying, but failing to fall asleep after about fifteen minutes.

Roman's phone kept vibrating on the dresser and it was getting on her nerves. He always did take long showers and she still heard the water running. When he didn't answer her after the fourth time, Malia jumped up and grabbed his phone from the dresser. Roman didn't like her answering it, but she was tired of hearing it buzz.

"Yes," Malia said when she picked up, but the person on the other end just held the phone.

Malia looked at the screen, but the person's number wasn't saved. Whoever it was hung up, but Malia had a funny feeling in the pit of her stomach. She knew that it had to be a woman because they wouldn't have felt the need to hang up if it wasn't. Since Roman's phone was unlocked since she answered it,

Malia decided to scroll through his text messages. The same number that had just called had also text him several times. The woman obviously knew he had a girl because she mentioned it several times. Malia felt the tears stinging her eyes as she read over the conversations. She no longer had to wonder where Roman was the night before because the proof was staring her in the face. The unknown woman was asking him what he wanted her to cook for him tonight or did he want the same thing that he had the night before. Malia was furious. She didn't even realize that Roman was done taking his shower until she heard him say something to her.

"The fuck is you looking through my phone for?" Roman barked as he snatched the phone from her hand.

"You lying muthafucker! I knew you were with a bitch last night!" Malia yelled as he pushed him.

Roman only had a towel wrapped around his waist, but he dropped it to the floor and stepped into his Ralph Lauren boxers. Malia was screaming and crying, but he ignored her and proceeded to get dressed. He didn't care that she knew about him cheating and he prayed that she decided to leave him. He was tired of doing the relationship thing. He tried it twice and failed both times.

"Keep your hands to yourself man," Roman calmly replied when Malia pushed his head.

"Fuck you! You had me sitting in here worried about your dog ass while you were out there laid up with another bitch," Malia cried.

She felt like a fool standing there naked with dried-up cum on her body as her man got dressed and prepared to leave the house, probably to be with his other woman again. Roman wasn't even tired when he got home that morning and, now, she knew why. He wasn't out making money like he claimed to be. He was sleeping peacefully with his side bitch.

"Aye Ro!" Roman's brother, Chad, knocked on the door and yelled.

Chad had a key to his older brother's apartment and he often showed up without knocking or calling first. Chad had a million women that he lived with, so he didn't call one particular place home. If ever he wanted time to himself, he would just occupy his older brother's spare bedroom or get a hotel room. He and Malia didn't get along, but she knew better than to step to him.

"Roman is busy!" Malia yelled out in anger.

"I'm coming bruh," Roman said while shaking his head at Malia.

"You're not going anywhere Roman. You better tell me what's up," Malia demanded as she slipped on her robe and blocked the door.

"Didn't you just go through my phone? Shit, you already know what's up," Roman chuckled.

"I don't find shit funny Roman. I swear, if you don't come home tonight, I'm leaving," Malia threatened.

"Cool, just leave my key on the dresser," Roman said as he grabbed his hat and tried to walk pass her.

"I hate you!" Malia screamed as she started swinging on him.

She felt like a fool to have left her family for Roman and be treated like shit. That wasn't his first time getting caught messing around and Malia was sick of it. Her situation was the prime example of the grass not being greener on the other side. She thought she wanted to be on the arm of a bad boy, but it was proving to be more trouble than it was worth.

"Stop putting your hands on me, man!" Roman barked as he towered over her.

"What time are you coming back home Roman? I'm not playing with you. That sleeping out shit is over with. You need to be home in bed at a decent hour," Malia said as he stood guard by the bedroom door.

"Didn't you just say that you were leaving? Get your shit and get the fuck on then," Roman said as he tried to move her out of the way.

"I'm not going nowhere. You better bring your ass back to this house tonight Roman!" Malia yelled.

"I'll think about it," Roman smirked, toying with her emotions.

"This is not funny Roman!" Malia screamed as she swung and hit him in the mouth.

Roman tasted the blood inside his mouth and became enraged. He was tired of Malia putting her hands on him every time she got mad. She had just gotten rid of a black eye the month before for the same shit.

"Bitch! I told you to keep your fucking hands to yourself," he snapped as he slapped Malia across her face twice and watched her drop down to the floor.

She was still blocking the door, so he kicked her legs to make her move.

"The fuck is that stupid bitch on today?" Chad asked when his brother walked out of the bedroom.

"Man, fuck that hoe!" Roman barked as the two men made their way outside.

"What happened?" Chad questioned once they were in Roman's car.

"Her stupid ass went through my phone and saw some shit that she didn't want to see. I just knocked fire from that silly hoe. I keep telling her to keep her hands to herself," Roman answered.

"That's good for her stupid ass. You know I never did like that bitch. She gets no respect from me," Chad replied.

He never liked Malia from day one and nothing had changed. He couldn't respect a woman who left her kids behind just to be with a man. He and his brother never really had a mother growing up and his heart went out to kids who grew up the same way. He had mad respect for Malia's ex-husband for doing his part and raising his sons. He and Roman didn't even know who their father was. They'd met Malia's ex-husband before and he seemed like a cool dude. He had his head on straight and they had to respect that.

"I already know you can't stand her ass," Roman laughed.

"I can understand if she wanted to leave her husband. He's a grown ass man and he'll get over it eventually. But for her to just leave her kids like that is just fucked up. I'll never like or respect her ass for that," Chad replied.

"I told the bitch that I didn't want kids. I wasn't telling her to leave her kids behind to be with me though," Roman acknowledged.

He and his brother had met Malia's sons several times when they came over, and Chad really liked them. He felt their pain and he tried his best to make them feel comfortable. Roman liked them too, even though he was ready to be done with their mother.

"Put her stupid ass out," Chad said, making his brother laugh.

"No worries lil brother, her time is almost up," Roman said as he looked down at his ringing phone that displayed Malia's number.

"Didn't you just slap that bitch around in there? The fuck is she calling for now?" Chad asked with a frown.

"The fuck you want Malia?" Roman barked as the call connected through his car speakers.

"My sons are coming over until tomorrow. Can you bring us something to eat later?" she asked him.

Although Roman didn't want kids of his own, Malia knew that he liked her sons. She hoped that by telling him that they were coming over, he would come back home that night and stay.

"Yeah, I'll stop and grab something," Roman replied, making her smile through her busted lip.

"Okay, thanks baby," Malia said before hanging up.

She called Landon next, to let him know of her plans. Admittedly, Malia didn't spend as much time with her sons as she should have. She called them all the time, but she was too busy trying to keep up with Roman. Malia didn't know much about the lifestyle that Roman lived, but she had to learn fast if she wanted to keep him happy.

"That bitch think she slick. She's only getting her sons over there, so you don't sleep out again. Sad ass bitch always trying to use her kids for some shit,"

Chad said with a frown once his brother was done with his call.

"I already know, but she ain't slicker than me. I'm going drop some food and snacks off for my lil dudes and I'm going chill with Jessica. Fuck Malia," Roman said as he and his brother fell out laughing.

It was good while it lasted, but the single life was the only one that Roman wanted to live. Malia needed to go back home to her family or find her somebody new. Whatever she did was all on her and Roman didn't care one way or the other.

Chapter 4

"The fuck did that stupid bitch want?" Aiden asked his nephew when he got off the phone with Malia.

"Chill out with the name calling bruh. She's still my son's mother," Landon replied.

"Man, fuck that bitch. She don't act like nobody's mama with her trifling ass. What is she calling for anyway?" Aiden asked again.

"She wants the boys to spend the night with her," Landon replied.

"And you trust that shit? Do you even know the nigga that she's living with?" Aiden inquired.

"Yeah, I met him and his brother before. They're cool, and my boys said they treat them right. That's all that matters to me." Landon shrugged.

"Ain't no damn way," Aiden said, shaking his head.

"What?" Landon questioned.

"I just don't see how you do it. I can't be cool with no nigga that my bitch left me for," Aiden noted.

"Man, I don't have nothing against that dude. I wasn't married to him and he don't owe me shit," Landon replied.

"Yeah, I guess you got a point. But, aye, since that hoe coming get the boys, you need to come hit the club with me this weekend," Aiden said.

"Nah, hell no bruh. I'm good on going to the club, especially with your ass," Landon replied.

"The fuck you mean? What's wrong with going to the club with me?" Aiden questioned.

"You always into some shit bruh. I got kids and a career to think about. I can't be out there getting caught up in no bullshit with you," Landon replied.

"Nah nephew, I'm good on all that now. I ain't been on that dumb shit lately," Aiden swore.

"Nigga, you were just running from the police two weeks ago," Landon reminded him.

"I know, but I'm a changed man now. And you should want to get your ass out of this damn house. You ain't had pussy in over a year. You gon' fuck around and get somebody pregnant when you do get some," Aiden noted.

"Nah man, I'm good," Landon maintained.

"Bruh, you got money, a big ass house, a nice car, and a few businesses that keep your accounts looking right. You're my nephew, so being handsome runs in the family. You got the whole Saks Fifth Avenue in your closet, so clothes ain't a problem. All this shit you got going for yourself and you still don't have a woman. The fuck is you waiting on? Bitches don't just fall from the sky. You gotta get out there and find one," Aiden advised.

"First off, I don't want a bitch. If I get somebody, it's gon' be a grown ass woman with something going for herself. Secondly, I'm not going to no club to find nobody. If it's meant to be, she'll come to me," Landon replied.

"I feel that, but you still need to get out of this house bruh. All you do is work and come home," Aiden said, right as Landon's sons walked into the sitting room.

"My mama just called and said she's coming to get us," Lennox said excitedly.

Landon had purchased both his sons a phone and Malia always called to talk to them. Lance never answered for her, but Lennox looked forward to her calls.

"Yeah, she just called and told me. Y'all go pack a bag. She's on her way," Landon replied as he watched Lennox run back upstairs.

He was entertaining the idea of a night out with his uncle since his sons were leaving. Landon hadn't done anything by himself in a long time. He always spent his weekends with his boys doing whatever they wanted to do. Even when they were with Malia, which wasn't often, Landon would stay inside or do some overtime at work. He wasn't even thirty years old and he had no life outside of his kids.

"Dad, can I talk to you for a minute?" Lance asked, sounding like a mature young man.

"What's wrong?" Landon asked as he walked away, following his son into the kitchen.

"I don't want to go with my mama. Can I stay here with you or go by GG?" Lance asked.

Landon remembered Faryn telling him how his son felt when he made him spend time with Malia. That was one of the reasons why he started acting out. Lance had been seeing Faryn for a little over a month and he was doing much better in school. He hadn't had a fight since he started counseling and that was a bonus. Even his principal was impressed, and she called and told Landon just how well he was doing. He didn't want to send him with Malia and ruin all the progress that he was making.

"You don't have to go if you don't want to. You can stay here with me," Landon replied, abandoning his plans to go out for the night.

"Really? I can stay here instead of going over there?" Lance asked excitedly.

"Yeah, we can find something to do here while Lennox is gone." Landon smiled.

"Thanks dad." Lance smiled as he ran to tell his little brother the good news.

Lennox still wanted to go and that was fine with his father. Landon checked to make sure his bag was packed, right before they all went outside and sat on the huge wraparound porch. Aiden was still in

Landon's ear about going out, but he wasn't changing his mind.

"Lance is staying home, so I can't go nowhere anyway," Landon said.

"Man, you know my mama will watch Lance while we go out. Stop making excuses," Aiden argued.

"I can go by my auntie," Lance said, referring to Makena.

"Call her and see if you can stay the night over there Lance," Aiden replied.

"Okay," Lance said as he ran inside to get his phone.

"Man, it ain't that damn serious," Landon chuckled while shaking his head.

"It's very serious nigga. I'm trying to make sure you get some pussy tonight," Aiden said, as Lennox giggled at his use of words.

"Nigga, I know you see my son standing right here," Landon fussed.

"That lil nigga alright. He know what's up," Aiden said as he started air boxing with Lennox.

"My auntie said that I can come over there. She said she's coming to pick me up when she finishes getting her nails done," Lance said when he came back outside.

"It's on now nigga. We're going hit up the clubs tonight," Aiden said excitedly.

Landon was about to reply until he saw Malia's all white Benz coming down their street. He'd just purchased the car for her two months before she left, and it was the only thing, besides her clothes, that she left with.

"Didn't I tell y'all not to give nobody the code to that gate? I've already changed it three times and y'all keep giving it out," Landon fussed as he looked at his sons.

"Lennox gave it to her again," Lance ratted.

"She needed to get in to pick me up," Lennox replied.

"The guard could have let her in or I could have buzzed her in with my phone. Nobody is supposed to have the code to the gate unless I give it to them or they live here," Landon said, stressing the same thing to his sons once again.

"Yeah and that bitch don't live here," Aiden replied.

"Chill Aiden bruh, damn," Landon fussed.

They all watched as Malia drove up the winding stone driveway and stopped her car in front of the house. Landon remembered when she left how his heart would damn near beat out of his chest whenever he saw her again. He always held on to the hope that she would change her mind and want to be a family again. As the months passed on, that feeling of nervousness stopped and seeing her had no effect on him at all. She was just another woman on the streets and any love that he once had for her was gone. He didn't think that he would ever get to that point, but he was happy that he did. He and Malia were cool and cordial, especially for the sake of their kids. They clashed occasionally, but that was only when she didn't come through like she was supposed to. Landon hated when she made promises to them that she didn't keep.

"Hey, my babies." Malia smiled when she walked up and pulled Lennox into a hug. Lance stood behind his father and didn't even bother trying to go to her.

"Come here and give me a hug Lance. You see your daddy all the time. Stop acting like you see me every day," Malia said.

"It ain't his fault that you left home to go be a dope man's kept bitch," Aiden spoke up.

"But anyway," Malia said rolling her eyes," Come give your mama a hug."

Lance didn't want to, but he slowly walked over to his mother and gave her a hug. As soon as she let him go, he walked back over to his father and stood next to him.

"What's up Landon?" Malia asked as she locked eyes with her ex-husband.

Hands down, Landon was the sexiest man that she'd ever had the pleasure of meeting. Roman was handsome in a thugged-out kind of way, but he didn't have shit on Landon. Malia always loved to see how he dressed because he knew how to put his clothes together very well. He even dressed their sons and they were always fresh. Landon only had on jeans and a t-shirt, but the outfit looked like it was tailored just for him. If Malia thought that she could have had him and Roman at the same time, she wouldn't have hesitated to try. She did have them both for a while, but that was becoming too much to handle.

"Ain't shit. What's good with you?" Landon asked, breaking her away from her thoughts of him.

"Nothing much, I just wanted to spend some time with my babies. Y'all ready to go?" Malia asked them.

"Lance ain't coming," Lennox informed her.

"What? Why not?" she asked while looking at her oldest son.

"I don't want to come," Lance answered while looking right at her.

"You don't have no wants boy. Come on here and let's go," Malia replied.

"Dad," Lance said, looking at his father with pleading eyes.

"Nah Malia, he ain't coming," Landon replied.

"Really Landon? He's a child. You're letting him make the decisions now," Malia fussed.

"That dude don't have to go nowhere with your ass. You're the one who left him, not the other way around," Aiden noted.

"Aiden, chill bruh, please," Landon begged.

He knew how his uncle was and he didn't need that kind of drama in front of his kids. Malia had a slick tongue, and Aiden wouldn't hesitate to knock her out.

"Man, let me bring my ass in this house before I be getting locked up again. Come on lil man," Aiden said, calling out to Lance.

"Go get in the car and wait for your mama, Lennox," Landon instructed his son.

"What's going on Landon? What's his problem?" Malia asked, referring to Lance.

"He doesn't want to come with you anymore Malia. I used to make him go with you and it was doing more harm than good. He started getting into fights and acting up in school," Landon replied.

"Okay and what does that have to do with me?" Malia asked.

"You can't be serious right now," Landon said as he looked at her like she was stupid.

"I'm very serious," Malia replied.

"Malia, he's a child. He didn't understand why you left the way you did. He thought it was something that he did wrong. I tried explaining everything to him the best way I knew how, but he still didn't get it," Landon said.

"I know that my leaving was hard on them, but I'm trying Landon. I'm trying my best to make up for that," Malia said as tears came to her eyes.

"That's just it Malia; you can't," Landon replied honestly.

"So, what am I supposed to do Landon? I love my kids and I do want to spend more time with them," Malia cried.

"Just give him some time Malia. He's been seeing a behavior specialist and things are already starting to look up. Maybe you can try calling to talk to him sometimes, to make things a little easier," Landon suggested.

"I call him all the time, but he never answers," Malia noted.

"I'll see what I can do about that. Just give it some time. He'll come around eventually," Landon assured her, as she nodded her head sadly.

"Thanks Landon. I appreciate you. You're a great father and you always have been." Malia smiled.

"I'm just doing what I'm supposed to do. They're my first priority and they always will be," Landon said, making her feel low.

She knew that he wasn't directing his comment towards her, but it still hit home. Malia was selfish, and it showed by her actions. She never thought about how her leaving was going to affect her sons. She did what made her happy and that was all that mattered. She would never admit it out loud, but she regretted her decision to leave home. Roman was not who she thought he was and it just wasn't worth it. Landon proved to be the better man and she wished she could go back and do things differently. Unfortunately, she had fallen in love with Roman and that was hard to let go off. As much as she hated to admit it, she was still in love with her ex-husband too.

Chapter 5

"What's up beautiful? Can I buy you a drink?" a man walked up to Faryn and asked.

It was her third offer in less than an hour, but she wasn't interested. Someone else had just purchased her third glass of wine a few minutes before and she was still sipping on it.

"No, I'm fine, but thanks anyway." Faryn smiled as she held up her glass for him to see.

"Okay, maybe later then," he replied before walking away.

"The fuck did she come for if she gon' be acting all stuck up?" Monica said to Harley, loud enough for Faryn to hear.

"How is she acting stuck up? She was polite and she smiled. Besides, she already got a drink," Harley said, defending her girl.

"Who comes to a club and orders wine?" Monica asked, making Harley frown.

Harley and Monica had met at the nail salon two years before and they had been cool ever since. Monica had three kids with three different men and she was a true hater. If she saw someone doing just a little better than her, she always had something negative to say about them. The first day she laid eyes on Faryn at Harley's apartment, she decided that she didn't like her. Monica didn't even know the other woman's name at the time. Her sister, Felicia, was the same way, but she wasn't as bad as Monica. Felica had two kids as well, but they were by the same man. She was supposed to be with them that night, but she couldn't find a babysitter. Monica left her kids home with her newest man, which was crazy in Harley's opinion.

"Maybe she would fit in more if she guzzled down a few Heinekens and Corona's like you," Harley laughed after a while.

"I'll pass on that. I'm not trying to get no beer belly," Faryn said as she looked over at Monica's swollen gut.

Monica had five empty beer bottles in front of her and had just ordered another one. No one had offered to buy her a drink and she was salty about that as well.

"I know she ain't trying to talk about me!" Monica yelled angrily.

"Chill out with all that Monica. Let's just enjoy ourselves without all the extra," Harley replied.

Faryn had turned her head and tuned out the entire conversation. She was ready to go, and she regretted not taking her own car. Hell, she regretted agreeing to go with Harley to the club at all. She had been getting hit on and groped all night and she was over it all.

"I wish my sister was here. I know I would have had a good time for sure," Monica said.

"I thought you said that Felicia didn't have a babysitter," Harley reminded her.

"Not Felicia, my other sister. Her son is at her house, so she couldn't make it," Monica said.

"Oh," Harley said with a roll of her eyes.

Monica and Felicia looked up to their younger sister, Malia, for some reason. Harley didn't know why because she was a sad ass woman in her opinion. She had never met her, but Monica told her all about how she'd left her husband and kids to be with some nigga who sold dope and beat on her. Monica said that her husband had a good job with money, but her sister still wasn't satisfied. Some women had more luck than sense and their sister sounded like the type. Malia apparently drove a nice car and wore expensive clothes and Monica thought that was the life. She didn't see anything wrong with what her sister did, and she always told her so. Harley thought she was a little envious of her sister, but Monica always denied it.

"What time are we leaving?" Faryn asked as she tapped Harley's arm, interrupting their little private conversation.

"We just got here a little while ago. And you don't have to work tomorrow, so you can't use that as an excuse," Harley replied.

"I know I don't have to work. I was just asking," Faryn replied.

"You got mad niggas trying to get at you, bitch. You need to let somebody knock the cob webs off that coochie," Harley laughed.

"Bitch, please. These niggas got on more fake jewelry than a two-dollar hoe. I've never seen so many imitation labels before in my life. The bitch at the end of the bar used red tape to make her red bottoms. I'm over it," Faryn said, making Harley double over with laughter.

"Well, everybody ain't able to live in fancy apartments and wear thousand-dollar shoes," Monica butted in with an attitude.

"And that's fine, but why pretend? It's a lot of stuff that I can't afford and I'm okay with that. But, what I'm not gonna do is try to recreate the shit on my own. I'm not wearing Miguel Kors if I can't afford to buy Michael," Faryn said, taking a shot at Monica's knock-off hand bag.

The inauthentic Louie Vuitton leggings with the matching shirt screamed flea market, but Monica thought she was the shit. Add her burgundy wig and cheap leather boots to the equation and she was a hot ass mess. Harley was cute in a black cat suit that she paired with a coral blazer. Her hair was parted down the middle and flat ironed straight. Faryn was cute and classy in some wide legged pants and the matching crop top. The outfit was navy and white, so she put on her canary yellow red bottoms to make it pop. Her makeup was light, and her hair was wind curled and bouncy.

"Bitch, you got the right one. I'll mop the floor with your conceited ass!" Monica yelled as she made a move towards Faryn.

"Do I look scared bitch?" Faryn questioned as she stood her ground and waited.

"Oh no, ladies, we need to calm down. We're grown ass women and there will be no fighting," Harley said as she got in between them.

She was happy that the music was loud because they were doing too much. Monica was always coming for Faryn and she was obviously sick of it. Harley didn't blame her for clapping back, but she didn't want them to fight or make a scene.

"I'm going to the bathroom," Faryn said as she shook her head in disgust.

"Are you okay? You want me to come with you?" Harley offered.

"I'm good, but I'm sick of that bad built gorilla looking bitch. I'm tired of pretending that I don't hear the slick shit that comes out of her mouth. She better not let the cute face fool her. I'll fuck her up and fix my makeup after," Faryn replied.

"Don't let Monica get to you. She's jealous and we both know that. Give me your phone and purse while you go to the bathroom. These hoes are master pickpockets around this way," Harley noted.

Faryn handed her friend her stuff and made her way through the crowd. She got stopped a million times along the way, but she finally made it to the bathroom. The line was long as hell, but Faryn couldn't wait. She looked over at the men's bathroom and was tempted to go inside. That was like stepping into the lion's den, so she quickly abandoned that idea. The three glasses of wine that she drank were running through her and she had to cross her legs to keep from pissing on herself. It wasn't that bad at first but, the closer she got to the bathroom, the stronger the urge to go became.

"Ugh! This bitch is throwing up all over the bathroom!" some girl yelled when she walked out of the bathroom frowning.

"Y'all can't use that bathroom. There's vomit all over the floors," another girl walked out behind her and said.

Faryn, along with some of the other women who were waiting, sighed in frustration. A few women stayed there and waited, but most of the women in line turned and walked away. Faryn was stuck for a minute, but she finally decided to walk away too.

"Shit!" Faryn hissed as she turned around and ran right into someone.

"Whoa. Slow down my baby," a masculine voice said while grabbing her arm.

Faryn looked up ready to apologize, when she looked into Landon's smiling face. He looked like a walking orgasm with his smooth like butter chocolate skin. The Versace polo style shirt that he had on hugged his muscles, and Faryn wanted to jump on him right there in public. His jeans hung low on his waist, but it wasn't trashy like some of the other men who she saw. Most of the men in the club tried hard to look the part, but Landon was born for the role. There was nothing fake about his designer labels and he wore them well.

"I'm so sorry Mr. Reynolds," Faryn apologized.

"Girl, if you don't knock it off with that Mr. Reynolds stuff. You make me sound like an old ass man. Just call me Landon," he replied.

"Sorry, Landon," Faryn apologized again.

"It's cool, but where are you rushing off to?" Landon asked.

"I was going to the bathroom, but somebody threw up in there. I feel like I'm about to pee on myself," Faryn said as she crossed her legs and rocked back and forth.

"Come on, I got you," Landon said as he grabbed her hand.

"Landon no, wait a second," Faryn protested when she saw him walking towards the men's bathroom.

She'd briefly entertained the idea of going in there, but she abandoned the idea just as quickly as it came. The men's bathroom was probably worse than the women's and she didn't want no parts of it.

"Your outfit it too cute for you to be pissing on yourself. Come on, I got you," Landon said as he opened the door and looked inside.

There was only one person in there, so he waited by the door with Faryn until the other man washed his hands and came out.

"Come on," Landon said as he grabbed her hand and made his way inside.

"I'm scared," Faryn admitted as she looked around nervously.

"I got you, baby girl. Nobody is gonna come in here," Landon promised as he stood guard at the door.

"Are you sure?" Faryn asked him.

"I promise," Landon assured her.

"Okay," Faryn said as she ran to one of the stalls and locked the door.

Surprisingly, the bathroom was cleaner than she thought it would be. Her bladder was full, and she appreciated Landon more than he knew. Faryn pulled down her pants and squatted over the black porcelain right, as someone started banging on the bathroom door. She was a nervous mess as she relieved herself as quickly as she could. It felt like she would never stop and the banging on the door had her shook.

"Move around nigga! The bathroom is occupied!" Landon yelled out to whoever was trying to come in.

Faryn giggled as she finished using the bathroom and used her heeled foot to flush the toilet. She saw that Landon was still standing guard by the door with his muscular arms folded across his chest.

"Thank you so much Landon. I really appreciate this," Faryn said as she washed her hands.

She felt so relieved and she was done drinking for the night.

"No problem. You look like you really had to go." Landon smiled.

"You have no idea. I'm ready to go from here period," Faryn replied, referring to the club.

"Shit, I don't even know why I came. I let my uncle talk me into this shit and I'm not even feeling it," Landon replied.

He and Faryn walked out of the bathroom together as people stared at them and whispered. Faryn didn't give a fuck and, apparently, neither did Landon. They continued with their conversation like it was nothing.

"I let my friend talk me into coming and she drove. Now, I have to wait until she's ready to leave," Faryn said.

"No, you don't. I can bring you home," Landon offered.

"No Landon, it's okay. I don't want to rush you. That's what I get for riding with someone else," Faryn replied.

"You're not rushing me. I'm leaving if I take you home or not. The club scene just ain't my thing," Landon admitted.

"Mine either," Faryn agreed.

"Cool, let's get up out of here then," he suggested.

"You don't have to tell me twice. Just let me get my phone and purse and tell my girl that I'm leaving. I can meet you out front," Faryn said.

"Okay, I'll be out there," Landon said, right as Aiden was walking over to him.

"That bitch is fine. Who is that?" Aiden asked as he watched Faryn walk away.

"Stop calling every female you see a bitch," Landon scolded.

"Nigga, I'm the uncle and you better not forget that shit. You and that nigga Raheem better get y'all mind right," Aiden replied while pointing an unsteady finger in Landon's face.

Aiden was tipsy, and Landon knew that he was just getting started. Raheem was there with him, so Landon knew that he would be okay. Raheem drove, and Aiden was probably going to stay the night at his house.

"I hear you, bruh, but I'm getting out of here," Landon informed him.

"What! We just got here a few hours ago nephew," Aiden replied.

"I know, but I have to bring Faryn home," Landon said.

"Who the fuck is Ferret?" Aiden slurred.

"Faryn bruh, the chick that I was just walking with," Landon answered.

"Oh shit, the fine one. Yeah nigga, you move fast like a muthafucker. Just like your uncle. You finally bout to get some pussy!" Aiden yelled excitedly.

"Bye bruh. I'll call you tomorrow," Landon replied as he walked away and headed for the exit.

He waited for about five minutes before Faryn came out and joined him. They both walked to his black G-Wagon and got in. Faryn smiled when he opened the door for her because that had never happened before. Even when they got to her house, Landon got out of the car and walked her to her front door.

"Thank you so much Landon. You were a lifesaver tonight." Faryn smiled.

"No problem. Maybe you can return the favor one day," Landon replied, making Faryn look at him sideways for a second.

She didn't want to believe that Landon was that type. He didn't look like the kind of man who expected something from a woman at the end of the night. It wasn't like he and Faryn were on a date. He gave her a ride home and she would be happy to give him gas money.

"What do you mean?" Faryn asked after being stuck for a minute.

"Let me take you out. Maybe dinner and a movie or whatever you want to do," Landon replied.

"God, you just don't know how bad I want to say yes," Faryn said as she looked into his handsome face.

"Okay, so say yes." Landon smiled, making her weak in the knees.

"I can't. It's against the rules for me to date the family member of a client," Faryn replied.

"I understand that, but who's gonna know?" Landon questioned.

"Probably nobody, but I'm too afraid to take the risk," Faryn said honestly.

Landon didn't like her answer, but he understood her position. He was still happy that he asked her because he no longer had to wonder about the possibilities. He'd wanted to ask her out since he first saw her, but he hadn't approached a woman in a long time. He didn't even know what to say. He was happy when the opportunity finally presented itself tonight, even though it didn't work out in his favor.

"I understand," Landon said after a long pause. "Make sure you lock up and have a good night."

"Thanks, you have a good night too," Faryn replied as she walked inside and closed the door behind her.

It was morning, but no one cared about the time. Faryn stood with her back up against the door as she tried to control her breathing. She was very attracted to Landon and that was her first time being around him all alone. She had regrets about turning him down the moment the words flew from her mouth. Faryn always said that she wanted a good man and she'd probably run one of the best ones away because of her fear. Landon was right. There was no way for anyone to know if they'd gone on a date or not. For all Faryn knew, one date could be all that transpired between them. Even still, she would never know unless she took a chance. She was tired of playing it safe all the time. She had more fun in her wild teenage years. Lately, work and home were the highlights of her day, and she wanted a change. Deciding to take a chance for once, Faryn opened the door and looked down the hallway for Landon. He must have already gotten on the elevator, so she took the steps and saw him right as he got into his truck.

"Landon!" Faryn yelled out of breath.

"Yeah. Is everything okay?" he asked, looking around to make sure she wasn't being followed.

"How about right now?" Faryn asked.

"What about right now?" Landon questioned.

"The date. How about right now?" Faryn asked again.

"Um... okay." Landon smiled as he closed his car door and walked over to her.

Chapter 6

"I hope you're not allergic to seafood." Faryn said as she and Landon made their way back up to her apartment on the elevator.

When she agreed to an impromptu date, Landon didn't know what she had in mind. He had no idea that Faryn was going to invite him up to her apartment to cook for him. He didn't know too much about her, so he didn't know if she even knew how to cook.

"No, I'm not allergic to anything," Landon said as they walked up to her door.

When Faryn ushered him inside, he was impressed. Her entire living room was decorated in pink, black, and white, the same as her office. She had a Paris theme and it was very feminine. Just like her office, her apartment smelled like tropical fruit. Landon could tell that she was a good housekeeper because everything was neat and in its place.

"Nice apartment," Landon complimented.

"Thanks. You can have a seat. I just need to change right quick," Faryn said as she disappeared down the hall.

She was a nervous wreck. Aside from Harley's husband, Kyron, Landon was the only man who had ever been in her apartment. Redd had been begging for over a year, but Faryn was done with him. He'd been calling her from another number apologizing since she still had him blocked. Faryn was cordial with him, but her mind was still made up. She was sure he'd found another favorite at the club by now, so he could leave her alone.

After throwing on a pair of yoga pants and a tank, Faryn slipped her feet in a pair of fuzzy slippers and pulled her hair back into a loose ponytail. She took a few deep breaths to contain her nervousness before she headed back to the living room where Landon waited.

"Here's the remote. You can watch whatever you want while I fix our food," Faryn said when she walked over to him.

"I'd rather watch you cook," Landon replied, making her blush.

"Um, okay, I have two bar stools at the kitchen counter," she replied as he followed behind her.

Faryn turned on her radio that was built in under the counter, so they could listen to some music.

"You need some help?" Landon asked while she washed her hands.

"Nice try, but Lance already told me that you can't cook. He's very thankful for his GG and your sister cooking for y'all," Faryn laughed.

"That nigga be telling all my business," Landon said, laughing with her.

"He never has anything bad to say though. Not about you anyway," Faryn noted.

"Yeah, I'm sure the same can't be said about his mama," Landon said, shaking his head.

"What happened? If you don't mind me asking," Faryn said as she started cooking.

She had already prepped her Sunday meal and she was happy for that. She planned to have homemade shrimp alfredo with salad and garlic bread. She was happy that she didn't have to eat it alone or with Harley and Kyron like she usually did.

"No, I don't mind. I honestly don't know what happened. I mean, I thought I was doing everything right. I married and started a family with my high school sweetheart. I went to college and got my degree. I got a good paying job and made sure that my family was well taken care of. We always talked about investing to increase our income, so I did that too with the help of my stepfather. When she couldn't find a house that she wanted, I decided to get her one built from the ground up. We were a few weeks away from them breaking ground on our new home when she hit me with the divorce papers," Landon explained.

"Oh, my God. Why would she do that?" Faryn asked with a puzzled look on her face.

"She started out with some bullshit excuse about not having a life outside of me and the kids. Once she left, she tried to make it seem like it was my fault. I did make a lot of promises in the beginning, but I was too busy building for our future. I guess the long hours away from home started to be too much for her. I promised her vacations and a lot of other stuff, but it takes money to do anything. I was ready to make good on my word, but she was already done with the marriage by then." Landon shrugged.

Faryn could tell that he was over the situation now because he was almost emotionless when he talked about it. She knew it had to be hard on him because it was definitely hard on Lance.

"It had to be more to it than that. I would have been happy if a man had done half of what you did for her. You think she had another man or something?" Faryn asked as she stirred her pot.

"She moved in with him the same day she left and they're still together," Landon replied, making her mouth hang open in shock.

"Now, I see why you kept your sons. She just up and moved in with another man," Faryn said, shaking her head.

"That was her choice too. She said that they were boys and they needed their father to teach them how to be men. I didn't want them there to see her leave, so I asked her to go while they were at school. They came home looking for her and I had to break the news to them. Lance has been fucked up ever since."

"I'm so sorry to hear that," Faryn said solemnly.

"It's all good. My sons are my only concern. Lennox was a mama's boy, so he still likes to be around her. Lance is doing better since he's been seeing you, but his feelings towards her are the same. I'm just happy that he's talking more and not acting out as much."

"Yeah, I've been telling him to use his words and not his fist. He'll get better results that way. He said his teachers have been telling him how well he's been doing. That makes me feel good." Faryn smiled.

"That makes two of us." Landon smiled back.

"Are you ready to eat?" Faryn asked.

"Will I wake up in the morning?" Landon questioned with raised brows.

"It's already morning, smart ass. I know how to cook. I live on Pinterest," Faryn said as she grabbed two plates from her cabinet and washed them off.

"What's Pinterest?" Landon asked.

"It's a site that has recipes and anything else that you might want or need," Faryn said as she fixed their food.

She smiled when Landon told her to bow her head while he said grace. That was a first for her too. Faryn often dug into her food without ever giving thanks to the one who made it possible. She was just taught a valuable lesson and she vowed to change that.

"Damn, you got some skills," Landon complimented as he ate his first bite of food.

"I told you. You need to get on Pinterest and feed those babies," Faryn joked.

"Nah, I'm good on that. My sister and grandma got us covered," Landon replied.

"What about your mama? Is she still alive?" Faryn asked.

"Yeah, but it doesn't matter much to me," Landon replied.

Faryn listened as he told her a little about his childhood. She was surprised that he still managed to get a degree and a career. He told her about his anger issues as a child and his story sounded so much like Lance's.

"Damn," Faryn mumbled.

"What about you? What's your story?" Landon asked.

"Nothing special. I'm the youngest of four, born to a crackhead who overdosed when I was sixteen. I haven't seen my siblings in years and I don't have any other family that I know of. I've been on my own since I was eighteen. I danced at JB's Gentlemen's Club to keep a roof over my head and put myself through college. I got my bachelor's first before graduating with my master's in learning and behavior analysis and here I am," Faryn rambled.

"You used to strip?" Landon asked in shock.

"For four years, but is that all you heard?" Faryn laughed.

"No, but that's shocking. I would have never guessed that about you. I've heard of that JB's place before, but I've never been there," Landon replied.

"You didn't miss anything. It's just a cover up for a whore house," Faryn said as she took their dishes to the sink.

She was surprised when Landon got up and helped her clean up their mess.

"Damn, if I would have known you were working there, I would have come through. I would have been one of your regulars too." Landon winked.

"I had one of those who's now turned into a potential stalker," Faryn replied.

"Why am I not surprised?" Landon smirked.

"I'm an open book Landon. I have nothing to hide. I'm not proud of some of the things I did, but it is what it is," Faryn said as they retired to the living room.

She was happy that he didn't have a look of judgment on his face. That made her relax and open up to him even more. Faryn grabbed her throw blanket and snuggled up on the sofa. Landon sat on the floor in front of her as they continued to talk about their past. Faryn was open and honest about everything and so was he. They both admitted to not being intimate with anyone for over a year and they were both shocked at the others revelation. Before long, they had finished off the rest of the food as they watched a few movies. A little while after that, they had both drifted off to sleep.

When Faryn got up hours later, Landon was still stretched out on her living room floor fully clothed with shoes and all. It was almost noon and she was sure that he had to get home to his kids. His phone had been ringing like crazy, but he didn't even hear it.

"Landon," Faryn said as she shook his arm.

"Yeah," he replied as he sat up and looked around. He looked a little confused about where he was until he looked up into her smiling face.

"Your phone has been ringing off the hook," Faryn noted.

Landon grabbed his phone and saw that he had a bunch of missed calls from Malia, Lennox, and his grandmother. Malia was probably ready to bring their son home, but no one was there.

"Shit! I gotta get going," he said as he jumped up from the floor.

"Okay, let me walk you out," Faryn offered.

"I need your number and not the same one that you gave Lance. I want your personal number," Landon said as they walked to the door.

"Give me your phone," Faryn requested.

She called her personal phone from his, so that she would have his number too.

"Make sure you lock me in," Landon said, as she walked him to the elevator.

"I will," she replied.

"And even though I appreciate the food and conversation, this was not a date. I want to take you somewhere and I'm not taking no for an answer," Landon said.

"Who said that I was gonna say no?" Faryn asked, right as his phone rang.

"Awe shit. This is my grandmother again. She probably put out a missing person's report on me," he laughed.

"Call her back, so she won't worry. And make sure you call me later," Faryn replied.

"No doubt," Landon said as he gave her a hug and got on the elevator.

Faryn smiled all the way to her apartment, until Harley opened her door and started up her drama.

"Bitch, you said you had a ride home, but I didn't know it was with a nigga. And you let him spend the night too. I want the tea on his cute, sexy ass!" Harley yelled.

"There is no tea, bitch, and I'm too tired to talk about it right now. I need a nap." Faryn yawned.

"You make sure you call me as soon as you wake up," Harley demanded.

"Okay nosey," Faryn agreed.

"What time are you gonna cook today?" Harley questioned.

"I already cooked, and the food is gone," she replied as she walked inside, closing and locking her door behind her.

She heard Harley cursing her out, but she was too tired to entertain her.

Chapter 7

Landon pulled up in front of his grandmother's house and sat in his car for a while. His boys jumped out and ran inside, while he talked on the phone with Faryn. It had been exactly three months since he stayed the night at her house and they still hadn't gone on an official date. He went to Faryn's house all the time when his boys weren't home but, most of the time, they talked on the phone all day. Faryn was still nervous about them dating, but Landon was running out of patience.

"You sure you don't need me to bring anything?" Landon asked her.

"Nope, just you," Faryn replied with a smile evident in her voice.

"Okay, I just got to my grandmother's house, so I'll be there in a little while," Landon replied, right before they hung up.

He walked into the house and found his sister, grandmother, and uncle Aiden all in the kitchen talking. His nephew and Ava's daughter were also standing there talking to his sons.

"Daddy! Look at what my auntie got us!" Lennox yelled excitedly as he showed Landon the hand-held video game that he had.

"That's what's up," Landon replied with a smile.

His sister was always buying them something and he did the same with his only nephew. Makena had asked for her nephews to spend the night with her son, and Landon happily obliged. He didn't have anything planned, so he was happy to be going spend the day with Faryn.

"Sit down and let me fix you something to eat," Ella said when her grandson walked over and kissed her.

"No, I'm good. I'm going eat in a little while," Landon replied.

"Going eat where?" Makena asked as she eyed him suspiciously.

"By a friend," Landon replied.

"A fine ass friend," Aiden smirked, making Landon frown.

"It's Ms. Clark," Lance blurted out.

"She's pretty too," Lennox replied.

Lennox had met Faryn one night when they went to her house for dinner and he wasn't shy about admitting to the crush that he had on her.

"Y'all go in the room and play so the adults can talk," Ella said to her grandkids.

"I met somebody grandma. It's not a big deal," Landon said, trying to move away from the situation.

"Boy, you ain't had pussy in over a year. It's a very big deal," Aiden replied as he sat down at the table with a plate of food.

"Watch your mouth muthafucker," Ella fussed, making them all laugh.

She had a mouth like a sailor and so did all her kids and grandkids. She usually let them express themselves freely but, occasionally, she would fuss at their use of language.

"Who is Ms. Clark?" Makena asked.

"Her name is Faryn and its Lance's counselor. Well, she's a behavioral specialist," Landon noted.

"How long have you known her?" Makena questioned, jumping right into her role as the overprotective big sister.

"A few months, but I didn't really talk to her like that until about three months ago. That's who I was with a while back when Malia dropped Lennox off over here. The time you were ready to call the police because you thought I was missing," he laughed while looking at his grandmother.

"You stayed the night at her house?" Makena questioned, remembering how nervous her grandmother was when Landon wasn't answering his phone.

"Yeah, that was our first time talking to each other outside of her counseling Lance," he replied.

"And she let you stay the night?" Makena inquired with a frown.

"I don't like that hussy already. She gave it up on the first night. She didn't even make you work for it," Ella fussed as she stood to her feet.

"What! No grandma, it wasn't even like that. She cooked, and we talked while we ate. We watched movies and just fell asleep. I was on the floor and she stayed on the sofa."

"All these months and you still ain't hit it?" Aiden yelled.

"Shut up Aiden. That's just why your nasty ass always need antibiotics," Ella argued.

"Can she cook?" Makena questioned.

"Yeah, she's a good cook," Landon replied.

"So, is she your girlfriend?" Makena inquired.

"No, man. She's scared to mess with me like that. It's against the rules for her to date anybody associated with her clients," Landon noted.

"Man, ain't nobody gon' know that shit. Tell her to stop acting like that," Aiden replied.

"That's the same thing I said, but she's not trying to jeopardize her career." Landon shrugged.

"Tell her that your big sister said you're worth the risk." Makena smiled. Her brother was a great catch and she just hoped whoever this new woman was realized it.

"Oh, well, I changed my mind. She sounds like a keeper," Ella said right as Ava walked through the door, making her grandkids and son frown in disgust.

"Hey mama. What's up?" Ava asked, not bothering to speak to her niece and nephew or brother.

"Nothing much girl, just talking to Landon about his new girlfriend." Ella smiled.

"It's about damn time. He acts like he was waiting for Malia to come back home. Either that or he gave up on women altogether," Ava laughed.

"Bitch!" Makena yelled as she jumped up and lunged at her.

"Chill out niece. It ain't even that serious," Aiden said as he held Makena back.

"I wish Makena would. Don't get mad at me for spitting facts," Ava said as she stood behind her mother.

She wasn't stupid. She and Makena had fought twice before, and she lost each time. Kane and Landon were always put in the middle, but Landon always had his sister's back.

"Keep talking shit and watch I let her go," Aiden threatened.

"What's going on in here?" Kane asked when he walked into the kitchen.

"You better get your wife before she gets her ass beat," Aiden replied as he continued to hold Makena back.

"That ain't gon' happen," Kane said as he stood in front of Ava like he was bad.

"The fuck you mean pussy ass nigga? I'll drop your punk ass in here too," Aiden threatened as he walked over to him.

He never did like Kane from the first day that Ava introduced them. He was a fraud, but his sister was blinded by dollar signs. Aiden knew he wasn't right, but Ava would have to find that out for herself.

"Stop it! That's enough of this foolishness," Ella argued as she and Landon held Makena and Aiden back.

"I'm sorry grandma. I'm about to get the kids and go," Makena replied.

"You don't have to rush out of here for nobody. We're family and y'all better start acting like it. Ava, you better watch that slick ass mouth of yours. I'm not gonna always be around to protect you," Ella warned.

"I don't need anybody to protect me. I can say what I want. I'm a grown ass woman," Ava replied.

Makena walked off to go get the kids, while Ella continued to fuss at her daughter. Aiden was ready to knock his brother-in-law out, but Landon pulled him out to the porch before he could make a move.

"That fuck boy gon' keep playing with me and Ava gon' be burying his punk ass," Aiden fumed as he pulled out a cigarette and lit it. He knew that he wouldn't be able to live with himself if he took his niece's father from her, but he was tempted.

"Man, fuck that dude. He be doing all that like he's so in love with her and know he be living foul. Stupid ass always claiming to be working at night and ain't never there," Landon replied.

"I told you that he be fucking with some bitch in the projects. Tricking ass nigga be acting like he's the best husband in the world. I can't wait until that bitch Ava get her face cracked. You know I could have been hurt her feelings with what I know, but darkness always finds light. The truth is gonna reveal itself."

"Man, you already know how Ava is. Her stupid ass probably already knows what's up, but she won't say shit. It's too embarrassing if she does. Besides, as long as he keeps the money flowing, she ain't going nowhere," Landon replied.

"I just want to knock his fake ass out one good time. Mama always saving their asses though," Aiden fumed.

"I never did have a problem with him. It's his wife that I'm tired of. He's supposed to have her back as her husband, but he can get it too. I already told him what it is. I don't want them to let the calm demeanor fool them," Landon replied.

"The calm before the storm," Aiden said as he laughed.

Landon was always cool and collected, and Aiden respected that about his nephew. He wasn't to be fucked with, but a lot of people underestimated him. He didn't pop off like Aiden did, but they were one in the same. Landon had never been to jail and that was probably the only difference. Once he did get started, it was hard to make him stop. His knockout game was something serious and several niggas found that out the hard way.

"We're leaving Landon. Call me tomorrow whenever you're ready for me to bring them home," Makena said when her and the kids walked out of the house.

"Alright and y'all be good and listen," Landon said as he walked his sons to his sister's car and saw them off.

"Boy, you got the rest of the day and all night to have fun. You need to go bust a big ass nut and go to sleep," Aiden said.

"Unless I can bust a nut by kissing, that ain't happening," he replied.

"Kissing!" Aiden yelled. "The fuck? Are y'all in high school or what?"

"Maybe she's not ready and I'm not rushing her."

"Damn bruh, you got more patience than me," Aiden said.

"Shit, it's been over a year. I can't help but be patient," Landon replied.

"I'm getting blue balls just thinking bout' that shit." Aiden shuddered.

"Nigga you did three years behind bars one time. Unless you got something that you want to tell me, you went without longer than me," Landon said while looking at his uncle sideways.

"Fuck you, boy. That was by force. This shit is by choice. You choose not to get no pussy. I've seen several broads throw the shit at you and you turned it down."

"You damn right I turned it down. I don't want nothing that I don't have to work hard to get. That's exactly why your dick be leaking green shit all the time," Landon laughed.

"Fuck outta here nigga. It can leak whatever color it wanna leak. I ain't going no whole year without pussy," Aiden noted.

"I guess you were getting boy pussy when you were locked up for them three years then," Landon laughed as he ran to his car when Aiden chased him.

"Your punk ass better run," Aiden laughed as he watched Landon pull off.

Landon blew his horn as he sped up the street and headed to Faryn's house for the night.

Chapter 8

"**Y**ou need to stop being so scary Faryn. That man gon' get tired of waiting for you to stop playing," Harley said as she sat on the bar stool and watched her friend prepare her food.

"How am I playing? I like him but, honestly, I'm scared," Faryn admitted.

"What are you scared of?" Harley asked.

"It's like he's almost too perfect. He's doing everything right and I can just see myself falling in love with him. I'm just having a hard time trying to figure out why he's been single for over a year. Like, why did your wife leave you if you're so well put together? Then, there's my job. I can risk getting fired just by being with him. What if it doesn't work out and I have nothing to fall back on?" Faryn said, revealing to Harley all the thoughts that had been going through her head.

"Stop being so negative all the time Faryn. Nobody is gonna know that y'all are together. It's been three months and all you do is invite the man to your house and cook for him. Hell, you could have at least let him knock the cob webs off your coochie," Harley fussed.

"Bitch, please. And why do you care so much? He's not complaining, and neither am I," Faryn noted.

"He's not complaining yet, but it's only a matter of time. It's obvious that he wants more. He even brought his kids over here to meet you."

"First off, I met Lance a long time ago. He's my client, remember? Secondly, I invited his kids over here, so he didn't do that on his own," Faryn acknowledged.

Lance had been making great progress in school and home since he started seeing Faryn. Landon told her about the good reports that he'd been getting from school and she wanted to reward him. She didn't want to leave his brother out, so she invited them both to her house with their father for dinner. They asked her to make some Philly cheese steak sliders with fries, and Faryn granted their wish. She loved to see Landon interacting with his kids and she couldn't understand how any woman would leave such a perfect setting.

"All that is irrelevant Faryn. You said yourself that Landon is a good man. Stop trying to find fault when there obviously is none. There's no such thing as being too perfect. You know how many women wish they had a man like him? Are you willing to miss out on a chance at happiness because you're afraid to take a small risk?" Harley asked, giving her a lot to think about.

Faryn never got a chance to respond because Kyron was texting Harley's phone before she had a chance to. Harley frowned and stood up, preparing to go back to her own house.

"What's wrong?" Faryn asked as she took in the look on her friend's face.

"He gets on my nerves always bringing these random ass niggas to my house. I'm going off on his ass as soon as his company leaves. I'm sick of this shit," Harley fussed.

"Who is he bringing over there now?" Faryn questioned.

"He just asked me where I was because he wants me to meet one of his friends. Some nigga that he hasn't seen since he was a damn teenager and he got him up in my damn house," Harley fumed.

"Kyron better stop being so trusting. He saw what happened when he invited one of his friends to y'all house the last time," Faryn reminded her.

"That's my point. Nigga was a damn wanted fugitive and he had him sitting up in our house drinking beers and shit. Crazy thing is, he had just robbed a gas station the day before he came there. How fucking stupid can Kyron be?" Harley fumed.

"Not too much on my boy now. You know Kyron got a heart of gold and he loves to entertain company," Faryn defended.

"Don't take up for his ass when he tried to hook you up with the criminal," Harley laughed.

"He tries to hook me up with everybody," Faryn said as she walked her to the door.

They stood in the hallway and talked for a while until Kyron opened the door and interrupted.

"I was just about to come get your ass," he said when he walked out of the apartment followed by another man.

Faryn's eyes widened in surprise as she stared into a familiar face from her past.

"Faryn?" the man questioned as he looked at a slightly older, prettier version of his first love.

"Hey Jo-Jo. How have you been?" Faryn asked the man who she'd given her virginity to when she was only fifteen years old.

"Man, I know you ain't acting shy. Give a nigga a hug girl," Jo-Jo said as he walked up to her and pulled her into his tight embrace.

"Well damn, Faryn. I thought you were a good girl. How do you know this nigga?" Kyron joked.

He introduced Harley to his friend as he watched him openly admire Faryn. Kyron and Harley were oblivious to Faryn's past, but she could see that Harley was wondering. Faryn was going to tell her friend everything. She was just waiting for the right time.

"Man, this was my baby back in the day. I couldn't stay my ass out of jail back then and we lost contact. This must be my lucky day," Jo-Jo said as he admired Faryn's curvy frame.

She used to be slimmer back in the day, but she had filled out nicely. Faryn was always pretty, but she was beautiful to him now. Jo-Jo had thought about Faryn a lot over the years, but he had no way of contacting her. He heard that she started stripping, but he didn't know how true that was. Faryn had earned a name for herself in high school when he started messing with her, but that was a long time ago. He knew for a fact that she was still a virgin because he was the first to get a taste of her. Looking at her now, he wouldn't mind having another sample.

"You used to mess with Joseph?" Kyron asked, calling him by his real name.

"That was a long time ago. I was only fifteen years old," Faryn replied.

"Yeah, but we can change all that. Unless you got a man living up in there with you," Jo-Jo said as he nodded his head towards her apartment.

Faryn hated that anyone knew where she lived and that was what she always tried to avoid.

"Nah man, she don't have nobody living with her," Kyron said, making Harley look at him and frown.

"Faryn is a grown woman, Kyron. She doesn't need you to speak for her," Harley said angrily.

She had just met Jo-Jo and she already knew that she didn't like him. Something about him rubbed her the wrong way. She needed to get Faryn alone to see just how well they knew each other. Kyron was always trying to hook Faryn up with one of his boys, but Harley wanted her to give Landon a chance.

"So, what's up Faryn? You got a man, or can we pick up where we left off a while ago? You know I never did have a problem taking care of you and nothing has changed," Jo-Jo said as he stepped closer to her.

Harley smiled when she heard the elevator ding and saw Landon step off and make his way down the hall to Faryn's apartment.

"Good evening everybody," Landon spoke as he leaned down and gave Faryn a soft peck on her lips.

"Hey boo." Faryn smiled, happy that his timing was so perfect.

Harley and Kyron spoke back, but Jo-Jo just looked him up and down like he was an intruder.

"You done with the food?" Landon asked as he looked down at her.

"Almost. I'm going inside Harley. I'll talk to you later," Faryn said as she grabbed Landon's hand and disappeared inside her apartment.

"What's wrong?" Landon asked as soon as they were alone.

"I'm so happy that you came when you did," Faryn said as he followed her to the kitchen.

"Why? What happened?" he questioned.

"You remember the dude Jo-Jo that I told you about? You know, the one who I used to mess with when I was younger? My first and all that stuff," Faryn said, reminding him of one of their many conversations about her past.

"Yeah. What about him?" Landon asked.

"That was him out there. He's one of Kyron's old friends that he hasn't seen in a while. I wish I wouldn't have gone out there. Now, he knows where I live," Faryn replied.

"Why you say that? You think he might try to do something to you?" Landon asked.

"No, nothing like that. He was always cool, but I just don't want him thinking that we're anything like we used to be. I don't want to be his friend or nothing like that."

"Tell that nigga that you already got a friend," Landon said, making her blush.

"Come taste the food," Faryn said as she stirred her pot roast and put some gravy on a spoon. She let it cool off for a minute before she put it up to Landon's mouth for him to taste.

"Put some more garlic power in it," Landon advised.

"Okay, that's all?" Faryn asked as she grabbed the garlic power from the cabinet.

"Salt too," Landon replied.

Faryn seasoned her food some more until Landon gave it the green light. She whipped up some mashed potatoes and waited for the vegetables to steam. She and Landon talked the entire time until the food was done. Once they ate and cleaned up, Faryn flipped through some movies on Netflix until they settled on something that they wanted to watch. She and Landon cuddled on the sofa under a blanket, and Faryn was content.

"Are you staying over tonight?" she asked after they were quiet for a while.

"Do you want me to?" Landon questioned.

"You ask me that all the time and my answer is always the same. Yes, I want you to stay," Faryn laughed.

"I ask you to go out with me all the time and that answer is always the same too. I'm done asking though," Landon replied.

"Landon-" Faryn started before he cut her off.

"No Faryn, fuck all that being nice stuff. I'm bout' to start demanding some shit. The movie that you want to see is coming out in two weeks and we're going," Landon informed her.

"We are?" Faryn asked, trying to hide her smile.

"Yep. Lennox is going to the fair with his mama and Lance can go by my sister. We're going to dinner and a movie and I'm not taking no for an answer. I feel like a damn teenager sneaking around to see his girlfriend. I don't even know who we're hiding from. This shit is dumb," Landon argued.

"So, I'm your girlfriend now?" Faryn asked him.

"I don't know. I'll let you know how I feel about that after we have our first date. I gotta make sure you know how to act in public," Landon joked.

"What if I want you to be my boyfriend?" Faryn asked as she looked at him.

"First off, I'm never gonna be your boyfriend. We're not in high school. If anything, I'll be your man," Landon corrected.

"Okay, so what if I want you to be my man?" Faryn quizzed.

"Ask me then?" Landon smirked.

"Ask you what?" Faryn questioned.

"Ask me to be your man," Landon replied.

"You can't be serious," Faryn said as she looked at him.

"Why not? Apparently, that's what you want, so ask for it," Landon replied.

"I guess I'll be single for the rest of my life." Faryn shrugged.

Being with Landon was indeed what she wanted, but she wanted him to make the first move. Faryn had never been the one to initiate a relationship and she didn't want to start. Landon was being an ass, but she wasn't going to give in.

"Alright, don't be mad when somebody else snatch me up first," he smirked.

"Don't play with me, Landon. Are you trying to get cut?" Faryn asked him.

"Awe, hell no. I don't think I want you anyway. I don't do violent women," Landon replied.

"Just shut up and watch the movie Landon," Faryn pouted as she turned her back to him.

"Stop acting like a baby girl. You just better make sure your ass is ready for our date in two weeks," Landon said.

"Stop acting like it's our first. We've been dating for three months now," Faryn said with a roll of her eyes.

"This ain't no damn dates girl. All you do is feed me and kiss on me all day. Trying to get me fat and shit," Landon replied while running a hand over his abs.

"You started kissing on me first," Faryn said as she turned around and pressed her lips up to his.

Landon opened his mouth and welcomed the impromptu kiss and pulled her on top of him. Faryn's heart was beating out of her chest, wondering just how far things were going to go. Landon could have stripped her and fucked her on the floor and she wouldn't have stopped him. She didn't have to wonder for long because the ringing of her phone killed the mood soon after. Since her phone was face up on her coffee table, they both looked down at the screen. Faryn wanted to scream when she saw Redd's name pop up. She had blocked his other number, but he had been calling her from another phone. Faryn didn't know what made her save the new number, since she barely answered for him anyway.

"Nah, you ain't ready for me to be your man," Landon said as he grabbed the remote and found something else to watch.

"You act like I answered the phone for him or something," Faryn said while sitting up to look at him.

"It's your phone Faryn. You can answer it if you want to," Landon said nonchalantly.

"Here, I'm blocking the number. Will that make you happy?" she asked.

"Nah, don't do it on my behalf. The fact that you didn't do it before says a lot," Landon replied.

"Why do you always have to be so complicated? This is all new to me, Landon. You've been married before and I've never really had a boyfriend. Cut me a little slack," Faryn pouted.

"It's not rocket science Faryn. If this is really what you want, you'll figure it out on your own," Landon noted as he settled on a movie for them to watch.

"Are you mad at me?" she asked after a long pause.

"Not at all," he replied while giving her a kiss to let her know that he was telling the truth.

Faryn was satisfied with that, as she snuggled up with him again and started watching the movie. It was weird how just a few months ago, she was happy when she was home alone. Since the first time that Landon came to visit her, she now hated the solitude. She didn't know how serious Landon was about her asking him to be her man, but Faryn was contemplating it. Harley was right and men like Landon didn't come along very often. Faryn didn't want to miss out on an opportunity to be genuinely happy. She also didn't want him to get tired of waiting for her to make up her mind and move on. For all she knew, his ex-wife could possibly try to come back into the picture. Faryn would die if that happened. She had only known Landon for a short period, but she wanted him to become a permanent part of her life. She had to put on her big girl thongs and make her move before someone else did. She had to talk to Harley to get her advice, even though she already knew what she would say. Harley always encouraged her to take chances and she was ready to do it. Even if it didn't work out, she could at least say that she tried.

Chapter 9

Malia looked in the mirror and blew a kiss at her reflection. She had on a black and hot pink teddy with the matching lace thongs. It was a Thursday night, but she had prepared a meal fit for a king. Roman said that he was on his way home and she couldn't wait until he got there. Malia was a great cook and she had prepared seafood pasta with crab cakes and garlic bread. Roman wasn't big on sweets, but he could have her for desert.

"Hey baby," Malia said when she answered the phone for Lennox.

"Hey mama. My daddy wants to know what time you're coming to get me Saturday, so he can make sure I'm ready," Lennox replied.

There was a local fair that came to the area once a year and Malia wanted to take her boys. Lance still didn't want to go anywhere with her, but Lennox was excited about it. Malia tried taking Landon's advice and taking things slow with Lance, but he seemed to be pulling further away. He barely said two words to her when she called him, but Malia was thankful that he answered at all.

"Tell your father that I'll get you around noon and bring you back the next day around the same time. It's not like he has anything to do anyway," Malia chuckled.

It was wrong for her to feel that way, but she was happy that Landon hadn't moved on when she left him. That was proof enough that he still loved her and would probably take her back if she wanted to go back home. If things didn't work out with Roman, that was exactly what she had planned to do. She didn't mind begging if it meant getting her family back.

"Okay, I'll tell him," Lennox replied.

"Okay baby, I'll see you day after tomorrow. I love you and tell Lance that I love him too," Malia said.

"I love you too mama, bye," Lennox said before they disconnected.

As soon as she hung up with him, Malia sent a text to Roman to see where he was. When he said that he wasn't too far, she jumped up and started to get things together. Malia had a folding table set up in the living room with candles lit and Hennessy on ice. The food was warming in the oven, so she slipped on her oven mitts and removed everything. Once she had her table set up to her liking, she ran to the room and sprayed on perfume before rushing back to the living room.

Ten minutes later, she heard Roman's key entering the locked door right before she pressed play on the remote, making their surround sound system come alive with soft music. He paused when he opened the door and saw Malia standing there in next to nothing. His manhood jumped to attention as his eyes lazily roamed over her body. The candles were the only light in the room, but he had no trouble seeing what he needed to see. When his eyes fell on the table and the food that she prepared, Roman's stomach started growling. He realized that he hadn't eaten all day and he was ready to dig in.

"Surprise baby." Malia smiled as she walked up to him and wrapped her arms around his neck.

"Surprise? It ain't my birthday or nothing. What's the special occasion?" Roman questioned.

"I don't need a special occasion to cater to my man," Malia said as she walked him over to a chair.

Once he sat down, she poured him a glass of his favorite drink and fixed them both a plate. Roman was ready to smash his food, but Malia had other plans.

She took her time and fed him and herself, carefully wiping his mouth after each bite. When they were done, Roman downed his drink and was ready to bend Malia over the table. She straddled him, ready for what was next, when the front door burst open and the light was turned on.

"The fuck is going on in here? How you invite a nigga to dinner and you in here bout' to get your dick wet?" Chad asked as he walked into the apartment.

"Excuse you! We have a doorbell, just in case you forgot. I'm not even dressed properly for you to just be barging in here!" Malia yelled as she tried to shield her half-naked body with her hands.

"Bitch, please. I wish I would knock on my brother's door. I got a key for a reason. Where the food at Ro?" Chad asked.

"The food and liquor is right here. Help yourself," Roman replied as he pointed to the folding table.

"Roman!" Malia yelled as she looked at him, hoping that he would put his brother in his place just once.

"Shut up man. It ain't like we gon' eat all this shit," Roman said as he stood up with Malia still in his arms.

She squealed as he threw her over his shoulder like a sack of potatoes and carried her to their bedroom.

"Ugh." Chad frowned when he looked up and caught a glimpse of Malia's bare ass. He couldn't deny that she was sexy, but he hated everything about that bitch.

"Baby, you need to put your foot down where Chad is concerned. Not only does he disrespect me, but he disrespects our house too," Malia said once they were alone.

"Man, I don't want to talk about Chad. Take all that shit off and let's get it," Roman replied.

He peeled his shirt off as he watched Malia strip down to nothing. Besides a few faded stretch marks, she looked damn good to be a mother of two. Her body was still tight and so was her pussy. Roman was only her second sex partner so that was more than likely the reason. Malia was all smiles when she walked over to him, until he forcefully pushed her down on her knees. She hated how rough Roman was with her at times but complaining didn't get her anywhere. He ignored her protests because that was what he was used to. Dealing with mostly hood rats in the past had that effect on him. Malia's eyes watered a little when Roman pulled her hair and forcefully shoved his dick down her throat. She gagged a little, but she quickly recovered and proceeded to please her man. Roman seemed oblivious to her discomfort as he held her in place and fucked her face. Malia had drool coming from the sides of her mouth as she focused on breathing and trying not to suffocate.

"No teeth!" he growled as he slapped the back of her head as a warning.

Malia was ready to tap out and the food that she'd just eaten was on its way back up. Roman was moaning in satisfaction, but she was in agony. It felt like he was never going to cum, and she felt like she was dying.

"Shit! I'm bout' to come!" Roman hissed, sounding like music to her ears.

Malia tried to move, but he had other plans. He held the sides of her face as he pumped faster and harder.

"Don't move bitch. You bout' to swallow all this shit!" Roman barked through labored breaths.

Malia had swallowed several times before, but she felt disrespected for some reason by his choice of words. Roman was treating her like a bitch on the streets and nothing like the woman who he claimed to love.

"Uhh," Malia gagged, as Roman continued to assault her face.

When she tasted the first few drops of his semen, she could no longer control her gag reflexes. As soon as he started releasing in her mouth, she pulled him out, making him squirt all over her face and hair.

Roman looked like he was pissed, but Malia felt too sick to care.

"The fuck!" Roman yelled, as she jumped up and ran to the bathroom.

Malia dropped down to her knees in front of the toilet and released the entire contents of her stomach. Roman rushed in behind her with a scowl covering his face. He pulled up his boxers and jeans as he watched her in disgust.

"Stop all that damn performing. I didn't even do the shit that hard," he fussed.

"Are you serious right now Roman? I felt like I was dying just now," Malia complained.

"You act like it was your first-time swallowing," Roman replied as he grabbed a towel and wet it for her.

"That's not the point Roman. I just ate, and you were acting like a wild animal. Are you high or something?" Malia asked, knowing that he and Chad liked to partake in snorting lines every now and then.

"The fuck that got to do with anything?" Roman asked while wiping his running nose.

Malia had her answer right there and that explained his behavior. Roman was always overly aggressive when he was high, among other things.

"Thanks," Malia said when he handed her some mouthwash and helped her stand to her feet.

"Come hop in the shower with me, so you can finish what you started," Roman said while starting the warm shower water.

Malia was already naked, so she climbed inside and started washing her hair while he undressed and joined her.

"This was not what I had in mind. We were supposed to have a romantic dinner and make love like a normal couple. Your brother showing up and you choking me to death with your dick was not a part of the plan," Malia replied as she washed him up.

"I'm sorry baby. I appreciate everything that you did," Roman said as he kissed her cheek and began to wash her the same way she had done him.

Malia was all smiles as they cleaned each other up and talked. She was happy that Roman hadn't initiated sex because she wasn't in the mood. It had been a while since they had a decent conversation without arguing, and she was enjoying it. It reminded her of when they first met, before he started showing her the real him. When they got out of the shower, Malia slipped on one of Roman's t-shirts and put her semi-damp hair in a ponytail. She frowned when she heard Chad in the living room talking loudly on his phone. She decided not to even say anything because she didn't want to ruin the mood. Even when she saw Roman sneaking to look at his phone, she pretended not to pay attention. He was home with her and that was all that mattered.

"Have you thought about us taking a trip somewhere?" Malia asked as she snuggled up with Roman when he got into the bed. He moved away from her, but that was nothing new.

"I told you to give me a few months Malia. I'll give you whatever you want, no questions asked," Roman replied, hoping that his response satisfied her.

He wasn't in the mood to be nagged. He didn't have any plans on coming home at all that night until Malia told him that she had a surprise for him. He had to turn his phone off because he knew that his other chick was going to blow him up like crazy. Trying to please two women in two different houses was beginning to be a bit too much for him to handle, but the other woman didn't mind his absences. She had other men too, so she was cool with it.

"I can't wait," Malia said while cuddling up next to him again.

"Take this shit off man," Roman said while tugging at her shirt.

He started kissing Malia's neck and she already knew what he wanted. He was trying to pull her shirt up, but she kept pulling it back down.

"No Roman. I don't feel good," Malia whined.

"The fuck you mean no? You shouldn't have no more food left in your system after all that throwing up you did. You should be straight now," Roman said while groping and grinding on her.

"It wasn't the food," Malia confessed.

"The fuck was it then?" he asked while gliding his hand down in between her legs.

"I'm pregnant," Malia blurted out, making him halt his movements.

She felt Roman's entire body stiffen before he moved away from her and sat up straight in the bed.

"What?" Roman asked, just to be clear.

"We're having a baby," Malia said as she sat up and smiled at him.

"The fuck is you smiling for? I thought you were on the pill Malia," Roman pointed out.

"I am, but it's not like we use protection. Things happen Roman," Malia noted.

"So what? I always pull out!" Roman yelled.

"You sound like a damn fool. Aside from teenage boys, who still uses the pullout method?" Malia questioned.

"Man, fuck! You must not have been taking your pills like you should have. Over a year of us doing the same thing and you just so happen to pop up pregnant."

"You act like I did it by myself," Malia said, ignoring what he said about her missing pills.

She hadn't taken her pills in two months, but she always took one out of the container as if she did. She wanted to cover her tracks, just in case Roman wanted to check up on her. Roman was adamant about not wanting kids, but he was great with her boys. She knew that if he had one of his own, he would see just how beautiful fatherhood could be.

"How far along are you?" Roman asked as he paced back and forth in their bedroom.

"Six weeks," Malia answered, happy that he seemed to be interested.

Roman walked into the closet and came out a few minutes later. Malia was a nervous wreck when she saw him walking over to her.

"Get rid of it!" Roman barked as he threw some money on the bed.

"What?" Malia asked as her heart fell in her chest.

"You heard me. Get rid of it before I pay some bitches in the hood to get rid of it for you," he threatened.

"You're threatening to kill your own child," Malia gasped in horror. Roman could be cold, but she didn't think he could be that cruel.

"You know I don't want kids and you knew that from the start. You don't even take care of the ones you have. Why the fuck would I want to have another one with you? You left your kids to be with another nigga. Even if I did want kids I wouldn't want your ass to be the mama," Roman admitted, making her heart break into a million pieces.

"Where are you going?" Malia asked when she saw him putting on clothes.

"Don't worry about where I'm going. You just better handle your business. Don't even think about playing with me, Malia," Roman warned.

"You need to stay here, so we can discuss this Roman!" she yelled as she got up and blocked the bedroom door.

"Ain't shit to discuss. Make an appointment and do what the fuck I said," he replied.

He grabbed his keys and wallet and pushed her out of the way. Chad looked up at him in confusion when his brother walked out of the room fully dressed, with Malia chasing behind him. He thought Roman was in for the night, but something must have changed.

"What's up bruh?" Chad asked as he began to put his shoes back on.

If his brother was leaving, there was no way that he was staying there with Malia's pathetic ass. Chad frowned when he saw her standing there in nothing but a t-shirt, crying and begging his brother not to leave.

"Let's go man," Roman replied angrily.

"You want me to drive?" Chad asked him.

"Baby please, just hear me out," Malia cried as she fell to her knees in desperation.

She was pulling at Roman's leg, making a complete fool of herself. Malia had never experienced anything remotely close to that with Landon. He had always put her first and loved her unconditionally.

"Get the fuck off me!" Roman bellowed as he stepped over her and left her on the floor, screaming and crying.

"The fuck is that all about?" Chad asked when they got outside.

"Stupid bitch is pregnant," Roman answered with a frown.

"Man, I told you that she was going to do that. Every time her sons come over here, she be throwing hints about how good of a father you would be. That bitch probably been planning to trap you for a while. Stupid hoe don't even take care of the ones she got and she's trying to have more," Chad fumed.

"That's what I'm saying, but I'm done with her ass. I wouldn't fuck her with another nigga's dick after this shit," Roman swore.

"You're saying that shit now but, when it's time to bust a nut, you ain't gon' care who you get it from," Chad laughed.

"She better get on the phone and beg her husband to take her back because it's a wrap with us," Roman replied.

"That dude probably don't want her trifling ass back. He would be a damn fool to be with her after she left him and his kids for another man. Dude cool as fuck, but I don't see how he ended up with that hoe."

"I don't even care no more. I'm going back to my home away from home for a while. I need to clear my head. That bitch got me stressed the fuck out," Roman replied.

Jessica's house was usually where he chilled at when he wasn't at his own. Jessica was a dancer, so she wasn't even home most of the time. Sometimes, she stayed out with other men, but Roman could care less.

He encouraged Jessica to do her because he was always going to do him.

"I'm going get me a room. I don't even want to be bothered with none of them hoes tonight," Chad said.

"Come chill with me by Jessica's house," Roman requested.

"Nah man, I'm not in the mood to be bothered with her friend. Every time I go over there, she calls her. I just wanna be by myself tonight."

"Fuck it, I'm rolling to the room with you then. Fuck all these hoes," Roman replied.

He and his brother both got into their cars and headed to their favorite hotel. They rented a room and smoked all night until they both passed out from exhaustion.

Chapter 10

It was almost noon and Malia still hadn't gotten out of the bed. She was severely depressed and morning sickness was kicking her ass something serious. It was Saturday, and Roman hadn't bothered to call or come home since he left that Thursday night. Malia didn't feel like doing much of anything, but she'd promised Lennox that she'd take him to the fair. She was supposed to get him at noon, but there was no doubt that she was gonna be late. Although she knew that he wouldn't answer, Malia grabbed her phone from the nightstand and dialed Roman's number once again. She'd been calling him nonstop since he left, and he sent each of her calls straight to voicemail. He didn't even bother letting the phone ring for a while.

"Fuck it," Malia mumbled as she got up and went to their walk-in closet to find something to wear.

Maybe going to the fair was exactly what she needed to take her mind off her problems. It also wouldn't hurt to spend some time with her baby boy. She only wished that Lance would start to join them like he used to.

It only took about thirty minutes, but Malia was dressed comfortably in her Victoria's Secret PINK leggings and matching shirt. She wore a pair of Nikes, since she knew that they would be doing a lot of walking. She grabbed her purse and keys, preparing to leave, right as her phone started ringing. As much as she wanted the caller to be Roman, she knew that it was probably Lennox trying to see where she was. When she saw her sister Monica's name flashing across the screen, she answered the call as she headed out of the house.

"What's up Monica?" Malia asked while locking her front door.

"Bitch! Where are you?" Monica asked excitedly.

"I'm just leaving home to go get Lennox. I'm taking him to the fair. Why? What's up?" Malia asked.

"You need to scrap that shit and get your ass over here to Oakwood Mall with me and Felicia," Monica replied, referring to their other sister.

"Did you hear what I just said? I'm not ditching my baby to go shopping with y'all." Malia frowned.

"We're not shopping. We only came in here to pay our phone bills, but that's not why I called. That nigga Roman is in here walking around with another bitch like it's all good," Monica informed her.

"He... what?" Malia questioned as her heart rate sped up and the butterflies went crazy in her stomach.

"Yes bitch," Felicia said when she grabbed the phone. "Nigga parading this hoe around the mall like he don't have a pregnant girlfriend at home."

"You need to get your ass over her right now!" Monica yelled in the background.

"I'm on my way," Malia assured them as she hopped in her car and sped to the mall.

She had quickly abandoned her plans to spend the day with her son when she got the call about Roman. Malia was at home losing her mind and his pathetic ass was out in public with the next bitch. Malia still hadn't gotten around to making her appointment and she wasn't sure that she should. Having a baby was exactly what Roman needed to calm his wild ass down. Kids had a way of changing people and she wanted him to see that.

"We're following his ass. Him and Chad just went in Foot Locker with them ugly hoes," Monica said as she instructed Malia on where to come.

"I should have known that he was with him," Malia replied as she parked and jumped out of her car.

She locked her purse and phone up in the trunk of her car and only took her keys. Roman was about to get the shock of his life when she walked down on his cheating ass. Malia powerwalked through the mall until she saw her sisters standing outside of the shoe store. She was fuming as she made her way into Foot Locker, followed by her sisters. Roman was asking the salesperson for a size six women's shoe right as she walked up to him.

"So, you leave your pregnant girlfriend at home, so you can run the streets with the next bitch! I guess you didn't see me calling either!" Malia yelled, making people in and out of the store stop to look at her.

"Oh shit!" Chad yelled as he fell out laughing.

Roman had spent that first night in the hotel with him, but he left the next day to go by his other girl, Jessica. Chad decided to stay another night, but he'd gone over there that morning when Jessica's friend, Cian, asked him to. Roman and Jessica had been off and on for years and she knew all about Malia. She had a few niggas on the side as well, so she didn't care about what Roman did. She was like the female version of him, so they understood each other well. They were more like good friends with benefits who didn't expect too much of each other. They smoked, drank, and got money together and it was all good. Jessica was more of his speed and the only woman that he'd ever been with to truly have his back. She was down for whatever and Roman liked that about her. She was his little black China doll with a banging body and a hood swagger.

"This bitch," Roman hissed as he shook his head in aggravation.

He was hoping that Malia got the hint and would have left by now, but she was dumber than he thought. Things with them hadn't been the same for months, but she was still trying to hold on.

"Who is this?" Malia said while pointing to Jessica.

"That's my people," Roman replied coolly.

"Your people?" Malia repeated. "Besides Chad, you don't have any people."

"Give me the money to pay for my shoes while you talk to her," Jessica said as she held her hand out expectantly.

"I wish the hell you would," Malia said as she pushed Roman when she saw him reaching into his front pocket.

"Keep your hands to yourself and get the fuck out of my face," Roman said calmly.

'That's fucked up," Monica said while Felica co-signed.

"Man, get y'all sister before this shit turn out bad," Roman warned.

"Fuck you! You out here doing me dirty with this hoe while I'm pregnant," Malia said as tears came to her eyes.

"I'm not your enemy sis, so don't come at me like that. If I were you, I would take that money that he gave you and have an abortion. Ro ain't cut out to be nobody's daddy. Why would you want to have a baby by a nigga who you admit is doing you dirty anyway? We gotta do better," Jessica said, shaking her head in pity.

"And you're telling that bitch our business too Roman. Huh?" Malia questioned as she pushed him again.

"Keep. Your. Hands. To. Yourself." Roman gritted, trying hard to stay calm.

"Let's just go bruh," Chad suggested.

"And fuck your homeless, broke ass too Chad. I'm not even surprised about you being here with him," Malia fumed.

"Bitch, you better pick your battles. Go get that baby sucked up out your ass and move around. The man don't want you. What else he gotta do to show you? That's what your dumb ass gets for leaving your husband and kids for the next man. You played the game and loss. Take that L and get the fuck on," Chad snapped.

The store employees rushed over and asked them to leave. Jessica was pissed because that was the only store that had the shoes that she wanted. She'd checked three other ones and had no luck. She didn't care what Roman did with his girlfriend, she wasn't leaving the mall without her shoes.

"This is some bullshit! I just want my shoes," Jessica huffed as they left the store.

"I hope you got money because Roman ain't buying them," Malia said with finality.

"I really need you to stop directing your anger this way love. You need to be humble. If it wasn't for me, you wouldn't even have a place to stay. I hope you don't think Ro can get an apartment in his name," Jessica said as she, Roman, and Chad laughed.

Malia felt like a damn fool and she was sure that she looked like one too. She had abandoned her husband and kids for a man that she didn't even know. Roman was nothing like who he pretended to be in the beginning. If she would have saw the Roman that she was seeing now, she would have never given him a second thought.

"Bitch, don't try to play my sister like that. You're the stupid one if their apartment is in your name and another woman is living in it," Monica spoke up.

"No boo, I don't need an apartment when I have a house. Why am I even entertaining these bad body hoes? Let me get my shoes, so I can go. Y'all can meet us back at the house when y'all finish up with this mess," Jessica replied while pointing to Malia and her sisters.

"The fuck you mean this mess?" Monica asked while walking up on Jessica.

"Ro, you better get these hoes. I'm not in the mood," Jessica warned.

"Man, y'all need to move around with all this unnecessary, drama. Malia, stop embarrassing yourself and go home baby girl. I'm not the man for you, ma. The life that I live is not a good fit for a mother. That's why I told you that I didn't want any kids of my own. You're a good girl and you need to find a man that matches your personality. That man ain't me. The streets are all that I know and you ain't built like that. Go back home to your family and be a mother to your kids," Roman said as the tears streamed down Malia's face.

Roman wasn't a bad man, but he wasn't the relationship type. He didn't know how to love and that was another reason why he didn't want kids. It wouldn't be fair to have a family knowing how he felt. There were only two women in the world to ever have a place in his heart and he didn't have room for anyone else.

When he turned to walk away, Malia felt rage like she'd never felt before. Her entire body was shaking as heat radiated throughout her. When she saw Jessica grab Roman's hand, she went into full attack mode. Malia was like an animal in the wild as she ran up to them and started swinging. Being that she was pregnant, neither Jessica or Roman wanted to hit her. When Roman grabbed her arms, Malia's sisters stepped up and started hitting him as well. Jessica wasn't gonna let them do him dirty, so she did what she was known to do and started throwing jabs in their direction. Cian hadn't said anything since they first got there, but she didn't think twice about jumping in to help her girl. The mall was in full pandemonium as the four women fought like they were paid professionals. Malia was still trying to swing on Roman, as Chad tried to break it all up.

When mall security came running over with a group of police officers behind them, it was hard to see who was doing what. Once the brawl was broken up, all seven of them were handcuffed, despite Chad and Roman's claims of innocence. They were heated as they were led out of the mall and placed in the back of the squad cars. Malia and both her sisters were placed in one car, while Jessica and Cian were placed in another. Roman and Chad were driven away first and the other two cars followed.

"I can't believe this shit. I left my kids with the neighbor until I ran here to pay my phone bill. That lady has to go to work and my stupid ass is going to jail," Felicia ranted.

"These damn cuffs are cutting off my circulation," Monica whined.

Malia tuned her sisters complaining out as she stared absently out the window. Never in her life had she ever been to jail and she was embarrassed about it now. In a little over a year, Malia's life had gone from sugar to shit and she had no one else to blame but herself. Leaving Landon was the worst mistake that she'd ever made, and she wasn't ashamed to admit it. As if she'd heard her thoughts, Monica spoke up and voiced her opinion about the situation.

"You should have stayed with Landon and continued to creep with Roman on the side. He is not main nigga material," Monica said to Malia.

"His dog ass ain't right for that shit. Get an abortion and go back home to your husband and kids. Thank God Landon ain't moved on yet. He's gonna be so happy to be a family again," Felicia said, making Malia smile.

The thought alone was enough to lift her spirits. Malia never stopped loving her husband and it was time that she let him know it. The first thing she had to do was get him to bail her out of the situation that she was in. Once she got rid of Roman's demon seed that was growing inside of her, she was packing up her shit and going back home to her family.

Chapter 11

"**M**an, Malia, call me when you get this message," Landon said as he left his ex-wife another voicemail. Lennox had been calling her since one that afternoon, and it was now after three and she still hadn't answered. She was supposed to be there to get him hours ago and she hadn't shown up or called yet. He was supposed to be picking Faryn up at six, but that didn't look like it was going to happen. It was their first official date in Landon's eyes and he was going to have to cancel. His son looked so pitiful as he walked around the house and peeped out of the window every so often. He wouldn't feel right going anywhere and leaving him home like that. Malia had disappointed them enough. Landon wasn't about to keep it going.

"Aye!" Landon yelled upstairs. "Y'all come down here right quick!"

He heard his sons walking down the stairs and they were standing right in front of him a few seconds later.

"Is it time to go?" Lance asked as he carried his duffle bag in his hand.

"Nah, you can go put your clothes up. You're not going by your auntie. We're gonna go to the fair," Landon replied.

"Really? Did my mama call?" Lennox asked excitedly.

"No, I'm gonna bring y'all," Landon replied.

"Can Ross come with us?" Lance asked, referring to Makena's son.

"Yeah, I'll tell his mama that we're coming to get him," Landon replied.

"Can he stay all night?" Lance asked.

"Yeah, he can stay," Landon replied.

"Yes!" Lance cheered as he ran back upstairs to put his clothes away, with Lennox following behind him.

Landon hated to do it, but he dialed Faryn's number, preparing to cancel their date. He was starting out bad already, but his hands were tied. He had to make sure his sons were straight, even if it meant neglecting himself. He had basically demanded that Faryn go to dinner and a movie with him and, now, he was calling to cancel. It seemed as if he was destined to be alone, but he had to be okay with that. His boys came first, no matter what.

"Hey handsome," Faryn said when she answered the phone.

"Hey," Landon replied.

"Why do you sound like that?" Faryn asked, sensing that he wasn't his normally happy self.

"I got some bad news," Landon said solemnly.

"What's wrong?" Faryn asked, concerned.

"I have to cancel our plans. Malia was supposed to pick Lennox up and she never showed up. Her stupid ass ain't even answering her phone. He was kind of down, so I'm gonna take them and my nephew to the fair," Landon replied.

"Okay, so I need to trade in my dress and heels for some jeans and kicks," Faryn said as more of a statement than a question.

"Huh?" Landon asked in confusion.

"Huh my ass, nigga. You said that I better be ready for our date today and I will be. I don't give a damn if we go to the fair or McDonald's to share a value meal, I'll be ready," Faryn replied.

"You're serious? You wanna go to the fair with us?" Landon questioned.

"What time do you want me to be ready?" Faryn asked, making him smile.

"Right now. I'll get you first and then we'll get my nephew, since he's closer to where we're going," Landon replied.

"Okay, call me when you're downstairs," Faryn replied.

"I will," Landon said before they disconnected.

"Ms. Clark is coming with us too?" Lance asked as he and Lennox heard the end of their father's conversation.

"Call her Faryn, like she told you to. She's only Ms. Clark when y'all are in the office," Landon answered.

"Okay, well, is Faryn coming with us?" Lance asked, correcting his error.

"Yeah, she's coming with us. Are y'all okay with that?" Landon asked while looking at them for an answer.

"Yes, I'm okay with it," Lennox was the first to say.

"I'm okay with it too. Ms. Clark... I mean, Faryn, is nice." Lance smiled.

"Cool," Landon said, happy that his sons were good. "We'll get her first and then get Ross."

"Ross and Auntie Makena are at GG's house," Lance informed him.

"Shit," Landon hissed under his breath, hating that he would have to go to his grandmother's house with Faryn.

They were going to be all over her and he knew it. Makena was like a mother hen and there was no telling what was going to come out of his grandmother's mouth. It still made more sense to get her first because they were closer to the fair from his grandmother's house.

"Let's go," Landon said as he ushered his boys outside and locked up his house.

Once they got Faryn, Landon made his way over to his grandmother's house. He warned her about the possible interrogation from his family, but he was trying to avoid it. When they pulled up, he called his sister and told her to send his nephew outside. Landon dropped his head and shook it when Makena stepped outside with him.

"Calm down Landon. I can handle myself," Faryn assured him.

"Is this Faryn?" Makena asked loudly when she walked up to the car. She was all smiles as she looked at the beauty in the passenger's seat of her brother's truck.

"Yes, this is Faryn. Faryn, this is my sister, Makena," Landon said, making the introductions.

"Grandma! Come out here and meet Landon's girlfriend!" Makena yelled at the partially opened front door.

"The fuck. Why you called her out here man? We ain't never gon' leave once she get to talking," Landon fussed.

"I'm so happy to meet you, Faryn. I've heard a lot about you." Makena smiled, ignoring her brother's complaints.

"Look how pretty she is," Ella said when she walked out of the house and up to the truck.

"Hi, it's nice to meet you, Ms. Ella. You too Makena." Faryn smiled.

"Girl, you better get your ass out of that truck and come hug us. You must be special if my baby is letting you meet the family," Ella said.

"Come on grandma. We have to get going," Landon complained.

"Shut your ass up and wait," Ella snapped, as Faryn got out of the car.

"Man," Landon drawled as he turned his car off and waited while they talked.

"When are you gonna come over and have dinner with us?" Ella asked.

"Um, I'm off every other Saturday and every Sunday," Faryn replied.

"What about next Sunday?" Ella asked.

"Okay, I can come over next Sunday," Faryn agreed. She was a little nervous, but she stood out there and talked with them a little while longer until Landon started fussing.

"We'll let you go before he has a fit, but it was nice to meet you, Faryn. We'll talk more when you come over next weekend," Makena said.

"Okay, I'll see you then," Faryn replied while getting back into the car.

"You know you don't have to go over there if you don't want to," Landon said as they drove to their destination.

"I don't mind getting to know my in-laws." Faryn smiled.

"Yeah, okay," Landon replied.

"What does that mean?" Faryn asked him.

"I was still single last time I checked," he replied as he continued to drive.

When they finally made it to the fair, it was crowded as hell. Landon drove around for twenty minutes before he got lucky and found a perfect place to park. The boys were excited to get out, but the line to get wristbands was long as hell. It was moving at a decent pace, so Landon let them get out and stand in it. He and Faryn sat in the truck, but they didn't say anything. It felt kind of awkward and it wasn't like them not to talk.

"You good?" Landon asked as he observed Faryn staring out the window at nothing.

"Yeah," she snapped angrily.

"What's with the attitude?" Landon asked her.

"I don't have an attitude," Faryn replied.

"That's not what it looks like to me."

"Whatever," Faryn said with a roll of her eyes.

"Say what you have to say Faryn. What's on your mind?" Landon questioned.

"First off, I was just joking with you about the in-law thing. I know you're single and you don't have to keep reminding me of that," Faryn announced.

"So, what are you upset about? We're both single, so what's the problem?" Landon questioned.

"Okay Landon, you win! You wanted me to ask, so I'm asking!" Faryn yelled.

"What are you asking?" Landon asked, making her look at him like he was crazy.

"I should have known that you were gonna be an asshole about it, but fine. I'm asking you to be my boyfriend, okay?"

"Okay," Landon replied.

"Okay what, Landon? Is that a yes or a no?" Faryn quizzed.

"It's a no for me," he answered, making her heart skip a few beats.

They'd had countless conversations about being together and now he was turning her down. Faryn felt like she was about to start hyperventilating, but she kept her composure as best she could. She didn't know what she had done wrong to make him change his mind so suddenly. Maybe Harley was right, and he got tired of waiting for her to make up her mind.

"Why?" Faryn asked, needing to know the reason for his rejection.

"I'm a grown ass man and I don't want to be nobody's boyfriend. Now, if you're asking me to be your man, then I'll be happy to," Landon said with a smile.

"Oh, my God, Landon! I can't believe that you just did that to me," Faryn said as she punched his arm.

"Stop being so scared of everything Faryn. You told me shit about your past that you were probably too embarrassed to tell anybody else. Yet, you were scared to ask me to be with you. It's not like I didn't want to. I told you that from the beginning," Landon replied.

"And just so you know, you are my boyfriend, but that doesn't make you a boy. It's just a word Landon. Nobody walks around saying that's my man," Faryn laughed as they got out of the car.

Landon walked around to her side of the car and kissed her before they went to stand near the boys. When they got to the window, Landon paid for five wristbands and they were granted access into the park where the fair was being held. Faryn had no intentions on getting on any rides, but Landon didn't give her a choice.

After more than three hours of running around like a kid, Faryn had officially tapped out. Landon got her a bottle of water and she sat on the nearest bench that she could find, while he took the boys on a few more rides. Landon was a great father and uncle, and Faryn loved that about him. She was sitting there texting Harley to tell her that she'd finally made her move with Landon, when someone walked up and called a name that she hadn't heard in more than a year.

"Is that you Candy Girl?" a woman said, making Faryn snap her head around to see who it was.

She smiled when she recognized Slim, her former co-worker at JB's, standing there smiling at her.

"You can call me Faryn now," she said as she stood up and hugged her.

"Zina," the other woman said, telling Faryn her real name. "How's it going?"

"I can't complain. Working and trying to maintain. Are you still at the club?" Faryn questioned.

"Girl, I left last month. I couldn't do it no more. JB is running a damn prostitution ring up in there. It ain't even about dancing no more. It's straight fucking and nothing more. It's only a matter of time before he gets shut down. I made sure I left before that happened," Zina replied.

"Are you serious?" Faryn asked as her mouth hung open in shock.

"Yes, and your boy Redd be all up in it."

"He's still a regular there?" Faryn questioned.

"He doesn't come as often as he used to when you were there, but he comes enough. You were his favorite, but he fucks anybody who's available now," Zina replied.

"He still calls me, but I'm done with all that. I haven't seen him since I left the club and I don't plan on it."

"I don't blame you. Who are you here with? You didn't have any kids last time I checked," Zina noted.

"I still don't have any. I'm here with my boyfriend and his kids and nephew," Faryn said, feeling good that she was finally able to give Landon a title.

"Oh okay. I'm here with my son too. I know he's probably looking for me, so I better go. It was nice to see you again," Zina smiled while giving Faryn another hug.

"You too." Faryn smiled.

She stayed where she was for a while longer until Landon and the kids came back. He looked like he was worn out and Faryn understood how he felt.

"You wanna come back to the house for a little while?" Landon asked as they walked back to his truck.

"Okay," Faryn replied nervously.

"What are you nervous about? It's okay if you don't want to. I promised my nephew that he could stay the night, so I won't be able to come by you," Landon pointed out.

"No, it's okay. I just need to stop home and grab some clothes.

"Oh, so you wanna spend the night?" Landon smirked.

"I thought that's what you meant, but I don't have to," Faryn replied.

"I'm just fucking with you, baby. I want you to stay," Landon admitted.

"I hope you have food," Faryn said.

"We might have to swing by the store if you wanna cook something," Landon replied.

"I'm too tired to cook anything tonight, but I'll do it tomorrow," Faryn said as he drove away from the park.

She and Landon held hands as he drove to her apartment and talked to the kids about them being in a relationship. They seemed to be excited about it and that made them both feel good. Faryn knew how much Landon loved his sons and she was happy to have their blessing. When they got to her house, Faryn hurriedly packed a bag while they waited downstairs in the car. She ran into Harley's nosey ass, so she had to give her a brief rundown of everything that happened. Harley was more excited than she was, and she couldn't wait to tell Kyron.

Once they left Faryn's apartment, they went the store to get food and snacks for the house. For the first time ever, Faryn felt like she was normal as she walked around the store holding Landon's hand while the kids went down the aisles throwing things in the basket. She had never had a real boyfriend as an adult and it felt good. She didn't know why his wife had decided to leave, but Faryn didn't plan to make the same mistake. She was in it for as long as he wanted her, and she hoped that it was forever.

Chapter 12

"This is your house?" Faryn asked in shock when they pulled up to the huge living quarters.

She didn't realize that the long brick street that they were driving on was a part of his house. Faryn had seen big houses before, but Landon's house almost looked like three in one.

"Yeah," he replied like it was no big deal.

Maybe it wasn't a big deal to him, but Faryn was in awe. It was dark outside, but the house and the grassy land surrounding it was very well lit. Faryn admired the small pond and waterfall out front, but that was nothing compared to when she went inside. Landon gave her a tour and she was lost.

"Wait, I need to take a break. This house is overwhelming," Faryn confessed.

"You can chill in my room while I make sure they take a shower," Landon laughed.

Landon's room was the biggest in the house. The color scheme was black, royal blue, and white, and he had a small leather sofa and chair situated on one side of it. Faryn kicked off her shoes and fell onto the sofa as soon as Landon left her alone. She closed her eyes to relax and was knocked out a few minutes later. She thought she was dreaming when she heard someone calling her name, until Landon started shaking her lightly.

"Shit, you scared me. I didn't realize I fell asleep. That damn fair wore me out." Faryn yawned.

"I can tell. You sound like a grown ass man in here with all that snoring," Landon laughed.

Faryn's mouth watered at the sight of him shirtless with basketball shorts clinging to his freshly showered body. He had even more tattoos on his chest and back and he looked good enough to eat. Faryn was never big on oral sex, but she wanted to suck the skin off him. He seemed oblivious to her lust as he moved around the room like he normally would.

"I need to take a shower," Faryn said as she stood up and stretched.

"Let me show you how to work it," Landon offered.

"Boy, bye. I know how to work a damn shower," Faryn said, waving him off.

"Okay," he smirked knowingly.

Faryn grabbed some clothes and liquid soap from her bag and walked into the bathroom. Landon already had fresh towels in there for her, so she stripped down and stepped into the huge walk in shower. The space looked big enough for ten people, with a small bench mounted to the wall. Faryn went to turn the shower on and there were no handles visible. She opened the clear frosted door and still couldn't find anything to turn on the water. There was a small screen with buttons mounted on the shower wall, so Faryn pushed one of the keys to see if the water would come on.

"Oh shit!" she shrieked as music started playing in the bathroom.

She pressed another button and a series of small colorful lights came on and started blinking. Another button lowered the shower head and Faryn was over it all.

"Landon!" she opened the shower door and yelled.

"What's up?" he asked from the other side of the bathroom door.

"Come here. What kind of back to the future shit you got going on in this bathroom?" Faryn asked.

"I offered to show you how to work it," Landon laughed as he walked into the bathroom.

He paused momentarily when he caught a glimpse of Faryn's naked body. Landon was stuck, and he didn't even try to look away.

"You can stare all day if you want to. Just help me with the shower first please," Faryn smirked. She was very comfortable with her body. She had danced in front of strange men for four years, so she had to be.

"Damn," he mumbled as he continued to stare.

He undid everything that Faryn had done and showed her how to turn the water off and on. Faryn turned the water on to a temperature that she was satisfied with and stepped under the warm stream. Landon was stuck staring at her and she was staring right back at him. The ringing of his phone snapped him back to reality. He knew that it was his sister, just by the ringtone that she had set for herself. Once he was gone, Faryn enjoyed the warm water as it massaged her tired body. She washed herself up twice, but the water felt too good for her to rush.

She didn't know how much time had passed, but she eventually turned the water off and got out. After drying off, Faryn oiled down her body and slipped into her pajamas. She went into Landon's room thinking he would be there, but the room was empty. Venturing out into the hallway, Faryn called his name. She kept walking trying to find him and she ended up in a part of the house that she had never seen. She kept walking as she continued to call his name, but she never got an answer.

"Fuck this. I don't even know where I'm going. This is just too much house for only three people," Faryn fussed as she tried to retrace her steps and go back to his bedroom.

"We can make it four if you want to move in," Landon smirked as he appeared out of nowhere.

"Shit! Landon! You scared the hell out of me!" Faryn yelled as she held her chest.

"My fault," he laughed. "Where were you trying to go?"

"I was looking for you, but I got lost. Where the hell am I?" Faryn questioned as she looked around.

"On the other side of my room. I can come and go to different parts of the house without walking down the main hall. You should have let me finish giving you the tour."

"That's ridiculous Landon. I shouldn't have to have a map just to get around my boyfriend's house," Faryn said when they walked back into his room.

Landon looked down at her tight-fitting pajama shorts and licked his lips. He tried hard to be a gentleman and let her make the first move, but she was taking too long. Faryn was still fussing when he walked up behind her and inhaled her scent. He placed soft kisses on her neck, and Faryn froze. She stopped talking and closed her eyes, enjoying the feel of his soft lips on her flesh. Tilting her head back, she gave him more access to what he wanted. When he turned her around, the look in his eyes mirrored hers. They were both ready, but Landon had to be sure.

"Now is the time for you to stop me if you're unsure," he said, hoping that she didn't.

Standing on the tips of her toes, Faryn pulled him closer and stuck her tongue in his mouth. There was no uncertainty and she tried to convey that through her kiss. That was all the reassuring that Landon needed. He stripped her out of her clothes before discarding his own. They engaged in another heated lip lock before Landon pushed her back onto the bed. Faryn closed her eyes and gripped the sheets, as he kissed down her body until he got to her feminine parts.

"Open your eyes and look at me, Faryn," Landon demanded.

Faryn opened her eyes and found him looking right at her. She arched her back and grabbed the back of his head right before he disappeared between her legs.

"Oh shit," Faryn hissed as she pulled him in deeper. She rotated her hips, as Landon expertly sexed her with his tongue. Redd was the last man to go down on her and that was a while ago. Still, Faryn didn't remember it feeling that good. Landon flicked his tongue up and down like a light switch, driving her crazy. Faryn tried to be quiet, but she couldn't contain her screams. The house was huge, and she prayed that the kids were somewhere far and couldn't hear them. They were probably sleeping and that was even better. Faryn tried to ease away from him, but his hold on her thighs didn't allow her to. She felt her orgasm building up as her entire body shook and convulsed. She sounded like a wounded animal when she came, letting out a high-pitched screech. Faryn tried to get away from him again, but he was relentless. He kept licking and sucking her sensitive middle until she hoarsely begged him to stop.

"You good?" Landon asked as he looked up at her with a cocky smirk.

Malia was the only other woman that he went down on, but he was pleased to see that he still had skills. Faryn was spent as she laid there trying to catch her breath. Landon didn't even give her a chance to answer. He flipped her over onto her stomach and positioned himself behind her.

"Landon, wait, I need a minute," Faryn weakly protested.

"I got you, baby," Landon replied while grabbing a pillow and putting it underneath her stomach.

The pillow made her feel better, but that wasn't what Faryn was talking about. She needed a minute to recover from that vicious tongue assault that he'd just given her. All doubts were removed when she felt Landon start to enter her, inch by inch. They both moaned in satisfaction once he had filled her all the way up.

"Damn baby," Landon groaned as he started to move inside of her.

His movements started out slow and easy. When Faryn started backing it up on him, that was his cue to speed things up a little. Before long, Landon was putting a beating on Faryn's kitty, but she wasn't complaining.

"Fuck!" Faryn yelled as she gripped the sheets and threw her ass back at him violently.

Landon pulled her hair from behind, forcing her up to him so that he could kiss her neck. He then pulled out of her briefly and laid on his back. Faryn took the hint and climbed on top, squatting down on his erection. Landon slapped her ass, but she didn't need any coaching. Faryn had to find her rhythm, but she had his eyes rolling behind his head as soon as she did. He sat up on his elbows and locked eyes with her as she bounced on him. Both her hands were on her breasts and she was the sexiest thing that Landon had ever laid eyes on. He wished it could last forever, but he knew that wasn't possible. The end of round one was near, and he felt it.

"Fuck Faryn!" Landon growled as he pulled out of her and came on the sheets.

Faryn had already found her release twice and she was just waiting on him. It felt like the entire room was spinning when Landon was done, and she was dizzy. She laid on his chest preparing to go to sleep, until he tapped her a few minutes later.

"What's wrong?" Faryn sat up and asked.

"Wake up. You can sleep later," Landon replied.

He rolled over, putting her on her back and positioned himself between her legs.

"Baby, I'm tired. Give me a few minutes," Faryn whined.

"I just did. I waited fifteen minutes before I said anything," he replied while kissing her lips.

"No, I need more time than that," Faryn begged.

"Just lay back then," Landon replied as he opened her legs and entered what had quickly become his favorite place to be.

***

Faryn's body was programmed to wake up at a certain time, but that wasn't why she popped her eyes open at only six the next morning. The vibrating of Landon's phone on the nightstand was driving her crazy, but he was knocked out. They were both still naked and he had his muscular arm draped around her torso, making it hard for her to move. Faryn's entire body ached from some of the positions that he put her in just hours before, but she wasn't complaining. Landon was the truth in and out of the bedroom and she had to give credit where it was deserved.

"Landon," Faryn whispered, trying not to startle him too much.

He stirred a little, but he still didn't wake up. His phone was closer to her, but she didn't want to take it upon herself to answer it. They had just made things official the day before and she didn't want to start out the wrong way.

"Landon, your phone is ringing," Faryn said, shaking him harder.

"Answer it," he mumbled groggily, making Faryn smile.

She picked up the phone and looked at the unavailable number before she answered the call. She never even got a chance to say hello before the automated operator started to talk.

"It's somebody calling from jail," Faryn informed him.

"That's probably that nigga Aiden. The fuck did he do this time?" Landon asked aloud.

He sat up in bed and wiped the sleep from his eyes as he looked over at the clock. It was entirely too early for him to be up and dealing with his uncle's bullshit. He knew that he would probably have to get up to go bail him out and he had already prepared himself.

"It's Malia," Faryn said once the person said their name. She knew that Malia was Landon's ex-wife because Lance had told her his mother's name.

"The fuck!" Landon yelled in shock.

Faryn accepted the call and handed him the phone. As soon as the call was connected, Malia started talking.

"Oh, my God, Landon. I'm so happy that you answered the phone," Malia said, sounding relieved.

"What the hell are you doing in jail Malia?" Landon asked.

"I really need your help Landon," Malia said desperately.

"I'm listening," he replied.

"Me and my sisters were arrested for disorderly conduct. I only need like five hundred dollars to get out. I promise I'll pay you back every cent once I get released," Malia replied.

"You better call your nigga to get you out. I can't do nothing for you," Landon said.

"Roman is locked up too. Landon, please, I feel like I'm losing my mind in here. I've been in a pissy smelling cell all night and they're just now letting me use the phone. Please don't leave me here like this," Malia begged.

"Man-" Landon started before she cut him off.

"Baby listen, I know I messed up a lot in the past and I'm sorry for that. I made a lot of stupid decisions that I now regret," Malia said, throwing Landon off when she called him baby.

"Malia-" Landon said when she stopped him again.

"I just... I just want my family back. I'm ready to be the wife and mother that I should have been over a year ago. Please forgive me, baby. If you take me back, I promise you won't regret it."

"I'm in a relationship now Malia and I'm happy. I'm sorry, but I don't want you back," Landon replied, making her heart plummet in her chest.

"You are not in a relationship. You don't have to lie Landon. I know that I hurt you with my actions and I'm sorry," she apologized.

Malia knew without a doubt that Lennox would have told her if his father had a girlfriend. She asked him all the time and he always said no.

"I don't have a reason to lie to you, Malia. I wouldn't want you back even if I wasn't with somebody else," Landon noted.

"We can talk about all that later. I'm just focused on getting out of here right now. This place makes me sick to my stomach." Malia frowned.

The life that she had growing inside of her didn't help all that much either, but Landon didn't need to know that. She would have that problem rectified as soon as she could. There was no way that she could go back home to her family with another man's baby inside of her.

"That ain't my problem Malia. My son sat around calling and waiting for you all day yesterday. I had to cancel my plans to make good on something that you promised him. You know I never have a problem with you unless it comes down to my boys. I've been cleaning up your messes with our kids for over a year and I'm sick of that shit."

"I'm in jail Landon. I couldn't come get him or answer my phone. I know that I have to do better with our kids. I promise that I will, but I can't do anything from behind bars. How do you think your sons would feel if they knew I was here?" Malia questioned, hoping to play on his soft side.

"They probably won't even care. You act like you being out of jail is benefiting them in some way."

Faryn threw the covers back and attempted to get out of bed. Landon's conversation was getting heated, and she was trying to give him some privacy. He grabbed her before she could get too far and pulled her back.

"Where are you going?" he asked as he pulled her close and kissed her neck.

"I was trying to let you talk in private," Faryn giggled.

"Ain't no such thing as private phone conversations. We don't keep secrets and I need you to remember that," Landon replied seriously.

"Are you serious right now Landon? You can't come get the mother of your sons out of jail because you're laid up with a bitch? It's not like you don't have the money. You blow more than that on clothes and shoes," Malia noted.

She was in her feelings when she heard a female's voice in the background. Maybe Landon was telling the truth about being in a relationship after all. Landon forgot all about Malia being on the phone when he started talking to Faryn. That was exactly how irrelevant she was to him. Malia calling Faryn a bitch didn't even get the reaction that she was looking for. The fact remained that she was locked up and Faryn was laid up with the man she loved.

"I never said I didn't have it. I'm just not giving it to you. Your problems stopped being mine the minute the ink dried on the divorce papers. I hope somebody bails you out, but it damn sure won't be me," Landon snapped as he hung up in her face.

Malia had him all the way fucked up if she thought they were going to get back together. Landon didn't want her even before he met Faryn. She made her choice and she had to live with it. Landon was good without her and had been that way for over a year.

"Are you okay?" Faryn asked as she rubbed his arm.

"Nope," Landon replied while lying down on his back.

"What's wrong? You wanna talk about it?" Faryn asked, letting the counselor in her come out.

"Yeah, look," he replied as he moved the covers to expose his growing erection.

"You damn freak. I wasn't talking about that," Faryn laughed.

"That's the only problem that I'm having right now. You unleashed the beast, so I hope you're prepared," Landon replied.

"I'm always ready," Faryn said as she rolled over and climbed on top of him. She leaned down and pressed her lips to his while guiding his erection into her opening.

"Shit," Landon hissed when she started gliding her body up and down his length.

Faryn didn't know it yet, but she was taking off from work the following day. Landon had planned to send his boys to his sister's house and let her see them off to school. He had a whole year to make up for, and he and Faryn were off to a good start.

Chapter 13

"**I** don't give a damn how long it takes, I want every damn dime back from all three of y'all. Fifteen hundred dollars of my hard-earned money to get y'all asses out of jail for some bullshit. Thank God, I was able to get my grandkids and make sure they ate and got to school safely," Cora fussed at her three daughters who she had just bailed out of jail.

Her daughter Felicia's neighbor had called to see if she could pick up her grandkids because she had to go to work. When she asked where her daughter was, the neighbor had no idea. Apparently, Felicia asked her to keep the kids while she went to pay her phone bill and that was the last that she'd seen or heard from her. Cora tried calling Monica and Malia, and she didn't get an answer from them either. She was heated when she heard from Felica the following morning and learned that they'd all been arrested. Cora already had picked up the kids, so there was need for her to worry about them. Monica had left her kids at home with some random nigga, so Cora went and got them too. She was pissed when her grandkids told her that they hadn't eaten anything the day before. She was even more upset when she found out the reason that her daughters had been arrested. Malia was a damn fool and Cora always reminded her of that. She left a good man for a nigga who didn't give a damn about her. Cora was so disappointed in her youngest daughter. Malia had never given her any trouble, so she was surprised at her actions lately. She had turned into a person that her mother no longer knew.

"You'll have your money before the day is out," Malia flippantly replied.

"Don't try to get an attitude with me. I could have left your ass in there until your court date came up," Cora replied.

"I don't have an attitude. I'm just letting you know that you're gonna get your money back," Malia said.

"I told you when I first met that Roman character that he wasn't right. Men like him don't know what it is to have one woman. You left your family to be with his ass and look at how he did you. Got you out here fighting random bitches and going to jail. This is only the beginning of your karma," Cora fussed.

Malia didn't have time for the 'I told you so' talk and she had more important things on her mind. Landon and his so-called relationship bothered her, and she wanted to know who the woman was. Malia tried calling him back a few times after he hung up on her, but he never answered. She ended up staying in jail another night. Then, there was Roman. Malia didn't know if he had been bailed out or not and she was a nervous mess.

Her mind was all set on going home to her family, but Landon was being difficult. She was sure that Roman was going to be pissed and possibly want her out of his apartment. Malia had to buy herself some time, at least until Landon came to his senses. She had nowhere else to go and living in the projects with her sisters wasn't happening. Her only other option was living with her mother and that was just as bad. Cora had too many rules for a grown woman to have to follow.

"Make sure I see you with my money before the day is out," Cora said when she dropped Malia off to her car that was still in the parking lot of the mall.

"I'll be over there later," Malia said as she got out of the car.

Felicia and Monica followed behind her because they didn't want to hear their mother's mouth. Cora was always a force to be reckoned with and they knew not to play with her.

"I don't care if I have to suck dick every day for a month, I'm gonna pay her back every dime of that five hundred dollars. I don't need her to be on my back about no money," Felicia said when they got into Malia's car.

"I have a few dollars saved up and I'm gonna go drop it off to her later. I need to go get my baby for a little while. I know he's upset that I didn't bring him to the fair," Malia replied.

"What do you mean get him for a little while? I thought you were going back home. I know damn well you ain't staying with Roman's dog ass after this!" Felicia yelled.

"First off, you need to calm down with all the yelling. And, secondly, Landon is on some bullshit right now. He claims he got a girlfriend, but I know the nigga is lying. Lennox would have been told me that," Malia noted.

"He's just probably trying to teach you a lesson for leaving him. Niggas be in their feelings more than bitches sometimes. His ass knows he wants you to come back. He just wants you beg." Monica frowned.

"Well, if that's what I have to do, so be it." Malia shrugged as she pulled up to their houses.

Felicia lived a few buildings over from Monica, but she got out and walked to her apartment. She was happy that her kids were in school because she needed a nap. As soon as Malia pulled off, she pulled out her phone and called Landon. She was happy that she hadn't got locked up with it and it was still halfway charged.

"Yeah Malia," Landon said when he answered the phone.

She wanted to scream when she heard a woman's laughter in the background. It was Monday morning, so Malia knew that her kids were in school. She wanted to get Lennox when he got out and keep him overnight. She had a lot of making up to do for standing him up. Plus, she wanted the info on this mystery woman that his father was now claiming.

"I know Lennox is at school, but I wanted to get him until tomorrow. I'll bring him to school in the morning and he can catch the bus back home. I'll pick him up this evening, so let Ms. Ella know that he won't be getting off the bus today," Malia said.

"Okay, that's cool," Landon replied as he kissed Faryn's neck and chest.

True to his word, he made sure that Faryn called off from work that morning. Once the kids went off to school, they got it poppin' in just about every room in the house. The kids' rooms and bathrooms were off limits, but everything else was fair game.

"Okay, I'll be there in a little while to get his stuff," Malia said, hoping that she could get a glimpse of the new woman in his life.

"Nah, I'll drop it off to him later. I have to pack it up and I'm busy right now," Landon replied.

"Busy doing what?" Malia asked.

"I'll call you later when I'm on my way," Landon replied before hanging up. He wasn't about to entertain Malia and her foolishness. He didn't know what kind of bullshit she was on, but he didn't have time for it.

"Asshole," Malia hissed once the phone hung up.

She made her way to the apartment that she shared with Roman with her heart beating erratically. She didn't know if he was home or not and she was scared to find out. She was able to breathe a little easier when she pulled up and didn't see his car parked out front. She visibly exhaled when she got inside of the apartment because her key still worked. Malia had all kinds of thoughts going through her head. Since learning that another woman had made it possible for them to get the apartment, Malia thought she would play dirty to keep her out. Although she was happy that she still had a place to stay, she still wondered about what was going on with Roman.

Malia grabbed her laptop from the dresser and decided to play detective. After going to the site and putting in Roman's information, she learned that he was still locked up. He had an attachment on him from another parish, so he would still have to be transferred before being released. Malia checked on Chad and it was the same thing with him. She could care less about Chad being in there, but she wanted Roman to come home, at least until she could get back right with Landon. Thinking quickly, Malia came up with a plan that would get her boo out of jail and hopefully solidify her place in his heart. After taking a shower and changing clothes, she made a few moves until it was time to get Lennox out of school.

***

"Are you full baby?" Malia asked as she looked over and smiled at her son.

She had picked Lennox up from school and taken him to the movies. Afterwards, they went to the Game Stop and picked up a few new games for him and Lance to play with. Lance still didn't want to be bothered with her, but she made sure to get him whatever she got his brother. She was confident that he would come around eventually, but he was still being stubborn.

"Yeah, I'm full. Can I take the rest home?" Lennox asked.

"You sure can. Let me call the waiter," Malia said as she looked around the Chinese restaurant that they were eating at.

"Is my dad coming to pick me up?" Lennox asked.

"No baby, you're spending the night with me." Malia smiled.

Her smile faded when she saw that her son didn't look too happy about the news that she'd just delivered. Lennox usually lit up when he would stay the night with her. He looked like he would rather be anywhere else now. She was sure it had a lot to do with her broken promise and she had to make things right.

"Lennox, baby, I'm sorry about not taking you to the fair. Something came up that was out of my control. Believe me, I would have rather been with you and Lance than anywhere else," Malia said while holding her son's hand.

"It's okay. My dad and Faryn took us. We had fun," Lance noted.

"Who is Faryn?" Malia asked, happy that she didn't have to bring up the other woman first.

"She's my daddy's girlfriend and she's pretty." Lennox smiled.

"Does she live with y'all?" Malia questioned.

"No, but her house is pretty too," Lennox answered.

"You've been to her house?" Malia inquired.

"Yeah, she cooks for us all the time. We were supposed to make banana splits tonight, but I can't since I'm staying the night with you."

"Does she sleep at your house?" Malia inquired.

"Yeah, she did last night."

"Do you like her, Lennox?" Malia asked, feeling like she wanted to cry.

"Yeah, she's nice to us. Lance likes her too. She's his counselor," Lennox noted.

"His counselor?" Malia asked in confusion.

"Yeah, he was fighting at school and Faryn helped him to stop. He's been being good, and my daddy said that it's because of Faryn," Lennox noted, making things clearer.

Malia remembered Landon saying that Lance was seeing a behavior specialist, so that must have been the woman in question. Hearing that Lance was fond of the other woman had Malia in her feelings. He was shunning her and opening up to his father's girlfriend

"Well, I'll probably be coming back home soon," Malia informed him.

"You are?" Lennox asked, confusion written all over his little face.

"Yes. Your father and I have been talking and we think it's best if we all live together again. Wouldn't you like that?" Malia questioned.

"What about Faryn?" Lennox asked.

"What about her? I'm your mother, not Faryn," Malia replied.

"But, my daddy likes her. She's gonna be sad if you move in our house and she can't come over anymore."

"Faryn will find herself another man. Your father and I are married. Husbands and wives are supposed to live together."

"My GG said that you and my daddy are divorced," Lennox repeated what he'd heard several times before.

"Your GG doesn't know what she's talking about." Malia frowned.

"But, I thought you had a boyfriend. What about Mr. Roman?" Lennox asked.

"Roman is still my friend, but your father is my husband. Do you understand?" Malia asked him.

"Yes," Lennox lied.

His little young mind couldn't comprehend all that he was hearing. He was seeing one thing and being told something different. His father never told them anything about their mother coming back home and he didn't know how he felt about it. Malia tried to sound confident, but she was conflicted too. On one hand, she wanted Roman to come to his senses and do right by her. Then, she wanted Landon to drop the bitch that he was with so that they could be a family again. Since she had gone above and beyond for Roman, she was hoping that he saw how much she had his back and showed his gratitude. Either way, Malia was going to get one or the other. Nothing or nobody was going to stand in the way of that.

Chapter 14

"**S**hit," Landon hissed as he pumped in and out of Faryn's mouth.

She had him almost in tears as she tried to suck the life out of him. Faryn was a pro at breathing through her nose as she took him to the back of her throat. Landon tried to ease up when he thought he was going too deep, but Faryn pulled him in deeper. She moved her tongue like a snake as Landon threw his head back and played in her hair.

"Fuuuuck!" Landon growled when Faryn started alternating between stroking and sucking.

He was feeling lightheaded as he held on to the dresser to steady himself. He was only trying to grab a t-shirt from his drawer when she dropped to her knees without warning and started sucking him up. His climax was approaching fast and he knew it was going to be a big one. When Faryn tasted the first few drops of his liquid candy, she pulled him in deeper and used her mouth like a suction cup. Landon's mouth was in the shape of a circle and words seemed to escape him.

"Its... shit... damn..." Landon moaned as he unloaded in Faryn's mouth and watch her drink it like water.

It was official; he was in love. Faryn was the definition of the truth in every sense of the word. She cooked, cleaned, and sexed Landon like a porn star. She had a degree and her own money, not that he cared. He wouldn't mind taking care of her, even though Faryn would never allow him to.

Landon dropped down to the floor, spent from busting a big ass nut. He watched as Faryn got up and went into the bathroom to brush her teeth. It was a little after six that morning and she had to be at work. She hated driving, so Landon always dropped her off after he took his boys to school. She was still skeptical of people knowing who he was, so she never let him drop her off in front. He dropped her off on the side of the building and she walked around to the front.

"Happy four-month anniversary baby," Faryn said with a smile when she walked back into the bedroom.

Landon was sprawled out on the floor, so Faryn kneeled and planted a kiss on his lips.

"It's only been a month," he replied as he pulled her down and kissed her again.

"No, it hasn't Landon. Today made four months since you gave me a ride home from the club and came to my house," Faryn noted.

"Okay, but it's only been one month since we made it official. That other shit don't count," he replied as he tried to lift her shirt over her head.

"Get off me. I have to go to work," Faryn snapped while pushing him away and standing to her feet.

"Alright baby, I'm sorry. It's been four months. Just let me get a quickie," Landon begged while grabbing her leg.

"Forget you, Landon. Stop trying to tell me what I want to hear just to get some ass," Faryn replied.

"Stop acting like that girl. I don't even know why you're keeping track of that shit. We're together and that's all that matters. It feels way longer than its actually be1en anyway," Landon said as he got up and pulled her into his embrace.

She smiled as she wrapped her arms around his neck and kissed him. Landon was right. It did feel like they'd know each other longer than they did. Lance had been her client for about six months, so that was technically when they met. Faryn and Landon had slept under the same roof every night since the first time she stayed at his house. She usually stayed at his house, unless his kids were gone, and he came by her. Landon told her that it had been a while since he'd slept next to a woman and he loved it. He now craved Faryn's body next to his and she felt the same way.

"Stop before you have us all late," Faryn giggled when he started kissing her neck and chest.

"Yeah, let me get dressed, so I can go see what Clarence is talking about," Landon replied.

His mother's ex-husband had requested his presence, but Landon didn't know why. It really didn't matter. Whenever Clarence told him and Makena to do something, it was done with no questions asked. Once he and Faryn got dressed. He made sure his sons were together as well. Lance had been in a foul mood for the past few days, but Landon didn't know why. Faryn said he seemed fine when she saw him the week before, so he didn't know where the sudden change had come from.

"Y'all wanna eat something before we leave?" Landon asked his sons.

"Can I have a pop tart?" Lennox asked.

"Yeah. What about you, Lance? You want something to eat before you go to school?" Landon questioned.

"No," he mumbled, sounding like he was aggravated.

"What's up with you, bruh? What's with the sudden attitude?" Landon inquired.

"I don't have an attitude," Lance snapped.

"Who you talking to like that boy? Don't make me whip your ass in here," Landon threatened.

"Baby," Faryn said as she softly rubbed his arm.

"Nah, fuck that Faryn. Ain't but one man in this bitch. I'll be damned if I let my own kids run shit in my house," Landon fumed.

Faryn quickly learned that Landon had a temper identical to Lance's. He gave his children the world, but he didn't tolerate disrespect.

"You okay Lance? You wanna talk about it?" Faryn asked softly.

"Can we talk when I get out of school? Will you be here?" he asked, void of the attitude that he'd just had.

Landon noted how he was always nice and sweet to Faryn, but he was always frowned up when he talked to him.

"Yeah, I'll be here," Faryn replied.

Landon shook his head as he grabbed his keys and headed for the door. Lance was begging for an ass whipping and he had no problem delivering. Once he dropped Faryn and the kids off to their destinations, Landon made his way to Clarence's house. He spotted an unfamiliar car in the driveway and he was curious as to who it was. Clarence told him that he had a female friend that he'd been seeing for a while, but Landon had never met her. Instead of using his key to enter the house like he normally would, Landon rang the doorbell. He didn't know if Clarence's woman friend was there or not and he didn't want to intrude.

"Your key not working or something," Clarence commented when he opened the door for him.

"Yeah, it works. I just didn't want to walk in on nothing. I see a car out there, so I figured you had company."

Landon walked into the house and immediately noticed the difference. It had been over a month since he'd been there, but things had been moved around. Clarence wasn't the best house keeper and Makena often had to go over there to wash and clean up for him. That wasn't the case anymore. Clarence's entire house was immaculate, and Landon's mouth watered when he smelled whatever was cooking.

"I got my lady here, but feel free to use your key any time. She knows that you and Makena are my babies," Clarence replied.

"Baby? Your son or your boy is cool, but that baby shit ain't gon' fly," Landon laughed.

"You always did hate when I said that. How's the new relationship going?" Clarence asked.

Landon had invited him to his house to meet Faryn a few days before and he really liked her. She made his stepson happy and that was all that mattered.

"It doesn't feel new, but it's going good. I have no complaints."

"That's always good to hear," Clarence nodded.

"So, what's up with you and this lady? Are y'all in a relationship or something?" Landon questioned.

"We are now. She had some shit to get right before I made that move with her."

"What do you mean?" Landon asked.

"She's younger than I am, but she didn't have nothing going for herself. I made sure she went back to school and got her GED and, now, she's enrolled in college. She's starting a new job next week and she seems to be on the right track now. I have too much going for myself. I can't have no dead weight around me," Clarence replied.

"When do I get to meet her?" Landon inquired.

"In a minute. I wanted to run something by you first."

"What's up?" Landon questioned.

He watched as Clarence got up and retrieved some information from his file cabinet. To anyone else, Clarence looked like a common drunk, but he was far from that. He was a damn genius, and Landon soaked up as much of his knowledge as he could. Clarence learned the business of investing at a young age and he was a pro at it.

"I've been doing my research on this for a while and it's a damn gold mine," Clarence said as he handed some papers to Landon to look over.

"Laundromats?" Landon asked with wrinkled brows.

"Fix your face and listen. Depending on how many machines you have, you can generate an income of seven to ten thousand a month. Not to mention the cost to purchase an equipped building is a steal. You won't even have to be there to do anything. Hire a part time person to keep the places clean and make sure it's running smoothly and you're all set. It's a no brainier," Clarence noted.

"Are you considering doing this for yourself too?" Landon asked.

"No, I've been doing my research for you and Makena," Clarence replied.

"Why not yourself?" Landon asked.

"Nah, I'm good with the real estate that I have now. I'm sixty years old and I have enough money coming in to be comfortable for the rest of my life. You know how Makena is. She doesn't like commercial real estate, even though that's where the real money is. She could have just as much as you in her accounts if she stops being so scared. I just wanna make sure that y'all are good."

"You always do, but I don't know about this laundromat thing," Landon said.

"Have I ever steered you wrong?" Clarence asked.

"Never," Landon acknowledged.

"Exactly and I'm not about to start. I don't go into anything blindly. I've been looking at this for months," Clarence noted.

"What am I looking at in terms of cost?" Landon asked.

"Flip to the last page," Clarence requested, watching as Landon did as he was told.

"Damn. That's not bad," he replied.

"Not at all and all three of them are in high traffic areas. You might make even more than I said," Clarence said.

"How long before I have to make a decision?" Landon wanted to know.

"Today," Clarence replied sternly.

"Damn. I can't even think about it for a while?" Landon wondered.

"I've already done all the thinking for you. Stop always procrastinating. You did the same thing with your office buildings and almost missed out on a golden opportunity."

"Yeah, I know," Landon agreed.

"I try to make this as easy as possible. You don't have to do research or nothing else. What do I always tell you?" Clarence asked.

"You can give me fish, but you'd rather teach me how to fish," Landon replied, repeating Clarence's favorite quote.

"Exactly. I have no problem giving you money, but I'd rather teach you how to make your own. Now, I have everything in place and all you have to do is write the check. What's it gonna be?" Clarence questioned.

"Do you even have to ask? You know I'm in," Landon replied, making him smile.

"That's my boy," Clarence said proudly.

Clarence had never led him astray and he trusted him with his life. Landon had more money in the bank than he'd ever seen in his life and even more was rolling in. It was all thanks to Clarence, and he loved and appreciated him for that. Clarence had done more for him and Makena than their mother ever had, and they were grateful.

"Now, let me meet this mystery woman and see if she can pass my test," Landon joked.

Clarence got up and walked away. He returned a few minutes later with a pretty, younger woman who looked like she could be his daughter, instead of his girlfriend.

"Son, this is Akira. This is Landon, Akira. The one that I'm always talking about," Clarence said, making the introductions.

"Hey Landon. It's nice to finally meet you." Akira smiled.

"Yeah, same here," Landon said as he stood up and shook her hand.

"I feel like I already know you and your sister. He talks about y'all all the time," she acknowledged.

"All good I hope," Landon said while looking at Clarence sideways.

"Yes, all the time." She smiled.

"Okay, I just wanted to make sure I didn't have to lay hands on him," Landon joked.

"Don't let the gray hair fool you," Clarence warned.

"I know it's still early, but I just finished cooking dinner. You're welcome to have some," Akira offered.

"Trust me, you won't be disappointed," Clarence said.

Upon his urging, Landon decided to take Akira up on her offer. He was happy that he did because Clarence was right. Akira's food was the shit and he was not disappointed. He ended up handling some business with Clarence regarding his new business venture. Landon had to wire money to make the purchases and that was done in a matter of minutes. Clarence offered to help him find a part-time employee whenever he was ready, but that wouldn't be for a few weeks. He had a lot of other legal things to do before he even thought about opening the businesses. Clarence rushed him because he didn't want him to miss out on the opportunity, but he didn't mind.

"I'm happy we got that out of the way. Now, I can relax since the hard part is over," Clarence said.

Landon was about to reply until his phone started ringing. He recognized the number as Lance's school and he blew out a breath of frustration. School was almost over and he didn't have time for the foolishness with Lance.

"Hello," Landon answered.

"Mr. Reynolds, it's Mrs. Jennings. I know it's been a while, but I need to see you in my office," the principal of the school replied.

"What did he do this time?" Landon asked.

"He got into another fight, but he's not suspended. I'm letting him off with a warning, but I told him that we don't want the old Lance back. He's been doing so well, and I don't know what set him off this time. He's still upset, so I just need you to pick him up and talk to him."

"Okay Mrs. Jennings, I'm on my way," Landon assured her.

"What happened?" Clarence asked.

"Lance got into another fight at school. I'm done talking. I'm whipping his ass on sight," Landon fumed.

"Whipping him is not the answer Landon," Clarence said.

"Yeah, well, obviously talking ain't the answer either. He got a bad ass temper and I'm about to get that shit in check."

"I wonder where he got it from," Clarence replied sarcastically.

"Man-" Landon started before being cut off.

"Man, my ass. How many times did Ella and I have to come to the school for your ass for the exact same thing? We never laid a finger on you and you eventually got it right. Imagine how you felt when Robin dropped you and Makena off to Ella. Lance has you, but he's probably feeling the same way. Just be patient with him Landon," Clarence advised.

Landon nodded his head in understanding, as Clarence walked him out of the house. He was trying to understand what his son was going through, being that he had gone through something similar. Lance had it better than him because he had a father, something that Landon didn't have. Talking to Faryn had done him good for a while, but he seemed to have reverted to his old ways. He said he wanted to talk to Faryn later, so hopefully that would help. Landon picked up his phone to call and tell her what was going on. Hopefully, she could get Lance back on track. If not, Landon was ready to take off his belt and get him in line the old-fashioned way.

Chapter 15

After picking Faryn up from work, Landon stopped to get them all something to eat. Faryn usually cooked, but he wanted her to focus on Lance. He was in the back seat staring out of the window and he hadn't said anything since his father picked him up from school. Landon wanted to go off on him, but he looked so pitiful sitting in his principal's office. He was starting to feel like a failure as a father, even though he tried to do everything right. Once they ate, Landon helped his boys do their homework. Afterwards, he lounged around on the sofa and watched an old football game.

"Lennox is playing his video game and we're going to take a walk out back," Faryn said as she and Lance walked into the living room.

"Okay," Landon said while nodding his head.

He appreciated Faryn more than she knew. She had a genuine heart and that was hard to come by.

"So, what's new?" Faryn asked as she draped her arm around Lance's neck.

"Nothing," he mumbled as they walked alongside the pool.

"Why were you fighting at school today?"

"Because the other boy got in my face." Lance shrugged like it was simple.

"Okay Lance, you said you wanted to talk, so what's up?" Faryn asked, getting right to the point. It was obvious that Lance wasn't going to say much unless she initiated it.

"Are you going to tell my dad about whatever we talk about?" Lance asked her.

"Not if you don't want me to," Faryn replied.

"No, I don't want you to tell him."

"Okay, I won't. What's up?" Faryn asked.

"Are you and my daddy breaking up?" Lance asked, making Faryn stop walking.

"Um, no, not that I know of. Why do you ask?" Faryn inquired.

"My mama told Lennox that her and my daddy are getting back together, and she was moving in with us. I don't want her to live here and neither does Lennox. My uncle Aiden said that she left us for another man, so she needs to stay with him," Lance said angrily.

"When did she tell him that?" Faryn questioned.

"When he stayed the night at her house that last time. She keeps saying that her and my daddy are still married, but they're not. My GG said that they're divorced."

Lance was ranting and raving, while Faryn just stood there in stunned silence. She didn't know if what Malia told her son was true, but she was physically sick at just the thought of it all. Her and Landon's relationship was still new, but she didn't want it to end any time soon. She could feel herself falling in love with him and the thought of not being with him had her scared.

"Is that why you've been upset for the past few days?" Faryn asked.

"Yeah. I don't want you and my dad to break up. Me and Lennox like it when you're here," Lance noted.

"I like being here too Lance, but you can't keep acting out like you've been doing. You're big enough to say how you feel. Your father and I are fine, so you have nothing to worry about."

"Are you sure?" Lance questioned skeptically.

"I'm very sure. We're happy with each other and we're not breaking up," Faryn said, trying to convince herself as well.

"Okay," Lance said as he smiled and visibly relaxed.

"And I think you owe your father an apology. He doesn't deserve the attitude that you've been giving him lately."

"You won't tell him what I told you though, right?" Lance asked.

"I told you that I wouldn't," Faryn replied.

"Okay, I'll apologize," Lance said.

He and Faryn talked for a while longer before they went back inside. Lance went to talk to his father while Faryn took a shower. She had a lot on her mind after talking to Lance and she didn't know what to do. Landon had never given her a reason to doubt him and she didn't want to start. She wanted to believe that he wouldn't do her wrong, but only time would tell.

✳✳✳

After being locked up for an entire month, Roman was finally released from jail. He had gone from one parish to another because he had warrants on him from both. Chad had the same problem, but he was still locked up. Roman was curious as to who had bailed him out, until he saw Malia's name on the paperwork. Jessica and her girl had been released the same day they went in and he tried to convince her to get him out. Just like he imagined, she was pissed and wasn't fucking with him like that right now. She had signed a month to month lease for his apartment, but she wanted that out of her name too. It wasn't the first time that he and Jessica had a big falling out and he was sure it wasn't the last. They had gone for an entire year without speaking once before, but it was like no time had passed at all when they reconnected. Roman didn't have anyone else to call, so he used the free phone in the lobby and called someone who he really had no desire to see again.

"Hello," Malia said when she answered the phone from the unknown number.

"Come get me, man," Roman demanded, sounding angry.

"Oh, my God, baby, you're out?" Malia asked.

"I must be if I'm telling you to pick me up," Roman snapped.

He told her where he would be standing, and she assured him that she was on her way. Malia was too excited that he was home and she needed to do everything in her power to make things right. She sped all the way to Orleans Parish Prison and saw Roman standing in the exact spot that he told her he'd be in.

"Hey baby," Malia said as soon as he got into the car.

"What's up?" Roman said, as she pulled off and drove away.

Malia wanted to kiss him so badly, but he didn't look like he wanted to be bothered like that.

"Ro, I know that you're probably still upset with me, but I'm sorry about everything that happened. I shouldn't have listened to my sisters and came to the mall like that," Malia apologized.

"It's all good man. I need to make some moves and make some shit happen. I gotta get my brother up out of that bitch," Roman replied.

"I had your car towed from the mall. It's parked at the house," Malia said, hoping to gain some brownie points.

"Yeah and what about that other thing? Did you take care of our little problem?" Roman asked.

"I couldn't. I had to pawn some of my jewelry and use the money that you gave me to get you out. I had to pay a bond in two different parishes," Malia replied.

"So, you're still pregnant?" Roman barked.

"What was I supposed to do Roman? I thought of everything that I could to get you out and you're still not satisfied. Would you have rather me let you stay in jail?" Malia asked as tears welled up in her eyes.

"I'm sorry baby. We got a lot of shit on our plates. The first thing I need you to do is renew our lease and put it in your name. Jessica is getting the apartment out of her name."

"You should have told me to do that when I first moved in with you. I can't believe that you had me living up in another woman's apartment." Malia frowned.

"That was my shit," Roman maintained, as they pulled up to the complex and parked.

"I don't have any income though, Roman. They might not let me do it," Malia noted.

"I can get you some check stubs made like I had to do for Jessica," he said, making her frown at the mention of the other woman's name again.

"When do I need to go to the office and do it?" Malia asked excitedly.

She was happy that the apartment was going to be in her name now. That meant that Roman couldn't put her out of it. She would also make sure to have the locks changed so that Chad wouldn't be able to come and go as he pleased.

"Wait until I come back," he replied.

"Come back from where?" Malia questioned.

"Didn't I tell you that I need to get my brother out of jail? I need to go shower and get to my stash. I need my damn hair cut too," Roman said when he got out of the car.

"Why can't one of his many women get him out like I did for you?" Malia questioned with a frown.

"Fuck them hoes. That's my damn brother," Roman said while pointing to himself.

"You want me to fix you something to eat before you go?" Malia asked.

"Nah, I'm good. Give me the paperwork for the pawn shop, so I can go get your shit back too," Roman replied, making her smile.

He immediately put his phone on the charger and went to go take a shower. Malia gathered up the paperwork from the pawn shop and sat it on the dresser. She hated that she had to pawn her wedding ring that Landon had given her, but she was happy that Roman was going to get it back. Landon paid a lot of money for her ring and she really didn't want to part with it. Malia got a nice chuck of change for all her jewelry and she still had over three grand left after she paid all of Roman's fees. She needed something stored away for a rainy day, just in case he decided to act a fool again.

"I put the paperwork on the dresser," Malia said when Roman came back into the room.

"Cool," he replied as he continued to get dressed in silence.

He grabbed his phone, even though it was still dead and put it in his pocket.

"Your phone isn't even charged yet," Malia pointed out.

"I'll charge it in the car," he replied as he grabbed his keys and left.

Malia heard the front door slam and she wanted to cry. She could tell that Roman was still mad with her, but she hoped he would get over it soon. After all, she'd gone above and beyond to get him out of jail. That should have counted for something.

Once she was alone, Malia stripped out of her clothes and went to sleep. She didn't realize that she had slept so long, but being pregnant had her more tired than usual. It was after midnight when she got up and she was still in bed alone. Roman had been gone for hours and she hadn't heard from him since he left. Malia got up and searched the house to make sure he wasn't in another room before she picked up her phone and called him. After calling three times back to back, she still hadn't gotten an answer. Warm tears cascaded down her cheeks as realization set in. Roman had played her and had her looking like a damn fool yet again. Malia grabbed some clothes to take a shower and hopefully wash all her pain away, if only temporarily.

***

After not hearing from Roman for two days, Malia woke up to the sounds of male laughter coming from the living room. She hurriedly went to the bathroom and handled her morning hygiene before slipping into her black silk bath robe. She smiled when she looked on the dresser and saw that all her jewelry was there. There was also some money next to it with a note explaining that Roman was paying her back for what she had done. Malia couldn't contain her excitement as she rushed out of her bedroom in search of her man. Her smile turned upside down when she got to the living room and saw Chad's stupid ass sitting there. He frowned when he looked up at her and she was sure that her face mirrored his. She ignored his miserable ass and walked right over to Roman. She wanted to grill him about where he'd been for the past two days, but she decided to leave it alone.

"Thanks baby," Malia said as she sat on his lap and kissed his lips.

"Thank you, too. I appreciate you getting me up out of there," Roman replied, as his brother let out a disgusted sigh.

"But anyway," Malia said while rolling her eyes, "did you eat anything yet?"

"Yeah, but you need to go get dressed, so we can go."

"Where are we going? We're hungry," Malia said, rubbing her still flat stomach.

Chad couldn't take it anymore. He grabbed his cigarettes and lighter and made his way outside.

"My hookup gave me the check stubs. We need to go to the office and do this paperwork," Roman replied.

"Okay," Malia said as she jumped up and hurried to the room to get dressed.

She wasn't showing yet, so she put on a two-piece stripped skirt set with a small portion of her belly visible. She pulled her hair up in a messy bun and put on her comfortable wedges.

"I'm ready boo," Malia said when she walked out of the room.

She and Roman passed by Chad as they headed to the car. Malia was nervous when they went to the leasing office, but the manager was cool. She didn't ask too many questions about them renewing the lease in someone else's name and that made everything easier. Once that was done, Roman stopped to get something to eat. It felt like old times as they rode around and talked like they did when they first hooked up. Things were going great until Roman pulled up to an unmarked building and parked the car.

"What is this?" Malia asked.

"The women's clinic," Roman replied as he got out of the car.

Malia was still sitting there until he walked around and opened her car door.

"The fuck you still sitting there for? Get out!" Roman barked, showing his true colors once again.

He and Chad had stayed by one of Chad's many girlfriends the night before, and she gave Roman some info on abortion clinics. She'd even made some calls for him and helped him set things up. Malia thought she was slick, but she had him fucked up. There was no way in hell that she was keeping that baby, even if he had to beat it out of her.

"I can't believe you did this," Malia said as the tears rolled down her cheeks.

"Fuck you thought. Ain't shit change and I still don't want no kids," Roman replied.

Malia shook her head in defeat and walked inside the clinic, with Roman following right behind her. She was heartbroken when she learned that he'd already made the appointment for her and paid the deposit over the phone. Malia sat through the counseling phase of the procedure in a daze. She didn't care about what they were saying, and she didn't bother trying to pay attention.

Two days later, she had the abortion and cried herself to sleep that night. To make matters worse, Roman didn't bother coming back once he dropped her off. He never even bothered to answer his phone either. Malia didn't know much about karma before, but she was getting a double dose of it now. Landon and her boys came to mind and she knew that she was getting back what she had done to them.

Chapter 16

An entire week had passed since Malia had her procedure and she was going in for a follow-up appointment. Roman had finally made his way back home, but they didn't say much to each other. He seemed to be avoiding her, but she didn't even care. Making her get rid of their child was the ultimate low and she hated him for it. She was surprised that he'd offered to take her to her follow up appointment, but she was happy at the same time. She didn't even have to ask, and she was shocked when he offered.

"Everything all good?" Roman asked when Malia came from the back of the clinic and said that she was done.

"Yeah, I'm good," she replied sadly.

"Don't look like that man. This was for the best. Kids complicate shit and my life is complicated enough," Roman said.

"I guess," Malia replied, not agreeing with anything that he said.

"You hungry?" Roman asked, surprising her once again.

It had been a while since he was nice to her, but she was enjoying it. He grabbed her hand in his and Malia felt a little relieved.

"I'm starving," Malia replied.

"What do you feel like eating?" Roman asked.

"It doesn't matter," Malia said as she looked out of the window.

She felt the depression creeping in, but she felt better knowing that Roman was there with her. He seemed to be feeling just as bad, but it was all his idea. Malia was going to play on his sympathies for as long as she could.

"What about Texas Roadhouse?" Roman asked.

"That's cool," Malia replied.

Thankfully, the restaurant wasn't crowded, and they were seated right away. Their food was out, and they were enjoying their meals about thirty minutes later. Usually, Roman would be in a hurry and rushing her to finish. He seemed to be calm and he didn't look like he was ready to go any time soon.

"You want some dessert?" he asked once they were done eating.

"No, I'm stuffed," Malia replied.

"Let's go to Best Buy right quick," Roman requested.

"For what?" Malia asked.

"I need another big screen for the bedroom," Roman replied.

He threw some money on the table, and Malia followed him out. After going to Best Buy, they went to Walmart for household necessities. Roman was never one to shop, but he got tons of soap, toothpaste, and other things that they needed. The store was more crowded than usual, and Malia was drained. They had been gone for hours and she was ready to get in her bed.

"Where are we going now?" she asked once they got back into the car.

"Home," was his simple reply.

She didn't want to nag him, but she was happy to hear it. When they pulled up to the house, Chad was sitting on the porch, but he stood up when he saw Roman's car pull up. Chad wasn't there when they left, and his car wasn't out front like it usually was. He had a smirk on his face when he walked up to the car that Malia would have loved to slap off.

"Where are you about to go?" Malia questioned while looking over at Roman.

"I got a few moves to make," was his simple reply.

"How long are you gonna be?" Malia asked as Chad stood there, impatiently waiting for her to get out.

"I don't know. I'll call you," Roman answered.

Gone was the nicer Roman who wanted to spend time with her and seemed to enjoy it. In his place was the one who just didn't give a damn and didn't want to be bothered. Malia was over his attitude already. She knew once he got with Chad that he would probably be out all night. That was probably his reason for being so sweet to her. It was all good though. He was going to pay for how he treated her and that she was sure of.

"About damn time," Chad hissed when she opened the door and got out.

"You want me to get the bags from the trunk?" Malia offered.

"No," Roman snapped in aggravation.

"What about the tv? I know you're not gonna ride around with a big ass tv on your back seat," Malia replied.

"I'll help him bring it in the house. He's good," Chad laughed, making Roman laugh with him.

"Whatever," Malia said, obviously not getting the joke.

She took her food that she had left over from the restaurant and made her way inside. The door was unlocked, so she didn't have to use her key. Malia stopped in her tracks as soon as she entered the apartment and looked around in shock.

"What the fuck!" Malia gasped as she looked around the bare living room that once was full of furniture.

She searched the spare bedroom and bathroom as well as the kitchen and got the same results. It wasn't until she got to her own bedroom that she could breathe a little easier. The bedroom was still the way she left it earlier and all the furniture wall still there. It wasn't until she opened the closet that she started to panic again. Roman's clothes and shoes weren't where he usually kept them and his drawers where he kept his underclothes was empty. Malia felt like she was getting lightheaded as she grabbed her phone and sat down on the bed. She dialed Roman's number and hoped he had enough sense to pick up.

"Yeah," he drawled into the phone.

"What the hell is going on Roman? Where is all of our furniture?" Malia yelled.

"My furniture is in my new apartment," he replied, as Chad laughed hysterically in the background.

"What new apartment?" Malia asked.

"Man, you dumb, but you ain't that damn dumb. The fuck you thought Malia? You got me and my brother locked up and you thought I was gon' stay with your disgusting ass. If we're keeping it real, I was done with you way before then," Roman answered.

"After everything that I've done for you, Roman? This is how you treat me?" Malia sobbed.

"I appreciate you making moves to get me out of jail, but it was your fault that I got locked up in the first place. Be happy that I made it possible for your ass to have somewhere to stay," Roman replied.

He was heated when he first got locked up and he vowed that he was done with Malia. He planned to kick her out of the apartment and make her fend for herself. His heart softened a bit when she did what she did to get him out. His mind was still made up about being done with her, but he took a different approach. He gave Malia the opportunity to put the apartment in her name and he left everything in the bedroom, so she'd have somewhere to sleep. He even purchased himself another tv and let her keep the one that was there. He let her keep all the toiletries and went to Walmart to purchase his own. When Chad told him that one of his girls agreed to get them a place in her name, that was music to Roman's ears.

"What am I supposed to do Roman? You know I don't have a job. I can't afford to pay this rent," Malia cried.

"You got two months to figure it out. That's how long it's paid up for."

"What did I ever do to you, Roman? I loved you unconditionally, even though you treated me like shit most of the time. I stayed with you through all the different hoes calling and the sleeping out all the time. I tolerated your brother's disrespect, even when you never stood up for me. When you said that you wanted to be with me, but you weren't ready to be a stepfather, I made that possible too," Malia rambled through her tears and runny nose.

"But who asked you to Malia? I specifically remember telling you not to leave your family because I wasn't ready for what you wanted. Even after you did the shit anyway, I still stepped up and did the right thing and moved you in with me," he acknowledged.

"But, we still made it work for over a year Roman."

"And that was the most miserable year of my life. All you do is bitch and complain about everything. We don't run in the same circles and we don't have shit in common. Hell, we don't even fuck the same way. Nigga don't have time to be all soft and gentle with your fragile ass!" Roman barked, making Chad laugh even harder.

"Tell his stupid ass to shut the fuck up!" Malia yelled angrily.

"Man, bye Malia," Roman replied.

"Ro, wait! Please! Can we just talk about this? I know that I have to make some changes, but you have to give it some time. Nothing is going to happen overnight like you want it to."

"Nah, Malia. You need to go back home to your family or get a job and take care of yourself. I keep telling you that I'm not the man for you. Stop trying to force shit that don't fit. I'm not a family man and that seems to be what want. I hope you find what you're looking for, but I'm not that nigga," Roman replied right before hanging up the phone in her face.

"Roman! Roman!" Malia yelled as she dropped down to the floor and started crying.

She couldn't believe how her life was turning out, but she had no one to blame but herself. She knew from the start that she and Roman were from two different walks of life, but the thrill of being with a bad boy overshadowed her common sense. She went from almost having her dream home built from the ground up to living in an almost empty apartment. She and Landon had three bank accounts with money pouring into all of them every month. Now, she had a little over three thousand dollars to her name. She was screwed, and she didn't know how she was going to get herself out of the mess that she had created. She couldn't even call Landon for help because he too had moved on and found someone else. Malia still wasn't giving up on her marriage though. Landon still loved her and that much she was sure of. She just had to find a way to make him see it.

Chapter 17

"**G**o wash all that sweat and funk off you and call me when you're ready," Landon said as he talked on the phone with Faryn.

"Where are we going?" she questioned, slightly out of breath.

She was in the gym at her apartment complex running on the treadmill. Faryn had picked up a lot of weight over the past two months and she had slacked up with her workouts.

"I don't know. Wherever you want to go is cool with me," he replied.

"Okay," Faryn replied as she turned off the machine and grabbed her bottle of water.

"I don't know why you always go home just to work out."

"Because I'm getting fat as fuck and you act like you don't see it," Faryn argued.

"Girl, you ain't getting fat. You gained weight in all the right places, but that's not what I meant. You could have worked out by me," Landon said.

"I know Landon, but you don't have a treadmill or an elliptical. That's mostly what I use to exercise," Faryn noted.

"Don't trip, I'll have them both in the basement no later than tomorrow," he replied, making her smile.

Landon's basement looked like a small one-bedroom apartment. Besides his weights and other masculine workout equipment, all he had in there were household supplies. He had more paper towels, tissue, and other household items than one person needed. Makena was a couponer and she kept his basement fully stocked. She was trying to teach Faryn how to do it, but it was more difficult than she thought it would be.

"Anything to keep me at your house, huh?" Faryn chuckled.

"You already know," Landon replied.

He and Faryn had been going strong for four months and he couldn't be happier. Not only was he happy, but his boys were happy as well. They had fun cooking and baking with Faryn and they looked forward to their weekend treats that she made with them. Faryn always said that they were seven months into their relationship, so Landon let her have that. She counted the first time that he came to her apartment as their first date and he was tired of disagreeing with her. If that made her happy, then he was all for it. They hadn't slept without each other since they first made it official and that was all that mattered to him.

"Okay baby. I'm going hop in the shower and get ready. Use your key to come in if you get here before I'm done," Faryn said.

"Okay, I'll see you in a few," Landon replied before they hung up.

As soon as she disconnected with him, Faryn's phone rang again, displaying Harley's number.

"Hey friend," Faryn answered as she downed the rest of her water.

"Where are you, Faryn? We just knocked on your door looking for you," Harley said.

"Who is we?" Faryn asked.

"Me and Patrice. She's here with the baby," Harley said, referring to her cousin.

"Aww, I can't wait to see her. I'm on my way back up from the gym, but I need a shower first."

"She'll be here for a while, so come over whenever you're done. And I want you to look at a few of these paint samples that I chose for the house," Harley said.

"Okay," Faryn said before she hung up.

Harley and Kyron had just closed on their new house and they were in the process of making a few changes before they moved in. Faryn was happy for her girl, but she was going to miss her being right across the hall. Once she left the gym, she took the elevator up to her apartment. As soon as Faryn got to her door and was about to open it, Harley's door swung open and Jo-Jo came walking out. He had an unlit cigarette dangling from his mouth that he removed so that he could smile at her.

"What's up beautiful?" he asked as he walked closer to her.

Faryn quickly abandoned the idea of going into her apartment because she didn't trust him. She didn't remember Jo-Jo looking so sneaky before or maybe she was just too young to pay much attention.

"Hey Jo-Jo. Is Harley in there?" Faryn questioned as she tried to go around him and enter her friend's apartment.

"What's up with you, Faryn? Why you acting like you don't know a nigga no more? I know you got a man and everything, but I won't tell if you don't." He grinned slyly.

"There's nothing to tell Jo-Jo. I have a man and I'm happy with him," Faryn said as she tried to ease by him again.

She flinched a little when Jo-Jo came up to her and backed her into the wall. He put his arm up over her head and leaned down closer to her ear.

"I still remember how you taste, how you smell, everything. Is it still as tight as it was when I first hit it?" Jo-Jo asked her as he licked his lips.

"Unfortunately, you'll never find out," Faryn replied as she went under his long arm and rushed into Harley's apartment.

She rolled her eyes to the celling when she saw Monica's hating ass sitting there talking to Harley, Kyron, and Patrice. She heard a lot of talking in the background when she talked on the phone with Harley and, now, she knew why.

"I thought you were going to take a shower first," Harley said when she walked in.

"I was," was all Faryn said while giving her a knowing look.

Harley knew that meant that they would talk about it later, so she didn't push the issue.

"This bitch is bad even in workout clothes. Come give me a hug heifer. I don't care if you're sweaty or not," Patrice said as she stood up and walked over to Faryn.

"Aww Patrice, she is so cute," Faryn cooed as she looked down at her sleeping baby in her car seat.

"Thanks boo. She's a crybaby too, so she'll probably be the only child for the rest of her life," Patrice laughed.

"And guess who's going to be the Godparents?" Kyron asked proudly.

"Oh Lord, they are going to have your baby spoiled rotten. You already know how Kyron feels about kids," Faryn laughed.

Monica was sitting there with a sour look on her face until Jo-Jo walked back inside. She fluffed up her dry looking weave and tried to make herself look presentable. Faryn already knew what that was about. Harley already told her that Monica tried to push up on every friend that Kyron ever had over. A few of them fucked her a time or two, but that was as far as it went.

"And I heard you got a new man in your life. I need to meet him, honey. If he got you to give him a chance, he must be something serious," Patrice said while looking at Faryn.

"He's such a sweetheart," Harley commented.

"He'll be here to get me in a little while. I'll introduce you," Faryn blushed.

"I'm so happy for you, Faryn. You look so happy." Patrice smiled.

"He's a lucky man. Trust me, I should know," Jo-Jo said.

"Jo-Jo please, stop acting like we were together recently. I was fifteen years old. That was a long time ago," Faryn snapped angrily.

She was sick and tired of him bringing up the past. She had forgotten about most of what happened between them, but it was obvious that he hadn't.

"It doesn't matter how long ago it was. You can never forget your first, no matter who you're with." He winked.

"Chill out bruh," Kyron warned with a stern look.

He knew that Harley was going to go off on him later if his boy kept up the foolishness. She already expressed her dislike towards him from the first day they met, but she was always cordial. He never did anything out of the way, so she tolerated his presence.

"Fifteen? Not how she be acting like she's better than everybody else," Monica spoke up.

She wanted Jo-Jo and she was willing to play dirty to get him. She'd given him oral sex the first day they met, but she was trying to take it further.

"No, I'm not better than everybody else, but I'm damn sure better than you. I don't understand how an uneducated bitch who have three babies with multiple daddies and wear knockoffs from head to toe, always got some slick shit to say. I gave you several passes on the strength of Harley, but don't get shit twisted. Ain't nothing weak or scary about me," Faryn assured her.

"Damn!" Jo-Jo yelled as he fell out laughing.

Patrice was snickering under her breath, while Harley tried her best to hide the smirk that was on her face. Kyron was shocked that Faryn popped off the way she did because she was always so laidback. Everyone had a breaking point and she'd obviously reached hers with Monica.

"What's up then bitch? Ain't shit scary about me either. What you wanna do?" Monica asked as she stood to her feet.

Patrice grabbed her baby's car seat and moved out of the way. Faryn stood up, ready to lay hands on Monica until Kyron and Harley pulled them both back.

"I'm sorry friend. You know I would never disrespect your house like this, but I'm tired of playing nice," Faryn noted.

"It's okay boo. Calm down and go wait for Landon," Harley said, making Monica snap her head around to look at her.

That wasn't a very common name and her ex brother-in-law was the only Landon that she knew. Monica prayed that he wasn't messing with Faryn. Landon was too good for her, in Monica's opinion. Besides, her sister was trying to get her family back and that would throw a wrench in her plans.

"Girl, yes, I need a drink," Faryn replied, as Harley walked her to the door.

As soon as they walked out of Harley's apartment, Faryn's front door opened and Landon was walking out.

"I was just about to knock on the door to see if you were over here. What's up Harley?" Landon smiled.

"Hey Landon," she spoke back.

"I just came over here to see Patrice's baby, but I was about to lay hands on Harley's ratchet ass friend," Faryn said.

"What happened?" Landon asked.

"The bitch got a slick ass mouth that she needs to get punched in," Faryn replied.

"Wait a second Faryn, let me call Patrice out right quick," Harley said as she yelled inside for her cousin to come out and meet Landon.

Landon didn't care that she was sweaty; he pulled Faryn close and leaned down to kiss her. She was giggling like a school girl until Monica's ratchet voice interrupted their tender moment.

"What's up brother-in-law?" Monica said with a smirk.

When Harley yelled for her cousin to come out, Monica beat her to the door to see for herself. She wanted to die when she saw that her suspicions were confirmed.

"Brother-in-law? Nah, you must have me confused with the next nigga," Landon replied.

"Play dumb if you want to. You know exactly what I'm talking about," Monica said, trying to make Faryn mad.

"Baby, this is my friend and Harley's cousin, Patrice. Patrice, this is my boyfriend, Landon," Faryn said while ignoring Monica and introducing Landon to Patrice.

"It's nice to meet you, Landon. You must be very special. Faryn turned down every man who's ever tried to get with her. You must be the one." Patrice smiled while shaking his hand.

"I better be the one," Landon replied while staring at Faryn.

"Don't worry boo, you are." Faryn smiled.

"How are my nephews Landon?" Monica asked, making sure that Faryn knew that she was connected to her man in some way.

It was childish as hell, but she really didn't give a damn.

"Nephews?" Harley questioned.

"Yes, that's my sister Malia's ex-husband and my nephew's father," Monica smirked triumphantly now that the cat was out of the bag.

Faryn's expression remained the same, but Harley wanted to jump for joy with happiness for her friend. If the stories that Monica told her about her sister's ex-husband were true, Faryn had found herself a winner. She always said that she was waiting for the right man to come along, and Landon was the one. She couldn't believe how all the dots were connecting. Landon might have been Malia's trash, but he was a treasure to Faryn.

"I'll wait for you inside baby. It was nice meeting you Patrice and nice to see you again Harley," Landon said as he completely ignored Monica.

"Faryn, bitch, you hit a home run. You better not let his fine ass out of your sight," Patrice said as soon as Landon closed the door.

"I don't plan on it," Faryn replied as she locked eyes with Monica and winked.

"Well, you go tend to your man and we'll talk later," Harley said.

"Maybe I can invite y'all to Landon's house soon, so we can chill and have drinks by the pool," Faryn replied.

"Bitch, just tell me when and where," Patrice said excitedly.

They said their goodbyes right before Faryn went inside to go get ready for her outing with Landon.

"I'm guessing that Monica was Harley's friend that you had it out with," Landon commented when she walked into the house.

"Yes, and I can't believe that she's your ex-wife's sister. I can't see you being married to a hood rat like that."

"I wasn't. They were nothing alike, or so I thought," Landon said.

"I can't stand that bitch with that dry ass outdated wig on. Looking like the head usher in church," Faryn said, making him laugh.

"You play too much," Landon chuckled.

"Jo-Jo is over there too. Something about him just rubs me the wrong way," Faryn replied.

"I don't trust that pedophile." Landon frowned, making her laugh.

"How you just gon' assume some shit like that about that man?" Faryn quizzed.

"I'm not assuming a damn thing, that's facts. You were fifteen and he was nineteen and had you sleeping up in his house, having sex with you. You might not have known better, but his grown ass did. Like I said, he's a fucking pedophile," Landon repeated.

"Yeah, I guess you're right," Faryn replied as she lowered her head.

"Don't do that Faryn. Hold your head up. Fuck that nigga and everything about your past. That shit is dead and gone. You could have used your upbringing as an excuse not to do better, but you didn't. Most chicks would probably still be swinging from a pole, but you wanted more than that. You got two degrees and a good job. The fact that you did the shit all on your own is an even bigger accomplishment," Landon said while looking into her eyes.

"You always know just what to say to make me feel better." Faryn smiled.

"That's my job. Now, go get dressed and let's go. I'm hungry," Landon said as he pecked her lips.

Faryn jumped up and ran to her bedroom to find something to wear. She had a big smile on her face and, for the first time ever, she could honestly say that she was happy. It was all thanks to Landon and their relationship. Truthfully, Faryn had doubts after her talk with Lance a few months ago. She was scared that Landon's ex-wife was going to come back into his life and want to be a family again. After another month or two had passed with no drama, Faryn had started to relax a little. Landon had never given her a reason to doubt him and she didn't want to start. Although she had never expressed it verbally, she loved him, and she couldn't even try to deny it. It was probably too soon to tell him, but the feelings were there, and they weren't leaving any time soon.

Chapter 18

"Yes! Shit! Fuck me!" Faryn screamed as she came once again.

"That's what I'm doing," Landon replied as he gripped her hips and went even deeper.

Her body was twisted at an awkward angle, but she wasn't complaining. She didn't think there was a name for the position that she was in, but Landon was tearing her shit out the frame. Faryn loved to see the look on his face when they were intimate. That was the sexiest thing in the world to her. Landon's eyes were low, and his bottom lip was caught between his teeth.

"Shit, I'm gonna come again," Faryn squealed.

"Me too, baby. Fuck!" Landon grunted as he released his seeds deep inside of Faryn.

Her body twitched as another orgasm took over and she was spent after that. Two hours of an intense workout and she was done for a while. Landon collapsed on top of her and tried to regulate his breathing, as Faryn did the same. A few minutes later, he started kissing her neck and she felt his erection growing inside of her.

"I'm tapped out Landon. I can't go no more," Faryn mumbled groggily.

"Come on baby, one more time and I'll leave you alone," Landon begged, as he started moving inside of her once again.

"You said that two hours ago and we're still at it," Faryn replied.

"Girl, stop acting like both of us ain't go without sex for a whole damn year," Landon reminded her.

"I know Landon, but damn. We've made up for lost time; don't you think?" Faryn questioned.

"We can never make up for lost time. Stop complaining and just lay back," Landon said as he continued to grow and move inside of her.

"You're a sex addict," Faryn accused.

"Maybe, but I'd rather be addicted to pussy than anything else," Landon noted.

The sudden ringing of his phone did nothing to stop him and he didn't care who was calling. His sons were home and the phone wasn't ringing to any specific ring tone. He knew it was nobody special, so they would have to wait.

"Baby, your phone is ringing," Faryn said as if he didn't hear it.

"I know," Landon replied uncaringly.

"You need to answer it. It might be something important."

The phone had rung three times back to back and Landon didn't flinch.

"It can wait," Landon moaned as he moved deeper inside of her.

"What if it's an emergency?" Faryn asked as she enjoyed their connection.

Landon pressed his lips to hers and stuck his tongue in her mouth to silence her. They were in sync as their bodies moved to the rhythm that they had created. Landon's phone had gone quiet for a while, but that didn't last very long. When it rang again, he paused momentarily because it was his cousin Raheem's ringtone. Landon's hated ringtones but, at Makena's urging, he used them for immediate family. If the tones weren't familiar to him, he didn't bother answering his phone most times.

"What's wrong?" Faryn asked when he stopped moving.

"That's Raheem. Something must be up," he said as he pulled out of her and reached for his phone.

"I told you," Faryn replied as she sat up in the bed.

"What's up Raheem?" Landon asked when he answered the phone.

"That nigga Aiden got locked up last night. He's been trying to call you, but he didn't get an answer," Raheem replied.

"The fuck did he do this time?" Landon questioned.

"Man, I don't know what he did, but I can't do shit for him. I'm at work and I don't get off until late tonight."

"Where is he? I'll go get the nigga," Landon sighed.

"He's in Jefferson. He gave me two phone numbers for bails bondsman that you can call," Raheem replied.

"Hold up. Baby, give me something to write with," Landon requested while looking at Faryn.

"Oh shit, that's why that nigga didn't get an answer. He caught you at a bad time," Raheem laughed.

"Hell yeah, he did," Landon replied, as Faryn handed him a pen and paper.

He took down the information that his cousin gave him and started making calls soon after. Faryn used that time to take a shower, and Landon was still on the phone when she got out. She threw on some joggers and a t-shirt and headed to the kitchen. They had already eaten breakfast, so she looked in the freezer to see what she was going to cook for dinner. Once she had a meal in mind, Faryn made sure she had all the ingredients before she started prepping everything.

"Hey Faryn," Lance said when he walked into the kitchen and sat at the island.

"Hey boo. What's up?" She smiled at him.

"Nothing, just finished playing the game with Lennox," he replied.

"Can we make something for dessert tonight Faryn?" Lennox asked when he walked into the kitchen a short time later.

"Yeah, but it depends on what y'all wanna make. We might have to go to the store," Faryn replied.

"Go to the store for what?" Landon asked when he walked into the kitchen.

"Faryn said that we could make dessert tonight," Lance replied excitedly.

Faryn was too busy staring at him to even answer his question. Landon was dressed down in jeans and a t-shirt, but he made the simple outfit look so good.

"Stop eye fucking me when you be acting stingy with the pussy," he whispered in her ear before kissing her lips.

He laughed when Faryn gasped at his choice of words.

"Where are you going dad?" Lance asked.

Landon didn't know what he and Faryn had talked about all those months ago, but he was back to his old self in no time at all. School was out for summer break, and Lance hadn't gotten into any more trouble since the last time. His grades were good, and Landon always let him know that he was proud of him.

"I'm going to get your uncle Aiden," Landon replied.

"Where is he?" Lance asked.

"In jail," Landon replied.

"Again?" Both of his sons asked at the same time, making him and Faryn laugh.

"Baby, is it okay if they stay here until I come back?" Landon asked.

"Do you even have to ask?" Faryn questioned.

"Yeah, I do," he answered.

"You know it's cool. They never give me any trouble," Faryn replied.

"I'll be back as soon as I get this clown straight and we can go to the store," Landon said.

Faryn hated to drive, so Landon had become her personal chauffer. He didn't mind, and he loved doing things for her. Her car had been in his garage for months with no movement.

"Okay," Faryn replied.

He and Faryn shared another quick kiss before he grabbed his keys and walked out the front door.

***

"Okay, thanks for meeting with me," Malia said as she threw her phone on the bed next to her and buried her head in her hands.

That was her third time going on a job interview and her third call informing her that she didn't get the job. She was slowly losing what little mind she had left, and she didn't know what to do. She had paid her first month of rent on her own and would soon have to pay another. The money that she had in the bank was almost gone and she was surprised that it lasted as long as it did. Roman had done her dirty, but he was going to get his in the end. Malia had seen him twice before and, both times, he was with a different chick. Being that she still loved him, Malia made a scene each time. She always walked away looking like a fool because Roman never paid her any mind. Malia hated to do it, but she would probably be moving in with her mother sooner than she thought.

Living with one of her sisters was out of the question. Their apartments were filthy, and they barely had enough room for their own kids. Cora's house was old and outdated, but it was clean and comfortable. The only thing she hated was the rules that she knew her mother was going to have. Cora was already trying to help her find a job. She had a good friend who owned a busy soul food restaurant and she put in a good word for Malia. Cora's friend wanted her to start as soon as possible, but Malia was stalling, hopefully to find something better. Her mother worked there whenever her friend needed help and she always made great tips.

Malia regretted not taking Landon up on his offer to go back to school. Having only a high school diploma was hurting her chances of finding a decent job. Landon always tried to encourage her to do better and she missed that about him. If she were being honest, she missed everything about him. One more chance was all that Malia needed to show him that he was where she wanted to be. She still loved Roman, but she loved Landon more. Having her heart torn between the two of them was driving her insane.

"Yes Monica," Malia said when she answered the phone for her sister.

"Bitch, I've been calling you since yesterday," Monica replied.

"I know, but I wasn't in the mood to talk. I'm stressed the hell out looking for a job," Malia replied.

"I thought Felicia said that she could get you on at her job."

"You must be crazy. I'm not going to work in no damn nursing home. I'll sell dope before I get paid eight dollars an hour to wipe somebody else's ass," Malia snapped.

"Excuse me, but you're the one who needs money boo. I don't see how you're still living in that empty ass apartment by yourself anyway."

"What do you want Monica? I know you didn't call to talk about my living arrangements," Malia said.

"No but, bitch, do you remember me telling you about Harley's neighbor who I can't stand? You know, the bitch who thinks she's too much? Lil conceited hoe who always wears the red bottoms," Monica said, trying to make her sister remember some of their conversations.

"Yeah, I remember you telling me something about her," Malia said, not knowing or caring where the conversation was going.

Monica and Felicia were haters and they talked about everybody. Malia lost count of how many people they talked about and no one person stood out in her mind.

"Girl, me and that bitch was about to fight in Harley's apartment," Monica noted.

"What's new Monica? You and Felicia are always fighting with somebody."

"But, that's not all bitch. Harley's cousin was saying that she wanted to meet ole girl's boyfriend and you'll never guess who it was."

"I'm listening," Malia said, dreading the answer.

"It was Landon bitch!" Monica yelled, making her sister's heart drop.

"You saw him there?" Malia asked with a newfound interest in the conversation.

"Yes, he was all hugged up and kissing on the bitch. It looks like they've been together for a minute too. She was telling them that she was going to invite them to the house for drinks by the pool like she got it like that."

"Who is she? What's her name?" Malia asked, praying that it wasn't the same person who Lennox had told her about.

"The bitch name is Faryn," Monica said, as Malia dropped her head.

"She's Lance's counselor," Malia spoke up.

"How do you know that?" Monica questioned.

"Lennox told me about her a few months ago."

"And you didn't say anything?" Monica asked.

"I really didn't care too much at the time. I was still pregnant, and I was focused on getting Roman out of jail. I really thought that things were going to work out with us," Malia admitted.

"So, now what? I know you ain't gon' sit back and let that shit fly. You put in too many years with Landon to just let another bitch think she can have him. You were there before the money. If anybody deserves to live the good life with him, it's you, not that bitch Faryn," Monica snapped.

"Let me call you back Monica," Malia replied.

"Wait..." Monica said, but Malia hung up anyway.

She called her son's phone and waited for him to pick up.

"Hey mama," Lennox said when he answered his phone.

"Hey baby. What are you doing?" Malia asked.

"Nothing, I'm on the computer in my bedroom," Lennox replied.

"Where's Lance?" Malia asked.

"He's in the kitchen talking to Faryn," Lennox replied, making her frown.

"Does Faryn live there with y'all?" Malia asked.

"Yeah, sometimes," Lennox answered as honestly as he could.

"I miss my babies. It's been two weeks since I saw you and Lance," Malia said, moving on to another subject.

Malia had been picking Lennox up, but he never wanted to spend the night with her anymore. She would spend the day with him and have him back home that night. She tried her best to get a look at Faryn whenever she went there, but Landon was always outside alone when she arrived. She never even saw a second car parked out front, so she never knew if someone else was there or not.

"I miss you too," Lennox said after a long pause.

"I wanna come see you," Malia replied.

"You can't right now. My dad is not here to let you in."

"Where is he?" Malia asked.

"He went to get my uncle Aiden out of jail," Lennox answered.

"And he left y'all there with her?" Malia asked, jealousy dripping from her voice.

"Yeah, Faryn is always here with us," Lennox acknowledged.

"Oh, well, you can let me in when I get there," Malia pointed out.

"I can't. My dad said that I can't do that anymore. I'm gonna get in trouble," Lennox replied.

"No, you're not baby. I just talked to your father and he said that it's okay. I told him that I want to see you and Lance, and he said that's it's fine."

"He did?" Lennox asked.

"He sure did. I also heard about how nice your room is, so I'll finally be able to see it," Malia lied effortlessly.

It was easy because she was manipulating a child. She should have been ashamed of herself, but she wasn't.

"It is nice. My dad put a basketball goal up behind my bedroom door," Lennox said excitedly.

"I can't wait to see it. What's the code to get in?" Malia asked.

She wrote down the information that Lennox had given her before they disconnected. They had a guard at the gate, but he had to alert the residents to see if they were okay with a visitor being there before they were let in. She was sure that Landon's little girlfriend would never be okay with her coming there. Besides, she wanted her visit to be a pleasant, yet unsuspecting surprise.

Malia got up and found a cute outfit to put on. She unwrapped her shoulder-length hair and applied a little makeup to her face. She wanted to make sure that Faryn's first impression of her was a lasting one. Once she was satisfied with her appearance, Malia grabbed her wedding ring from her jewelry box and slipped it on. She wasn't going in there to play. She was a woman on a mission and she was determined to accomplish it.

Chapter 19

"What time is my dad coming back?" Lance asked as he watched Faryn finish cooking.

"Why? Are you tired of me already?" she joked with a smile.

"No, I never get tired of you," he replied.

"I know I tell you this all the time, but I'm so proud of you and so is your father," Faryn said.

"Thank you," Lance blushed. "Maybe my dad will finally take us to Disney World again like he promised."

Landon took them to Disney World a few months after Malia left, hoping to make them feel a little better about what was going on. They had a good time, especially since Ross and Makena had joined them on the trip.

"Maybe he will. You and Lennox deserve it."

"What about you? Will you come with us?" Lance asked.

"Only if your father wants me to," Faryn replied.

"You're his girlfriend. He's gonna want you to come with us," Lance assured her.

"Are you ready to eat?" Faryn asked him.

"Yes," Lance replied, right as Lennox came running through the kitchen.

"Boy, you know your daddy would kill you for running in here. Are you ready to eat?" Faryn yelled after him.

"Sorry Faryn. Yes, I'm ready to eat!" Lennox yelled back as he went to open the front door.

Malia's face hit the floor when she stepped inside of the home that was supposed to be hers. She knew without a doubt that Landon didn't decorate the place because he wouldn't have known where to start. It had to be professionally done because the color scheme was perfect. Everything blended together well, as if it was torn from the pages of an elegant magazine.

"Hey baby," Malia said as she leaned down and kissed her son.

She had Lennox to open the door for her, so she wouldn't have to knock or ring the bell. He was so excited to show her his room that he didn't realize all what he had done wrong. Malia frowned when she smelled the aroma of food wafting through the house because she knew that Faryn was responsible for it. She was living the life that was meant for Malia, but she was about to put a stop to it.

"Lance is in the kitchen," Lennox said as he grabbed her hand and pulled her along.

Malia continued to marvel at the beauty of Landon's home and regret set in soon after. That feeling intensified as soon as they got to the kitchen and she laid eyes on Faryn. Malia was far from being ugly, but Faryn had the kind of beauty that would make other women feel insecure. She had a shapely, toned body, and Malia found herself sucking in the stomach that she didn't have. It was crazy because she was always the prettiest girl in the room. Faryn had her feeling like an ugly duckling and she hated that.

"Hi," Faryn spoke with confusion written all over her face.

"What is she doing here? Did you let her in Lennox?" Lance frowned.

Malia's feelings were hurt by what her son had said, but she tried to remain unaffected. Lance was all smiles when he was alone with Faryn, but his mood turned cold once he laid eyes on her.

"Daddy said that I could," Lennox replied, repeating only what his mother had told him.

"Hi, Faryn right?" Malia asked, sounding more confident than she felt.

"Yeah, I'm Faryn, and you are?" Faryn asked.

"I'm Malia, Landon's wife," Malia said while extending her hand.

Faryn looked at her hand like it was covered in dirt before she cast her eyes on her face once again.

"I wasn't aware that Landon had a wife," Faryn replied as her heart beat in her chest like a drum.

"My daddy ain't married to her! My GG told us so!" Lance yelled.

"I guess he didn't tell y'all yet," Malia smirked.

"Tell us what?" Faryn questioned.

"Mama's back home." Malia smiled as she held up her finger and showed off her ring.

"I told you, Faryn. He's a liar," Lance fumed as he jumped up and stormed out of the kitchen.

"I'm sorry, I thought he talked to everybody already," Malia replied.

"No need to be sorry love. Welcome home," Faryn said as she fought back her tears.

She hated that she couldn't get to her car, but that wasn't going to stop her. Landon had the garage opener, so she couldn't get in to get it. She ran upstairs and grabbed her phone and purse and headed out the front door, while Malia smiled triumphantly. Faryn walked towards the front gate as she called for a Lyft to pick her up. She wanted to get as far away from Landon's house as quickly as she could. Tears were clouding her vision and she stopped trying to hold them in.

The dam broke, and she let the flood waters flow down her cheeks. She was hurt, embarrassed, and a mixture of other emotions that she was trying to identify. Landon had made a fool of her and lied to her for months. Faryn thought sure that whatever Lennox had told Lance had to be a lie. After all, months had passed, and the subject was never mentioned again. Maybe Landon and Malia had been talking about reconciling and they finally decided to do it. Faryn's mind was racing with lots of possible scenarios. She was even doubting Landon's story about why he had to leave. Saying that Aiden was in jail was probably just his way of getting out of the house without seeming suspicious. He was a coward who used a woman to do his dirty work for him.

"Where to ma'am?" the driver asked when Faryn got into the car.

Faryn gave him her address, as she sent Landon a text message. It was at those times that Faryn wished that she had some family around to talk to.

✱✱✱

"Man, it's always some bullshit with you," Landon fussed as he and Aiden turned on his grandmother's street.

"That shit wasn't even my fault though, bruh. That bitch burned me. Had my dick feeling like it was in the pits of hell," Aiden fussed.

"You need to be mindful of the women that you lay down with and start strapping your shit up. Fuck around and catch some shit that you can't get rid of."

"I would have killed that bitch. She better be lucky that all I did was slap her hoe ass around," Aiden noted.

"Seven hundred fifty dollars, all because you can't keep your dick in your pants and your hands to yourself," Landon fussed as if he was the uncle.

"I got you, nephew. You know I'm good for the money."

"Nigga please, you're already about five grand in the hole with bail money," Landon pointed out as they sat in front of Ella's house.

"I know bruh, but I'm done. I'm about to do like you did and reclaim my virginity until a good woman comes along. These hoes is dirty out here in these streets," Aiden replied.

Landon laughed as he watched his uncle get out of the car and go inside. When his phone beeped with a text message from Faryn, he smiled until he read what it said.

You could have been man enough to tell me that it was over to my face, but fuck you! I'll be there to get my car and the rest of my shit later.

"The fuck!" Landon yelled out in confusion.

He dialed Faryn's number, only to learn that she had him blocked. Landon was more confused now than ever. When he left a few hours before, everything was fine. He hadn't done anything wrong to make her have a change of heart so suddenly. He couldn't even lie, Faryn had him nervous as hell. If she was trying to break up with him, she better have a damn good reason. Landon didn't even try to dial her number again. He called his son instead to see what he knew.

"Dad! Where are you?" Lance asked as soon as he picked up the phone.

"Where is Faryn, Lance?" he asked.

"She left, but why is my mama here?" Lance questioned.

"Your mama? In my house?" Landon questioned, not wanting to believe that what he was hearing was true.

"Yeah, Lennox let her in and Faryn left. Where are you, dad? You need to make her leave."

"I'm on my way right now bruh," Landon assured him.

"She's walking all through our house like she lives here. Dad, please don't let her move in here," Lance pleaded.

"Calm down bruh. She is not moving in with us," Landon swore.

Malia must have lost her damn mind to show up at his house on some bullshit. She had to be crazy to show up uninvited at all. There was no telling what she told Faryn and that explained that stupid ass text that she sent. He was pissed with Faryn too because she should have known better. She knew better than anyone else how he felt about Malia. Landon didn't hate his ex-wife, but he didn't want her either. It was as if him rejecting Malia was making her go harder.

"I don't want you and Faryn to break up," Lance said sadly.

"We're not breaking up Lance," Landon said, praying that he was right.

He had fallen in love with Faryn and his feelings weren't going to change any time soon. He just hoped that he could undo any damage that Malia and her drama had caused before it was too late. Landon felt his anger rising, and Malia was going to feel his wrath if she kept up with her bullshit.

Chapter 20

Faryn was all cried out by the time she made it home. There was a little traffic getting from Landon's house to hers, but she was happy that she'd finally made it. As soon as she sent him that text, she blocked his number. She just wished that she could do the same with her feelings.

"Thanks," Faryn said as she handed the driver a tip and exited his car.

She hated to think that she would be spending more time at home and Harley was about to be moving. She didn't have any other friends and she was going to be all alone once again. Harley was out furniture shopping, and Faryn was feeling the loneliness already. She had hung out with Makena a few times before, but that was a thing of the past now that she and Landon were over. After dragging her depressed body onto the elevator, Faryn headed up to her apartment to sulk in peace. That was exactly why she steered clear of love and relationships. Having her heart broken wasn't on her to do list. Landon had the ability to break her down and she knew that from their first encounter.

Once she located her keys inside of her purse, Faryn unlocked her door and prepared to go inside. Harley's front door opened before she did and out stepped Jo-Jo, cigarette in hand.

"What's up beautiful?" he asked while looking Faryn up and down.

"Hey Jo-Jo," Faryn said as she kept her hand on the knob of her door.

"Why you ain't out shopping with your girl? That nigga must have had you on lock."

"No, I had something to do," Faryn replied nervously.

No matter how much she told herself that she was being paranoid, she just couldn't shake the creepy feeling she got whenever Jo-Jo was around.

"What's been up with you? Why you be acting like you don't know a nigga no more?" he asked.

"We're cool Jo-Jo, but I've grown up since we were together. Both of us have."

"Nah, you just think you're better than a nigga now," Jo-Jo accused.

Since finding out that Monica knew Faryn's boyfriend personally, Jo-Jo asked her all about him. Faryn had hit the jackpot and her man was paid. Jo-Jo felt some kind of way about how Faryn had been treating him. He was the one who stopped her from doing hand jobs at school and started taking care of her. That alone should have counted for something.

"Whatever," Faryn said as she tried to hurriedly enter her house and close the door behind her.

She was quick, but Jo-Jo was quicker. He used his foot to stop her door from closing and entered the apartment behind her.

"Bitch, you should be grateful that I rescued your ass when I did. If it wasn't for me, you probably would have ended up selling pussy just like your crackhead mama," Jo-Jo sneered.

"Fuck you! Get out of my house before I call the police," Faryn said as she nervously fumbled with her purse, trying to locate her phone.

Jo-Jo grabbed her purse and threw it across the room before he pulled her hair and made her come closer to him.

"You probably did start selling pussy once I got locked up. You can pretend for that nigga all you want to, but I know the real. You had to give hands jobs just to get something to eat," Jo-Jo taunted.

"Get the hell out of my house Jo-Jo!" Faryn yelled while trying to pull away from him.

"Or what? The fuck can you possible do to me. I tried to be nice and ask you for another taste, but it looks like I might have to take what I want," Jo-Jo said with an evil smirk.

He pushed Faryn back against the wall and used his knee to pry her legs open. She closed her eyes and cried silent tears when his free hand started roaming her body. Faryn swore on everything that he would have to kill her if he wanted to rape her. There was no way that she was giving it up to him again unless she was a corpse.

"I hope you're prepared to fuck some dead pussy. That's the only way you're gonna get it," Faryn said as she started swinging and going crazy on him. She was screaming to the top of her lungs hoping that someone, anyone heard her.

"Bitch!" Jo-Jo yelled as he slapped her down to the floor.

Faryn had scratched his face up and it was burning like hell. He was used to Faryn being slightly shy and timid, but she was an entirely different person now. He had to keep reminding himself that she wasn't the same fifteen-year-old girl that he'd met and manipulated all those years ago. She had grown and matured. Jo-Jo was ready to slide down to the floor and have his way with her, but Faryn was up on her feet in no time at all. She tried to run for the door, but he grabbed her by her hair again and threw her to the floor. Faryn was kicking and screaming as he led her down the hall to her bedroom. Jo-Jo had never been there before, but he was sure he could find it with ease. Faryn's head was pounding from having her hair pulled, but she was in survival mode. Jo-Jo was having a hard time with her because she was putting up a good fight.

"The fuck," Faryn heard right before Jo-Jo's grip on her hair loosened and he released her altogether.

She jumped up from the floor just in time to see Landon pummeling Jo-Jo's face. Faryn had never seen him look like that before and she was shocked. His sister told her that he had a dark side, but Faryn never had to witness it. Seeing as how he was doing Jo-Jo, she was happy that she didn't. Faryn didn't even hear him come in, but she was thankful nonetheless. Landon's handsome face was a mask of anger as he pounded Jo-Jo's face with his closed fist.

"Landon, no! You're gonna kill him!" Faryn screamed as she ran over to him.

Jo-Jo had fallen to the tiled floor and Landon started stomping him. He was out cold and his face was a bloody mess, but Landon still wasn't satisfied.

"Move Faryn!" Landon barked.

"Baby, please! I'm scared! You're gonna kill him!" Faryn screamed as she cried hysterically.

Thankfully, Landon finally backed away, but he was breathing like a raging bull. He was pacing the floor like a mad man, leaving his bloody shoe prints on the light-colored tile.

"The fuck is this Faryn? Huh?" Landon boomed as he showed Faryn the text message that she'd sent him.

"I-" she started before he cut her off.

"You blocked my number and I don't even know what the hell is going on," Landon fumed.

"Landon, please, I don't want to be here with him passed out on my floor," Faryn said while pointing to Jo-Jo.

"Fuck that nigga!" Landon barked as he kicked Jo-Jo's unconscious body for good measure.

"Oh, my God! Can we just go? I really don't want to be here," Faryn begged as she grabbed her purse from the floor.

Landon grabbed her hand and was heading for the door until she stopped him.

"What about him? I can't leave him in my house," Faryn panicked.

Landon let her hand go and grabbed Jo-Jo by one arm, dragging him out of Faryn's apartment. Once he had him out in the hall, he let him go and left him right there for someone else to find him. After he locked up Faryn's apartment, they took the steps to the first floor and went to his car.

"Start talking and don't leave shit out," Landon demanded as he drove.

Faryn knew it was the wrong time to be lusting, but Landon was sexy as hell when he was mad. She immediately shook the naughty thoughts from her head when Landon looked at her expectantly.

"You remember when Lance got in trouble at school that last time and we went out back and talked?" Faryn questioned.

"What about it?" Landon countered.

"Well, he was upset because Lennox told him that their mother was moving back in with y'all. Apparently, Malia told Lennox that y'all were getting back together and they thought we were breaking up."

"And you believed that shit Faryn? They're kids, so I can see how they were manipulated, but you should have known better."

"I'm sorry Landon, but I didn't know what to think. I didn't tell you because I was too scared of it being true. Then, when she showed up there today and said that she thought you told me that y'all were back together, I believed her. Hell, she still had her wedding ring on and everything."

"That's some straight up bullshit! And you call yourself a counselor?" Landon questioned.

"What the hell is that supposed to mean?" Faryn snapped.

"It means exactly what I said. How can you help other people talk about their feelings and you can't even talk about yours? I never hid anything from you, Faryn. I was straight up from day one and I still am. Even if I wasn't with you, I wouldn't be with Malia. I just don't understand how you and my sons let one person come in and flip shit upside down in a matter of hours. I wasn't even gone that damn long. This shit doesn't even make sense to me right now. It's like everybody was keeping a secret that wasn't even true," Landon fussed.

"I'm sorry baby, but what did you expect me to do?" Faryn asked.

"I expected you to talk to me like you always do Faryn. Do you realize how much worse shit could have been? I started to go straight home, but I'm happy that I came to you first. I told you that I didn't trust that nigga. Fucking pedophile rapist," Landon fumed.

"Everything happened so fast. It was like he just snapped all of a sudden. He barged inside my apartment and started wilding out," Faryn replied.

"Yeah, well you can consider yourself moved out," Landon informed her.

"I can't do that Landon. I still have at least six more months left on my lease. If I don't fulfill it, that's going on my credit report."

"I'll take care of the lease Monday," he assured her.

"You can't just move me out of my apartment like that," Faryn argued.

"Try and stop me!" he barked angrily, making her jump in fear.

"Why can't I just move to a different apartment?" Faryn questioned.

"Now ain't the time for you to test me, Faryn. You must be crazy if you think you're going back there after this shit just happened. I'm already pissed off, so you better be mindful of what you say to me right now. And unblock my damn number," Landon fussed.

"What about my stuff?" Faryn asked as she removed his number from her block list.

"We'll figure that out later Faryn. You just need to get all your clothes and personal stuff for now," Landon replied as he pulled up to his house.

When he saw that Malia's car was still parked out front, his frowned deepened even more.

"She must be out of her muthafucking mind," Landon mumbled angrily.

He and Faryn got out of the car and was greeted by Lance's angry face. He was sitting on the sofa watching tv, but he perked up a little when he saw that Faryn had come back. He stood up and walked over to them, but Landon stopped him before he could say anything.

"Both of y'all sit down. We need to have a family meeting," Landon ordered, sounding like his grandmother. Ella was forever calling a family meeting whenever she felt like something was wrong.

"Excuse me?" Faryn questioned with her hand on her hip.

Landon was talking to her like she was one of his kids and she wasn't feeling that. When he turned around and gave her a look, Faryn and Lance sat down at the exact same time. Landon took the steps two at a time to get upstairs. He checked his bedroom first, just in case Malia was bold enough to be in there. Once he saw that she wasn't, he checked the hallway bathroom and one of the other spare bedrooms. He heard voices coming from Lennox's bedroom, so he made his way there next. When he opened the door, he saw Malia sitting comfortably on one of his son's bean bags. She had her shoes off and she seemed nice and comfortable. Too bad Landon was about to cut her stay short.

"Go downstairs in the front room with your brother and Faryn," Landon said to Lennox.

He knew not to question his father, so he jumped up did as he was told.

"Landon, I can explain. We need to talk," Malia said.

"We don't have shit to talk about. Put your shoes back on and get the fuck up out of my house," Landon snapped.

"Landon wait, please, just listen to me. Didn't you see how happy our son was just now? They want their family back together. I'm sorry about breaking us up in the first place," Malia replied.

"Man, Malia, I'm trying not to drag you down those stairs and pull an uncle Phil on your stupid ass," Landon said, referring to The Fresh Prince of Bel-Air when Jazz always got thrown out the front door.

"This was supposed to be the home that we grow old in," Malia noted.

"Yeah, until you decided that a six-month affair was worth more than that," Landon reminded her as he grabbed her arm.

He picked up her shoes and purse from the floor and led her down the stairs. He didn't have time to keep going back and forth with her, and he wasn't.

"I'm so sorry about that Landon. If I could take it all back, I would. You and my children mean the world to me."

"Yeah, and I'm sure you figured that out after that nigga dogged your stupid ass. Fuck out my face with that dumb shit!" Landon barked.

"Are you really gonna do this is front of our sons?" Malia asked as they got to the living room where her sons and Faryn were seated.

"As if they give a fuck," Landon replied as he continued to the front door. He honestly hated to do that in front of his sons, but Malia left him no choice.

"That bitch ain't their mama. You got that hoe around my kids and I don't even know her," Malia fumed, as Landon walked her out of the house and up to her car.

"Let this be your warning. The next time you pull some shit like this, your sons will be seeing more than just you getting thrown out. I've always tried to be cordial with you for the sake of our kids and I want that to continue. Don't fuck with me, Malia. You, of all people, know that it won't be pretty. Get it through your head once and for all, I don't want you back and I never will. I would be a damn fool to let a snake bite me twice," Landon sneered as he threw her purse and shoes at her.

Malia wanted to protest, but it was a lost cause. Landon's mind was made up and it didn't seem like he was going to change it. She had to let him calm down, but she still wanted to have a talk with him. After all the years that they'd been together, he had to still have love for her. There was no way that he couldn't. She'd given him two beautiful sons and that had to count for something. Malia could admit that she went about it wrong. She had to give Landon time to come around and that was exactly what she was going to do. After getting into her car, she pulled away from the home that should have been hers and headed back to her barely furnished apartment. Landon walked back into the house and started going off as soon as he did.

"Let me clear this up right now, so we won't have any more problems. Your mother is not moving in here. Not now, not ever. Faryn and I are still together, and we are not breaking up. And since neither one of you have a car, I'm not giving y'all the code to the gate anymore. If somebody is dropping you off, Faryn or I will buzz you in," Landon said.

"I'm sorry dad, but my mama said that you said it was okay," Lennox replied sadly.

"I'm not mad at you, Lennox. You're a child and your mama shouldn't have done that. But, from now on, I need y'all to come to me if y'all want to know anything. Don't listen to what nobody else says. If it didn't come from me, then it's a lie," Landon said as he looked at Faryn to make sure she understood what he was saying.

"Okay," his sons said, happy that he had cleared everything up.

"Y'all go upstairs and take a shower," Landon ordered his sons.

They jumped up and walked upstairs to their bedrooms.

"I need a drink," Faryn said as she got up and headed to the kitchen where she kept her wine.

"Get the bottle and bring it to the bedroom. You got a lot of making up to do," Landon said as he winked at her.

She smiled as she grabbed a bottle of wine from the fridge and two champagne glasses. Landon didn't do wine, so she grabbed his bottle of Cîroc and headed to the bedroom to wait for her man.

Chapter 21

"**I**'m so fucking mad right now," Harley fumed as she and Faryn talked on the phone two days later.

Harley had called to tell her how Kyron had found Jo-Jo passed out in the hall right in front of their house. His friend had gone outside to smoke, and he was trying to see what was taking him so long. What he didn't expect to see was his friend's bloody, battered body instead. Kyron didn't know if he'd been shot or stabbed, so he called an ambulance, instead of bringing him to the hospital himself. When Faryn told them what happened, Harley was pissed and Kyron felt like shit. They were her best friends, so Faryn told them all about her past and how she knew Jo-Jo. They weren't judgmental, and she appreciated that more than anything.

"Faryn, I'm so sorry baby girl. You know I would have never let that nigga nowhere near you or my wife if I knew he was living foul like that," Kyron swore, letting Faryn know that she was on speakerphone.

"It's okay Kyron. You didn't know that he was a psycho. It's not your fault," Faryn replied.

"No, it's not okay and it is his fault. I kept telling him about bringing all those shady ass niggas to our house," Harley fussed.

"Baby, I said that I was sorry. I promise that it won't happen again," Kyron said.

"You damn right it won't because I don't want none of their asses at our new house and I mean that shit. This is the second time that one of your so-called friends did some dumb shit," Harley fumed.

"You're right, baby, and I can't even argue with you. I'll be good with just my brothers and my cousins," Kyron replied.

"You better be, with your over friendly ass," Harley said, making Faryn laugh.

"Well, Landon has banned me from coming back over there, even though he paid the lease out this morning. If y'all want anything out of there for the new house, you're welcome to have it," Faryn offered.

Harley was moving into a four bedroom, so she could probably use some extras for the other rooms. Most of her furniture was only a year old and still looked brand new. Faryn lived alone, so there was no one there to tear it up.

"Bitch, are you serious? You got some bad ass furniture in there," Harley pointed out.

"Yeah, but I don't have anywhere to put it unless I get a storage," Faryn noted.

"I can definitely use another bedroom set for one of the spare rooms. And your living room furniture would look great in the sitting room," Harley said excitedly.

"It's all yours honey," Faryn replied.

"We can pay you for it Faryn. I wouldn't feel right just taking your stuff like that," Kyron said.

"Hell no, Kyron. Before I met Landon, y'all were the only family that I had. Landon and his uncle and cousin are getting my clothes and stuff out one day this week. Y'all can have everything else. Harley, you have a key whenever you want to get it," Faryn replied.

"Thanks, Faryn. I appreciate it," Harley said.

"Anytime friend." Faryn smiled.

"Man, but that nigga Landon is the truth. I didn't know he got down like that," Kyron chuckled.

"What do you mean?" Faryn asked.

"He fucked Jo-Jo up bad. Nigga jaw is wired shut and everything," Kyron informed her.

"Oh, my God! Are you serious?" Faryn asked.

"Yeah, man, that nigga is fucked all the way up. He got knots all on his face and shit. Ain't no doubt about who won the fight," Kyron laughed.

"It wasn't really a fight. I don't even remember Jo-Jo getting any licks in," Faryn admitted.

"Yeah and it shows," Kyron laughed again.

"Faryn got herself an undercover bad boy," Harley joked.

"He's so sweet, though. That was my first time ever seeing that side of him," Faryn acknowledged.

"Girl, but the way you say he escorted his ex-wife out was hilarious. The nerve of that bitch," Harley said.

"I know, but that hoe was convincing. I guess the seed was already planted when I talked to Lance, so it was easy for her to water it. Landon was so mad," Faryn laughed.

"I wonder what Monica's messy ass have to say about that," Harley said.

"Fuck Monica. She makes me so sick."

"She's another one who won't be invited to my new house. I don't want any negative energy in my space."

"I know that's right," Faryn cosigned.

"I can't wait until you see it friend. The painters did a great job and the decorating is coming along nicely."

"You know I'll be one of the first to visit, but I gotta get going. My break is over, and I have an appointment in a few minutes," Faryn said.

"Okay, call me later," Harley requested.

"I will," Faryn assured her before they disconnected.

She was sleepy as hell and happy that she didn't have to cook anything. Ms. Ella was cooking a big pot of gumbo and she invited them over to eat some. Faryn had her a container in the back of Landon's car because she needed her some food to go as well.

***

"Man, let me hold the spot down until the lease is up. It's already paid up, so you might as well," Aiden said as he rode with Landon back to Ella's house.

He and Raheem had helped Landon move all Faryn's personal items from her house to Landon's. Faryn's apartment was nice as hell, and Aiden wanted to use it as a spot to entertain females.

"The fuck you want to stay there for? Her girl is taking all the furniture and stuff to put in her new house. Faryn already gave everything away," Landon noted.

"I don't give a fuck. All I need is a blow-up mattress and a shower," Aiden replied.

"I really don't care, but it's not my decision to make. You gotta ask Faryn about that."

"My niece is cool. She'll be okay with it. I only need it a few nights a week to entertain. It's not like I'll really be living there," Aiden replied.

"I thought you were done entertaining random females. What happened to you settling down?" Landon asked.

"That must have been the antibiotics talking. I'm not trying to settle down with nobody right now."

"You better start strapping up boy," Landon warned, right as he pulled up to his grandmother's house.

Aiden frowned when he saw Kane standing out front smoking a cigarette.

"I just want to stomp his bitch ass one good time. That's all I need," Aiden sneered.

"Let that shit go bruh," Landon said as they got out of the car.

"What's up with y'all?" Kane said as he walked over to both men with his hand extended.

"Pussy," Aiden spat as he walked pass him without bothering to shake his hand.

"Crazy ass nigga," Kane mumbled as he and Landon shook hands.

"What's good bruh?" Landon asked.

"Shit, I should be asking you that," Kane replied.

"What you mean?" Landon questioned.

"I keep hearing everybody talking about the newest member of the family, but I haven't had the pleasure of meeting her yet. Even my wife has seen her before me. She must really be pretty if Ava said so. You know she never gives compliments," Kane laughed.

"As if I give a fuck what your wife thinks," Landon replied.

"When do I get to meet her?" Kane questioned, ignoring what Landon had just said about his wife.

"She's always over here with or without me. You know how Makena is. She be dragging her all over the place. If you don't see her before then, you'll see her for grandma's birthday dinner next month," Landon answered.

"She must be special to make you settle down," Kane said.

"You act like I was in the streets heavy or some shit. Unlike you and Aiden, I can't just stick my dick in anything with a pussy," Landon smirked.

"The fuck you mean nigga? I'm a happily married man," Kane argued.

"Play dumb if you want to. Just because I don't say shit don't mean that I don't know. I mind my business, but the streets talk," Landon informed him.

"I ain't about to sit here and tell you that I've never fucked up, but that was only during the first year or two of my marriage," Kane swore.

"Alright bruh, if that's your story, then stick to it. You don't have to explain shit to me. I can walk down on you fucking another bitch and I won't say shit. Ava probably won't believe it anyway." Landon shrugged.

"You know I love my wife but, shit, y'all ain't the only ones who nerves she get on. I just need a break from that shit sometimes," Kane admitted.

"No explanations needed," Landon said as he raised his hands in surrender.

He and Kane stayed outside a little while longer until it was time for him to get Faryn from work. She had already said that she didn't feel like cooking, so he planned to take her and his boys out for dinner and a movie.

Chapter 22

"Y'all like it?" Faryn asked as she watched Lennox and Lance sample the gravy steaks that she was preparing for dinner. She had loaded baked potatoes and broccoli with cheese to go along with it.

"Yes, it's good," Lennox said with a smile.

"I can't wait to eat," Lance said, rubbing his stomach.

"What's for dessert?" Lennox asked.

"Your father went to the bakery to get a German chocolate cake," Faryn replied.

"Yes," Lance said excitedly.

"My GG said you're gonna make all of us fat," Lennox laughed.

"Yeah and my auntie Makena said that we put her food down for yours," Lance chimed in.

"I can't wait to see those heifers. They been talking behind my back, I see," Faryn joked.

"My GG likes you. She said God answered her prayers," Lance replied.

"Yep and my auntie said she likes you too. She's happy that you cook for us and stuff," Lennox spoke up.

"Aww, I like your GG and your auntie too." Faryn smiled.

"Nobody likes my auntie Ava. My grandma said she's a spoiled... you know, the b word," Lennox chuckled as he repeated what Ms. Ella had said.

Faryn didn't reply, but Ella had her daughter right. Ava was a piece of work, and Faryn wasn't too fond of her either. When they first met, Ava turned her nose up at Faryn like she was beneath her. She asked her a bunch of questions, until Makena intervened and told her to mind her damn business. Faryn had never met her husband, Kane, but she could tell that he wasn't a favorite either. Aiden couldn't stand him, but he and Landon were cool. Raheem seemed to be neutral in everything and was the more laidback one of the crew. Faryn had even seen Landon and Makena's mother a few times when she was over there. It baffled her how Robin waved at her kids and grandkids as if they were neighbors and not her blood. She was a very attractive woman, and Faryn saw where Landon and Makena got their looks from.

"My dad is back," Lennox said when he heard the front door open and close.

Landon walked into the kitchen carrying a cake box in one hand and another plastic bag in the other. He sat the cake down on the island and dared his sons to touch it. He went upstairs for a few minutes and came back down wearing basketball shorts and no shirt. Just like always, he grabbed and washed a spoon before he dipped it into the pot that was on the stove to taste the food.

"It needs a little more salt," Landon said as he dropped the spoon in the sink.

"What?" Faryn questioned angrily.

"Salt, add just a little more salt to it," Landon repeated.

"Fuck this! If you don't like the way I cook, then maybe you should do it yourself. Since you always wanna complain, you can finish the meal," Faryn snapped as she dropped the cooking spoon on the counter and stormed upstairs.

"What the hell just happened?" Landon asked himself out loud.

"Why did you have to say that? Nothing was wrong with it," Lennox said as he got up and walked away.

"It doesn't need salt. We tasted it and it was good," Lance said as he too got up and left his father in the kitchen alone.

"The fuck did I do?" Landon questioned as he stood there in shock.

From the first day that Faryn ever cooked for him, she always asked him to sample the food and give his opinion. Her food was always on point, but she just needed to tweak a little something occasionally to make it better. Landon never complained about her cooking because he didn't have a reason to. Faryn was a great cook and he always told her so. After standing there in shock for a few minutes, Landon headed up the stairs and into their bedroom. He found Faryn lying across the bed wiping her teary eyes.

"I'm sorry baby. You know I wasn't complaining. I love your cooking," Landon said as he laid down next to her and pulled her close.

"Yeah, well that's not what it sounded like to me," Faryn replied as tears continued to fall.

"What's really going on Faryn? I've been your taste tester in the kitchen for months. Why are you making a big deal out of it now?" Landon questioned.

"You basically said my food tasted like shit, that's why," she said as she cried harder.

"Are you serious right now Faryn?" Landon asked as he laughed hysterically.

"It's not funny Landon!" Faryn yelled.

She tried to pull away from him, but his grip was too tight. He was laughing his ass off, and she was ready to swing on him.

"When's the last time you saw your period?" Landon questioned with a smirk.

"What does that have to do with anything?" Faryn asked, when she couldn't come up with an answer.

"Maybe my grandma was right," Landon replied.

"Right about what?" Faryn asked.

"She thinks you're pregnant and I think so too. Shit has been crazy with you lately and I'm sure that's why. You cry for dumb shit and your attitude is ridiculous," Landon noted.

"How would your grandmother know?" Faryn asked.

"She's always the first to know that kind of shit. She knew when Malia was pregnant both times and she told Makena and Ava too. She even knew what everybody was having before we found out. She got some kind of sixth sense about that shit."

"And she's always been right?" Faryn asked.

"She hasn't been wrong once," Landon replied.

"Oh God. I can't be pregnant," Faryn sighed.

"Why not Faryn? All we do is fuck and you ain't on no birth control. Shit, I was backed up for a whole damn year. I'm surprised it didn't happen the first time we had sex."

"That's probably why I've been gaining so much damn weight. I guess I need to make a doctor's appointment," Faryn said.

"Yeah but, in the meantime, I need you to go handle this for me," Landon said as he handed her the plastic bag that he walked in with not too long ago.

Faryn opened the bag and pulled out the boxes that were inside.

"Why do I need to take three pregnancy tests?" she questioned.

"I just got three different ones. I didn't know which one was the best or more accurate. It's been a while since I had to do this," Landon replied.

He looked at her sideways when she put the boxes back in the bag and started playing on her phone.

"What?" Faryn questioned when she saw the look that he was giving her.

"You need to go take at least one of them right now," he replied.

"I'm not ready yet. What if it's positive?" Faryn asked.

"Then, we're having a baby." Landon shrugged.

"I know that, smart ass. I just don't know if I'm ready to find out right now," she noted.

"But, I need to know Faryn. It's gonna kill me if I have to wait any longer," Landon said anxiously.

"Okay, but I don't think I have to pee right now," she replied.

"Stop stalling and come on girl," Landon said as he got up and picked her up with him.

Faryn was moving in slow motion as she watched him open one of the boxes and read the instructions. She had mixed emotions about having a baby, but she knew that Landon would have her back. The way that he took care of his kids was remarkable and that alone eased her fears. She didn't have the best mother, but she was going to do things differently. Unlike her own mother, Faryn was prepared to put her child first. She already found herself doing that with Landon's sons.

"You ready?" Landon asked her.

"I guess so," Faryn replied.

Landon told her what to do, even though she already knew. She never had to take a pregnancy test before, but it seemed simple enough just by looking at it. She grabbed some tissue and sat it on the counter for when she was done. After making Landon get out, Faryn squatted over the toilet and relieved her bladder on the test. Once she was done, she sat it on the tissue and washed her hands before rejoining Landon in the bedroom.

"What did it say?" Landon asked anxiously.

"I didn't look at it yet. I think we have to wait a few minutes," Faryn replied.

Landon was pacing the floor like he didn't already have two kids. Faryn sat on the edge of the bed wringing her hands as she awaited her results.

"Fuck it. It's been long enough," Landon said as he walked into the bathroom and looked at the test.

"What does it say?" Faryn yelled a minute or two later.

"It says that you're stuck with me for life." Landon smiled when he walked out.

"It's positive?" Faryn questioned.

"Yep and Makena is gonna go crazy. You better give my sister a niece too," Landon said while kissing her.

"I need to ask her about a doctor," Faryn replied.

"We'll figure that out later but, right now, you need to get me out of the dog house."

"What do you mean?" Faryn asked.

"You overreacted about that food situation and got my sons mad with me and shit," Landon informed her.

"Oh no, I wasn't trying to do that. I really don't know why I got mad," Faryn admitted.

"Hormones," Landon replied.

"Let me go tell them that I'm okay," Faryn said as she walked away.

"Maybe we should tell them about the baby. They've always wanted a baby sister, so that might make them smile," Landon suggested.

"It's too soon. You really think we should?" Faryn asked.

"Hell yeah. I'm telling everybody. I'm happy as hell," Landon replied.

"Me too." Faryn smiled as she looked over at him.

"I love you, baby," Landon said for the first time since he and Faryn had been together.

"I love you too," Faryn replied happily.

She was happy that they'd finally expressed how they felt about each other. They showed their love through actions, but it was good to hear it sometimes as well.

"Come on, I got a lot of phone calls to make," Landon said as he helped her up from the bed.

Aside from Harley and Kyron, she didn't have anyone else to tell. She knew that they would be happy for her. If Faryn never believed in prayers before, she believed in them now. She prayed to God for a good man and Landon was her prayer come true.

Chapter 23

Eight weeks, the equivalent of two months, was how long the life had been growing inside of Faryn. With the help of Makena, she and Landon had found a good doctor, and everything was good so far. Faryn was concerned because she had drunk some wine before she knew that she was pregnant, but he assured her that she would be fine. Now, there was another problem that she had to deal with. Four days in a row, Faryn had experienced the worst morning sickness ever. It started out feeling like an upset stomach until she began to throw up any and everything that she'd eaten. She had taken off from work the day before and stayed home in bed. Landon and the kids were so attentive. They kept bringing her ginger ale and crackers all day to make sure she felt better.

"We don't have to go anywhere baby. My grandma will understand," Landon said as he rubbed Faryn's back.

"No Landon, I'll be fine. I just need to let that medicine kick in," Faryn replied.

Her doctor had prescribed her some medicine for nausea and it worked wonders. He told her that the feeling would subside the further she got into her pregnancy and she couldn't wait. It was Ms. Ella's birthday and she was doing her traditional dinner with her immediate family. Landon had all the food catered from a soul food restaurant and Makena got her a huge three-tiered cake. Landon said that his grandmother liked to do her birthday dinner at her house, instead of a restaurant. That way, they wouldn't have to rush or be on anybody else's schedule. A knock on their bedroom door shook Faryn from her thoughts, as Lennox and Lance entered the room.

"Are you feeling better Faryn?" Lance asked her.

"I got you some more crackers," Lennox said as he handed her another pack of saltines.

Landon smiled at the way his sons catered to Faryn. He was happy that they loved her as much as he did. He couldn't be with a woman that his sons didn't approve of.

"Aww, y'all are so sweet. I feel much better, but I'll put the crackers in my purse, just in case," Faryn replied.

"You ready to go or do you need a little more time?" Landon asked her.

"No, I'm ready. I don't want us to be late," she replied as she got up and stretched.

"Damn," Landon mumbled as he looked at Faryn's ass.

"I heard you, freak," Faryn laughed.

Landon and his sons grabbed the gifts that they had for Ella and prepared to leave. Faryn felt much better than she did before, and she was happy for that. She was ready to eat, and Landon had ordered lots of food for her to choose from. It took them about twenty minutes, but they were parking in front of Ella's house soon after.

"Happy Birthday GG!" Lennox and Lance said when they walked into their great-grandmother's house.

"Thanks, my babies. Put the gifts on the table over there. I'll open everything later," Ella replied.

Landon and Faryn greeted her with hugs and kisses before joining Makena and her husband in the kitchen. Landon was happy to see his brother-in-law because he didn't get to see him that often anymore. Ross Sr. drove trucks and he was always on the road.

He'd only been doing it for a year, but he and Makena hated it. They had rental property, thanks to Clarence, but Ross still felt like the man of the house should always work. Landon had purchased and upgraded the laundromats that Clarence told him about, but he had never opened them. He didn't trust just anyone to manage them. He wanted to offer the job to his brother-in-law before he looked anywhere else. That way, he would have someone that he trusted running the businesses and Makena would have her husband at home every night like they both wanted. He had no problem matching his pay if he decided to do it.

"Look at my niece," Makena said as she rubbed Faryn's flat stomach.

"What the hell are you rubbing? There's nothing there," Faryn laughed.

"So what? I want her to know her auntie's voice," Makena replied.

"How do you even know if it's a girl?" Faryn questioned.

"It better be," Landon chimed in.

"My grandma will tell me once you start showing," Makena noted.

"Don't even encourage her with that mess. The doctor will tell us when the time is right," Landon replied.

"Say what you want, but I've never been wrong even once. I knew the sex of all my grandkids and great-grandkids before the doctor even said anything," Ella acknowledged.

They were a few minutes early, so they just sat around and talked for a while. Makena had already set everything up and there was nothing else left to do. The food was warming, and the cake and gift tables were set up nicely. Ella let Faryn eat before anyone came because she couldn't wait.

"Damn. How y'all start eating and everybody not even here yet?" Ava asked with her usual snobbish attitude when she walked inside with her daughter.

As usual, she was dressed in designer labels from head to toe and her makeup was flawless. Ava was beautiful on the outside, but her attitude took away from her beauty. It was as if she was on a pedestal looking down at everyone else. At least, that's how she acted to Faryn.

"Faryn is the only one eating. My great-grandbaby is hungry." Ella smiled.

"Oh yeah, congrats on the baby. I see you and Landon ain't waste no time. How long have y'all been together again?" Ava asked.

"Why does that matter? How long were you and Kane together before he started cheating?" Makena asked, making Ava flush with embarrassment.

"Not today! It's my birthday and y'all will not ruin my dinner with no bullshit," Ella warned. "Where is Kane at anyway?" Ella asked.

"He's at work, but he'll be here a little later," Ava replied.

"How is he always at work, but Landon does most of his work at home from the computer? They still do the same job, right?" Makena asked.

"Chill out Makena," her husband warned with a stern look.

"Okay baby, but it was just a question," Makena replied innocently.

A few hours later, everyone had arrived, and the dinner was in full swing. Ella only wanted her immediate family there, so two of her sisters and one of her brothers were in attendance as well. Faryn was meeting most of them for the first time, but they gave her a warm welcome. Landon's mother passed through briefly to drop off a gift. She fixed herself and her man a plate to go and left soon after. Landon invited Clarence and his girlfriend, but they were coming after they attended another party.

"I'm so full," Faryn said as she sat back in her chair and sighed. She was happy that she'd worn her Adidas leggings and matching shirt. She would have had to unbutton her pants if she hadn't.

"I guess you don't want no cake then," Landon replied.

"Yes, I do. I saved room for that," she said, making him laugh.

Landon had been outside most of the time talking to his brother-in-law. Ross was happy about the offer and he couldn't wait to stop leaving his family for days at a time. Raheem was playing the game with the kids and Aiden barely came out of his room. He was nursing a hangover from the night before. He came out to get food and talk for a minute before going right back to bed.

"Makena is taking them home with her, so just let me know whenever you're ready," Landon said as he pushed his chair close to Faryn's and kissed her.

"I'm not in a hurry. Besides, I thought you were waiting for Clarence," Faryn pointed out.

"I was, but he's taking too damn long. I'm tired as hell." Landon yawned.

"I should have known that I was pregnant. You sleep more than I do," Faryn laughed, right as Ella's front door opened.

Landon was about to reply to her comment until he saw Kane walking in. His lying ass claimed to be at work, but Landon knew for a fact that he was off that day.

"Look at this sneaky ass nigga," Landon said, making Faryn look up to see who he was talking about.

The twilight zone was real and Faryn felt like she was in it. Her breathing increased and so did her heart rate when she saw him. Landon must have felt the change in her mood because he looked at her with a worried expression on his face.

"How do you know him?" Faryn asked as she locked eyes with Kane.

"That's Ava's husband, Kane. The one that I told you I work with," Landon replied.

"I... I gotta go to the bathroom. We can leave when I'm done," Faryn said as she jumped up and rushed off.

Landon was about to go after her until Kane walked over and started talking.

"That was wifey?" he asked with a smirk.

"Yeah," Landon replied, feeling funny for some reason.

"Landon, come get some candles from this top self for me! We're about to sing happy birthday and cut the cake!" Makena yelled to him.

He abandoned his idea to go check on Faryn for a minute and went to help his sister. Faryn was in the bathroom down the hall shaking like a leaf on a tree. Her life was just starting to look up, but something always had to go wrong. There was no way that she was going back out there. Ella had a side and a back door, and she was about to use one of them. She would just have to explain her actions to Landon once they got home. Once she got herself together, she walked out of the bathroom and ran right into the one person that she didn't want to see.

"You hit the jackpot, huh? Not only did you manage to snag a nigga with money, but you got pregnant by him too. You're smarter than I gave you credit for."

"Fuck you, Redd. Please do me a favor and act like you don't know me," Faryn begged.

"I guess that's why you never wanted to hook up with me when I asked. Who would have thought that you were the chick that my boy has been talking about all this time? Faryn, right?" Redd questioned with a smirk, calling her by her real name, a name that he never had the pleasure of knowing. Even when Landon talked about her, he wouldn't have known that it was the same person. He knew her by Candy Girl at the club and she wanted to keep it that way. No real names and nothing personal was the rules that she lived by.

"You have a wife. You shouldn't have been trying to hook up with me anyway," Faryn said as she tried to walk away.

"I bet that nigga don't know that I was balls deep in that pussy for a whole year before you up and disappeared on me," Redd said as he pulled her back.

"Let me go!" Faryn yelled as she pulled away from him.

"Don't try to get loud, bitch. That nigga can't hear you anyway," Redd teased.

They were all singing happy birthday to Ella and the kids were loud. Ella's house was big, so they probably wouldn't have heard her anyway.

"Keep your hands off me," Faryn said as she pulled away again.

"Why? You never had a problem with me touching you before," Redd said as he pinned her up against the wall.

He put his face in the crook of Faryn's neck and inhaled her scent just like he used to. He missed her, and he was green with envy to know that Landon now had her. She was having his baby and living under his roof. He knew that he was playing with fire by being so close to her in his mother-in-law's house, but he didn't care. He couldn't believe how close Faryn had been to him the whole time and he never even knew it.

"Leave me alone!" Faryn yelled as she slapped him hard across his face.

"Bitch!" Redd yelled as he raised his fist high in the air, ready to strike. He knew that he would have Landon to deal with, but he didn't give a damn.

"I was just waiting for your pussy ass to give me a reason!" Aiden yelled as he pushed Faryn out of the way and started throwing jabs at his sister's husband. He had been in his bedroom listening and he came out at just the right time.

"Aiden, no!" Faryn yelled as she moved out of their way while they tussled.

Redd talked all that shit, but Aiden was beating the dog shit out of him. They had put a huge hole in Ella's wall and she was going to have a fit when she saw it. Faryn didn't know who it was, but somebody was walking down the hall and saw them fighting. It only took a few seconds for everyone else to come running to the back.

"These muthafuckas must be crazy. Look at my damn wall. Aiden, let that boy go before you kill him," Ella fussed.

Redd's light-colored skin was a bloody mess by the time Raheem and Landon came in to break them up.

"What the fuck is wrong with you, Aiden? Look at his face!" Ava yelled as she rushed to her husband's side.

"His bitch ass was trying to put his hands on Faryn, but he couldn't fight a real man. Fuck that nigga," Aiden spat angrily.

"Fuck you, nigga. And fuck that bitch too. The fuck you mad for? You hitting the pussy too? You fighting over Landon's bitch like she's yours," Redd fumed.

"Nigga, what?" Landon spoke up in confusion, wondering how he and Faryn knew each other.

"That bitch got community pussy. Everybody at the strip club got a piece of it. My dick been in her mouth more than her dentist. You wifed a hoe, my nigga!" Redd yelled.

"Kane!" Ava shrieked in embarrassment.

She wasn't the only one who was embarrassed. Faryn wanted to disappear when Redd put her on blast like that. Landon knew all about her past, but his family didn't. He didn't know that Kane and Redd were one and the same, but Faryn knew that he was curious. He looked like he was out for blood as he watched Ava help her husband up and clean the blood from his face. As soon as they passed by Landon, he hauled off and punched Kane in his face, knocking him out cold.

"Bitch ass nigga. Make that your last time disrespecting her. Since he can't hear me, make sure you relay the message when he wakes up," he said while looking at Ava.

"Oh, my God! Baby! Wake up!" Ava yelled as she kneeled beside her husband and slapped his face.

"Girl, get your stupid ass up and leave his dirty dick ass down there. He just admitted to cheating on you in front of everybody," Ella said, shaking her head.

"Raheem, help me get him to the car," Ava begged.

Being the nice one in the family, Raheem picked Kane up and threw him over his shoulder. He was dripping blood all over his white t-shirt, but he didn't care. It was going right in the trash when he was done.

"Don't you feel bad Faryn. All of us have a past that we're not too proud of. Hell, I had to give five different men a blood test when I had my first baby," Ella confessed.

"Man, come on grandma. Nobody wanna hear that," Landon fussed.

"Boy, shut up. We all had a lil hoe in us back in the day. I was the queen of hoes when I was in my twenties," Ella replied, making everybody laugh.

"Ava needs to be the one beating his ass if you ask me," Makena spoke up as everyone, but Landon and Faryn walked back to the front of the house.

"I'm so sorry Landon, but I can explain," Faryn sniffled.

"I saw the change in your attitude the minute he walked through the door. How do you know that nigga?" Landon asked as he wiped the tears from Faryn's eyes.

"That's Redd from JB's, but I swear I didn't know that he was married to your auntie. I didn't know anything about him," she replied.

"That's Redd? The nigga from the strip club that you told me about?"

"Yeah," Faryn admitted.

"Who the fuck calls him Redd?" Landon questioned.

"The men that he was with the night we met kept calling him Alpha Redd or something like that," Faryn noted.

"That must be some fraternity shit." Landon shrugged.

"Can we leave through the back door? I don't want to go back out there Landon. This is so embarrassing," Faryn said shamefully.

"Fuck what anybody says or thinks Faryn. I didn't come into this relationship blind. I knew what it was from day one. My opinion is the only one that counts and I'm good," Landon assured her with a kiss.

He got a message on his phone soon after with Clarence saying that he was on his way. Landon sat in one of the spare bedrooms and talked with Faryn for a while to ease her mind. She was worried about what everyone was going to think of her, but she felt better knowing that he wasn't upset. Most of the guests had gone home and Faryn was ready to go too. She made another trip to the bathroom before saying her goodbyes to everyone. As soon as she and Landon got outside, a black Benz with dark tints pulled up and parked in front of the house.

"That's Clarence. Let me tell him that we're leaving," Landon said as he walked over to the car.

The passenger's side door opened, and Clarence's girlfriend got out and rushed right pass him. Landon wondered where she was going until he saw her stop in front of Faryn.

"Akira?" Faryn questioned when the woman walked up to her.

"Faryn!" Akira yelled as she pulled her into a hug and fell to the ground.

"The fuck!" Landon yelled as he rushed over and tried to help Faryn up.

She was pregnant and had no business doing so damn much. He felt like Mister in The Color Purple as he tried to pry the two crying women apart. They were locked in a tight embrace that they refused to break free of. It took a few minutes, but they eventually got up. They were a ball of tears as they continued to hug each other and smile.

"What did we miss?" Clarence asked.

"This is my baby sister," Akira said as she lovingly kissed Faryn's cheek.

"Seriously?" Landon questioned skeptically. He didn't see the family resemblance, but that didn't mean anything.

"Oh, my God, Akira. I missed you so much," Faryn said, looking happier than Landon had ever seen.

I Don't Want You Back

"I missed you too, baby sister. I can't believe this. God answered my prayers and I'm so grateful," Akira cried as she squeezed Faryn tight.

"Look, we were just about to go home. Y'all follow us there, so y'all can talk and catch up," Landon suggested.

"Okay, let me give Ella this card I got her and I'll be right behind you," Clarence said as he walked away.

Akira finally let Faryn go and got back into Clarence's car, as Landon and Faryn got into his.

"Anything else I need to know? I mean, damn, you've been full of surprises tonight," Landon joked.

"I had no idea that Clarence's younger girlfriend was my sister. You told me that her name was Ashley," Faryn laughed.

"Hell, I know it started with an A. But you did say that your sister liked older men. You weren't lying about that," Landon replied.

"This is so unbelievable," Faryn replied with a bright smile covering her face.

"This entire night was unbelievable, if you ask me," Landon replied.

He and Faryn went home and waited for Clarence and her sister. The two men sat in the house while Faryn and Akira sat outside by the pool for hours and talked, exchanging their stories since they hadn't seen each other in years. Akira had lived with another older man in Baton Rouge for a few years until he had a stroke. One of his daughters took him to live with her, but Akira couldn't go. She got a job and stayed out there for two more years, until she met Clarence at the gas station where she worked. He was out there closing the deal on a piece of property that he had just sold.

Even after they'd talked for months, Akira still stayed in Baton Rouge. Clarence would drive down to visit her, but that was as far as it went. He felt like Akira was too old not to have anything going for herself and he didn't take her seriously at first. She wanted more than just sex and an occasional visit, but he wasn't interested. That was, until she started to take his advice and went back to school. Once she got her GED and enrolled in college, Clarence started letting her come to his house. She left her job in Baton Rouge and eventually found one in New Orleans. They made their relationship official soon after and now lived together.

Faryn told her sister all about herself and how she'd put herself through college. She told Akira about Harley and how she met Landon and his family. Faryn was so happy when she went to bed that night. The events that happened at Ella's house were a thing of the past once she laid eyes on her sister. They exchanged numbers and promised to hook up for lunch the following day. Akira vowed to keep in contact with her, and Faryn wouldn't have it any other way. Landon was happy as long as she was and happy was the only emotion that Faryn was feeling.

Chapter 24

Malia let out a breath of relief when the large crowd left the restaurant and only a handful of people remained. The tips that she made were great, but she was dead on her feet. She hated to do it, but she'd finally accepted the job offer that was extended to her. She was running out of options, so she didn't have a choice. The apartment was too much for her to maintain, so she gave it up and moved in with her mother. Monica begged her for the bedroom set, so Malia let her have it. She was too depressed about her circumstances to put up much of a fight.

"Take a break Malia. You've earned it after handling that large crowd. You caught on so fast. It feels like you've been here longer than a month," the owner, Melba, said.

Melba and Cora were good friends, and Malia appreciated the opportunity. It wasn't her dream job, but it kept money in her pockets. Malia would have loved to go back to the days when she was a stay-at-home mom with money at her fingertips for whatever she needed. She wanted those days back, but Landon was being an ass. When the door chimed, signaling the arrival of a customer, Malia prayed that it wasn't another huge crowd. Her back was aching, and her feet felt like they were on fire from walking so much. That was not the life that Malia had envisioned, but she had no one to blame, but herself.

"Malia?" a male voice came up to her and asked, as if he was unsure it was her.

"Hey Kane." Malia smiled as she got up to hug Landon's good friend and uncle by marriage.

Kane was light skinned, so it was easy to see the faint bruises that covered his face. They looked to be healing, but they were still very noticeable.

"When did you start working here? Me and Ava come through a lot and I've never seen you here," Kane said.

"I haven't been working here very long, but it's usually early mornings when I do. I needed some extra cash, so I took on somebody's else's shift. I'll probably never do that again. This night crowd ain't no joke," she replied.

"The fuck you need money for? Landon's bitch ass got enough money to end world hunger. I know he ain't playing you like that," Kane said.

"Yeah, well Landon's money ain't doing me no good. I have to work to get mine," Malia flippantly replied.

She would never tell him that she gave up every dime in their joint bank account to be with a no-good ass nigga who dogged her out.

"Nigga got that hoe living the good life while his baby mama is waiting tables." Kane frowned.

"I guess you met the new girlfriend too," Malia said with jealousy dripping from her voice.

"I did more than meet her. I was fucking her long before he was," Kane pointed out.

"What! Are you serious?" Malia questioned.

"Dead ass," Kane confirmed.

"What about Ava? You cheated on your wife?" Malia questioned.

"Like you got room to talk," Kane said, looking at her like she was crazy.

"How did you end up messing with her?"

"Bitch was a dancer at a club that me and my boys used to go to."

"She was a stripper?" Malia asked in shock.

"The bitch did more than strip. How do you think I started fucking her?" Kane asked.

He was bitter, but Malia had no way of knowing that. Truth was, jealously was eating him alive. When he went to JB's with some of his frat brothers, it was only to enjoy his birthday. He looked forward to getting a few drinks and lap dances, but he didn't anticipate meeting Faryn. He saw her giving a customer a lap dance and he told another dancer to call her for him. His frat brothers called him Alpha Redd because of his light-colored skin, so Redd was the name that he gave when they made their introductions. When she gave him his first lap dance, Kane was hooked. He became a regular at the club and Faryn was the only dancer that he wanted to see. Unlike some of the others, her costume choices were always classy and she always smelled good.

She was quiet and didn't say much at first. As time went on, she started to open up a little more, but she was very vague with her answers. She told Kane that she was working at the club to put herself through college, but she never said what she was going for. Feelings weren't supposed to be a part of the equation, but he couldn't help it. Faryn had been an intimate part of his life for an entire year. He fell for her and he didn't try to deny how much he loved her. Sadly, the feelings were one sided.

He loved Ava to death, but she was too stuffy at times. Ava was a spoiled princess and he had to take the blame for some of that. He never told his wife no for any reason, but she got under his skin at times. With Faryn, he never had that to worry about. He gave her money all the time and she never had to ask. When she graduated college, he spent over a thousand dollars to purchase her a pair of red bottoms so that she could graduate in style. He just knew without a doubt that he and Faryn were going to continue what they started once she left the club. He was shocked and disappointed when she refused to meet him and barely answered his calls.

"That nigga got my kids around a stripping prostitute!" Malia yelled angrily.

"Basically." Kane shrugged.

"And that bitch is my baby's counselor. I need to call the agency and make them fire her ass," Malia fumed.

"Who's a counselor?" Kane asked.

"That bitch Faryn is Lance's counselor. That's how her and Landon met," Malia confirmed.

"That nigga stupid as fuck." Kane frowned, storing the info that he'd just received in his memory. He did remember Landon telling him that once before, but the information wasn't important at the time.

"What happened with y'all? You and Landon were best friends at one time. I know y'all ain't beefing over a bitch."

"Man, fuck that nigga. He sucker punched me behind that hoe, but it's all good. If it wasn't for Ava and Ms. Ella, him and Aiden's bitch ass would be in the morgue by now," Kane threatened.

He had to take a leave of absence from work because of his bruised face and ego. He also didn't want to run the risk of running into Landon again until the smoke cleared just a little. Malia only listened, but she knew that Kane was full of shit. She had been in that family for years and talking was all that he ever did. Kane was born with a silver spoon in his mouth and he loved to throw his money around. Both his parents were attorneys and they ran a very successful law firm. He played tough, but he was a spoiled pretty boy. He and Ava were the perfect couple. He was no match for Landon or Aiden and he knew it.

"He got that bitch trying to replace me. I haven't seen my kids in a whole month now. First, Lance stopped wanting to come with me and I noticed that it was around the time that he started seeing her. Lennox still came all the time, but that started to change. He would come for a little while, but he wouldn't want to spend the night. Now, he doesn't want to come at all. Every time I call, he always says that his daddy is bringing them somewhere. I called yesterday and Lennox said that they were leaving to go on a cruise today."

"Stupid ass nigga wining and dining that hoe like he got something. He better do a blood test on that baby. Lil bastard might not even be his," Kane said.

"She's pregnant?" Malia asked louder than she meant to.

"Yep," Kane replied smugly.

He could see that he was getting under Malia's skin and that was his goal. Malia was the perfect person for him to use against Landon. It was no secret that she still wanted him because Landon told him about her always begging him for another chance.

"Wow," Malia replied, feeling that her attempts to get her family back were pointless now.

She was really going to be a nobody to Landon now. She prided herself on being the mother of his only kids. Now, Faryn was going to have that title as well. If she knew Landon as well as she thought, marriage was next on his agenda. He was a stand-up guy and he was going to marry the mother of his child, no questions asked. He believed in doing things the right way and he loved being a family man. Malia felt like crying. She had already lost Landon to another woman. She didn't want to lose her kids to Faryn too.

"That's fucked up about your kids though. You need to get a lawyer and fight for custody," Kane said, trying to plant a seed of confusion.

"Hell no, Kane! Do you see where I work? I can't afford to hire an attorney. Besides, I left them. I'm an unfit mother in the eyes of the courts."

"That's what that nigga wants you to think. Now, they might not give you full custody, but you can definitely get joint custody. You can make him pay child support for the times that they're with you. It's not like you can't use the money and he has plenty of that," Kane noted.

"Maybe, but I'm not in the best position to go to court right now. I'm not prepared financially or emotionally," Malia admitted.

"Stop worrying about money Malia. Getting a lawyer ain't nothing for me and you know that," Kane assured her.

"Damn. Landon must have really pissed you off," Malia said.

"This has nothing to do with his punk ass," Kane lied.

"Why do you wanna help me then?" Malia questioned.

"You made a mistake just like a lot of people do. I don't think you should be punished for the rest of your life for it though. And you damn sure shouldn't be kept away from your kids. Ain't no telling what kind of shit they be putting in their heads about you."

"You might be right because Lance hates me now. Landon blames me for his behavioral problems in school and Lennox called me a liar one time when we spoke," Malia said sadly.

Lennox was upset with her for lying about his father saying that she could come to their house. Malia tried to apologize and explain, but he called her a liar and hung up on her. It took her a week to get him to forgive her and she promised to never do that again.

"That's fucked up. Nigga gon' have your kids calling another bitch mama soon," Kane said, trying to make a bad situation worse.

"Fuck her and him. I get it, he doesn't want me anymore, but I want a relationship with my kids. They can't deny me of that," Malia argued.

"I agree. But, here, take my card and hit me up whenever you're ready to make something shake. Stop talking about it and handle your business. Your kids aren't getting any younger," Kane noted.

If he thought that Landon cared anything about her, Malia would have been his latest conquest. Since Landon no longer had feelings for her, that would have been defeating the purpose. Malia was pretty, but she wasn't his type. He liked his women thick and shapely. Malia was too thin for him. Besides, he was already trying to buy his way out of the dog house with Ava. She was pissed when she learned of his dealings with

Faryn. He didn't need to add any more charges to his case. Fucking her nephew's ex-wife would not have been a good look. Kane had just redeemed himself from another affair that Ava had found out about not too long ago.

"Thanks Kane. I appreciate it. We've been talking for so long, I never asked you what you came in here for," Malia replied after a short pause.

"Oh yeah. I need to order some food for my wife. She didn't feel like leaving the house tonight," he said.

Malia took out her notepad and wrote down Kane's order. He sat down at one of the empty tables, while she went the back to give it to the cook. Malia was happy that it was almost closing time. Working at night made her appreciate the morning shift that much more. When her phone rang, she was tempted to let the call go to voicemail. When she saw that it was Roman calling, she was happy that she didn't.

"You must have dialed the wrong number," Malia said with a smile evident in her voice.

"What's up with you?" Roman asked as he laid across the bed in his new apartment.

"I'm working Roman. How can I help you?" Malia asked, happy that he called.

"Damn ma. You got a job now?" he asked with a chuckle.

"It's not like you left me with much of a choice. I had rent to pay, remember?"

"What time you get off? I'm trying to slide through and see you," Roman said.

"Slide through where?" Malia asked.

"The fuck you mean where? The apartment," Roman answered.

"I gave that apartment up. I live with my mother now," Malia embarrassingly admitted.

"Damn. I miss you, man. I'm trying to see you. I'll get a room then. Come spend the night with me," Roman requested.

He was experiencing a serious drought and on the verge of desperation. He was back fucking with

Jessica, but she was out of town with one of her other niggas. The chick that he was dealing with the most was on her period and his backup side piece was at work until morning. Roman needed some female companionship and Malia quickly came to mind. Roman had access to every hole on her body and he was ready to unload in them all.

"I thought you had an apartment. Why can't I come there?" Malia questioned.

"You know Chad ain't fucking with you like that. This is his shit and you already know you're not welcomed here," Roman lied.

The apartment belonged to them both, but he would never invite Malia there. She would make his life a living hell if he did. He saw her out in public a few times and she always caused a scene.

"As much as he was at our apartment, he shouldn't have nothing to say," Malia replied.

"What's up Malia? You trying to hook up with a nigga or what?" Roman asked.

"Where?" Malia asked.

"I'll text you the info," Roman answered.

"Okay, I'll be there," Malia assured him as she hung up the phone with a smile.

Her entire attitude shifted once she ended the call. She was tired and dragging a minute ago, but she was full of life and energy now. It had been months since Malia had any male companionship and she was looking forward to it. Maybe Roman was finally maturing and trying to settle down. She was trying hard not to get her hopes up high, but it wasn't easy. Roman had lots of women that he could choose from, but he chose her. That had to mean something. He could have gotten sex from anywhere, but he wanted it from her. That alone had Malia smiling from ear to ear. She had learned her lesson from before though. She was no longer on birth control, so she had to take extra precautions. Roman hated wearing condoms, so the Plan B pill was going to be Malia's back up plan. Hopefully, their one night together turned into more.

Even if it didn't, Malia was happy that he'd called her at all.

Chapter 25

As the season changed, so did Faryn's body. She was now five months pregnant and she had no idea when her huge belly had appeared. She went to bed one night with a little pudge and woke up looking like she'd swallowed a watermelon. Landon and the kids were happy, and they rubbed her belly all the time. Everybody was hoping for a girl, but Faryn had become partial to boys. They seemed easier to care for, from what she could see when helping with Lance and Lennox.

"Y'all have a good day!" Faryn yelled to the boys as they got out of the car in front of their school.

Landon was so thankful that he could get Lance back into the private school that he had gone to before. Lennox was happy to have his big brother back there as well. The principal of the other school wrote a recommendation letter on his behalf. As his counselor, Faryn had to write one as well to let them know that he was seeing her bi-weekly for anger management and how he was progressing. Lance was already receiving compliments from the staff and Landon was happy for that.

They'd been begging him to go back to Disney World but, with Faryn being pregnant, he didn't want to chance her flying. Her doctor said that it was fine, but he wasn't taking any risks. Landon did something even better. He took them on a Disney cruise before they went back to school and that made everybody happy. His sons deserved it and so did Faryn. The boys had even gone to spend a week with Malia at Cora's house before school started. She asked Lance to come and, surprisingly, he did.

"You ready to lose your money?" Landon asked her with a smile as they drove away.

"Nigga, you better be ready to pay up," Faryn replied.

"I'm telling you, Faryn, that's my daughter. I can feel it."

"I don't feel nothing but heartburn," Faryn replied, making him laugh.

"You need me to stop and get you something?" Landon asked.

"No, I'll be okay," she replied.

Faryn was going into work late because she had a doctor's appointment. They were finding out the sex of their baby, and she and Landon had made a bet. He put up a thousand dollars believing that it was a girl. Faryn matched his bet because she assumed it was a boy.

"We're over an hour early for the appointment. You wanna go back home or by my grandmother?" Landon asked.

"We can go by your grandmother. If we go back home, I'll probably fall asleep." Faryn yawned.

She didn't usually get up so early, but they took the boys out to breakfast before taking them to school. At the mention of food, Faryn was up and dressed before they were.

"The fuck!" Landon said when he turned down Ella's street.

They had an ambulance, firetruck, and police cars cluttering the street. His heart dropped when he saw that they were right in front of Ella's door.

"Baby, calm down, look, Ms. Ella is fine," Faryn said as she pointed to his grandmother and Makena standing in the middle of the street.

Landon parked as close as he could before getting out and helping Faryn do the same.

"What happened?" Landon asked while giving his grandmother and sister a kiss on the cheek when they walked up.

"Hey y'all." Makena smiled as she rubbed Faryn's round belly.

"I don't know what happened. I heard sirens and I ran out here. I panicked when I saw them rushing into Robin's house. I thought something had happened to my child until I saw her come out and stand on the porch," Ella spoke up.

"We're not that lucky," Makena replied sarcastically.

"You stop that Makena. Robin is a no-good bitch, but that's still my child. And no matter how trifling she is, she's still your mother," Ella fussed.

"You're our mother," Landon corrected, right as the paramedics wheeled a stretcher out with Robin's boyfriend, Leroy, on it.

Ella rushed over to see what had happened. Robin locked up her house as she talked to her mother. Once they put Leroy in the back of the ambulance, Robin hugged her mother and got back there with him.

"They think he had a heart attack," Ella informed them when she walked back over and led them inside the house.

"Sorry to hear that. What time is your appointment Faryn?" Makena asked, changing the subject. She wasn't about to pretend to care about her mother or her man. They never cared about her or Landon, and she was returning the gesture.

"It's at ten. We stopped over here because it was too early to go," Faryn replied.

"Y'all better call me the minute they say something. I swear, I'm going shopping today if it's a girl. Hell, I'm going shopping either way, but I just need to know. One of my friends that I went to school with is taking care of the baby shower for me. She's an event coordinator and her work is amazing," Makena beamed.

"They don't have to tell me nothing. I already know what it is," Ella said as she rubbed Faryn's stomach in a circular motion and smiled brightly.

"Come on grandma, don't start playing Miss Cleo with all that psychic mess," Landon argued.

"Shut up bastard. Say what you want, but I bet I'm right," Ella replied.

"I wanna know grandma," Makena begged.

"Tell her when we leave," Landon ordered.

Landon didn't want her to ruin his surprise like she'd done the first two times. He wanted the doctors to deliver the news of his baby's sex. After talking with Ella and Makena for a while, Landon and Faryn headed to their appointment to find out what was baking in the oven. Once she signed in and changed into her hospital gown, Faryn laid back and waited for the doctor to arrive.

"You got time to change your bet before you lose," Landon smirked.

"I'm thinking about doubling the amount since I have such a good feeling about it," Faryn replied, right as the doctor walked into the room.

He took a few minutes to examine her and she was pleased to know that her pregnancy was going well. Landon winked at her and smiled when the nurse walked in with the ultrasound machine. Some gel was applied to Faryn's stomach before her doctor started moving the probe around.

"Boy or girl?" Dr. Evans asked as he looked at Faryn.

"Boy for me and girl for him," Faryn replied.

The doctor had a serious look on his face as he whispered something to the nurse who was present. She put a little more gel on Faryn's stomach and moved the probe around some more.

"One thing is for sure, somebody will get what they want and somebody won't," Landon chuckled.

"Maybe not," Dr. Evans replied.

"What do you mean?" Landon asked nervously.

Dr. Evans took the probe from the nurse and took over once again. They were whispering back and forth, and Landon was getting upset. Faryn grabbed his hand and squeezed it, letting him know that everything would be fine.

"Is something wrong?" Faryn asked after a while.

"Can you see if it's a boy or girl?" Landon asked impatiently as he stood right next to the bed that Faryn was on.

"It's both," Dr. Evens replied with a smile.

"What!" Landon and Faryn shouted at the same time.

He was happy that he was there to catch her because Faryn almost fell out of the bed.

"Whoa. Are you okay?" Dr. Evans asked her.

"I'm fine, but are you sure?" Faryn asked.

"I'm almost positive. I'm gonna do a three-dimensional ultrasound as well just to confirm the sexes, but you definitely have two babies in there," Dr. Evan replied.

"My stomach is not even that big," Faryn noted.

"It's big enough to say that you're only five months in, but that doesn't mean anything. You can carry in other places besides your stomach," the doctor informed her.

The nurse left and got the other room ready for them to go into. A few minutes later, Faryn had another ultrasound and got confirmation. She was pregnant with a son and a daughter, and she and Landon were in shock. They were both getting what they wanted and that was the best part. Getting them both at the exact same time was the kicker.

"Two babies at the same damn time," Landon sighed as he drove away from the doctor's office.

"They're coming sooner than we think too. Dr. Evans said that I won't go full-term with twins," Faryn replied.

"Yeah, we need to start getting shit together right now. We can't be caught off guard with two babies. Makena don't even have to do a baby shower. We can buy everything they'll need."

"I don't care about a baby shower. Besides my sister and Harley, I don't have anyone else to invite. I don't want to do that to your sister though. She really wants to do this. Maybe we can convince her to do something small," Faryn suggested.

"Let me call her anyway. She's gonna be shocked as hell," Landon laughed.

"You think your grandma knew?" Faryn asked.

"I don't know," Landon replied, right as Makena's voice came through over the speakers of his car.

"Is it true?" she yelled in excitement.

"Is what true?" Landon questioned.

"Are we having twins?" Makena asked, making Landon and Faryn look at each other in shock.

"A boy and a girl," Landon confirmed.

"I knew it! Didn't I tell you?" Ella screamed in the background.

"How do you be knowing that stuff grandma?" Landon questioned in confusion.

"I can't explain it baby. It's my gift from God. I told y'all that one of my grandbabies was going to have twins. I had a set and so did my grandmother. It skipped a generation with my mama and my kids, but I knew it was gonna hit one of y'all," Ella said, like it was a conspiracy theory.

"Damn man. I'm happy, but why couldn't it have hit Aiden? Then, it would have skipped me and my girl," Landon joked.

"That disease infested dick probably can't even make no babies," Ella said, making them laugh.

"That's not how it works anyway. The twin gene can't come from the father's side. Only the mother's genetics matter," Makena informed them.

"My mama was a twin to a boy. He got killed in a car accident when I was little though," Faryn admitted.

"Damn. You never told me that," Landon said while looking over at her.

"I was only about four or five when it happened, so I don't really remember him. My mama and my grandmother used to talk about him all the time and I saw the pictures that they had around the house," Faryn replied.

"Yep, so that explains it. I'm so excited! We get two for the price of one!" Makena yelled.

"Wait until y'all tell the boys. They are going to go crazy for sure," Ella replied.

"I'm getting my junior this time. Lance was supposed to be my namesake until Malia came with her bullshit. I don't know why I let her talk me out of it," Landon said.

"What do you mean? What did she talk you out of?" Faryn asked.

"I wanted to name Lance after me, but she came with some bullshit about wanting them to have their own identity. I don't know why I fell for that shit," Landon fussed.

"I don't know why either. Lil bossy bitch know she should have named your first son after you," Ella argued.

"Well, you can have your junior this time. You can pick the names if you want to," Faryn said, making him smile.

"That's so sweet of you, Faryn," Ella said.

"My baby is sweet," Landon said while leaning over to plant a kiss on her lips.

"Okay, I need to call my girl, so she can get started on the baby shower," Makena spoke up.

"That's what we were calling for too. We didn't really want you to do nothing too big for the shower Makena," Landon informed her.

"That's not for y'all to decide. This is a shower for the babies. This is their first party and we're doing it big," Ella argued.

"She's not even going full-term. The doctor said that twins don't go all the way to nine months," Landon noted.

"We can do it in two months from now. Faryn will be seven months then. And I'll respect y'all wishes and not make it too big," Makena promised.

"Cool, just tell me how much it is and I got you," Landon said.

"No Landon, I'm doing this all on my own. I don't need any help," Makena assured him.

"Are you sure?" he questioned.

"Yes, I'll take care of everything. If there's any special foods or anything that you want Faryn, just let me know," Makena said.

"Okay, we just pulled up to my office, so I'll call you later," Faryn replied.

"Okay," Makena said before they disconnected.

"You know you lost the bet, right?" Landon asked as he looked over at her.

"How? If I lost, then you did too. We were both right since it's a boy and a girl. If I owe you a stack, then you owe me one too," Faryn laughed.

"How about a car instead?" Landon asked.

"I already have a car that I'm still paying a note on," Faryn noted.

"Not that lil toy car. We're having two babies Faryn. Your Camaro is not gonna work."

"Aww, but I love my car. That's my first one," Faryn whined.

"I'll pay it off and you can keep it. You still need something bigger though, Faryn. Look at some SUV's and let me know what you like. Remember, it's gonna be the two of us and four kids most of the time. We need more room," Landon said.

"Yeah, you're right. I'll look at something and we can talk more about it later," she replied.

"I'll see you at five. I love you, baby," Landon said as he gave Faryn a kiss.

"I love you too," Faryn replied as she got out of the car and wobbled into the office to get her day started.

Chapter 26

Faryn was drained and she hadn't even worked a full day. She needed a nap and she couldn't wait to get home. Her case load was huge that day because she had lots of parents requesting her for their troubled kids. Faryn was good at what she did because she was once one of them. The other counselors gave advice from a book, but Faryn gave advice from experience. Her other clients were easy but, of course, they always saved the worst for last.

Daytona, a troubled thirteen-year-old with the attitude of a roaring lion, was a piece of work. She'd been coming to Faryn for two whole months and she still refused to talk. Faryn had just opened her folder and read over some new information that had been put inside. Her heart went out to the young girl because she saw beyond the attitude and rough exterior.

"So, Daytona, do you wanna talk about some of the things that's going on in school?" Faryn asked her.

"Do I ever?" the young girl countered with the usual attitude that Faryn had grown accustomed to.

"For this to work, you have to talk to me, Daytona. I can't help you if I don't know what's wrong," Faryn said softly.

"I don't need your help. I'm good," she snapped angrily.

"Okay, so why were you caught in the boy's bathroom charging for oral sex?" Faryn asked, tired of playing the same stupid game with her.

"I'm good at sucking dick and I needed the money." Daytona shrugged.

"Who do you live with Daytona?" Faryn asked.

"My mama, her boyfriend, and my brother and sister," she replied.

"What kind of drugs is your mother on?" Faryn asked.

"My mama ain't on no drugs bitch. Don't try to look down on me because you got a lil money. Fuck you and fuck this stupid counseling shit," Daytona cried as she jumped up and ran to the door.

"I'm not looking down on you, Daytona. At one time, I was you," Faryn said, stopping her in her tracks.

"What does that mean?" Daytona asked with a sniffle.

"Sit down and I'll tell you," Faryn requested.

Daytona reclaimed her seat, as Faryn told her all about her childhood. She didn't leave anything out as she gave her the sordid details of her past. Daytona gave Faryn her undivided attention as she spoke of an upbringing that sounded almost like her own.

"My mama and her boyfriend smoke crack," Daytona finally admitted.

"My mother did too," Faryn replied sympathetically.

"I don't want to do what I'm doing, but that's the only way that I can eat. My mama sells our food stamps and my brother and sister be hungry," Daytona admitted.

"I understand Daytona, I promise I do. I'm not here to judge you. I only want to help. The agency can help you with getting food without you having to do what you're doing for money. I didn't have that when I was growing up, so my options were limited. I have all the resources that you'll need. All you have to do is trust me. Are you willing to let me help you?"

"I don't want to be separated from my brother and sister," Daytona said as she started to cry again.

"You won't be, I promise. I at least want to make sure that you have food when you're hungry. If you need anything more than that, just call me. Even if I have to take my own money to help, I will," Faryn promised her.

"I can just call the number on the card that you gave me?" Daytona asked.

"Yes, and this is against the rules but, here, this is my personal cell," Faryn said as she handed her the paper that she'd written her number on.

"Thank you," Daytona said as she got up and hugged her.

Faryn was touched by the gesture, especially since she had never shown any emotions before.

"Is that a smile?" Faryn asked her once they broke away from each other.

"I didn't think I was going to like you," Daytona admitted.

"Why? I'm not so bad." Faryn smiled.

"So, nobody really came to your college graduation?" Daytona asked, remembering something that Faryn had said moments earlier.

"Nope. I had no one there to clap for me, so I clapped for myself. I was proud of me, even if nobody else was."

"That's what I want. I want to go to college and help people like you do," Daytona replied.

"I'm gonna hold you to that," Faryn said, right as the timer went off, signaling the end of their session.

It was five o'clock and Faryn couldn't have been happier. She knew that Landon was probably on his way because he was never there exactly at five. She walked Daytona out to her ride and bid her farewell until their next session. Daytona was a part of the boys and girls club and the van was outside waiting to take her back home.

"Faryn, Ms. Marcel wants to see you in her office," the receptionist said as soon as Faryn walked back into the building.

"At five o'clock?" Faryn questioned.

"You know how she is. She expects everybody to work on her schedule. I'm out of here, so I'll see you tomorrow." The receptionist smiled before she left for the day.

Faryn couldn't take in any more cases and she was sure that was what her supervisor wanted her for. It was going to be hell trying to pass off so many clients to the other counselors when she went on maternity leave. Faryn had never told them no before, but there was a first time for everything. She went back to her office and grabbed her purse and phone. She locked her office door and walked down the hall to her supervisor's office. Faryn tapped on the door and was granted access. She paused briefly when she walked in and saw the director of the agency seated in the office as well.

"Have a seat Faryn," Ms. Marcel said sweetly.

"Okay. What's up?" Faryn questioned, ready to get the meeting over with.

"We received some information today regarding you and one of your clients," the director, Mr. Pierce, said.

"Which client?" Faryn questioned.

"Lance Reynolds," he replied.

He didn't have to say anything else. Faryn already knew what the meeting was about. She sat there in a daze as he went over company policies and the rules that every counselor was supposed to follow. Faryn wasn't interested in a lecture; she wanted him to get to the point and get it over with. He was doing a lot of pointless talking and Landon was blowing her phone up. Thirty minutes later, the meeting was concluded and Faryn powerwalked out of the building and up to Landon's truck. She didn't care if he parked in front of the building anymore. No one knew who he was, or so she thought.

"Girl, I was about to act a fool. I thought you already left. I've been calling and texting you for thirty minutes," Landon said with a worried look on his face.

He went to give Faryn a hug, but she grabbed him first and burst out in tears.

"Baby, what's wrong?" Landon asked with a concerned expression on his face.

"Let's go. I wanna get the hell away from here," Faryn sniffled.

Landon helped her get into the truck before he pulled off and drove away.

"Talk to me baby. What's wrong?" Landon said while grabbing her hand.

"I just resigned from my job," Faryn sobbed.

"What! Why Faryn? You love that job," Landon replied.

"Apparently, somebody told them about my relationship with you. They were trying to open an investigation on me and put me on unpaid leave until they figured it all out. I don't even want them to waste their time when I know I'm guilty," Faryn cried.

"Damn baby. I'm so sorry about all this," Landon said solemnly.

"I knew that this was going to happen. This is the exact thing that I was afraid of," Faryn said, shaking her head.

"It sounds like you're having regrets. I hope that's not what I'm hearing in your voice," Landon said as he looked over at her.

"I don't regret being with you, Landon, but look at the position that I'm in," Faryn replied.

"What position is that?" he questioned.

"Are you serious?" Faryn asked.

"Yeah, I am. I'm sorry about your job baby, but you know I got you," Landon promised her.

"I appreciate that Landon, but I don't want you to have me. I shook my ass in a club for four years to get my degrees. I'm not letting them sit on the wall and collect dust."

"I understand that Faryn and I respect it. If you feel like that, open your own business. Your clients love you, so they'll follow you wherever you go. You have the certifications to make it happen. All you'll need is a building and I can help you with that," Landon replied.

"Seriously? You think I should?" Faryn asked.

"Why not? Be your own boss, so you don't have to answer to nobody else," Landon answered.

"Them bitches had me work all day up until five before they hit me with this bullshit. I wish they would have said something earlier, so I could have gone home and taken a nap," Faryn fussed, making Landon laugh.

"What I wanna know is how they found out about the shit. That ain't something that they would have known without being told. Nobody there knows who I am."

"That's the same thing I said. You think your ex-wife had something to do with it?" Faryn asked.

"I'm leaning more towards Kane's weak ass. That nigga ain't been to work in a minute, but I don't put nothing pass him."

"He doesn't know anything about me though," Faryn pointed out.

Besides her phone number, Kane had no other info on her. Faryn ended up changing her number too because he started sending her all kinds of crazy text messages since the incident at Ella's house. Landon wanted to beat his ass, but she begged him to leave it alone. Not many people had her number, so changing it was no big deal.

"It's not that hard to find out. He's married to my auntie," Landon reminded her as he pulled up to his grandmother's house to get his sons.

He and Faryn couldn't wait for them to find out about the babies. He knew that they were going to be excited about getting two babies instead of one.

"Tell Ms. Ella that I said hello. I'm too lazy to get out," Faryn said when he got out of the car.

Landon was gone for about five minutes before he and the boys came back out and they were on their way once again.

"What did the doctor say? Are we having a sister or a brother?" Lennox asked.

"What do you want it to be?" Faryn asked.

"I want a brother," Lennox replied.

"Dummy, you got me. We need a sister now. I want it to be a girl," Lance butted in.

"What is it? A boy or a girl?" Lennox questioned.

"Both. We're having twins. A boy and a girl," Landon answered.

"Like auntie Ava and uncle Aiden?" Lennox asked.

"Yes," Faryn replied.

"So, we get two babies?" Lance asked them.

"Yes, a boy and a girl," Faryn reiterated.

"That's a lot of crying," Lance said, shaking his head at the thought.

"That's what big brothers are for. Y'all are gonna help us, right?" Faryn inquired.

"I'm gonna help you, Faryn," Lennox said.

"I'll help too, but I don't know how to change diapers," Lance said, making them laugh.

"We'll take care of that part. Do y'all have homework?" Landon asked.

"Yes," they both answered at the same time.

"Anybody need help?" Faryn questioned.

"No," they both answered in chorus again.

"Dad, can we order pizza and wings tonight?" Lennox asked.

"Yes," Faryn answered before Landon could say anything.

He knew that she didn't feel like cooking, so whatever they wanted was fine. When they pulled up to the gate of their home, the security guard was out front speaking to a sheriff's officer. When Landon entered the resident's side of the gate, he saw the guard pointing his way before beckoning for him to come over. Leaving the car running, Landon jumped out and jogged over to where they were.

"Landon Reynolds?" the officer said as soon as he got close to them.

"Yes," Landon replied in confusion.

"You've been served. Have a good day," the officer said as he handed him a thick packet in a gold colored envelope and walked away.

"I'm sorry Mr. Reynolds. I didn't know what that was about," the security guard said.

"Nah, it's cool. I don't know what this is about either, but I guess I'll find out soon." Landon shrugged.

"What did he want with you? What's that?" Faryn asked when he got back into the car.

"I have no idea," Landon replied.

When they got into the house, his sons went straight to their rooms to do their homework like they always did. Faryn was anxious to see what was in the envelope that Landon had, so he tore it open to ease her mind.

"Man, this is some bullshit," he said as he laughed out loud.

He gave the papers to Faryn for her to read over, but she didn't find anything funny. Malia was asking for joint custody of the boys and she didn't find the humor in that. She wanted them to stay with her every other month, which equated to six months of the year.

"This is not funny Landon. Why is she doing this?" Faryn asked as her eyes filled up with tears.

Faryn missed them like crazy when they went by Malia for a week. That was their mother, so she was happy that they were spending time with her though.

"I'm not worried about that shit. She got her mama listed as a character witness. She already lost the case," Landon laughed as he locked their bedroom door.

"And then she wants child support for the time that she has them. This is crazy," Faryn argued.

"That's what this is all about. She needs money," Landon said as he started removing Faryn's clothes.

"Baby, stop. This is serious and you act like you don't care."

"I don't care. She let that nigga Kane get in her head," Landon replied while removing his own clothes.

"How do you know that?" Faryn asked, as Landon laid her down and climbed on top of her.

"Look at the name at the top of the documents. Carmen Monroe is Kane's mama. His mama and daddy are both attorneys who practice criminal and family law," Landon informed her as he slid inside of her and moaned.

"I can't believe that you're worried about sex at a time like this," Faryn argued.

"I'm always worried about sex. Now, hurry up before they finish and come knocking," Landon replied as he flipped her over so that she was on top.

Malia and her bullshit custody papers were the furthest thing from his mind. He didn't know how she'd hooked up with his newest enemy and he didn't care. Kane was a hoe and Landon knew that from the first day they met. Kane was being punked by a dude from another fraternity and Landon had to come to his rescue. He tried to get Landon to join the Alphas, but he wasn't interested. Kane was always on some catch back shit like a lil bitch and Malia was dumb enough to fall for it. Landon planned to give her a call later, but nothing was more important that what he was doing at that moment. All the other bullshit would just have to wait until he was done.

Chapter 27

"Uh, shit," Malia moaned, as Roman pounded into her from behind.

She was on her way home from work when he summoned her to a crime and drug infested area in the ninth ward that he was known to frequent. It was dark outside, but Malia was willing to risk her safety just to be with him. When she pulled up, she spotted Roman and Chad standing outside with a bunch of other men. He hopped in her car and instructed her to drive, giving her directions on where to go. Malia thought they were finally going to his house until they pulled up to a secluded park that barely had any lights.

When Roman got out of the car, he walked around and helped her out too. Malia got excited when he pushed her up against her car and began to roughly kiss her. Her excitement never lasted too long when it came to Roman though. A few seconds after kissing her, he turned her around and yanked down her pants and underwear. Malia was thankful that his kiss made her wet because he plunged inside of her without even checking to see. There was nothing romantic about the way he had her bent over the trunk of her car, fucking her outside in the park. Malia had never felt so low in her life, but she still didn't stop him.

"Fuck!" Roman grunted as he pulled out and released all over her ass.

"Really Roman? I don't have nothing to clean up with," Malia fussed.

"Damn, I needed that," Roman said, breathing heavily.

"Did you hear what I just said? I'm standing here with your babies all over my ass and I don't have nothing to clean up with," Malia fussed.

"You nag too fucking much. Here!" Roman yelled as he took off his white t-shirt and threw it at her. He had another shirt underneath it, so he didn't care. He and Chad were about to go home anyway, so it was cool. Malia cleaned herself up as best she could with the shirt, before throwing it to the ground. She felt dirty and she needed a shower bad.

"You wanna get a room?" she asked once they got back in the car.

"Nah, bring me back where you just got me from. I got moves to make," Roman said while looking at a message that Jessica had just sent him.

She was trying to get him to come by her, but he wasn't in the mood to be up under nobody. Malia got him straight for the night and all he wanted now was a shower and his own bed.

"When am I gonna see you again?" she asked.

"When I need to bust another nut," he laughed.

"That's not funny Roman. You keep telling me to be patient and I'm trying. Don't string me along if you know this isn't what you want. All we do is hook up to fuck and then you go on your way again."

"You're too old to be so naïve," Roman chuckled.

"What the hell is that supposed to mean?" Malia questioned.

"Nothing man, nothing at all," Roman laughed.

Malia was dumb as hell. He didn't understand how her sisters were so hood and street smart and she was so sheltered and fragile. Maybe the years she spent with her husband had done that to her because she was a real dummy to believe anything that Roman told her. Any other woman in her right mind wouldn't have wanted anything to do with him if he had done to them what he did to Malia. One call of whispering sweet nothings in her ear was all it took for him to be back in like he never left.

"Make sure you call me," Malia requested when she pulled up to the house where she had picked Roman up from.

He got out of her car without a word or a backwards glance. Malia shook her head and pulled off, heading in the direction of her mother's home. Living with Cora wasn't as bad as she thought it would be, but she still wanted her own space. She was working and saving her money, but the need to do more was overwhelming her. She regretted not going to school when Landon encouraged her to and she had been thinking about going back. She wasn't even thirty years old and she had nothing going for herself. Malia was deep in thought as she pulled up to the house and parked next to her mother's car. As soon as she opened the front door to the house, Cora was standing there ready to go off on her.

"What the hell is this?" Cora yelled as she held up the subpoena that she had been served with earlier that day.

"I told you about that already ma," Malia replied.

"Yeah and I told you to leave that shit alone. And you got the nerve to have me subpoenaed as a character witness. You must be out of your damn mind," Cora fussed.

"I just want to be able to spend time with my kids! Is that too much to ask for?" Malia yelled.

"You better lower your damn voice in my house. When has Landon ever stopped you from seeing them Malia? They spent an entire week here with us not too long ago. You weren't worried about seeing them when you left home to go be with that nigga."

"This has nothing to do with Roman," Malia maintained.

"Girl, please. You must think I'm stupid. I saw him drop you off here at three in the morning a few nights ago. He didn't even think enough of you to wait until you got inside safely. You must be a special kind of stupid to even deal with his ass after what he did to you. You didn't give a damn about your kids, as long as y'all were together. Now that Landon has moved on and is happy, you want to try to cause confusion."

"I've always cared about my kids," Malia cried from the truths that her mother was telling.

"Tell that shit to somebody who don't know the real story. But, you can remove my name from your witness list. I'll testify, but it won't be on your behalf," Cora assured her.

"I'm your daughter, but you always take Landon's side like you gave birth to him," Malia sobbed.

"It's not about taking sides Malia. This is about my grandkids and what's best for them," Cora replied.

"And what makes you think being with him is best? He got my kids living up in the house with an ex stripping prostitute. I don't even know her ass and she's raising my kids."

"I don't give a damn if she sucked dick on the highway for passing motorists to see. Her past is her past and you have no room to judge. Your kids love her, and she must love them too. They didn't utter one bad word about her and they called her the entire time they were here. You know Landon wouldn't just move anyone in his house around his boys. You're jealous and that's where this custody mess is coming from. Another woman came along and appreciates everything that you gave up and walked away from. Being the mother to his only kids doesn't hold as much weight as it did before because he has two more on the way. Trying to make Landon miserable won't make you happy Malia. Stop playing victim to the circumstances that you created," Cora said as she walked off and left Malia in a pool of tears.

Malia didn't have a rebuttal because everything that her mother said was true. She let Kane, of all people, get into her head and convince her to do something that she would have never done on her own. She would never admit it out loud, but she was jealous. Faryn had come along and became to Landon what she was supposed to be. All the years they were together, and she threw it all away for nothing. Roman wasn't worth it and it didn't take her long to figure that out.

"Hello," Malia said, answering her phone without looking to see who it was.

"What's up with these bullshit ass papers that you sent me Malia?" Landon asked her, getting right to the reason for his call.

"Just forget it Landon. I'm going to the lawyer tomorrow and have them withdrawn," Malia replied in her hoarse voice. She had been crying for a while and she didn't even sound like herself.

"Why did you even send them? I've always communicated with you about our kids and I've never stopped you from seeing them."

"I know that," Malia admitted.

"If you know that, then what's the problem?" Landon asked.

"One of my problems is the woman that you chose to have my kids around."

"What about Faryn?" Landon asked.

"She was a prostituting stripper Landon!" Malia yelled.

"Yo, are you serious right now? That nigga Kane is foul as fuck for that shit," Landon laughed.

"So, it is true," Malia said.

"Kane knows as much about Faryn as you do. This shit is childish as fuck man. You need to meet her for yourself and form your own opinion. She's here to stay no matter how you feel, but you should meet the woman who's going to be around your kids every day. We're about to be a blended family and I don't need the added drama."

"We've already met, remember?" Malia asked sarcastically.

"I'm talking about a formal introduction Malia," Landon corrected.

"Just let me think about it Landon," Malia replied.

"That's cool. Just get back to me with your decision," he replied before he hung up.

He didn't understand how Malia didn't feel the need to meet Faryn. When she was living with Roman, that was the first thing that he wanted to do. He had to know who his kids were going to be around and the kind of environment they would be in. Their safety was his only concern. Maybe Malia didn't feel the same way. Like he'd just told her, Faryn was there to stay, no matter how she felt about her.

***

"Okay ma," Ava said as she rolled her eyes and hung up the phone.

"What happened?" Kane asked her.

"She wants a family meeting to discuss all this bullshit between you and Landon," Ava replied.

"Ain't shit to discuss. I don't fuck with that nigga and that's that."

"Did you have anything to do with Malia trying to take Landon to court for custody of their kids?" Ava asked him.

"What? Hell no," he lied.

"I guess you wouldn't know anything about somebody calling his girlfriend's job either," Ava said while looking at him.

"I don't even know where she works," Kane maintained.

"Don't lie to me, Kane. You've done that enough," Ava warned.

"I'm not lying to you, baby. Me and Landon don't talk no more, so I don't know what's going on with them," Kane swore.

"Well, that seems to be what everybody thinks. Your mama was the attorney who drew up the papers," Ava pointed out.

"What does that mean Ava? My parents represent lots of people that I know. That doesn't mean that I sent them there. You know how popular their firm is. Hell, they have billboards, commercials, and everything else," Kane noted.

"Yeah, okay. You embarrassed me enough with that mess with Landon's bitch. Don't bring no more shit to my doorstep because I'm tired of stepping it in," Ava fussed.

"I fucked up before baby, but I swear I'm not doing anything wrong now. I love you too much to keeping doing dumb shit."

"And you better not even think about helping that bitch Malia do nothing. She fucked up her own household and she has to deal with it," Ava said.

"I know that baby," Kane agreed.

Malia was a stupid bitch. Kane had to practically beg his mother to represent her for free, only for her dumb ass to go withdraw the papers. His plan to piss Landon off had backfired, thanks to her. He didn't know what Landon had said to her, but she was scared to do anything now. Kane couldn't even depend on her to call Faryn's job to report her, so he did it himself. It was easier than he thought it would be. Malia told him Faryn's last name and he found everything else that he needed online. Faryn's job had a website with all the counselor's pictures, so he knew that he was calling the right place. He skipped calling her boss and called directly to the human resources office that was listed on the site.

He knew without a doubt that Landon could take care of her. He just wanted to piss them off, especially Landon. Kane was done running from him and Aiden. He was going back to work and he'd accompanied his wife to her mother's house the week before. He made sure he kept his gun on him, just in case the crazy came out of Aiden. He would have hated to shoot him in his own home, but he would have if it came down to it. Landon had too much to lose to entertain him, but Aiden just didn't give a fuck. Even Ms. Ella was throwing him shade, but that was nothing new. Things would be forgotten soon and back to the way it was before.

"I know my mama is gonna want me to go to her baby shower, but that's not happening. I'll send some gifts for her babies, but I'm not going to that shit," Ava fussed, shaking Kane away from his thoughts.

"Babies?" Kane questioned with a frown.

"Yes, your ex stripper bitch is having twins for my nephew. What kind of bullshit is that?" Ava asked sarcastically.

"How long are we gonna do this Ava? I've apologized a million times?" Kane sighed in disgust.

"Were you the one embarrassed in front of his entire family? Were you the one who learned that their spouse was paying for sex from a stripper who is now a part of the family?" Ava quizzed.

She hated that Faryn was having kids by her nephew. That meant that she was going to be around all the time. Ella's house was the chill spot for the family, but Ava didn't want to see her husband's ex-mistress there of all places.

"Man," Kane drawled.

"That's what the fuck I thought. As a matter of fact, we need to be hitting up Saks today anyway. You still owe me a few pairs of red bottoms for this shit," Ava said as she got up walked to their bedroom, slamming the door behind her.

Ava's spoiled, nagging ways was the reason why he'd started messing with Faryn to begin with. She wanted to be treated like a princess and Kane was guilty of letting her get away with it. Ava had a million-dollar wardrobe and had never worked a day in her life. She wore the pants in their home and Kane was dumb enough to let her do it. They went where she wanted to go and did whatever she wanted to do. Even sex was on her time and that wasn't very often. It was cool though. Kane was still a regular at JB's. He didn't even bother watching them dance anymore. He walked in, picked out a girl and went straight to the private room for a little private fun. What Ava lacked at home, the girls at JB's Gentlemen's Club more than made up for.

Chapter 28

"We can name the girl Latasha. A girl in my class has the same name," Lennox spoke up from the back seat.

"Yeah and she's ugly too. Faryn don't name her that. I don't want my sister named after that girl," Lance fussed.

"Your girlfriend is ugly too," Lennox replied.

"What girlfriend?" Faryn asked.

"You got a girl Lance?" Landon asked.

"He better not. He's only eleven," Faryn answered.

"That's old enough," Landon smirked.

"I don't have no girlfriend, but she likes me," Lance noted.

"Yeah and she's ugly," Lennox repeated.

"I know. That's why she's not my girlfriend," Lance said, making them laugh.

They were headed to Ella's house to discuss a few details for the baby shower. Landon and Faryn had already picked out the furniture and were preparing the room. They chose the nursery rhyme theme because it was cute and unisex. Faryn was now in her sixth month and her stomach was much bigger than the month before. It was becoming more obvious that she had more than one life growing inside of her. Maybe it was a good thing that she was no longer working because she was already starting to move slower. It was only a matter of time before she and Landon would have to occupy one of the spare bedrooms downstairs. She wouldn't be able to walk up the stairs soon.

"Ross is here," Lennox said excitedly when they pulled up.

"Yes," Lance replied.

Makena's son was out front with one of the neighbor's sons, throwing the football around.

"Y'all don't go nowhere and stay out of the street," Landon ordered when his sons got out of the car.

He noticed a lot more cars on the block than usual and people were going in at out of Leroy's house. When Landon walked into his grandmother's house, he was surprised to see Ella sitting there with her arms wrapped around his mother. Robin's eyes were red and swollen when she looked up at him.

"Leroy passed away at the hospital today Landon. He had another heart attack, but it was massive," Ella said sadly.

"Oh word. Where's Makena?" Landon asked.

"I'm right here lil brother. Come on so I can show y'all what I came up with," Makena replied as she walked from the back of the house.

"What are you eating?" Landon asked her.

"A turkey sandwich. You want one?" Makena asked.

"I do," Faryn spoke up.

"Okay, I'll make you one," Makena replied.

"Insensitive asses. I'm gonna get y'all two for this," Ella threatened as she looked at them through squinted eyes.

"What is she talking about?" Landon asked when they got to the kitchen.

"She wants somebody to feel sorry for Robin. I left all my fucks at home, so I have none to give." Makena shrugged.

"Who felt sorry for us when that nigga said he didn't he want us living under his roof? Thank God for grandma or we wouldn't have had nowhere else to go," Landon replied.

"Exactly," Makena co-signed.

She fixed Landon and Faryn a sandwich as she got their approval on some things for the baby shower. Faryn had never had a party or anything that put her in the spotlight, so she was excited. The ideas that Makena's friend had were nice, and she and Landon loved it.

"Y'all two should be ashamed of yourselves. Your mother is grieving and y'all couldn't even offer a kind word," Ella fussed when she walked into the kitchen.

"I said good riddance. That's as kind as it will get," Makena replied.

"I know she was an awful mother to y'all, but this is not the time to dwell on that," Ella noted.

"Grandma, I love you, but I have to keep it real. It's not fair for you to tell us how to feel or what we should do. You took us in and raised us after our own mama didn't want to anymore. She put the same man that she's mourning before her own kids and I'm not about to pretend to feel sorry for her. We watched from your front porch how she bonded with Leroy's grandkids like we weren't shit. She formed a relationship with them and lost her connection to us. I forgave her a long time ago, but I'll go to my grave remembering what she did," Landon said.

"I'm sorry baby. I know that what Robin did hurt y'all and I would never try to downplay that. As much as I want turn to my back on her for how she treated y'all, I just can't do it. She's still my child," Ella replied.

"We would never want you to do that grandma. The way that me and Landon feel have nothing to do with you. She's still your child and she's still our mother. The difference in the two is that she continued to be your daughter. She just decided that she didn't want to be our mother anymore. She made the choice, not us," Makena pointed out.

"I understand, and I won't say nothing else about it," Ella replied.

"Say nothing about what?" Aiden said when he walked into the kitchen.

"Nothing, but I'm happy that I have both of y'all here at the same time. Y'all know that I'm cooking a big dinner in two weeks for when my sister comes in town and everybody will be here," Ella said.

"We know ma. You do the same thing every time your sister comes in town. What's the point?" Aiden asked as he looked in the fridge.

"Bitch, shut up and listen. Ava and Kane will be here and I don't want no mess in my house. Y'all understand me?" Ella asked while looking at them both.

"We already had this talk when you called that family meeting. I'm good on that grandma. I don't have nothing to tell that dude," Landon assured her.

"I'm not making no promises," Aiden said as he popped open a beer.

"Don't fuck with me, Aiden. I haven't seen my sister in three years and you better not act a fool in front of her. I'll lose my religion in here on your ass," Ella threatened.

"Man, you ain't been to church in years. You lost your religion a long time ago," Aiden said, making everybody laugh.

Landon and Faryn stayed by Ella's house for a while longer before going back to their own. Faryn didn't want to be anywhere near the man that she now knew as Kane, so she made up her mind to skip the family gathering. She had made plans to hang out with her sister and Harley for the day, while Landon and the kids went over there. Landon was cool with it and he promised her that he wouldn't be there long either.

***

Landon enjoyed seeing his grandmother smiling and happy all throughout the day. Her sister had arrived from New York and a lot of other family members were there to see her as well. Ella's house was the biggest, so it made sense for everyone to go there. Just like always, she'd prepared a huge Thanksgiving like feast to welcome her guests. Everyone seemed to be enjoying themselves and that's what Ella wanted. Landon was standing outside with Aiden and Raheem watching his sons play football and listening to what Aiden was saying.

"Man, that shit is crazy. I probably would have been dead if I was in there. It had to be that nigga that you had to knock out that one time," Aiden said, referring to Jo-Jo.

He had been using Faryn's apartment to entertain his female companions since the lease was already paid up. He tried to bring somebody there about two that morning, only to discover that the door had been kicked in. There was nothing for anyone to take, but that wasn't the point. Somebody obviously thought that Faryn was still living there. Needless to say, that was his last time going there.

"That's the only person that I can think of too. That nigga stupid as fuck if he thought I was leaving my girl in there with him knowing where she lived," Landon replied.

"Exactly, but I need to see who he is. He seems like he might be a problem one day," Aiden said.

"Man, fuck that dude," Landon said, waving him off.

"I'm just saying nephew. You put him to sleep temporarily. I'm trying to give him some permanent rest. You can't put nothing pass these niggas no more," Aiden replied.

"I don't put nothing pass nobody, but that nigga don't scare me," Landon said, right as Kane and Ava pulled up.

"Look at this lil bitch. Nigga wife got a bigger dick than he do." Aiden frowned when he saw Kane opening the car door for Ava to get out.

"Chill out bruh. I don't need to hear grandma's mouth," Raheem said.

Ava's daughter got out of the car and ran to the other kids who were outside playing, while her parents headed inside the house.

"Hey y'all," Ava spoke.

"What's up Raheem?" Kane said, sounding like a lil hoe.

He made it a point to let Landon and Aiden know that he wasn't speaking to them, as if they gave a fuck. He was petty just like a lot of females.

"Lil pussy ass!" Aiden barked loudly.

"Don't start Aiden. We didn't come here for all that," Ava replied.

"You better make that nigga strap up Ava. Them hoes in the project gon' give his ass some shit that he can't get rid of," Aiden warned.

"Fuck you, Aiden, bruh. You don't have room to talk about nobody catching nothing," Kane said angrily.

He was tired of Aiden thinking that he was punking him, especially in front of his wife. Landon had to grab Aiden before he could make it up the stairs and get to Kane.

"Calm down man. You already know grandma ain't feeling that shit today. Let his ass make it," Landon said.

"Fuck that nigga. Lil bitch, I see your tampon string hanging out your pussy," Aiden taunted, as Kane and Ava walked into the house.

Kane was furious and he couldn't even hide it. Ava gave him a look that could kill, but he wasn't in the mood for her shit either. He already knew that she was pissed about what her brother said about him being with other women. Kane loved his wife, but he was ready to put a bullet in her twin's head. There was only so much that a man could take before he snapped.

Once he got Aiden calm, Landon was ready to go. He'd stayed longer than he thought he would and he was tired. He went into the house to let his sister and grandma know that he was about to leave. Of course, leaving was harder than he thought it would be. Everybody kept stopping him to talk and, before he knew it, another hour had passed. Faryn and her sister had gone out to eat with Harley and Akira was going to bring her home afterwards. Landon was happy that Faryn at least had one family member to spend time with and she seemed to be just as excited.

"Here Landon," Makena said, handing him a bag with some containers inside.

"What's this?" he asked.

"Faryn told me to fix her some food," Makena replied.

"Her greedy ass. She's out eating right now," Landon laughed.

"How far along is she?" a familiar voice asked.

Landon looked over and saw that his mother had occupied the chair right next to his at the table.

"Six months," he replied flatly.

"Wow. Twins, huh?" Robin asked.

"Yep," Landon answered.

"That'll make five grandkids for me once they arrive. I can't wait to meet them." Robin smiled.

"Alright sis. I'm about to get going," Landon said while standing to his feet.

"Okay, let me walk you out," Makena offered.

She and Landon maneuvered through the crowd in the living room and made their way to the porch.

"The fuck was that about? Since when does she give a fuck about what's going on with us? Hell, I got two kids that barely know her, but she can't wait to meet the ones that's not even here yet," Landon ranted.

"That's what's it's all about lil brother," Makena said as she pointed across the street to Leroy's house.

"Oh shit. I didn't even pay attention to that," Landon said as he and Makena laughed.

There was a huge for sale sign outside of the house that he didn't even notice before.

"Ole Leroy was barely in the ground before his kids called the realtor. They let mommy dearest know just how much clout the live-in girlfriend has. She can't say shit and she can't get shit," Makena chuckled.

"Oh okay. That's why she's so full of conversation now, but I ain't got nothing for her. The same people that she put us down for is fucking over her."

"Karma has no menu. You get served what you deserve." Makena shrugged.

"And that's some real shit," Landon said as he called his boys and walked to his truck.

He took another look at the for-sale sign in front of the house and shook his head. He remembered how he and Makena would be sitting on the porch and their mother would wave to them as if they were just her neighbors and not her own kids. She never uttered a word, but she was full of conversation now. Too bad Landon had none to give. The same family that she put before her own had come back and kicked her in the ass. Landon didn't wish bad on anyone, but Robin asked for it.

The same with Malia. She was getting her karma too, for how she had abandoned her family. Now, she was in her feelings because Landon was building a life with Faryn. He tried to do the right thing and get them to meet face to face, but Malia declined. She claimed that she didn't want to meet the woman who was trying to replace her. She swore that Faryn was trying to turn her kids against her, but that was untrue. It was because of Faryn that Lance was even going around her again. She might not have had her office anymore, but she still acted as his counselor. Lance had made tremendous progress and Malia couldn't take credit for any of it.

Chapter 29

"Harley said that it's crowded, but they put their names on the list to be seated," Faryn said as she and Landon sat in the traffic that they were stuck in.

She and Landon were meeting Harley and Kyron for dinner and they were running late. Faryn had just entered her seventh month of pregnancy and she was seeing her doctor every week now. As soon as she left her appointment that afternoon, she went home and went straight to sleep. She was the reason that they were late, but nobody cared. Faryn felt like she was carrying around fifty extra pounds of belly and that wasn't easy to do. She couldn't get comfortable for nothing and heartburn had quickly become the enemy. Her baby shower was coming up that following weekend and she was feeling like she didn't even want to go. Aiden and Raheem helped Landon get the babies room together, and there was nothing left for them to do but wait.

"I don't know where all this damn traffic is coming from. It's after work hours," Landon complained.

"I hope they get seated before we get there. I'm hungry," Faryn whined.

"Always," Landon laughed as he reached over and rubbed her stomach.

Faryn's doctors were predicting the babies to be around five or six pounds each, which was ideal for twins. One baby was already bigger than the other, but that was normal too.

"My stomach feels like it's about to pop. I couldn't see it at first, but it looks like I'm carrying two babies now."

"Girl, I told you that I was backed up. Nigga shot a double load up in your ass," Landon laughed as they finally got off the bridge.

It took about ten more minutes before they were pulling up to the parking lot of the restaurant where they were meeting up at. The timing was perfect because Harley had just sent her a text and told her that they had been seated. Faryn and Landon had never eaten there before, but Harley swore that the food was some of the best that New Orleans had to offer.

"God Faryn, it looks like your stomach is twice as big as it was two weeks ago," Harley said as her mouth hung open in shock.

She had just hung out with Faryn and her sister two weeks before, while Landon attended his family gathering.

"Girl, I know and it feels like it too," Faryn said as she gave Harley and Kyron a hug.

Landon greeted them both before helping Faryn sit down and get comfortable. They picked up their menus and looked over them to see what they wanted to eat. As usual, Faryn didn't know what she wanted, so Landon ordered a few different items to satisfy her cravings.

"I know your greedy ass ain't about to eat all that food," Harley laughed.

"Half now and half later," Landon replied.

"Yep," Faryn agreed with a chuckle.

"When's the last time you talked to your boy Jo-Jo, Kyron?" Landon asked him.

"I haven't talked to that nigga in a minute, but he called me out the blue like two weeks ago asking me all kinds of questions. The shit seemed shady, so I was vague with my answers," Kyron replied.

"I didn't know that he called you," Harley said while looking at her husband.

"I thought I told you, but it wasn't important," Kyron replied.

"What did he want?" Harley asked.

"He was saying that he came back there to the apartments looking for me, but we were already gone by then," Kyron answered.

"Oh okay, so it was him that kicked in the door to Faryn's old apartment," Landon noted.

"What! When?" Harley asked in shock.

"That was about two weeks ago. My uncle went there and found the door kicked in. I told Faryn to go turn in the keys and just be done with it. My uncle wasn't going back there anyway," Landon said.

"But, he's in jail now," Harley said.

"How do you know?' Faryn asked.

"Me and Kyron saw one of his brothers in the mall and he told us. His own brother said that he was shady. He said that Jo-Jo had supposedly messed with one of their friends' seventeen-year-old daughter. Had the lil girl thinking they were in a relationship and everything," Harley informed them.

"I told you, baby. That nigga is a fucking pedophile." Landon frowned.

"His brother said that the dude was looking for Jo-Jo to kill him for messing with his daughter," Kyron said, shaking his head.

"That was your second strike. I swear on our unborn kids, you better not ever bring nobody to my house as long as you live," Harley fumed.

"We already discussed this Harley. Nobody is coming to our house," Kyron promised.

Once the food came, they all fell into a comfortable silence as they ate. Harley was on point with what she said because everything was good. Faryn sampled everything on her plate as well as Landon's and she wasn't disappointed.

"Damn man, we gotta come through here more often. This shit was good," Landon said as he finished the last of his meal.

"I know. I need some containers to take the rest of my food home," Faryn replied as she rubbed her chest.

"Heartburn?" Landon asked her.

"Yep, just like always," Faryn replied.

"Let me see if they have ginger ale," Landon said as he looked around for the waitress.

"Order it, I have to go to the bathroom," Faryn said as she stood to her feet.

"Let me come with you, friend. It's crowded as hell over there," Harley said as she got up and followed behind her.

The bathroom was on the other side of the restaurant near the take-out area. Everybody in New Orleans must have been hungry because the entire area was filled. Thankfully, they were nice enough to see Faryn's huge belly and move out of her way. Harley followed her into the bathroom and waited until she was done.

"Girl, these babies be on my bladder something serious," Faryn complained.

"You look so cute Faryn. I'm so happy for you, friend." Harley smiled.

"Thanks girl, I'm happy too. I just gotta get over the feeling that something bad is going to happen," Faryn admitted.

"Why do you think that something bad is going to happen?" Harley asked.

"Because it always does. Landon is the best thing that ever happened to me, but I don't want him to regret being with me. I feel like I'm bringing all my drama into his life."

"No, you're not Faryn. You had no idea of knowing that his auntie's husband and Redd were the same person. You said yourself that you didn't know his name or nothing else about him," Harley reminded her.

"That's true, but it still feels weird being around his family now that they know. His grandmother and sister are okay, but his auntie is always giving me the side eye," Faryn replied.

"Fuck that bitch, Faryn. That nigga is just a dog. If it wasn't you, it would have been somebody else."

"That's true," Faryn agreed as they walked out of the bathroom.

She and Harley were deep in conversation when Faryn felt someone tap her shoulder. When she turned around to see who it was, she almost lost her balance and fell from shock. Years had passed, but Faryn would know that face anywhere. She loved him too much to forget.

"Roman?" Faryn asked in a whisper.

He had the phone up to his ear, but he nodded his head with a huge smile covering his face.

"Girl, you better come here and give me a hug. Chad, bring your ass in here right now!" he yelled as he picked Faryn up, big belly and all, and planted kisses all over her face.

"Ahhhh!" Faryn screamed excitedly, making everybody in the restaurant look over to see what was going on.

"The fuck!" Landon yelled as he looked across the crowded room and saw what was going on.

Faryn's scream was like a siren, making him spring into action. He jumped up from his seat and almost knocked the waitress down, as she sat the ginger ale on their table. He felt his anger rising to new heights as he observed the man who his ex-wife had left him for, hugging and fawning over the woman that he was in love with now. His luck couldn't have been that fucked up to have the same nigga take his woman twice. Landon felt like he was moving in slow motion as he made his way over to see what was up. His attention was diverted for a minute when he saw Malia coming from the back of the restaurant and rushing over to them as well.

"Nigga, you got me fucked up!" Malia yelled as she pushed Roman, making him stumble and almost fall with Faryn in his arms.

She grabbed Faryn's hair from the back and Landon couldn't get to them fast enough. He hated to do it, but he was about to knock Malia the fuck out. He was just thankful that his sons weren't there to witness it. As soon as he got close enough, Landon gripped the collar of Malia's shirt, but Kyron grabbed him up into a bear hug before he had a chance to strike. He didn't even know that Kyron was following him, but he was pissed that he did.

"Bitch! Don't put your muthafucking hands on my friend!" Harley yelled as she grabbed Malia's thin body and slung her to the ground.

Malia was never much of a fighter, but she jumped up and starting swinging on Harley anyway. She wasn't scary, and she wasn't about to act like she was. She couldn't believe what was happening and on her off day at that. She only went to her job to get her mother something to eat, when she saw Roman and Faryn embracing. The smile that covered his face was like nothing that Malia had ever seen. He looked genuinely happy and that had her seeing red. Not only had that bitch taken her husband, but she was trying to take her man too. Malia didn't think before she reacted, which was why she was getting her ass kissed by Faryn's friend now.

"The fuck is going on in here?" Chad asked when he walked in and saw the chaos that was taking place.

People were leaving the restaurant without their food and, now, he knew why. He saw some dude holding Malia's ex-husband back, while some girl was beating Malia's ass. Roman was standing there shielding a pregnant woman, but Chad couldn't see her face.

"Baby, calm down. I don't need to be bailing you out of jail," Kyron said as he pulled Harley off the woman that he'd never seen before.

Since Landon was no longer being held back, he rushed over to Faryn and pulled her away from Roman. He didn't know what was going on, but he was damn sure about to find out.

"Fuck you, Roman! Your dog ass lied and said you were out of town!" Malia screamed as she used her sleeve to wipe the blood from her mouth.

She had just called Roman a few minutes before she got to the restaurant and he said that he was out of town handling business for a few days. Malia heard all the noise in the background, but she would have never guessed that he was at her job. Roman didn't know where she worked, so he would have been busted had she been at work that day anyway.

"This bitch here," Chad said as he looked at her and scowled.

"Fuck you too, Chad! Nigga made me get rid of our baby, only to get the next bitch pregnant. And I hope you don't think that's your baby, Roman. That bitch ain't nothing but a prostitute!" Malia shouted.

"Bitch! You better not ever fix your lips to say some shit like that about my little sister again!" Roman gritted as he walked up on her. Chad stopped him from getting too close because he knew how Roman's temper was.

"Sister!" Landon yelled as he looked at Roman in confusion. Malia looked confused as well because she didn't know that he had any other family besides Chad.

"Faryn?" Chad questioned once he got a good look at her.

Faryn had tears falling from her eyes as she moved away from Landon and went to give Chad a hug.

"I missed y'all so much," Faryn sobbed.

"We missed you too, baby. When did this happen?" Chad smiled as he held Faryn close and rubbed her swollen belly.

"Seven months ago," Faryn chuckled.

"Man, I'm so damn happy to see my baby," Roman said as he walked over and kissed her cheek.

Faryn always did have a special place in his heart, but the circumstances of how they were raised was the problem. Being born to a drug-addicted mother was hard on them all. Roman and Chad tried their best to keep up with their sisters, but it was hard. They were young boys out there trying to make money and they succeeded for a while. Roman used to bring his sisters money all the time, until their mother started stealing it. When that didn't work, he started buying them what they needed, but Alicia used to sell everything. It got so bad that Roman would have to meet his sisters at the gas station close to their house and let them change into their new clothes in the bathroom. Chad always made sure to take them out to eat before they went back home, and that worked out fine for a while.

Then, just like always, their good thing came to an end. Both brothers went to jail, and their sisters had to fend for themselves once again. Akira was the oldest, so she left soon after that. She found herself a sugar daddy and moved in with him. She kept up with Faryn for a while, but that didn't last very long. When their mother died, Roman got released from jail a few days later. The first thing he did was go get Faryn and move her in with him and the girl that he was living with. Chad got released soon after and they were back on their grind in no time at all.

The long arm of the law reached out and touched them a few years later and both brothers were locked up once again. When Roman called one day to check on his sister, his ex informed him that she had moved out and she didn't know where. He didn't have a number or an address and he didn't know where to look once he was released. The only two women to ever hold a place in his heart and he didn't even know how to find them.

"Out! Everybody get out before I call the police. The place is closed for the night!" the owner, Melba, came out and yelled, breaking up the impromptu family reunion.

She gave Malia a wet rag for her face and ushered her back into the kitchen. Malia was so embarrassed for her employer to see her behaving that way, and she knew that Cora was going to hear all about it.

Two men came from the back and started clearing out the restaurant. They never did pay for their food, but Harley went to grab her and Faryn's purses before they all walked outside. Landon looked as confused as ever and he wasn't the only one. Roman and Chad were both wondering why their baby sister was with Malia's ex. They all walked outside of the restaurant, hoping to get answers to the questions that lingered between them.

Chapter 30

"I'm confused as fuck," Landon said as soon as they walked outside.

"I am too, but what's up bruh? We never got a chance to speak when we were inside," Roman said as he shook Landon's hand and watched as Chad did the same.

"I told you that I had two brothers and a sister that I hadn't seen in a while," Faryn replied.

"Yeah, but... damn," Landon said as he tried to process everything that was going on.

"Hold up!" Chad said as he looked back and forth between the two of them.

"What?" Faryn questioned.

"Y'all are together?" he asked as he looked on in shock.

"Yes, this is Landon, my boyfriend and the father of my kids," Faryn said proudly.

"We know who he is. We've met before," Chad replied.

"Wait, you said kids. You have other children?" Roman asked.

"No, I'm having twins," Faryn replied.

"Damn. It looks like it too," Chad observed.

"How do y'all know each other?" Faryn questioned.

"Um... it's complicated," Roman said, not wanting to put Landon's business out there like that.

"Nah man, it's cool. She already knows everything." Landon shrugged.

"Obviously not," Faryn replied.

"Roman is the man that Malia was living with when she left," Landon said.

"What! That's your girlfriend?" Faryn asked her brother in shock.

"Hell no! That bitch is crazy!" Chad yelled.

"She was, but that's a wrap. Me and relationships are a no go," Roman replied.

"Some things never change." Faryn smiled, knowing her brother all too well.

"Man, we gotta hook up and talk Faryn. You just don't know how much I missed you and Akira. Shit was all fucked up when we got out of jail that last time," Roman admitted.

"I've been in contact with Akira too. We need to have a dinner date, so we can talk. I have so much to tell y'all. I'm just so happy," Faryn said as she hugged her brothers again.

"I'm scared to let your lil ass go. I feel like it might be a few more years before I see you again," Chad said.

"That shit ain't happening no more, if I can help it. I want your number, address, email address, social security number, and everything else," Roman said, making her laugh.

"Where do you live Faryn?" Chad asked.

"With my man," Faryn said, making Landon smile at her not calling him her boyfriend like always.

"This is some weird shit right here. What are the odds of this happening like this?" Roman said, shaking his head.

"You think this is crazy, Akira's boyfriend is his stepdaddy," Faryn laughed while pointing at Landon.

"Real shit?" Chad asked in surprise.

"Yep, that's how we reunited. I told you, we have a lot to talk about," Faryn said.

"Are you free tomorrow? Maybe we can go grab something to eat and catch up," Roman suggested.

"Are you okay with that baby?" Faryn asked while looking at Landon.

"Yeah, I'm cool with it," Landon replied.

It was weird how Faryn reunited with her brothers. It was even crazier who her brothers turned out to be. If he wasn't in the middle of the situation, he would have found it hard to believe. He thought that Malia leaving was the worst thing that could have happened to him and his sons. It turned out to be a blessing instead. Her leaving started a chain of events that seemed to work out in his favor.

"My baby shower is next weekend. I hope y'all can make it. I really want y'all to come," Faryn said as she and her brothers exchanged numbers.

"We'll be there, no doubt about it," Roman assured her.

He and Chad just couldn't stop hugging her, and Landon thought it was sweet. He was thankful for his grandmother keeping him and Makena together because he couldn't imagine them being apart for years like Faryn and her siblings.

"I'm so rude y'all, I'm so sorry. Roman, Chad, this my best friend Harley and her husband, Kyron. Until I met Landon, they took the place of being my family." Faryn smiled as she introduced them.

She forgot all about Kyron and Harley standing there, but they didn't mind. They were curious as to who the two men were as well, so they stayed around to find out.

"I owe y'all one. Especially you, lil mama. Malia needed that beat down in the worst way," Chad said as he shook their hands.

"Don't even mention it. My friend know I got her," Harley replied.

"I know y'all gotta go, but I'm calling you tonight," Roman said as he looked at Faryn.

"Where are y'all parked?" Faryn asked.

"Right there," Roman said as he pointed to Chad's car.

"I'll be right back baby," Faryn said as she handed Landon her purse and gave him a kiss.

Kyron and Harley decided to leave, so Landon stood by his truck and waited for Faryn to say her goodbyes to her brothers.

"You got a damn good nigga right there Faryn," Chad acknowledged while nodding his head towards Landon.

"I know," Faryn agreed with a smile.

"How did you hook up with him?" Roman asked.

"I was his son's counselor," Faryn replied.

"You're a counselor?" Chad asked.

"Well, I'm a behavioral specialist and he was one of my clients," Faryn answered.

"Damn baby girl, I'm so proud of you." Roman smiled.

"While that dumb bitch is running around here chasing dick, her son had to see a damn counselor," Chad fumed.

"Yeah and it was all because of her and how she left. They're so sweet though. Y'all will meet them at the baby shower." Faryn smiled.

"We met them already. That crazy bitch lived with me for over a year," Roman noted.

"That's my lil dudes." Chad smiled when he thought of Malia's sons.

"Listen, I don't want to keep Landon waiting, but y'all call me tonight. We can discuss where we're going to meet up tomorrow," Faryn said.

"Alright baby girl. We love you and always remember that," Roman said as he and Chad gave her a final hug.

"I love y'all too." Faryn smiled happily before walking away.

"And don't tell Akira nothing! Let her be surprised!" Chad yelled after her.

"Okay!" Faryn yelled back.

"You good?" Landon asked as he helped her into the truck.

"Better than ever." Faryn smiled.

"Cool," he replied as he started the truck up and drove away.

"And don't worry, I didn't tell them where we live. I'll meet them at the restaurant tomorrow. I know that it'll probably be weird having them come there."

"I don't have a problem with your brothers, Faryn. We've met several times before and they were always cool. Malia was responsible for what happened in our marriage. I don't place the blame on nobody else," Landon assured her.

"I hope you don't regret being with me, Landon," Faryn said out of the blue.

"Where did that come from?" he asked as he looked over at her.

"I just feel like I brought all my drama into your peaceful life. First it was the situation with Jo-Jo, then Redd, and now this," Faryn replied.

"Nothing that happened is your fault Faryn. Our paths crossed in a weird way, but that's life. I'll never regret something that makes me happy," Landon said while kissing her hand.

"I love you so much. I swear, I'm gonna marry you one day." Faryn smiled.

"I love you too baby and yeah, you are," Landon replied as they headed home.

***

Malia's head was pounding when she pulled up to her mother's house. She popped a few aspirins and swallowed them dry. She was dreading going into the house, but she couldn't sit in her car all night. After taking a deep breath, Malia slowly got out of the car and made her way inside. She barely had a chance to close the door before Cora started going in on her.

"You got to be one dumb bitch to get fired on your day off," Cora fussed while shaking her head in pity.

"I'm not fired," Malia snapped angrily.

"You're dumber than I thought if you think Melba is letting you come back after that shit. Your last check is being prepared as we speak."

"I found that job and I can find another one," Malia flippantly replied.

"I don't understand you, Malia. Of the three of y'all, you were the only one who had your head on straight. When your sisters were sneaking out to go be with boys, you stayed home and kept your head in the books. You were supposed to go to college and make something of yourself," Cora noted.

Cora had never said it out loud, but Malia was always her favorite. She never gave her mother any trouble and she was a homebody for a long time. When she and Landon got together, Cora didn't have a problem with her youngest daughter having a boyfriend. She was shocked when Malia got pregnant, but Landon did the right thing. He moved her into her own apartment and gave her his last name. They had a perfect, yet simple life, but Malia wasn't satisfied. She always felt like she had missed out on something, which was why she was so drawn to Roman. She was naïve and couldn't keep up with the life that Roman lived. He ran circles around her and left her with a broken heart soon after.

"Yeah, well things change and so do people," Malia replied, shaking Cora from her thoughts.

"How many ways does this man have to tell you that it's over Malia? He's cheated, beat on you, and even left you in an empty apartment to fend for yourself. What is it going to take?"

"Why do you assume that everything is about Roman?" Malia asked.

"Don't try to play me for a fool Malia. Melba heard you saying his name. It's over Malia. He doesn't want you and he's made that clear. Stop making a fool of yourself over this man. It's bad enough that you left your family to be with him. Focus on you for a change. Enroll in school and get your degree," Cora said, as her daughter burst into tears.

Cora wanted to cry with her, but she just pulled her into a hug and held her instead. Malia was going from one extreme to the next and she felt like she was losing her mind.

"I don't know what's wrong with me," Malia cried, as her mother rocked her back and forth.

"Nothing is wrong with you, Malia. You were selfish, and you made some poor decisions. You're human and you're not perfect."

"Everybody hates me, and I can't even blame them. My kids hate me and now Landon hates me too," Malia sobbed.

Sadly, Malia was used to Roman bracing up to her or trying to hit her. Her feelings were truly hurt when Landon grabbed her like he wanted to do the same. Admittedly, she was wrong for how she grabbed Faryn. She had no way of knowing that the other woman was Roman's sister. If she never knew it before, it was made clear that day, Landon had no love for her anymore. It was her own fault and she couldn't say that she blamed him.

"Landon doesn't hate you, but he's moved on. You left him unexpectedly and moved in with another man. What did you expect him to do? You can't create a storm and get mad when it rains," Cora said.

"I just wish I could start all over and do things right this time. I've made a mess of my life and I don't know how to fix it," Malia admitted.

"The first thing you need to do is learn to be by yourself Malia. For some reason, you and your sisters feel like y'all need a man. I don't know where y'all get that shit from. Just take some time and learn to love you. Spend more time with your boys and find out what you wanna do with your life," Cora suggested.

"I'm sorry ma. I'm sorry for everything that I've put you through since Landon and I split up. I'm sorry for just being a stupid bitch," Malia said, making her mother laugh.

"No apology needed. All kids go through a rebellious phase. You just waited until you were a grown ass woman to go through yours," Cora said, making Malia smile this time.

"Medical coding and billing. That's what I was supposed to go to school for before and that's what I'm going to do," Malia said, feeling a little better.

"That's what I like to hear. And listen, I know this is off the subject, but it needs to be said."

"I'm listening," Malia replied.

"Landon's girlfriend is not the enemy. You're gonna have to stop being childish and officially meet her one of these days."

"Ma-" Malia started before Cora cut her off.

"Malia, this is a woman who is around your kids more than you are. She's not going anywhere and that's obvious. Now, I'm not saying that you should do it today or even tomorrow, but you really need to think about it. Honestly, it shouldn't have taken you this long."

Once again, her mother was right, even if she didn't want to admit it. As crazy as it sounded, Malia wasn't ready for that just yet.

"Let me just take things one step at a time for now. Hopefully, everything else will fall into place," Malia replied.

"Okay, no pressure over here. I just thought I'd mention it," Cora said.

"Sorry that I didn't get your food," Malia apologized.

"Sorry my ass. Get your keys and let's go. We're gonna make a run for the border or something. I'm starving," Cora said, making her daughter giggle.

Malia felt better than she had in a long time. She was always smiling, but she was miserable inside. As much as it pained her to admit it, her relationship with Roman was over a long time ago. She was embarrassed that she'd left her family for him, so she tried her best to make it work. It was like she had a point to prove to everyone who told her that she had made a mistake. She tried to put on a brave front, knowing that she cried herself to sleep most nights. That part of her life was over with and she vowed to make better decisions from that day forward. From now on, it was all about her and her boys. She had to strengthen her bond with them before she did anything else. As far as she was concerned, that day was the first day of the rest of her life and she planned to make the best of it.

Chapter 31

"I thought Makena agreed to do something small. There's over sixty people here and I don't even know most of them," Faryn whispered to Landon as they sat at the front of the hall at their baby shower.

They had just arrived about twenty minutes prior and there were lots of people already in attendance. Three tables were filled with gifts and two clear boxes were filled with cards. Faryn thought Landon went too far when he rented a small moving truck to load up all the gifts, but she was happy that he did. They would have been making multiple trips to unload everything if he hadn't.

"I don't recognize some of them either," Landon replied as he looked around.

He saw a few of his co-workers that he invited and some of his family members. Harley, her cousin Patrice, and Kyron were there as well, but he didn't recognize some of the others. He assumed that it was Makena's friends, but he wasn't too sure.

"I'm trying to be cordial and not snap, but I can't make no promises," Makena said when she walked over to them.

"What's wrong?" Faryn asked.

"Girl, my mama is the problem. Walking around here like she went half on some shit. Then, she had the nerve to invite some of her friends. She better be happy that they came with gifts. I was escorting all of their asses out if they didn't," Makena fussed.

"She got the entire game fucked up if she thinks she got it like that. No need to try to be a mother now. We're grown as fuck," Landon replied.

"Exactly. I just told grandma to go make her ass sit down before I be putting her out. I'm not for the bullshit today," Makena said.

"What time do we eat?" Faryn asked.

"Whenever you want to honey. I already told the servers to feed y'all first," Makena replied.

"I'm waiting for my brothers and sister to come," Faryn said as she kept looking towards the front door.

She gasped a little when she saw Kane and Ava walk in instead. Ava had two gift bags in her hands that Lennox and Lance took from her. They were at the door accepting gifts from the guests and sitting them on the gift tables.

"That was my grandmother's doing too," Makena said as she watched them find a table close to the back of the room and sit down.

"Don't worry about them baby. That nigga better not even look at you wrong. And that goes for Ava too," Landon gritted.

"That bitch better sit there and shut up. I got my Nike's on for a reason," Makena said while showing them her colorful shoes.

"Oh God. I hope it won't be that kind of event," Faryn groaned.

"It won't be boo. I'm just prepared for whatever. And I reserved a table close to you for your brothers and sister," Makena said while pointing to a table that Faryn had never noticed.

"Aww, thanks Makena." Faryn smiled.

"There they go," Landon said while pointing at the front door.

Faryn smiled when she saw Roman, Chad, and Akira walking in together with their hands full of gifts. Never in a million years would she have imagined that she would once again be in the same room with her brothers and sister. When they went out to dinner the weekend before, Akira just assumed it would be her and Faryn. When Chad and Roman walked into the restaurant, she fell out of her chair trying to get to them. It was like the best day of their lives, just to be sitting down having dinner as a family. Chad and Roman kept apologizing for not being what their sisters needed them to be, but there were no hard feelings. They were the oldest and they tried their best. They kept up with each more than anything, but the same couldn't be said for their younger siblings.

"I guess they'll come over here whenever Lance and Lennox let them go," Faryn laughed.

They'd already taken all the gifts from them, but they were standing there talking them to death. The boys were shocked to find out that Chad and Roman were Faryn's brothers. Makena was also shocked when she found out that the man that her brother's wife had left him for was his new girlfriend's brother. She made Landon and Faryn tell her the story about four times before she finally got it. It sounded like a modern-day soap opera, but it was their life.

"What's up y'all?" Landon smiled as he and Faryn got up to greet her brothers and sister when they finally made their way over.

"This is so beautiful. Who put everything together?" Akira asked.

"That would be me," Makena spoke up.

Akira had heard all about Makena from Clarence and Faryn, but they had never met.

"Y'all, this is my sister, Makena," Landon said as he introduced everyone.

"It's nice to meet everybody. I've heard a lot about y'all already. I reserved this table for y'all to sit right next to Faryn. I'll have them to start serving the food in a minute," Makena said before she walked off.

Faryn was happy that Robin had finally sat down and so was Makena. The food was served, and Makena and two of her friends ran the shower and played a bunch of games. As usual, Ella was the life of the party. She was all over the place and played every game until she won a prize. Ava and Kane stayed in their little corner and didn't move or say much of anything to anyone. When it came time to open the gifts, Ella, Makena, and Akira had to help Faryn because Landon had disappeared. She was pissed that he wasn't there to see what they had gotten for the babies and she couldn't wait to curse his ass out.

"What's wrong Faryn?" Makena asked when she saw the shift in her demeanor.

"Where is your brother?" Faryn questioned.

"Forget him girl. He's probably somewhere around here with Aiden and Raheem," Makena said, waving her off.

"I know the fuck he's not!" Faryn yelled angrily.

Her brothers and some of the other men were carrying gifts to the U-Haul truck, while the father of her kids was off somewhere bullshitting with his family. She was livid and the smirk that was on Makena's face wasn't helping. Even Landon's sons were helping while he was nowhere around.

"Don't worry about that sis. You're almost finished opening your gifts," Akira spoke up.

Faryn had started opening and reading the cards when all the gifts were opened and put away. Makena had a bag that she put all the cash and gift cards in and she guarded it with her life. Once that was all done, Faryn had steam coming from her ears. Landon walked in with his uncle and cousin like he hadn't done anything wrong.

"We got a lot of stuff to put away when we get home," he said while kissing Faryn on the cheek.

"Don't kiss me and don't say shit to me," Faryn snapped angrily.

"What did I do?" Landon smirked.

"I don't find shit funny Landon. I was in here opening gifts for our kids while you were outside bullshitting with your people. I'm pissed the fuck off!" Faryn snapped.

"I love you, baby," Landon said as he kept kissing her face.

"Stop trying to make me laugh Landon. I'm mad and I don't want to smile. I felt like a single mother just now," Faryn pouted.

"Girl, stop being so damn dramatic," Landon said as he called his sons over.

They were both smiling from ear to ear as they stood in front of her and grabbed both of her hands until she stood up.

"Wait! Lennox. Lance. What are y'all doing?" Faryn panicked as they walked her to the middle of the floor.

The DJ started playing *All my life* by K-Ci and JoJo, making Faryn smile. That was her ringtone for Landon and she always told him that the words conveyed exactly how she felt about him. Faryn thought they were pulling her to the middle of the floor to dance like they sometimes did at home, but they had her confused when they just stood there. When Landon walked up, they left Faryn standing there and went to stand next to him. Faryn was about to ask what was up until she saw the three of them drop down on one knee. Faryn's hand went up to her mouth as the entire place erupted in cheers. Everyone had their phones out recording, as Landon opened the small velvet box and revealed the biggest diamond ring that Faryn had ever seen. Lance and Lennox opened a box of their own that held a diamond necklace with the matching earrings.

"I don't need to make a long speech because you already know what it is. I love you with everything in me and I would be honored if you would be my wife. Will you marry me, baby?" Landon asked with a smile.

"Us dad, will she marry us," Lennox corrected.

"Yes!" Faryn yelled as tears clouded her vision. "I'll marry you. All of you."

"I guess you forgive me now, huh?" Landon asked as he stood up and put the ring on her finger.

"As big as this rock is, I'll never get mad at you again," Faryn said as she planted a sloppy kiss on his lips.

"We got you something too, Faryn," Lance said as he and Lennox presented her with their gifts.

"Y'all are so sweet. I love them," Faryn said as she hugged and kissed them too.

"Okay, so since the babies have been showered with gifts, it's mama's turn now!" Makena yelled over the mic.

"What is she talking about?" Faryn asked Landon.

"Faryn, come on outside boo. Landon has a little something for you," Makena said, answering her question.

Faryn looked at him and smiled, as Landon grabbed her hand and walked her outside. Ava and Kane were already out there seemingly in a heated argument, but they played it off once everyone started exiting the building.

"What am I looking for? Where is my gift?" Faryn questioned.

Her question was answered when a brand-new silver Mercedes GLS 550 pulled up with a huge pink and blue bow on top of it.

"You might not be pushing, but your fiancé got you a push present!" Makena yelled excitedly.

"I'm fucking you up Aiden. I told you to stand out here and watch the truck. Nobody told your dumb ass to drive it," Landon argued.

"Nigga, please. You got me out here guarding a damn near hundred-thousand-dollar whip and you didn't think I was gon' push that bitch," Aiden laughed.

"And you ain't no better Raheem," Landon fussed when his cousin exited the passenger's side.

"Calm down bruh. We only went around the corner," Raheem replied.

"Oh, my God, baby! I love it!" Faryn yelled as she rushed over to her new truck. She moved slow every other day, but she was damn near running to her present.

"Slow down Faryn," Landon chastised.

The baby shower was over, but a few people stood around and took pictures and talked. Faryn was so happy, and that was Landon's goal. He was nervous as hell about proposing and that's why he was missing when she opened her gifts. Clarence had to talk some sense into him because he had changed his mind. Landon's first marriage didn't end very well, and he didn't want a repeat of that heartbreak. Clarence had to drill in his head that Faryn and Malia were nothing alike, and he was right.

After weighing his options, Landon knew that making Faryn his wife was the right thing to do. They loved each other, and their chemistry was on point from day one. Once he really thought about it, the decision was easy. His sons were excited about them getting married and that let him know that he was doing the right thing. They wanted to be a part of the proposal, so Makena helped him out with that as well. Landon had told everybody that he was proposing, so it would have been weird if he didn't do it.

"I'm getting married y'all!" Faryn yelled to her brothers and sister when they walked over to her.

"Congrats baby." Roman smiled as he gave his baby sister a hug, followed by Chad and Akira.

Roman and Chad were especially happy for her because they knew that she had a good man in Landon. Malia was dumb as hell, but they knew that Faryn would make a great wife.

"So, when's the wedding?" Akira asked while admiring Faryn's ring.

"That's the catch," Landon said, making Faryn pause and turn to look at him.

"Oh, hell no, Landon. Who proposes to somebody and has a catch to it? I knew this day was too good to be true. You better not say nothing stupid. I'll start swinging on your ass, babies and all," Faryn threatened.

"Damn baby. At least let me say what I have to say before you start going off. My babies got you mean as fuck," Landon laughed.

"Okay, I'm listening," Faryn replied with her arms folded across her swollen belly.

"I was just gonna say that I wanted us to get married before the babies come. If you want to do something big in a year or so, we can do that too," Landon said.

"Oh, well that's not a problem. We can do it tomorrow if you want to. And I don't need anything big. I'm not trying to impress nobody," Faryn replied.

"Shit, just let us know when and where," Roman spoke up.

"Let me see what my girl can do. She knows a lot of people and places that could probably do a last-minute event," Makena said, speaking of her friend who did the baby shower.

"Thanks, but no thanks Makena. You don't know how to do anything small. This baby shower was way bigger than we wanted it to be," Faryn replied.

"You better talk to your man. He was the one who told me to invite the entire family because he wanted to propose," Makena replied.

"Oh yeah baby, that was all me. But, see what your girl can do Makena. Money is not a problem if she can make it happen," Landon said.

"I got you, lil brother," Makena said as she walked away.

"Make sure you keep us posted Faryn," Chad said as he gave her a hug. Roman and Akira did the same before saying their goodbyes and leaving.

"Are we leaving now? I'm tired," Lennox asked when he walked up to them.

"Yeah, you and Lance can ride with Faryn. I have to bring grandma and her sisters home," Landon replied.

"What about that U-Haul truck?" Faryn asked.

"Raheem is gonna drive it for me and Aiden will follow him in his car. We'll unload it tomorrow sometime," he replied.

"I get to drive my new car. Thank you, baby. I love it." Faryn smiled.

"And I love you," Landon replied.

"Aww, I love you too, boo. We'll see you at home," Faryn said as she kissed him.

"Can we go take a ride somewhere in your new car Faryn?" Lennox asked.

"I thought you were tired," Landon said.

"I'm not tired no more," he replied as he hopped in the back seat and closed the door. Lance got into the front and buckled his seat belt.

"Don't worry. I'll just ride them around for a minute and we'll be home before you get there," Faryn assured him.

Landon removed the huge bows from the top of the car and watched while they drove away. Faryn was too excited as she tried to learn some of the features in her new toy. The kids helped her figure some things out as they drove around and listened to music. They stopped for ice cream and the time was the furthest thing from their minds. When Landon called to see where they were, Faryn decided to head home. Landon laughed when they pulled up because he had beat them there. He was happy to see them smiling and that alone made him smile in return.

Chapter 32

Aweek after the shower, Landon and Faryn were married at the Lakeside Country Club in Metairie. Makena's friend was a member there and she pulled some strings to help them out. The small ceremony was poolside and they had a small dinner like reception right after. Only immediate family and a few friends were in attendance and that was good enough for them. They had two to three weeks before the babies came, and both parents and big brothers were ready. Makena and Ella offered to stay with them for a few days after the babies arrived, but Landon declined their help. He didn't want to start out depending on anyone. He and Faryn wanted to do it all themselves. They decided that Faryn would stay home for a few months before going back to work. Landon still wanted her to be her own boss and she was really entertaining the idea.

"Congrats Faryn," Robin said as she walked over to her.

Landon was trying to find her some ginger ale because she was having terrible heart burn. They had a few more hours to go before the reception ended and Faryn was ready to go.

"Thanks," Faryn said with a smile.

"I've met your brothers and sister, but where are your parents?" Robin asked as she took a seat right next to her.

"My mom passed away when I was sixteen," Faryn replied. She didn't bother saying anything about her father, especially since she didn't know who he was.

"Aww, I'm sorry to hear that," Robin said solemnly.

"Sorry to hear about your recent loss as well," Faryn replied.

"Thank you, sweetie. And listen, I know it's gonna be rough on you with two newborn babies in the house. I know that Landon works and I'm sure you'll be going back to work eventually. If you ever need a babysitter for any reason, just give me a call," Robin offered.

"Nah, we're good on that," Landon replied as he walked up on the end of their conversation. He handed Faryn her drink while occupying the seat on the other side of her.

"It was just an offer Landon," Robin said.

"And I just declined it. Don't try to come at my wife on no friendly shit trying to snake your way back in. You already got three grandkids who don't even know you," Landon argued.

"I'm trying to get to know them, but you and Makena won't let me," Robin replied, right as Makena walked up.

"It took your man dying for you to even acknowledge them," Landon pointed out.

"Look, the only reason you're even here is because of our grandmother. Don't be trying to ruin my brother's day with that fake ass love. I have no problem escorting you out, if that's going to be a problem. You didn't want kids when you were with Leroy, remember? Your wish was granted a long time ago and you still don't have any kids now," Makena said angrily.

"I apologize for not being the mother that y'all needed me to be," Robin said as she tried to force out some tears.

"Girl, please! You can't even make yourself cry with that bullshit that you're spitting. We're adults boo. The fuck we need with a mother now," Makena snapped.

"I know, but-" Robin said before her daughter cut her off.

"But nothing. Right now, you have one of two choices. You can have a seat and enjoy the free food and drinks that my brother is paying for, or you can find the nearest exit and get the fuck out. Now, what's it going to be?" Makena asked calmly as she looked at her waiting for an answer.

"It was nice talking to you, Faryn," Robin said as she got up and reclaimed her seat right next to Ella and Ava.

"I know that we just got married, but I'm about to lay down the law right quick," Landon said while looking at Faryn.

"What did I do?" Faryn questioned.

"You didn't do anything, but a friendship between you and her ain't happening. I can already see that she's trying to use you to get back in and I can't have that. We don't need her to babysit or nothing else. I'll hire a stranger before I open my doors to her. Hell, as far as I'm concerned, she is a stranger," Landon ranted.

"Don't fuss at her, Landon. She didn't know," Makena said, coming to Faryn's defense.

"I'm not fussing at you, baby, but I know how my mama is. She's selfish as fuck. Anything that she does is done to benefit her and her only. We're good and let that be your answer every time she offers her assistance," Landon said as he grabbed her hand and kissed it.

"Okay." Faryn shrugged uncaringly.

She really didn't know Robin, but she would respect her husband's wishes. He told her all about how she did him and Makena, and she didn't want a relationship with her anyway. Ella was more than enough mother and grandmother for them all.

"Aye Landon, who is that chick with the red dress on?" Roman came over and asked.

Chad had already met somebody who he was entertaining, and Roman had his eyes on a new bedmate as well.

"No Ro. Don't even try it," Faryn replied.

"I work with her," Landon said when he looked in the direction that he was pointing in.

"Is she married?" Roman asked.

"Has that ever stopped you before?" Landon laughed.

"Damn bruh, that's cold," Roman said, laughing with him.

"Nah man, she ain't married," Landon replied.

"Cool," Roman said as he walked off and walked right up to her.

"That poor girl," Faryn said, shaking her head.

"Her snitching ass. I hope he do her dirty. Bitch always at work reporting shit," Landon replied.

"Why did you invite her then?" Faryn asked.

"I didn't. We're cool with some of the same people, so she must have come with somebody else. She tried to get with me when I got divorced and I turned her down. She's had it out for me ever since then," Landon chuckled.

"That's messed up, but she still doesn't deserve a man like Roman," Faryn said, laughing.

"Fuck her," Landon spoke up.

"I wonder what made that bitch Ava show up," Makena said as they looked over at their auntie sitting there looking bored.

She and Ava had just passed words and were about to pass licks at Ella's house the day before. She was always saying some slick shit out of her mouth and Makena was sick of her. It took Aiden and Raheem to hold her back from tagging her auntie's ass. She had gotten her last pass from Makena and that was a promise.

"You know how grandma is. She's always putting a guilt trip on somebody. It didn't matter to me one way or the other." Landon shrugged.

"I'm happy she left her punk ass husband at home," Makena replied.

"She could have stayed at home right with that nigga. I'm sick of her ass too," Landon acknowledged.

"Look at Lance following that lil girl around," Makena laughed while changing the subject.

"Where?" Faryn asked as she looked around the semi-crowded room.

"Calm down Faryn. He's gonna have a girlfriend eventually," Landon chuckled.

"I doubt it," Faryn said with a roll of her eyes.

She spotted Lance smiling hard, as he followed a pretty little girl all around the room. She was giggling as she looked behind her to make sure he was still following her.

"Her lil hot ass," Faryn said as she stood to her feet.

"Girl, sit your ass down. You better not go over there messing with them kids," Landon fussed.

"I'm not going by them. I'm going to the bathroom," Faryn said as she wobbled away.

She was counting down the minutes until she could be reunited with her bed again. She was happy to see everybody having fun, but she was ready to go. Akira and Clarence stayed on the dance floor the entire time they were there. Faryn didn't even recall seeing them eat anything. It didn't matter if the song was fast or slow, the two of them had to dance to it. Akira had an old soul and had been that way ever since Faryn could remember. It was no surprise that she preferred older men. Robin called herself trying to talk to Clarence, but he had nothing to say to his ex-wife. She was all about her family now that the man who she abandoned them for was no longer here. She'd scarred her ex-husband and kids and they weren't as forgiving as she hoped they would be.

Faryn was happy that all the stalls weren't occupied when she went into the bathroom. She was the only one who was in there, at least for a few seconds. As soon as she closed and locked the door to the stall that she was in, someone else walked in behind her.

"Girl yeah, I'm tired as hell. Kylie is with your mama and my husband was at home. I just called him to come pick me up. He should be pulling up in a minute. I could have been relaxing with my man tonight. My nephew decided to marry a hoe and I had to get out of my bed for this bullshit," Ava said loudly.

She was on the phone with her sister-in-law when she purposely followed Faryn into the bathroom. She wanted her to hear what she had to say and she was unapologetic about her feelings. In her eyes, Faryn was a hoe who lucked up on a good man.

"I'm right here boo. You can say what you have to say to my face," Faryn said when she walked out of the stall and washed her hands.

Ava ended her call before turning around to address the woman who she now hated with a passion.

"Don't flatter yourself boo. Calling you a hoe was me being nice." Ava smirked.

"Bitches like you really kill me. You seem to have a problem with everybody else, but your husband. He's the one who cheated on you boo, not me. And the shit wasn't even all that good anyway," Faryn replied, shocking Ava with her words.

Faryn seemed so laidback and calm and she never said much. Landon or Makena always came to her defense before she could say anything. The hood came out of her quick and her face owned no fear. Her voice was strong and confident, making Ava want to back down.

"It must have been if you went back for it for an entire year," Ava countered.

Kane had confessed to everything after she threatened to leave him. He told her how he and Faryn had met and how long they had messed around. Ava cried for two days straight, but she would never leave her man. She had too much to lose if she did. Ava was a pampered housewife and she would never give up that lifestyle, no matter what he did. Kane had cheated on her several times before, but never for that long.

That's what hurt her the most. His previous affairs never lasted longer than a month. To know that he had messed with Faryn for an entire year was like a knife being plunged into her heart. She could tell that feelings were involved, and he proved that the night of Faryn's baby shower. When Landon proposed to Faryn, she could see the envy in her husband's eyes. Kane got up and stormed out of the hall, and Ava followed him. He claimed that he went outside to smoke, but she knew that it was more than that. He couldn't take seeing his ex-best friend with the woman who he had fallen so hard for. They argued for a while until everyone started coming outside to see the new car that Landon had purchased for Faryn. They ended their argument briefly, but it started back up as soon as they got home. They were barely speaking to each other after that and not much had changed since then.

"Trust me, that lil toddler dick wasn't all that much to go back for. The head and the money was the best part of it all," Faryn said, shaking Ava from her thoughts.

"Bitch, please. You wish my husband did eat that worn out pussy of yours," Ava sneered.

"I didn't have to wish boo. That nigga was begging for another taste, even after I stopped fucking with him. I had to change my number because he turned into a stalker. I would hurt your feelings and show you the text messages, but you already look like you're ready to cry. I'm a happily married woman now, so your husband and his pinky-sized dick are a thing of the past. The bitches at JB's are who you should be worried about. He's paying for pussy left and right over there and they don't give a fuck about him having a wife at home. Keep some bail money handy. It's only a matter of time before that whorehouse gets raided with him inside. And a word of advice from me to you. Don't throw lemons at a bitch who knows how to make lemonade," Faryn said as she turned to walk away.

Ava was fuming at being dismissed by the other woman. Faryn was beneath her, in her opinion. Landon upgraded her, and she was acting like she didn't strip for a living at one time. Common sense was missing, as Ava grabbed Faryn by her hair and pulled her back. Faryn grabbed on to the sink to keep from falling, and Ava quickly let her go. The huge belly that Faryn carried around quickly snapped her back to reality. That was her great niece and nephew that she was carrying, no matter how she felt about her. Being that she was pregnant, Ava thought that Faryn was going to leave and run tell Landon what she had just done. She was mistaken when Faryn turned around with a murderous look in her eyes.

"Bitch!" Faryn yelled as she hit Ava with a quick two-piece that knocked her to the floor. She didn't stop there; she reached down and grabbed her hair, punching her in the head again. Ava's scalp felt like it was on fire, as Faryn dragged her out of the bathroom by her long, naturally curly hair. She had never seen a pregnant woman move so fast and act so wild before in her life. Faryn didn't act like she was carrying two babies or even one with the way she was behaving. Ava could see people running towards them, but Landon got there first.

"Let her go Faryn! The fuck is you doing fighting while you're pregnant. This is our damn wedding reception," Landon fussed as he picked his wife up and sat her down at the nearest table.

"Let that bitch go! I'm bout' to stomp them babies right up out that hoe!" Ava ranted as she ran behind Faryn, trying to hit her.

She was punching Landon in his back trying her best to get to his wife. A hard lick to the side of her face quickly put a stop to that.

"You got the right one today bitch!" Makena yelled as she ran out of the crowd and punched her auntie.

Ava tried to fight back, but Makena was doing her dirty. Landon called Roman and Chad over to sit with Faryn while he tried to break up yet another fight. Ella was yelling for them to stop, but no one seemed to be listening. Things only got worse when Kane walked through the door and pushed Makena off his wife. When Landon saw how hard his sister was pushed, he was ready for war.

"This nigga got me fucked up!" Landon fumed as he came out of his suit jacket and started throwing blows at Kane.

Someone was helping Ava up from the floor as her nephew beat her husband down to where she once was. Kane proved that he was a real hoe as he tried to protect his face, instead of fighting back. He had a feeling that something was going to pop off and he was prepared. Landon didn't notice the small gun that he pulled out of his pants, but Chad did.

"Kane!" Ava yelled when she saw her husband raise the weapon.

"Lord Jesus!" Ella screamed.

People started running and ducking for cover, as Chad came out of nowhere. He grabbed Kane's arm, ripping the gun from his hand and shoving it in his own pocket. It took Aiden and Raheem a minute to get Landon off him, and Kane was grateful. He only went there to get his wife, but he decided to be nosey. He wanted to see what Faryn looked like in her wedding dress and he was sorry that he did. He heard all the noise before he even walked in, but he didn't know what was going on. He never thought that he would see Makena beating the shit out of his wife and that had his blood boiling when he did. He was happy that he came strapped, even though it didn't do him any good.

"Shut this bitch down! The reception is over!" Landon roared angrily as he made his way back over to his wife.

"Are you okay baby?" Faryn asked as she inspected his face.

"The fuck was you doing fighting Faryn?" Landon barked.

"That bitch started with me. But yes, me and your babies are fine," Faryn replied sarcastically as she rolled her eyes.

"Don't start with me, Faryn. This is not a good time," Landon warned as he grabbed her hand and walked away.

"This is ridiculous. We can't even get together as a family without trying to kill up each other!" Ella yelled angrily.

"Fuck this family! Y'all don't ever have to worry about seeing my wife and daughter again!" Kane barked, as he limped to the door with Ava following close behind him.

"Nigga what!" Aiden yelled while trying to get at him. Raheem wasn't letting that happen though. They had fought enough, and it was over.

"I told you that they didn't give a fuck about you. They put that bitch Faryn before you and you're their blood. Nigga married a hoe and act like he did something special," Kane said while grabbing Ava's hand.

Roman's head snapped around in his direction when he made the comments about his little sister. He didn't know who Kane was, but he was damn sure going to find out. He had the entire game fucked up, coming to his sister's reception on that bullshit. And disrespecting her for any reason was a big mistake.

"You know that is not true Ava. You're upset with Faryn about something that happened in the past. Place some of the blame on your husband too. He's only trying to fill your head up with all that bullshit because he's guilty. I just want my family to get along. Is that too much to ask for?" Ella cried, as Makena tried to console her.

Ava left with her husband without so much as a backwards glance. Landon felt like shit as he walked over to his grandmother and pulled her into a hug.

"I'm sorry grandma. I didn't mean to upset you like this," he apologized.

"It's okay baby. I'm just sorry that your reception got ruined by all this foolishness," Ella replied.

"It's all good. As long as it wasn't the wedding." Landon shrugged.

"Are you okay baby?" Ella asked Faryn.

"I'm fine. At least somebody cared enough to ask," Faryn replied with a roll of her eyes.

"Stop being so damn dramatic Faryn. You drug that damn girl out of the bathroom by her hair while you were punching her. I know you're fine because I didn't see her get a lick in," Landon said.

"I can't believe that bastard pulled out a gun on you," Makena fumed.

"I didn't even see that shit," Landon replied while shaking his head.

"That muthafucker better not ever think about stepping foot in my house again. I'll make Ava a widow my damn self if he does," Ella threatened.

"I can make it happen tonight if you want me to," Aiden replied.

"Shut the hell up Aiden. Let's just go. I've had enough excitement to last me for a lifetime," Ella said as they all walked out together.

All the guests had already gone and they were ready to do the same.

"Come ride with us, Aiden. We'll bring you home," Roman offered.

He needed to pick his brain about his brother-in-law to see what the deal was between him and Faryn. They waited until Landon, Faryn, and the kids got into their car and pulled off before they did the same.

"Faryn beat up auntie Ava," Lennox said as he and Lance fell out laughing.

"How she let a pregnant lady beat her up?" Lance said as they continued to laugh and discuss the fight.

"Look at that, setting a bad example for your stepsons already," Landon said while shaking his head.

"Don't do that Landon. You know that was not my fault. I'm sorry y'all. I shouldn't have done that. Fighting is not the way to solve problems," Faryn explained.

"Uh-uh, don't try to jump into counselor mode now. Pregnant with two babies and fighting at your wedding reception. I need to get an annulment," Landon joked.

"Ain't no divorce nigga. You said I do and you're doing it for life. I'll be on the next episode of Snapped if you even try it," Faryn threatened.

"Damn," Landon said as he doubled over with laughter.

"Let's go get some ice cream," Faryn suggested.

"Whatever you want baby," Landon replied as he drove.

He and Faryn listened, as the boys talked about everything from the wedding to school and anything in between. Landon stopped to get them all some ice cream before heading home. He and Faryn's first day as husband and wife was full of drama, but that seemed to be the norm for them lately. He still wouldn't change anything about his life, even the bad parts. It was all worth it because he found his real soul mate and he and his boys were happy. In a few more weeks, he would have two more reasons to be even happier.

Chapter 33

"**D**o you feel any pain baby?" Landon asked as he held Faryn's hand.

"No, I don't feel anything," Faryn replied.

Three weeks after they got married, she was admitted into the hospital to give birth to their twins. It was only six in the morning and they had been there for an hour already. Both their families were in the waiting area, and Landon was a nervous wreck. He had been there to see both of his sons enter the world, but the situations were different. Malia had their sons naturally, but Faryn had to get cut. It was different having two babies and he didn't know what to expect. He tried to ease Faryn's mind, but he was just as anxious as she was. He would be meeting his first daughter and another son in a matter of minutes. The surgery had already started, but Landon was too afraid to look. He didn't know if his stomach could take whatever the doctors were doing.

"Okay Faryn, just relax. You'll feel a little pressure and then baby number one will be out. The same thing for baby number two. A little pressure, but no pain," the doctor said.

Just like he'd said, Faryn felt a little pressure both times and her babies had entered the world crying and healthy. Landon Jr. was out first weighing a little over six pounds, followed by London, who weighed a little over five. They both had a head full of hair just like Ella had predicted. She swore that Faryn's constant heartburn guaranteed that they would. Once Landon cut the cords, they finished patching Faryn up as the babies were escorted to the nursery.

"Four babies and six more to go." Landon smiled.

"What!" Faryn yelled.

"I'm just playing with you, baby. Calm down," he laughed.

"Four is more than enough," Faryn noted.

"Maybe one or two more and I'll be good," he replied while kissing her lips.

It was a little after ten that morning when Faryn was situated in her room and ready to receive visitors. Lennox and Lance were the first ones to enter the room wearing their proud big brother t-shirts that Landon had specially made for them. They swore that the babies looked just like them and nobody could deny that. They were excited when they sat in the chair and Landon let each one of them hold a baby. Roman and Chad were on their way and Akira was coming with Clarence as soon as she got off from work.

"That poor lil girl. Three big brothers and a crazy ass daddy," Makena said as she smiled at her niece.

"Yep and nobody better play with her," Lance replied as he looked down at her.

"That's right. That's the only time that you won't get in trouble for fighting. A nigga look at her wrong and you better knock him the fuck out," Landon ordered.

"Don't tell him that baby," Faryn fussed.

"Drop them niggas Lance and you too, Lennox," Landon replied, making her shake her head at him.

"Robin asked if she could come up here to visit," Ella said as she hung up the phone and looked at Landon.

"Send her a picture." Landon frowned.

"Okay, I was just asking," Ella replied.

"I'm really getting sick of hearing her name," Makena said, rolling her eyes.

"You know she has to move within ninety days. They sold the house and she has to leave. I told her that I can't help her. You pay all my bills, so I don't have any money to give her," Ella noted.

"You have lots of money. What's mine is yours," Landon replied.

"You know what I mean Landon. I don't want to see her on the streets, but I can't afford to help her get a place to stay. The only thing I can offer her is a room in my house," Ella said.

"Aww, hell no. She better not come in there on no bullshit," Aiden fussed.

"Shut your overgrown ass up boy. You barely sleep there, so you wouldn't know anyway," Ella fussed.

"I'm not taking care of her, grandma. She never took care of me, so why should I? Now, I can't tell you who to move into your house, but she better get a job and pay her own way. My responsibility is to make sure you're straight and that's it," Landon informed her.

"I know baby. I told her that you pay all the bills and I had to run it by you first," Ella said.

"Oh, well my answer is no," Landon replied.

"Landon!" Faryn yelled.

"Man, look, I'm not trying to have this conversation right now because it's only gonna piss me off. I wanna celebrate the birth of my kids without all the added drama," Landon replied, right as someone knocked on the door.

"Congrats my nigga. I'm a muthafucking uncle!" Roman yelled when he walked into the room with gift bags and balloons.

"Watch your mouth in front of Ms. Ella, nigga," Chad fussed as he walked in behind him carrying more gifts and bubble gum cigars.

"I'm sorry Ms. Ella," Roman apologized.

"Y'all are alright baby. Don't change your language for me," Ella said, waving him off.

"Y'all wanna hold them?" Faryn asked her brothers.

"Nah man, I'm scared of kids," Roman replied.

"Shit, me too," Aiden agreed.

"That's a damn shame," Faryn laughed.

"This is as close as I'll come to having some of my own." Roman shrugged.

"Don't worry brother-in-law, we'll have enough to get you right," Landon said while winking at Faryn.

"Nigga please," Faryn replied with a smirk.

She slept off and on all day while her visitors came and went. Akira, Clarence, Harley, and Kyron came with more gifts, and Faryn's room was getting crowded. It amazed Faryn how she went from being a loner to being surrounded by more love than she could imagine. Meeting Landon was a blessing that she vowed to never take for granted. Makena, her brothers, and the boys stayed until visiting hours were over. Lance and Lennox went home with their auntie, while Landon stayed the night with Faryn and the twins.

"What are you gonna do about your mama and her living arrangements?" Faryn asked Landon as he cuddled up in the hospital bed with her.

"Nothing," Landon replied.

"Don't be mean Landon. You don't have to take care of her, but I know you don't want her to be homeless."

"Me and my sister would have been homeless if our grandmother wouldn't have taken us in."

"I know, but-" Faryn started before he cut her off.

"If your mama was alive, would you have done it for her? Based on how you were treated as a child, would you have done anything to help her out if you could?" Landon asked.

Faryn was silent as she pondered over his question. She took a moment and traveled down memory lane, reliving every detail of her childhood from as far back as she could remember. The pain had subsided, but the memories would forever remain.

"No," she mumbled, giving her husband an honest answer.

"Get some rest. We'll talk some more tomorrow," Landon said as he closed his eyes.

"Okay, I love you." Faryn yawned.

I love you too, baby," Landon replied.

The bed was big enough for them both to sleep in, but he had to be careful since Faryn had just had surgery. Landon waited until she was in a deep sleep before he crept out of the bed and got in the recliner that was next to it. He watched a movie for a little while before he joined his wife in a deep slumber.

***

"I need a break y'all. I'm out of breath," Malia said as she flopped down on a bench.

Her boys had begged her take them go cart driving, and she happily obliged. She was just happy to be spending time with them, so she didn't mind. Landon had taken them several times before, so they knew what to do. That was her first time there, but she didn't know that the adventure park offered so much. They had Malia rock climbing and playing outdoor laser tag. As thin as she was, she was out of shape and it showed. She was breathing hard as hell and drinking water like she was dehydrated.

"It took you forever to make it to the top of the wall," Lennox laughed.

"I know. That was harder than I thought it would be," Malia chuckled.

"You did good on the go carts though," Lance complimented.

"I've been driving for years, so that part was easy," Malia said, smiling at him.

She was so thankful that Lance had come around and wanted to spend time with her again. Malia had to admit that she was surprised when she learned that it was Faryn who was responsible for it. Her kids spoke highly of their stepmother and she had to admit that she'd misjudged her. Just like she'd assumed, Landon made Faryn his wife and they now had two beautiful two-week-old babies. Her sons were so happy to be big brothers and they showed her lots of pictures of their brother and sister. Landon finally got his junior and he seemed to be happy. Malia had to admit that, if anyone deserved happiness, it was him. She messed up their marriage, but it wasn't fair for him to suffer because of it. It took a lot of long talks with her mother for Malia to realize that. She still hadn't been formally introduced to Faryn, but she was sure that the day was coming soon.

"I'm hungry," Lennox spoke up as he rubbed his stomach.

"Me too," Lance replied.

"Okay. What do y'all feel like eating?" Malia asked.

They didn't know what they wanted to eat, so they went to the food court to look around. After a few minutes of searching, they all decided on Philly cheese steak sliders and fries.

"Faryn's tastes better than this," Lennox spoke up.

"I know," Lance agreed.

"Is Faryn a good cook?" Malia asked.

"Yes, and she lets us help her make dessert too. Her banana splits are good." Lennox smiled.

"Her brownies are good too," Lance chimed in.

"Y'all are gonna get fat eating all that stuff," Malia chuckled.

"No, we're not. Our dad turned our basement into a gym for Faryn. She can't exercise yet because she just had the babies, but she will when the doctor says she can," Lennox replied.

"Did I tell y'all that I'm going back to school?' Malia asked them.

"No. For what?" Lance asked.

"Medical coding and billing. I'll be making more money than I make now, and we'll be able to do more together. I've been studying to get a head start on everything," Malia replied.

A month after being fired from Melba's, Malia lucked up and found a job as a bank teller. Her hours were perfect for her to attend night school. She was also off on weekends to spend time with her boys. She was slowly working on building a better relationship with them. She was adhering to Landon's advice and taking it slow. He and Malia's cordial relationship was back on track and she was happy for that. For the sake of their sons, they would always remain friends.

"That's good, but what's it like working at the bank?" Lance questioned.

"I like it a lot and I like the people that I work with." Malia smiled, happy that he was talking to her more.

"I'm gonna be rich like my daddy when I grow up. I'm gonna buy a big house like him and everything," Lennox said.

"You can do it too, baby. You and Lance are smart, just like your father. Can I come and visit when you get your big house?" Malia asked with a smirk.

"Yes, and you can have a key," Lennox said, making her heart smile.

"Aww, that's so sweet baby." Malia smiled while kissing his cheek.

"Yep, you, my daddy, and Faryn can have a key to come to my house whenever y'all want to," Lennox added.

"Y'all really like Faryn, huh?" Malia asked.

"We love her," Lance corrected.

Malia didn't feel the usual twinge of jealously that she used to feel. She'd grown to accept things for what they were. Faryn was just as important to her kids as she and Landon were. She treated them right and that showed by the love that they had for her. Malia was blessed that her kids had a stepmother who loved them as her own. Not many women could say the same.

"That's good baby. I'm happy that y'all love her and I know that she feels the same," Malia replied.

"I love you, too," Lennox spoke up as he looked at her and smiled.

"Aww, you're gonna make me cry. I know that I haven't been the best mother to y'all and I'm sorry for that. I did a lot of things wrong that y'all are too young to understand. I can't take back what happened in the past, but I promise not to make the same mistakes twice. I just ask that y'all forgive me and give me another chance to get it right. I promise not to let y'all down again," Malia said as tears came to her eyes.

Although she was still living with Cora, her goal was to save up enough money to get her own place for her kids to visit. Her mother loved when her grandsons were there, but Malia wanted them to have their own space. Cora's house was a matchbox compared to where they lived. They never complained, but Malia knew that it took some getting used to.

"I forgive you," Lennox said as he hugged her.

"Thank you, baby," Malia said as tears fell from her eyes.

Lance was quiet the entire time, but that was okay with her. She wasn't going to rush him to do anything and she didn't love him any less. The fact that he was even around her again was a blessing. Lennox was always a mama's boy, so things came easier with him. Lance had an attitude like his father and he was tougher than the average kid his age. He stood firm on his feelings and he didn't budge until he was good and ready.

"Okay, so what do y'all wanna do now?" Malia asked once their tender moment was over.

"Let's do the bumper cars," Lance spoke up.

"Bumper cars it is, but I'm warning y'all. I'm not taking no mercy just because y'all are my babies. I'm bumping anything that comes close to me," Malia said, making them laugh.

They all ran to the bumper cars and stood in line for their turn. Malia was having a ball with her boys and she missed spending time with them. Besides school and work, they were the only other things that she was focused on. She didn't have a man and she wasn't looking for one. She was learning to love herself and not depend on a man to do it. Aside from spending time with her boys, that was the best feeling in the world.

Chapter 34

Things had gone from bad to worse with Ava and Kane ever since the fight at Landon's wedding. Ava was used to calling the shots, but Kane had been on one lately. He had been working a lot more than usual and he seemed to be avoiding her as much as he could. Ava was basically estranged from her family thanks to him, and she was regretting it. She hadn't seen her family since the day Landon got married and she missed her mother more than anything. Ella was the glue that held them all together, and Ava felt lost without her. She didn't want to hear the backlash from what Kane had done and she was sure that Ella was going to bring it up. She felt stupid about it all and her husband didn't make things any better. Her daughter missed her grandmother and cousins, but Ava's pride wouldn't allow her to give in. Kylie had been spending a lot of time with Kane's parents lately, but it wasn't the same. She was the only grandchild on her father's side and she didn't have anyone else to play with over there.

"Stop fucking nagging me all the time man!" Kane yelled as he walked out of his and Ava's bedroom.

"Who the fuck are you yelling at?" Ava yelled back as she followed him into the living room.

"I'm going to work Ava, damn. I'm tired of being interrogated every time I leave the house," Kane argued.

"Some shit just ain't adding up Kane. You've never worked this much overtime since we've been married. Why now? It's like you hate being home."

"That's because you won't let me breathe. I'm stressed the fuck out and you're not helping," Kane replied.

"Where's all the extra money going? I damn sure don't see it."

"Maybe if you stayed out of the mall, then you would. I have to put in extra hours just to afford the lifestyle that you want to live," he replied.

Ava regretted letting him handle all the finances and important details when they got married. As long as Kane gave her whatever she wanted, she didn't care about what was in their account. When it was time for them to buy a house, she picked out what she wanted, and Kane wrote the check. That's the way it had been from the very beginning and that's the way she wanted it to stay. Ella told her that she was fool for doing that, but she didn't care what anyone had to say.

"Cut the bullshit Kane. Nothing about the way we live has changed, so come again," Ava said.

"You go get a job then, Ava. If you want me to stop working so much, then you get a job and take up the slack around here," Kane suggested.

Ava had a degree in communications, but she had never done anything with it.

"Bye Kane," Ava mumbled as she flopped down on the sofa and grabbed the remote.

"Yeah, that's what I thought," he replied as he grabbed his keys and walked out of the house.

Ava felt like crying as she absentmindedly flipped through the channels on the tv. Her marriage seemed to be falling apart and she didn't know how to fix it. Her woman's intuition was telling her that something wasn't right, but she was too afraid to find out. Her husband had been her world for years and she was scared to start all over. Ava appeared to be confident on the surface, but her insecurities ran deep.

"Hey sis," Ava said when she answered the phone for her sister-in-law, Kya.

"What's wrong with you?" Kya asked, picking up on how down she sounded.

"Your brother makes me so damn sick," Ava replied.

"What else is new? You and Kane have argued more this past month than you did for your entire marriage," Kya pointed out.

"Something is wrong Kya. I can just feel it. Kane has never worked this much before in his life. If I catch him cheating again, I'm done. I'm not gonna continue to be his fool just because he provides well."

"You say that all the time, but a pair of red bottoms will always change your mind. He got caught with his pants down a few months ago and a new car swept that under the rug," Kya said, calling her out.

She lost count of how many times Ava had called her and her mother crying about something that Kane had done. Ava never took their advice, so they stopped giving it. Kane had always been sneaky since he was a little boy and not much had changed. He was still Kya's only brother, so she always had his back.

"Fuck this shit. I'm about to do some investigating for myself. Even if I have to track that nigga's phone, I'm about to get some answers," Ava said as she stood to her feet.

"Don't go looking for shit Ava. You might not like what you find," Kya warned.

"It sounds like you already know something," Ava replied.

"I don't know anything. I just don't want you to get your feelings hurt again like the last time. You went searching and didn't like what you found," Kya reminded her.

"You wanna come take a ride with me?" Ava asked, ignoring what she had just said.

"Take a ride with you where?" Kya asked.

"I don't know. I need a drink or something," Ava replied.

"I can't sis. I have a few errands to run, but I'll call you once I'm done, if it's not too late," Kya said.

"Okay. Maybe I'll just watch a movie or something," Ava replied before she hung up.

Ava tried hard to take her mind off her husband and focus on something else. The nagging feeling in the pit of her stomach just wouldn't let her be. Ava hadn't tracked Kane's phone in a while and she didn't want to start that up again. She always ended up getting her feelings hurt whenever she did. Still, something was telling her that he wasn't where he was supposed to be. Instead of tracking his phone, Ava decided to take a ride to his job to see for herself.

It took her about thirty minutes before she was pulling up to the NASA assembly facility. There was an access gate at the front, so there was no way that she could get inside without a badge. She called Kane twice, but she never got an answer. She could see a few cars in the parking lot, but not all of them. When Ava saw a car coming towards the exit, she prayed that it was someone that she knew. Her prayers were answered when she recognized one of the women who had attended Landon's wedding. She was cool with her husband and nephew, so she smiled and waved when she saw Ava standing outside of her car at the entrance.

"Hey girl. What are you doing here? Your nephew is out on maternity leave with his wife," she said.

"I wasn't looking for Landon. I'm looking for Kane," Ava said, wiping the smile off the other woman's face.

She dropped her head and looked away like she was no longer happy to see her.

"What?" Ava asked, noticing the change in her demeanor.

"Kane doesn't work here anymore. He resigned about a month ago. I'm sorry, but I thought you knew," she replied solemnly.

Ava was happy that she was leaning against her car because she felt like she was about to fall. Kane had supposedly been working twelve and sixteen hour shifts for the past two weeks, but that couldn't have been true. If her calculations were correct, he resigned from his job around the same time as Landon's wedding, per what the other woman was saying.

"I'm so sorry. I didn't mean to cause any trouble," the other woman apologized.

"No need to apologize. I appreciate you for letting me know," Ava said as she got back into her car.

She pulled out her cellphone and logged into her iCloud account to track her husband's phone. Kane was nowhere near where he was supposed to be, but Ava was about to walk down on him wherever he was. He was always proving her family right, and she was tired. It was getting harder to smile when all she ever wanted to do was cry. She followed the directions that her phone was giving her, but she wasn't very familiar with the area. She was starting to think her phone was leading her to a dead end until she saw something that got her attention.

Ava's heart was beating out of her chest when she pulled up in the parking lot of JB's Gentlemen's Club. The place looked like a hole in the wall, but they seemed to have a lot of business. She replayed the argument that she had with Faryn in her head. There was obviously some truth to what she had said, and the proof was staring her right in the face. There were lots of cars in the parking lot, as Ava drove around trying to find Kane's. It didn't take her very long before she spotted it backed into a spot right near the entrance. The place looked like a dump, but Ava grabbed her taser and entered, along with a group of other women.

***

"Shit," Kane hissed as he watched his dick disappear down one of the dancer's throats.

Kane rested his hand on the back of her head as she sucked him up like a vacuum. It wasn't hard for her to swallow him whole because he wasn't very well endowed. He had been stressed out for the past few months and he needed some relief. Aside from the beef that he had with Aiden and Landon, Kane's marriage was another thing that was heavy on his mind. He loved Ava more than anything, but all the arguing was getting to be too much. Things hadn't been the same with them since the night of Faryn's baby shower. Admittedly, he was upset when Landon proposed to her, but he thought he hid his feelings well. Obviously, he didn't, and Ava was pissed at his reaction. He didn't want to go, but Ava insisted that he accompany her since Ella had basically guilted her into going. It seemed like all they did was fuss since then and he was tired of it.

Kane had a lot on his mind and he needed a wife, not another mother. He was sure that things were only going to get worse once he told her some of the things that he'd been hiding. Resigning from his job was one of them and he was sure that she was going to be pissed. Thanks to his parents, he and his sister were good on money, but Ava wouldn't care. The more the merrier was her way of thinking. She depended on that income to shop, as if she was the one working for it. Kane wanted to tell her when he first did it, but he wasn't in the mood to argue. Working with her nephew had become uncomfortable, and Kane no longer felt safe. He wasn't too worried about Landon, but Aiden and his threats weren't to be taken lightly. The last straw was when he went to work the Monday after Landon's wedding and saw his brother-in-law standing outside the gate with another man. He'd seen the dude before, but he couldn't remember where. When Kane locked eyes with him, Aiden made his hand into the shape of a gun, and Kane was shook. He resigned the very next day and never looked back.

"Keep going. I'm bout' to cum," Kane said as he pushed her head down further.

He bit his bottom lip hard as he spilled his seeds in her mouth and watched as she drank and swallowed. After getting head from a few of the others, Kane soon learned that she was the best. Just like he used to do with Faryn, he requested her every time he went there. Unlike his situation with Faryn, Kane didn't catch feelings and he only paid her for her services.

"You want me to hang around?" she asked, knowing that he would probably want sex at some point during the night.

"Nah, I'm good for now. I know where to find you if I need you," Kane said as he stood to his feet.

He fixed his clothes and reached into his front pocket. After counting out a few bills, he handed them to her and watched as she counted it.

"Thanks boo. You want a drink?" she asked while walking towards the exit.

Kane was a regular and JB never charged him for liquor. He spent enough money on everything else, so there was no need to.

"Yeah, you know what I like," Kane said as he followed behind her.

"I got you," she said as they exited the private area.

He was looking down at his phone at all the missed calls that he had. Ava had called twice, and she was the only one that he was worried about calling back.

"I don't even know why I'm surprised. A leopard will never change its spots," Ava said when she saw her husband following one of the strippers out of the private areas.

Kane stopped in his tracks, shocked beyond belief at seeing his wife in a place that he considered his guilty pleasure. The look of hurt and anger couldn't be missed as Ava shook her head at him in disgust.

"Ava-" Kane started before she raised her hand to stop him.

"Save your time and energy. I don't want to hear shit that you have to say. I'm so done Kane. Shit was already bad, and you just had to go and make it worse. My people had you right," Ava said as she turned to walk away.

"Baby please. Just let me explain," Kane begged.

"Explain it to the judge when I divorce your lying ass!" Ava yelled.

"Please don't do this Ava. I'm sorry baby, but I can explain," Kane replied as he pulled her over into a quieter area of the room.

"Explain how I just witnessed my husband coming out of a private room with a half-naked dancer. Explain how you've been lying saying that you're going to work, and you no longer have a job. I've been so busy lying to other people about my marriage that I'm starting to believe the shit myself," Ava said as tears fell from her eyes.

"I didn't want to resign from my job, but I didn't feel safe being there anymore. Your crazy ass brother came there and threatened to kill me," Kane said, exaggerating the truth.

"That's bullshit Kane. If that was true, you should have said something a long time ago. I can't do this anymore," Ava cried as she tried to walk away.

As much as she hated to admit it, she owed her family, including Faryn, an apology for her behavior. They were right, and she felt like a damn fool. Kane wasn't going to change, and she was sure that there was more that she didn't know about. She was quickly knocked off that high horse that she had climbed on so many years ago.

"Baby..." Kane said, before there was a loud crash and a commotion coming from the front of the building.

The music stopped, and another commotion was heard coming from the back of the building. Ava's heart dropped when she saw a gang of police officers rush in from two different directions with guns drawn.

"Keep some bail money handy. It's only a matter of time before that whorehouse gets raided with him inside," is what Faryn had said to her in the bathroom at her wedding reception. Another prediction that had obviously come true. Just like everyone else in the establishment, Ava was made to get on her knees with her hands on top of her head. She was humiliated and hate for her husband was quickly starting to develop. A police officer was on a bullhorn reading them their rights, so there was no mistaking that they were all under arrest.

"I'm so sorry baby. I swear, I'm going to fix this," Kane promised as he and Ava were cuffed and thrown into the back of a paddy wagon.

Ava shook her head in regret as they pulled away from the club and headed to central lock up. She knew that if Ella could see her now, she would be so disappointed. Not so much about her going to jail, but the circumstances as to why she was going. Kane wasn't shit, and Ella had said that only a year into their marriage when she first found that he'd cheated and made her youngest child cry.

Chapter 35

Mug shots, fingerprints, and booking were all new words in Ava's vocabulary. It took them forever to do anything and she ended up spending the night in jail. Thank God for her in-laws because she didn't have to call anyone to bail her out. Kane's parents, Carmen and Kyle, were right out front in the lobby waiting for her to be released. They were pissed when she told them what happened and they couldn't wait to confront their son. Kyle drove Ava and his wife over to JB's to get the cars while he went back to the men's prison to wait for Kane. They had bailed him out first, but Ava was release before him.

"Where's Kylie?" Ava asked when she and Carmen walked into her house to wait on Kyle to return.

"I dropped her off to your mother. But, don't worry, I didn't tell her what was going on. She was so happy to see Kylie that she didn't even ask," Carmen replied.

"I'll tell her myself. I'll probably be staying there until I can find me another place to stay," Ava said.

"This is your home and my granddaughter's comfort zone Ava. If anybody is leaving, it's going to be Kane," Carmen noted.

"I'm done with this marriage. I have a degree and I won't have a problem finding a job and taking care of myself. I can't do this anymore," Ava said as she burst into tears.

Carmen jumped up and pulled her into a hug, trying her best to comfort her. Ava was a bit of a spoiled drama queen, but she and her husband loved their daughter-in-law. The first few times Ava came to them crying over their son, they encouraged her to leave him. Of course, she didn't take their advice because she had been blinded by the material things that he provided.

"I'm usually not one to say I told you so, but I did. When he cheated on you the first time, you should have been done. My husband and I know thousands of people. Helping you find a good job in communications is a piece of cake. I just have to know that you're serious about this Ava. I love my kids and I'll give them the world. What I won't do is condone their imperfect behavior. Kane plays that secretive shit with Kya. He knows not to try it with me and his father," Carmen replied.

Ava had a feeling that Kya knew more than she was saying, but she couldn't prove it. She was always telling her to leave Kane too, but it was no secret that she was on her brother's side.

"I'm very serious about moving on. I'm tired Carmen. I can't even be mad with him because I sat back and allowed it. I let my love of material things take over my common sense. I feel like I don't even know who I am anymore. I barely have a relationship with my family because of Kane, but that's my fault too," Ava admitted.

It was time for her to start taking responsibility for the role that she played in everything. At one time, Ava and her twin were closer than close. It wasn't until Aiden started telling her stuff about Kane did they start to drift apart. She didn't want to believe it, but the truth just kept coming out.

"I knew that something was up with him when he showed up to my office with Landon's ex-wife. I've always known Landon to be a great father, but she was asking for joint custody of the kids. Kane and Landon were best friends at one time, so I knew that he was on some bullshit. My husband told me to give up the case, but she called and withdrew it before I had a chance to," Carmen admitted.

"Wow. I asked him if he had anything to do with that and he looked me in the eyes and lied. The shit just gets deeper and deeper and I keep stepping in it," Ava said as the front door opened.

Kane and his father walked in and he walked right up to Ava.

"Baby-" Kane said.

"Don't say shit to me, Kane. Just get your shit and go," Ava said as she waved him off, cutting off whatever lame ass apology he was about to issue.

"I'm not going nowhere. This is our home and I'm not leaving it," Kane replied.

"Cool, I'll leave then," Ava said as she turned to walk away.

"No Ava, he's leaving," Kyle said as he gave his son a stern look.

"You can come by us for a while until y'all can figure everything out," Carmen suggested.

"Can we just sit down and talk Ava?" Kane pleaded.

"In divorce court," Ava replied sternly.

"I'm not signing shit!" Kane snapped in anger as he walked pass her and went to their bedroom.

Ava shook her head at his nerve. He was dead ass wrong, but he was mad with her. If she were being honest with herself, she probably would have divorced Kane years ago. It took him a minute, but Kane stormed out of their bedroom with his duffle bag thrown over his shoulder.

"Don't waste your time filing for divorce Ava. It's not gonna happen and I promise you that," Kane said as he left and slammed the door behind him.

"Don't worry about him Ava. If a divorce is what you want, then he can't do shit to stop it," Carmen assured her.

"And you call us if you and Kylie need anything. And I mean it Ava," Kyle said as he kissed her cheek and left.

Ava locked up her house and took a shower as soon as they left. She put some clean clothes on and prepared to go see her mother. She was nervous at first but, as soon as she walked into Ella's house, she felt a calmness come over her that she hadn't felt in a while. Ella and Robin were sitting at the kitchen table eating, but her mother stood up and hugged her as soon as she saw her. Ava didn't get a chance to say anything before Aiden walked in carrying her daughter and the ice cream he'd just got for her.

"Who bailed you out?" he asked while looking at his twin.

"What!" Ella shrieked as she released Ava from her hold and looked at her.

"Kylie, go in grandma's room and watch tv," Ava instructed her daughter.

"What happened Ava?" Ella asked as soon as her granddaughter was gone.

"How did you know Aiden?" Ava asked.

"Stop asking stupid questions girl. People talk, and I listen. I told you that fuck boy wasn't right, but you didn't want to listen. How you get mad with us and we're the ones who tried to have your back?" Aiden questioned.

"I know, and I feel so damn stupid. Nigga quit his job a month ago and been lying like he's been at work," Ava confessed.

Aiden was wondering why he hadn't seen him the last few times he and Roman went back there. Ro had met a chick that worked with them at Landon's wedding, and Aiden hooked up with her friend. They waited outside the gate for them to get off work one night when he ran into Kane. Aiden was fucking with him hard, but Kane looked scared out of his mind.

"What did you go to jail for?" Robin asked.

Ava took a few minutes and explained to them the events of the night before. She didn't leave anything out and she answered her mother's questions truthfully for the first time in a while.

"That dude ain't right Ava. Don't change your mind about the divorce and try to work shit out. Be done with his ass and mean it," Aiden said.

"It's over. His mama said that she'll help me find a job and whatever else I need. He's at his parents' house and he's not coming back to ours," Ava swore.

"Maybe you and Robin can help each other out," Ella suggested.

"No ma, I'll be okay. I have a little money saved up. I just have to find me a job," Robin spoke up.

"Help each other out with what? What's going on with you, Robin?" Ava asked.

"You know Leroy's kids sold the house," Ella spoke up.

"No, I didn't know that," Ava replied.

She was so busy living in her fantasy world that she was missing what was happening in the real world.

"All those years with his ass and he couldn't even leave you a little change in his will. Thank goodness you had enough sense to keep a little stash," Ella said, shaking her head.

"Why can't you live here Robin? Mama has about four extra rooms that are empty," Ava noted.

She must have hit a sore spot because her mother and sister both looked a little uncomfortable when she mentioned it. Being who he was, Aiden wasted no time shedding light on the situation.

"Landon ain't having that shit and I don't blame him," Aiden spoke up.

"Alright Aiden. Now ain't the time for all that," Ella said, waving him off.

"No ma, it needs to be said, so I'm saying it. Y'all acting like that man is wrong, but he's not. When it comes to kids, you get back what you give out. You took care of him and Makena, and now they're taking care of you. Robin know she was wrong as fuck for choosing that nigga over her kids. Now, look at what happened. His old ass checked out and she don't have nothing to show for it. You can't expect Landon to give her something that she never gave him. Put yourself in his shoes," Aiden said, giving them all something to think about.

"I never said that he was wrong. I just told her that I had to respect his wishes. This is my house, but I haven't paid a bill in years. The bills don't even come here anymore," Ella admitted.

"I understand his feelings and that's why I didn't want you to ask him. I can afford a one bedroom for a few months until I get me a steady job," Robin said.

"Well, I don't know what's going to happen with the house once Kane and I divorce, but you're welcome to come there until you can figure something out. Hell, I don't even know how long I'm gonna be there," Ava replied honestly.

"I'm not sure if I'll need to or not, but thanks for the offer," Robin said, smiling at her baby sister.

"Do you have a picture of the twins?" Ava asked her mother.

"Yes honey, I have a bunch." Ella smiled as she pulled them up on her phone.

"Damn. They look just like Lance and Lennox." Ava smiled.

"They sure do," Ella agreed.

They all sat around and talked for a while until Ava's daughter said that she was sleepy. Ava wished they had some extra clothes over there because she would have stayed the night. She wasn't ready to go home, but she didn't have a choice. Ava wasn't prepared for the loneliness, but she had to get used to sleeping alone.

Chapter 36

An entire month had passed since Ava and Kane had separated and things were looking up. True to her word, Carmen had contacted some of her friends at a local radio station and helped Ava find a job. She had only been working for one week, but she loved her job as a communication's specialist. Her sister, Robin, had moved in with her temporarily and she had found a job as a switchboard operator for a towing company. They rarely saw each other because Ava worked days and Robin worked mostly nights. Thanks to Ella intervening, Ava, Landon, and Makena all ended up by her house at the same time one day. The tension was thick at first, but Ella did what she did best and started crying. Ava ended up apologizing to her niece and nephew and they begrudgingly accepted. Ella was no fool and she knew that things between them would never be the same. She just wanted her family to be in the same room without fussing and fighting all the time. They all agreed to be civil and that was all she wanted.

Kane was still living with his parents, but he came to their house to spend time with their daughter whenever she wasn't already at her grandparents' house. He was still begging Ava for another chance, but she stood firm on her decision. If she was being honest with herself, she entertained the idea, if only for a little while. She would probably have to kill Ella, but a part of her still loved her husband. Or maybe it was just her fear of being alone. Deep down, she knew that it would never work and that was the only thing stopping her. Kane couldn't be trusted, and he'd proven that time and time again. Ava knew that she was sending him mixed messages because she'd slept with him twice since their separation. It wasn't too deep; she just needed sex and he was there to deliver. Both times, she regretted it soon after it happened, but it was too late. Ava hadn't filed for divorce yet, but she hadn't changed her mind.

"Hey Carmen," Ava said, answering the phone for her mother-in-law.

"Hey boo. This granddaughter of mine is trying to stay over another night. I wanted to check with you before I agreed. I can get her to school in the morning, but she needs a uniform," Carmen said.

"She just probably wants to be close to her daddy," Ava assumed.

"Girl, Kane hasn't slept here since he left your house. He comes over whenever Kylie is here, but he claims that he's been staying with Kya," Carmen replied.

"Oh okay. I have to go to the store to get a few things, so I can drop something off to her," Ava said.

"Okay sweetheart. We'll see you soon," Carmen said before they disconnected.

Ava sat there deep in thought for a little while. Kane was never going to change. She specifically remembered him telling her that he was living with his parents, but he was ready to come back home. He was in tears one night telling her how he couldn't even sleep because she wasn't next to him. Ava hadn't talked to Kya much since she and Kane separated, but she was almost certain that he wasn't living with her.

"Lying ass nigga," she said as she got up and went to her daughter's bedroom.

She packed Kylie an overnight bag with a school uniform and left out of her house soon after. Ava was going to cook a nice Sunday meal but, since she was going to be there alone, she decided to grab some fast food. After dropping Kylie's clothes off by her grandparents, she decided to grab some takeout from the Chinese restaurant before going back home. While she waited at the light, Ava spotted Kya's car pulling out of the daiquiri shop drive-thru that was located across the street. Kya didn't drink, so Ava was surprised to see her there. She grabbed her phone and decided to mess with her since she was stuck at the red light across the street.

"Hey sis," Kya said when she answered the phone.

"What the hell are you doing heifer?" Ava asked with a smile, although she already knew.

"Nothing, at home about to take a nap," Kya said, wiping the smile from Ava's face.

"Oh, okay, well call me later," Ava said before she hung up.

Kya had no reason to lie to her, so she didn't understand why she did. Abandoning her previous plans to get something to eat, Ava turned around at the light and decided to follow her soon to be ex-sister-in law. It had just gotten dark out, but Ava made sure to stay at least two cars behind her. She followed her on the bridge for about ten minutes before she got off and continued to drive. Ava was surprised when she saw Kya turn towards the projects because she was unaware that she knew anyone who lived in that area. Kya was just as sheltered as she was and maybe more.

It was dark and Ava was a little nervous. She was about to abandon her mission until Kya pulled up to one of the houses and parked. The projects had been renovated to look like homes and they were nice and well kept. Not many people hung outside at night, but the house that Kya had just pulled up to was the exception. There were three women siting out front in folding chairs while kids played all around them. Ava had to do a double take when she saw Kane's car parked right in front. Aiden had his ass right all along. Her twin was always saying that he was messing with bitches in the projects and it was obviously true. Kya was a shady bitch, but it was all good.

"Damn Kya. It's about damn time," one of the women said when she got out of the car with two gallons of daiquiris.

The woman had a bold, gold colored weave that flowed down her back. The hair looked neat and professionally done, but it was too much in Ava's opinion. Every part of her exposed arms was covered with tattoos and she was loud as hell. Her big mouth was what allowed Ava to creep up on them without them even noticing.

"That line was long as hell," Kya replied, right as she spotted Ava in her peripheral.

"That must have been a short ass nap," Ava said sarcastically when they locked eyes.

"What are you doing around here Ava?" Kya asked nervously.

"Shit, I should be asking you and your brother that question. Carmen seems to think he's been living with you, but we both know that's a lie, since I see his truck parked out here," Ava sneered.

"Who is this?" the woman with the gold weave asked.

"That's my brother's wife, Ava," Kya replied.

"Girl, Kya, I know you didn't bring no drama to my house," the woman said as she stood to her feet, letting Ava get a good look at her.

She had a huge ass and a huge beer belly to match. Her legs were small, but her hips were wide, making her body look uneven and weird. Ava worked hard to keep her body and appearance together. Obviously, that didn't mean much to her husband as she looked over at the hood rat who she assumed he was messing with. She was the only one talking, so she had to be the other woman.

"I didn't have nothing to do with this," Kya swore.

"How does she know where I live then?" the woman asked.

"I don't know," Kya answered.

"Y'all can stop talking about me like I'm not standing here. I can answer for myself," Ava noted.

"Look, I don't know what's going on with you and Kane, but please don't bring your marital problems to my doorstep. Fuck around and get me and my kids put out," she replied, as her two friends folded up their chairs and walked away.

They were loud as hell and they didn't want their names to come up in no mess. The new owners of their complex were very strict. People got put out every day for one thing or the other. Truthfully, they weren't even supposed to be sitting out there like they were. They didn't need Ava to make matters worse.

"Ava, just leave. You and Kane are separated, so you have no reason to cause a scene," Kya said, pissing Ava off.

"Girl, fuck you and fuck your brother. You ain't nothing but a liar, just like his ass. But, you were the same bitch that smiled in my face the whole time, knowing what the fuck was going on. Now, I see why my brother fucked your sad ass and left you alone," Ava snapped, hurting Kya's feelings.

Kya was head over heels in love with Aiden at one time and that was a sore spot for her. People were standing around waiting to see if something was going to pop off, but Ava was calm. She just wanted to see everything for herself and not assume anything.

"I'm going inside and y'all need to leave. Janae, get your brother and sister and come on!" the woman yelled to her daughter as she folded up the chair that she was sitting in.

Both little girls took off running towards their mother, but the little boy kept riding his big wheel.

"I'm the wrong one for you to be mad at. Me and my mama told you to leave my brother a long time ago, but you chose to stay. This is not my fault," Kya said angrily.

"Kane! Get your ass off that bike and come inside!" the woman yelled, making Ava swallow the words that were about to come out of her mouth.

"K... Kane?" she stuttered as her heart beat erratically in her chest.

"Shit," Kya mumbled to herself, but Ava heard her loud and clear.

She looked at the little boy who shared the same name and, as she looked closer, the same features as her husband. There was no need to ask questions when the answer was staring her right in the face. The boy looked to be about two or three years old, so there was nothing that Kane could tell her. Ava didn't have a doubt in her mind about the state of her marriage now. It was over and there was no coming back from that. They must have been too loud because the front door swung open, and a shirtless Kane stepped out onto the porch. He had a frown covering his handsome face until he saw his wife standing there staring at a secret that he'd tried his best to keep hidden.

"Baby, let me explain," he said, sounding like a damn fool.

"Kane, you better get this stupid hoe from around here. I don't have time for this shit," the golden-haired woman fussed.

"Bitch, you better not ever disrespect my wife like that again. Fuck wrong with you, hoe," Kane snapped as he got in her face.

She flinched, but she didn't say anything. Instead, she went inside and got his keys and shoes and threw them outside before closing and locking her door. Kane had her fucked up for real. It wasn't like he did shit for her anyway. He spent the night and fucked her occasionally, but it wasn't that serious. He did take care of his son and that was good enough for her. Besides his sister, no one else in his family even knew that her baby existed. Kane never spent time with him, so he wouldn't be missed.

"Can we go home and talk baby? Please, just let me explain myself," Kane begged.

"Nigga, fuck you. You better go back inside with your bitch. Don't come back to my house unless it's to pack the rest of your shit!" Ava yelled as she walked back to her truck.

"Man, that's still my house too. Five minutes Ava. Just give me five minutes to explain," Kane begged her as he grabbed her from behind.

"Let me go! I don't know what took me so long, but I'll be going to file for divorce tomorrow," Ava cried.

"I'm not signing shit, so you're wasting your time. Please don't do this Ava. What are people gonna think?" Kane said, hoping to play on one of her insecurities.

Ava lived for appearances and she wanted people to think that her life and marriage were perfect. That was why she'd swept his other affairs under the rug and stayed with him.

"For the first time ever, I really don't give a fuck," Ava said as she got in her car and pulled off.

She was physically and mentally drained and she couldn't take anymore. As much as it pained her to admit it, her family was right. Ava felt stupid and she wasn't afraid to admit it. She drove around aimlessly for a while, as Kane blew her phone up with calls and texts. She finally made up her mind and drove to the only place that had ever felt like home. Ava's eyes were red and swollen from crying, but she didn't care. She got out of her car and used her key to enter her mother's house. She expected to see Ella in the living room when she entered, but she was greeted by Aiden instead. He looked at his twin sister with pity as he pulled her into a hug and let her cry on his shoulder. She didn't have to say anything because he already knew. Truthfully, he'd known for a while, but some things Ava just had to see for herself. That was the only way she was going to believe it. Aiden was supposed to go out that night, but something compelled him to stay home. It was like he knew that his sister needed him, and he was happy that he was there for her.

Chapter 37

"Okay baby, we probably got about thirty minutes," Faryn said when she rushed into the room and started taking off her clothes.

Landon already knew what was up and he started stripping too. Having two newborns in the house was no joke and they had to seize every free opportunity that they had. The twins were now two months old and caring for them was not an easy task. Faryn was so thankful for Lance and Lennox because they were a big help. She and Landon taught them how to wash and fix the bottles, so that was their job. Faryn alternated between breastfeeding and formula and that helped her to drop some of her baby weight faster.

"Let's get it," Landon said as he pulled Faryn close and started kissing her neck.

"No baby, we don't have time for foreplay. Just put it in," Faryn said.

"Damn. I feel so cheap," Landon joked as he climbed on top of her.

He and Faryn moaned at the same time when he entered her and started moving. Landon started off slow, but he had her legs bent back and touching the headboard soon after.

"Shit, yes!" Faryn screamed as he pounded into her.

As soon as she got comfortable in one position, Landon switched it up on her. He was making the best out of whatever time they had, and Faryn had no complaints. Her moans of pleasure bounced off the walls as Landon sucked, slapped, stroked, and pleased every inch of her body. They moved all over the room, from the bed, chair, dresser, wall and eventually ended up on the floor, where Landon finally unloaded inside of her. Faryn was happy that she was on the birth control shot because she would have probably been knocked up again.

"That was so good," Faryn panted as sweat rolled down her damp, naked body.

"It always is. And stop trying to rush me," Landon replied while getting up and pulling her up with him.

"I'm sorry baby, but you know our time is limited. Your daughter is a crybaby and your son is greedy as fuck," Faryn laughed.

"Not too much on my kids," Landon said while laughing with her.

He couldn't dispute the truth in her words because she was right. London didn't go to sleep unless she was in somebody's arms, and Junior was hungry every hour on the hour. It didn't help that Lance and Lennox wanted to hold them all the time. They were the ones spoiling them more than anybody else.

"I need to find us something to wear," Faryn said as she opened their huge walk-in closet.

"No baby, just leave them here," Landon replied.

"No Landon. You've been getting up with them by yourself for the past three nights and you need a break. The boys are going with their mama and I'm taking the twins to the mall with me and Harley. This will be their first time really getting out besides doctor's appointments," Faryn noted.

"Yeah, but we've never taken them anywhere without each other. That's gonna be too hard," Landon said.

"I have their stroller and Harley will be with me. I'll be fine," Faryn assured him.

"I might come with y'all." Landon yawned.

"No, Landon. I know you're tired and you need to relax. Grab the monitor and let's take a shower before one of them wakes up," Faryn suggested.

She and Landon took a shower before she resumed her task of finding them something to wear. She fixed breakfast for the boys before Landon saw them off to go with their mother for the day. Malia had been spending a lot of time with them lately and they seemed to enjoy it. She hadn't given Landon and Faryn any problems since the last stunt she pulled, and they were grateful. Once the boys left, Landon and Faryn fed the twins and got them dressed for the day.

"This nigga is getting fat as hell," Landon laughed as he watched his son sucking on his fist.

He looked like a butterball turkey lying there with his navy blue Ralph Lauren jumper on. He was way bigger than his sister because he ate twice as much. London had gone back to sleep, but she had on the pink version of the same outfit as her brother.

"That's because his greedy ass is always hungry," Faryn replied as she packed their baby bags.

Landon admired his wife in her fitted joggers and off the shoulder shirt. Faryn looked great to have had two babies only two months ago. Landon fussed at her because she lived on Slim Fast and water for the first six weeks after she had them. She couldn't exercise, so she did the next best thing.

"Are you sure you're good baby? If you need some time to yourself, just let me know. I don't want you to lose yourself in this house or me and the kids," Landon said as he walked up behind her and kissed her neck.

"Don't do that Landon. I told you that I'm not Malia. I love taking care of you, our house, and our kids. I have the family that I've always wanted and I'm not complaining. We're in this together," Faryn assured him.

"Okay, I just have to make sure you're okay," Landon replied.

He didn't want to make the same mistake twice. Things moved kind of fast with him and Faryn, and he didn't want her to get overwhelmed. Faryn had moved in with him and became a wife and mother to two babies in a little over a year. Not to mention becoming a stepmother to the two that he already had. That was a lot to take in, but she handled it all well. Landon was still encouraging her to open her own business, but she wanted to wait until the babies got a little older.

"Make sure you get some rest baby. Forget the video game and the tv. Just relax and enjoy your time alone," Faryn said as they strapped the babies in their car seats.

"Shit, you ain't said nothing. I'm going my black ass right back to sleep," Landon said as he yawned again.

Faryn gave him a kiss before she pulled off and left to go pick up Harley. When she pulled up, Harley and Kyron were already outside sitting on their porch. Kyron came to the car to speak and see the babies.

"Aww Faryn, they are so cute. They're getting so big," Harley cooed as she continued to look in the back seat at them while Faryn drove.

"I know girl. Landon was talking all that shit about wanting one more when they were first born. His ass changed his mind after the first week," Faryn laughed.

"Well, Kyron and I have finally decided to try. We got our home and now we want to fill it up with some babies," Harley said.

"I'm so happy for you, friend. I can't wait to get that phone call."

"Yes, but please let it be just one. Twins don't run in my family, so I should be fine."

"Besides my mama, I don't know of any other twins in my family. Hell, I barely knew anybody in my family," Faryn noted as they pulled up to the mall.

Harley helped her load the babies and their bags in the double stroller before they went inside.

"Bitch, that stroller is everything. It looks too pretty for them to even use," Harley complimented.

"I know, I love it. Makena ordered it from Saks, so I know it cost a grip," Faryn replied.

She and Harley walked from store to store, with Faryn buying something in just about all of them. She'd already put some of her purchases in her trunk and she would probably have to make a second trip. Besides buying a few things for the twins, she got Landon and the boys a lot of stuff too. The only person who she didn't shop for was herself.

"I'm tired as hell. My lazy ass needs to walk more," Harley said as they sat on a bench in the center of the mall while Faryn fed her son. Both babies were up, but London was just looking around while sucking on her pacifier.

"Being on the treadmill again is helping me with that. I'm trying to get the rest of this baby weight off. I gained over fifty pounds when I was pregnant," Faryn confessed.

"How did you lose it so fast?" Harley asked.

"Breastfeeding helped, but I lived off Slim Fast and water for a while too. I haven't lost all of it and Landon doesn't want me too. He likes my thicker frame, but I don't. My ass looks like it needs its own zip code," Faryn joked.

"Girl, you are sexy. Bitches pay top dollar to get an ass like that," Harley reminded her.

"I just want to lose about ten more pounds and I'll be satisfied," Faryn said as her son finished the last of his bottle.

"Let me burp him. I need all the practice I can get," Harley said as she reached her hands out for the baby.

Faryn happily handed him over as she put his bag back underneath the stroller. She and Harley were done shopping, so they were leaving just as soon as they grabbed a bite to eat.

"Hey stranger," someone walked up behind them and said loudly.

Both Faryn and Harley turned around at the same time and saw Monica's ratchet ass standing there. She had on a fire red wig with some too tight jeans and a tank that showed off her muffin top. The chick that she was with was no better with some faded leggings and a belly shirt. She had a bonnet on her head and a cigarette behind her ear. They didn't look like they were there to shop, and Monica rarely purchased anything from the mall. She preferred buying flea market knock-offs or beauty store leggings.

"Hey girl," Harley spoke back. "What are you doing in here?"

"I just came from paying my phone bill," Monica said as she pointed to the store behind her.

"Oh okay. So, what's been up?" Harley asked, making small talk.

"Shit, you tell me. I haven't seen you since you moved," Monica noted.

"Yeah, I've been busy getting my place together," Harley replied.

"Damn. Well, I guess I'm not invited to the new house," Monica said sarcastically.

"I guess you're right," Harley shrugged as she cradled the now sleeping baby.

"I bet all your other fake ass friends have been there though," Monica said, taking a cheap shot at Faryn.

"Bitch, talk to me when you stop rocking a pre-paid phone. High school kids don't even do that shit no more," Faryn chuckled.

"Okay, Faryn, let's get going. We can find somewhere else to eat," Harley said as she buckled Junior in the stroller.

She was trying to avoid a potentially bad situation. Faryn and Monica never did get along and she didn't want nothing to pop off in the mall. Harley wanted to scream when she and Faryn walked off and Monica and her friend followed them.

"Is this bitch following us?" Faryn questioned out loud.

"Bitch, my friend's car is parked this way. Fuck I need to follow your hoe ass for?" Monica said loudly, making people turn to look their way.

"Faryn, please. Think about your babies. Landon will kill you," Harley whispered to her friend.

She could see that Faryn was ready to pop off and she didn't blame her. Monica had been provoking her for a long time. The timing and the place was just all wrong. Harley was happy when they made it out of the mall but, as usual, Monica couldn't keep her mouth closed for too long.

"Whose ugly ass kids are those?" Monica smirked, as her friend laughed hysterically.

Harley knew right then and there that all her attempts to keep Faryn calm were in vain. Monica had just signed up to get her ass whipped and she deserved it. Faryn didn't bother replying to her. She just walked up to her and swung. The first lick caught her off guard and made it hard for her to recover. Harley moved out of the way with the babies, as Faryn gave Monica the beat down that she had been begging for. Monica's friend was easing over to them, but Harley stopped her before she could do anything.

"Don't do it boo. It's not even worth it," Harley said as she flashed her Taser and made it buzz for good measure.

The other woman quickly backed down as she watched her friend get manhandled. Harley was mortified as she watched people standing around with their phones out recording. When Faryn slammed Monica's face into her knee, Harley knew that she had to break them up. Blood gushed from Monica's nose as she dropped to the ground, moaning in pain.

"Bitch, let's go. We're gonna go to jail," Harley said as she looked around nervously.

Thankfully, the crowd had disbursed just as quickly as they came. Monica was back up on her feet talking shit just like she was known to do. Harley was happy that they were outside and mall security wasn't riding around. There was no way in hell that she could explain to Landon that his wife had gone to jail for fighting in public. They quickly walked away, as Monica yelled obscenities. She was telling Faryn that it wasn't over, but it should have been with the way she got her ass beat.

"Fuck!" Faryn yelled angrily as they made it to her car.

"What's wrong?" Harley asked while strapping one of the babies in the car seat.

"Bitch made me chip my nail. I just got my shit done yesterday," Faryn replied.

"Get your crazy ass in this car and let's go. Are you trying to get locked up?" Harley asked.

Faryn made sure that her babies were safely secured before she got into the car and pulled off. She checked her face for scratches or bruises and was pleased to see that she didn't have any. All that shit Monica talked, and she didn't even have any hands. That was the way it was most of the time. The loudest one in the room was usually the weakest.

"I'm so hungry," Faryn said, right as her phone started ringing.

"Let me connect it for you," Harley offered as she pressed the talk button on the dashboard.

"Hello," Faryn said, answering her phone.

"Faryn!" Roman yelled out loud.

"Yeah Ro. What's wrong?" she asked him.

"Who the fuck is you outside the mall fighting with? Me and Chad are on our way," Roman fumed.

"No, I already left. How did you find out about that so fast? The shit just happened," Faryn said.

"Me and Chad were at the barber shop just now. Some chick that was in there getting her hair done showed everybody. She was on Facebook when one of her friends went live. I wouldn't have even known it was you if I wouldn't have seen your girl standing there with my niece and nephew in the stroller," Roman said angrily.

"Damn, now everybody is gonna be looking at me sideways when I go in there next week," Faryn replied.

Faryn had started going to Harley's hair stylist a few months before she moved in with Landon, and she loved the way she did hair. Harley had been going to the same girl for years, but she had just moved to a new location. It was purely coincidental that the new location shared space with Faryn's brothers' barber shop. Faryn hadn't gone since a week before she had the babies and that would be her first time going back. She wanted to try a new color and the stylist told her that she had the perfect one in mind.

"Nobody is gonna look at you sideways, girl. People fight every day in the hood," Roman said.

"Yeah, but Landon is gonna kill me if he finds that out though," Faryn worried.

"You know we ain't saying shit, but word travels fast," Chad spoke up.

"I see that," Faryn muttered.

"Who the fuck was that bitch? That's all I want to know. I couldn't really see her face on the video," Roman said.

"That was that bitch, Monica. Malia's sister. I'm sick of that hoe always coming for me," Faryn argued.

"I know she ain't on no bullshit about you being with Landon," Chad stated.

"No, it's nothing like that. I knew her before I knew Landon. I didn't even know that she was Malia's sister when we got together. She's Harley's friend," Faryn pointed out.

"She was my friend," Harley corrected with a roll of her eyes.

"Bum bitch called my babies ugly and I lost it," Faryn replied.

"That bitch must have a death wish. Maybe she should have asked her sister about me," Roman added.

"Let it go Roman. She got what she asked for and it's over," Faryn replied.

"Yeah, she most definitely got that ass spanked," Chad laughed.

"Call us when you get home baby sis. Me and Chad want to see the kids," Roman requested.

"Okay. We're going to get food and then I'll be there right after," Faryn said.

"Bet, we'll see you later," Roman said before hanging up.

"Lil sis must be crazy. She got the whole game fucked up if she thinks this shit is over with," Chad spoke up.

"Shit, with the way Faryn beat her ass, it is over with," Roman laughed.

"Why couldn't it have been that bitch Malia instead?" Chad frowned.

"Give the damn girl a pass, bruh. She's been calm for the past few months."

"Fuck that bitch." Chad frowned.

"She's not the one that I really want. That fuck boy who Aiden's sister is married to is the one. I'm happy that she left his ass. That way, I won't feel bad about doing him dirty when the time comes," Roman replied.

Kane was still public enemy number one in his eyes. He and Chad knew all about his history with Faryn and they had asked around about him. He was lame just like they'd assumed, but he was a pretender. He was still going around bad mouthing Faryn, even though it had been over two years since they were together. Aiden wanted to do him in a long time ago, but he had his sister and niece to think about. Kane had done his sister dirty and had him reconsidering his decision. Roman and Chad knew just about everyone in the projects, so it was no coincidence that they knew the chick, Shantel, who Kane had the baby with. She got put out of her apartment after Kane's wife went there and caused a scene and his sad ass didn't even help her and his son find another place to stay. Shantel told them all about the things he was saying about Faryn, Aiden, and Landon. He was talking reckless, and Roman and Chad weren't feeling that. They promised Aiden that they would let it go, but they didn't know if that was a promise that they would be able to keep.

"If she wasn't Aiden's sister, I would have probably tried to get at her. I like that nigga though, so I don't want it to be no beef," Chad said as he rolled a blunt.

"Yeah, her stuck up ass is just your time, but I'm not interested," Roman replied.

"Since she's Aiden's sister, neither am I. What her husband did would be a walk in the park compared to what I would do to her. She ain't ready for niggas like us," Chad said, making Roman laugh as they drove around and waited for Faryn to get home.

Chapter 38

"A fucking baby Kane! Huh! You have a three-year-old son and you didn't think to tell me or your mother about it?" Kyle fumed as he paced back and forth in his living room.

"You had a wife and child at home Kane. What the hell were you thinking?" Carmen chimed in.

Kane sat there in silence as he got scolded like he was a child. That's exactly why he refused to move back home with them. His life had spiraled out of control and he didn't know what to do to fix it. Ava made good on her promise and filed for a divorce. Kane meant what he said and didn't sign the papers. In fact, he ripped them up into little pieces and mailed them back to her. He was sure that the divorce would be granted eventually, but he wasn't going to make it easy on her. They had to be separated for a year for anything to happen anyway.

Having his wife find out that he had an outside child was never a part of the plan. His son's mother, Shantel, was a ghetto bird who he got caught up with. She was four months pregnant when she revealed it to Kane and he immediately told her to get rid of it. When she informed him that she was having a boy, he quickly had a change of heart. Kane had always wanted a son, but his wife didn't want any more kids. One was enough for her and she'd already had the little girl that she wanted. Just like always, Kane let his wife have her way. She was the love of his life and telling her no was never something that he wanted to do. Ava was the only woman that he could truly say he ever loved. Well, she was, until he met Faryn.

Just thinking about Faryn put a frown on his face. In his mind, none of his misfortunes started until she entered the picture. He and Landon would still be best friends and he would still have his family intact. It wasn't her fault that he cheated, but her presence started a chain of unfortunate incidents. Then, to top it off, he'd learned through Ava, before they split, that the man he'd seen Aiden hanging with was her brother, Roman. He was the same man who Malia had left Landon for. Shit was getting crazier by the minute and Kane didn't know if he was coming or going. He already had to watch his back because of Aiden. Now, he had to add Faryn's brothers to his list of enemies.

"So, what do you plan to do Kane?" his father asked, shaking him away from his thoughts.

"About what?" Kane questioned.

"What the hell do you mean about what? Your son's mother called my wife saying that she didn't have a place to stay. You need to man the hell up and handle your business," Kyle fussed.

"We have a business Kane. I don't need random women calling my office telling me about grandkids that I didn't even know I had," Carmen noted.

"Man, she got two other kids. She's acting like I'm her only baby daddy. Why didn't she ask one of them other niggas? It ain't my job to find her a place to stay," Kane said, making his father look at him like he was crazy.

"Are you out of your fucking mind boy?" Kyle barked as he walked up on his son.

"Look, let's all calm down and try to figure this out," Carmen said as she placed a comforting hand on her husband's chest.

"This is not our problem to figure out Carmen. We've been fixing his messes since he got old enough to make them and I'm sick of it. Kane is a grown ass man and it's time for you to stop pacifying him. He's dragging our family's name deeper and deeper through the mud. His ass is selfish and only thinks about himself. I'm ready to wash my hands with him and this entire situation. If you wanna sit here and help him out of yet another mess, then be my guest. I'm done with this shit," Kyle said as he stormed out of room and out of the house, slamming the front door behind him.

"He acts like I asked for his help." Kane frowned once his father was gone.

"You need to understand the position that you've put us in Kane. Until today, we never even knew that this woman and child existed. For years, we were under the impression that Kylie was our only grandchild. Now, I have no problem putting her up in one of our rental properties rent free, but it'll be on her to pay her bills. Does she have a job?" Carmen asked.

"Yeah. She's a secretary or whatever," Kane replied.

"Well, you need to set up a time and date for us to discuss this. I don't want her here or at my office. Maybe we can meet up at a restaurant or something. I'll let you know when and where. I have to calm your father down before I can do anything else."

"Man. He be tripping for nothing," Kane said.

"It's not for nothing Kane. You might not think so, but this is a very serious situation. I know that you were trying to protect you wife's feelings, but you were selfish to keep that child hidden the way you did. Now, we have a grandchild that we don't even know and who doesn't know us. And before I do anything financially for anybody, I need something in black and white to prove that what she's saying is true."

"We already did that. A DNA test was the first thing that I did when he was born. I know he's mine," Kane replied.

He pulled out his phone and showed his mother pictures of the little boy who had features that were identical to his and Kylie's.

"Yeah, he's yours. God, Kane, you should have said something," Carmen fussed.

"Kya knew, but I couldn't tell that to you and daddy. I couldn't run the risk of Ava finding out," Kane admitted.

"Kya is not your parent, but I'm gonna get on her ass too. You were married, and she shouldn't have condoned that mess."

"I'm still married," Kane corrected.

"Not for long, but that's irrelevant right now. I want to meet him. I've already lost out on three years of his life at no fault of my own. Kylie needs to know that she has a brother as well. I'm sure she'll be happy about it, if nobody else is," Carmen replied.

Kylie was always saying that she wanted a brother or sister, so that was going to make her day. Ava was probably heartbroken, and she had every right to be. Carmen and her husband loved her like a daughter and they hated what their son had done to her. Thankfully, she had found a job that she loved, but they had no problem helping her out financially if she needed them to.

"I'll call his mama to see if I can get him for a little while Saturday. I've never taken him anywhere before," Kane admitted.

"And that's just sad," Carmen said as she shook her head and walked away from him.

Kane didn't care about his parents being upset. He had enough on his plate, and he refused to let them or Shantel add any more to it. She was a sneaky bitch for going behind his back and contacting his mother. She was looking for a come up, but he would be damned if he let her use his people to get it. He was already stressed, and she was trying to make it worse.

He wished he could go to JB's for a drink and some stress relief, but they were still closed. Apparently, the police had been watching the popular strip club for a minute and they had a lot of evidence against them. Undercover officers had pictures of the illegal activities and lots of other proof to go along with it. JB didn't even have a liquor license anymore, but that didn't stop him from selling liquor. He had a million violations that he had to fix and that was going to take a while.

"Yes?" Shantel snapped when she answered the phone for Kane.

"Have him ready Saturday. My mama wants to meet him," Kane said.

"I have to work. Saturday is the busiest day," Shantel replied.

"Dress him and bring him there with you. I'll pick him up," Kane suggested.

"I'll text you the address," Shantel said.

She didn't even give Kane a chance to respond before she hung up on him. She didn't regret her son, but she regretted the day that she'd met his father. Shantel knew that she was dead wrong for messing with a married man, so that was her own fault. Kane was out with some of his frat brothers one night when Shantel caught his eye. She was hood, but she had an ass that had him mesmerized. Kane got them a room that same night and they had been off and on since then. He wasn't the best father, but his sister Kya picked up where he lacked. Kane used to send her over with money for his son, and she and Shantel formed a friendship. When Shantel got put out of her apartment, it was Kya who encouraged her to reach out to their mother. Carmen had them spoiled rotten and she knew that she would help. Kane basically didn't give a damn, but she knew that Carmen wouldn't let her grandson go without. Shantel had sixty days to be out and she was praying for a miracle. Until then, she continued to work while looking at other options.

***

"Come on Robin, tell me where you want this shit to go," Aiden said as he walked in with another box full of stuff.

Leroy's kids had emptied his house and Robin was moving in with Ava. Although she and her little sister always did get along, Robin didn't want to stay with her too long. She wanted a place of her own and she hoped that she could get one soon. Robin loved living close to her mother and she wanted to see if she could get a place close by her again. Living with Ella would have been perfect, but Landon put a stop to that. Robin knew that she handled the situation with her kids wrong when they were younger, but she didn't just throw them away. She knew that her mother would take good care of them and she did. Robin gave them money whenever she could, and she saw them all the time. Leroy was an older man and he didn't have the patience for kids. His children were grown, and he didn't want to start all over again. Robin wanted it all. She wanted the man and the kids, so she found a way to make it happen. Her kids didn't see it that way though. They felt like they were thrown away, but that wasn't the truth. Clarence wasn't even their father and they treated him like more of a parent than they did her.

"Just bring it to the room that I'll be sleeping in. I'll unpack it later," Robin said after a long pause.

"Here, this is the keys to your new lock," Raheem said as he handed two keys to Ava.

He was in the process of changing her locks, making sure Kane didn't have access to enter or exit as he pleased.

"Thanks Raheem. Now, all I have to do is get the access code changed for the alarm," Ava replied.

"Don't let that nigga have you shook like that Ava. What, is he threatening you or something?" Aiden asked as he carried the last box into the house.

"No, but I don't want to take any chances. He's already fighting this divorce tooth and nail. There's no telling what else he's capable of. It's like I'm seeing a side of him that I never knew existed," Ava said.

"That part of him has always been there. You just didn't want to see it," Aiden noted.

"Yeah, maybe you're right," Ava sighed.

"Ain't no maybe about it," Aiden said, right as her phone started ringing.

"Hey Carmen," Ava said when she answered her phone.

"Hey honey. I'm at home stuck on an emergency conference call that I can't get out of. I had to send Kya to get Kylie from school and she's about to drop her off to you. Tell my baby that I'll call her as soon as I'm done. We were supposed to do something together this evening, but this came up unexpectedly," Carmen rambled.

Ava wanted to snap on her for asking Kya to come to her house, but Carmen didn't know that she now hated her daughter. Carmen and her husband had always been there for Ava and she would never do anything to hurt them. It wasn't their fault that their union produced two lying, sad ass kids.

"Okay, I'll tell her. Thanks, Carmen," Ava said before they disconnected.

"Where are you going?" Robin asked when she saw Ava heading for the front door.

"I'm going to sit on the porch. Kya is coming to drop my baby off and I don't want that bitch nowhere in my house." Ava frowned.

"Aww shit, let me come sit out here with you. I might luck up and get me some head if I play my cards right," Aiden said as he followed his sister out.

"I don't care what you do with her," Ava replied as she sat on her wraparound porch and played on her phone.

Aiden had dogged Kya out so bad at one time that he and Ava got into. Kya was her only sister-in-law and she felt bad that her brother had done her so dirty. Kya confessed to her that she was in love with him, but Aiden didn't care. She was one of many and he treated her as such. Kane warned her not to mess with him, but Kya did it anyway. Aiden wasn't boyfriend material and he knew that's what his little sister was looking for.

"Here that bitch come now," Ava said when she saw Kya's car turning onto her street.

She didn't budge from her spot on the porch as she watched Kya stop in front of her door. She expected her daughter to get out and come inside on her own, but she noticed that Kya was preparing to get out as well. She probably only did that because she saw Aiden standing there.

"Hey my baby," Aiden said when Kylie ran up and jumped into his arms.

"Do you have homework baby?" Ava asked her daughter.

"No," Kylie said as she ran over and hugged her next.

"Okay, go take your uniform off and get a snack until I finish cooking," Ava said, right as Kya walked up holding Kylie's overnight bag.

She had stayed the night with her grandparents the night before and Carmen had taken her to school.

"Here's her clothes. My mama said that everything is already washed," Kya said as she handed Ava the bag that was snatched from her hand.

A part of her wanted to apologize to Ava for the part that she played in keeping Kane's outside child a secret. That was her primary reason for getting out of the car in the first place. The look on Ava's face told her that it was not the right time or place to say anything. Having Aiden there wasn't a part of the plan either. Kya had never known him to be at his sister's house, not that she wasn't happy to see him.

"What's up Kya?" Aiden asked as he walked up on her.

"Hey Aiden." She smiled and blushed.

"I'm trying to get some head. You got me or what?" Aiden asked, wiping the smile from her face.

"Fuck you, Aiden. Don't disrespect me like that," Kya said as she turned to walk away.

"Fuck you, bitch. Don't talk stupid to my brother," Ava said as she stood to her feet.

"What's the problem? It ain't like you never did it before." Aiden shrugged.

"Look, I know that you're upset with me and you have every right to be. I'm sorry, okay? I was wrong for the part that I played in everything. We're adults and we should be able to talk as such," Kya said as she stopped walking and turned to face her sister-in-law.

"Bitch, please. The only thing for us to talk about is you sucking my brother's dick like he just asked you to," Ava replied angrily.

"What's up with it?" Aiden asked as he unbuckled his belt.

Kya had tears in her eyes as she power walked to her car and sped away. Ava used to be like the sister she never had. Her feelings were hurt by the way she had just talked to her. She tried to be the bigger woman and apologize, but that obviously wasn't good enough.

"Stupid bitch," Ava spat once she pulled off.

"Damn Ava, I didn't know that you had it in you. I guess you are Ella's child after all," Aiden joked.

"Yeah, I guess I am," Ava replied as she walked inside to go spend time with her daughter. Aside from Carmen and Kyle, everyone else in the Monroe family could kiss her ass. She couldn't wait to be rid of Kane and his last name too.

Chapter 39

"I think I'm gonna just cancel my appointment until next week," Faryn said as she and Landon sat in the nursery and fed the twins.

"Why baby? You've been complaining about how your hair looks for weeks," Landon reminded her.

"I know Landon, but I don't feel right leaving them here. I thought Makena was going to come over," Faryn noted.

Makena was stuck at home in bed with the flu. She'd originally agreed to come over and help Landon with the babies while Faryn went out for a while, but she couldn't do anything right now. Faryn and Harley were supposed to get their hair done and go to the nail salon, but she was having second thoughts. She didn't trust leaving her babies at home with Landon and the boys while she was gone for so long.

"I know how to take care of my kids, Faryn. I leave them here with you and I don't feel no kind of way about it. What's the difference?" he questioned.

"I'm a mother, Landon," she noted.

"And I'm a father, Faryn," he countered.

They stared at each other for a while, neither refusing to back down. Faryn was doing exactly what he didn't want her to do. She was losing herself in him and the kids, and he didn't like that. She needed time to herself and he wanted her to get it. Even when she went shopping with Harley, she didn't come back with anything for herself. Everything she purchased was for him and the kids. Landon felt so bad that he went on the Saks website and ordered her three pairs of red bottoms. She was so surprised when they came, but she was happy. She couldn't stop smiling and that made Landon smile too.

"Okay Landon, I'll go, but you better answer the phone every time I call. And don't let Lennox and Lance hold them all day. That's what their swings are for. And don't overfeed Junior because he'll start throwing up. Make sure you put cream on them after each diaper change because I don't want them to get rashes. I pumped some milk this morning and I'll let the boys make a few formula bottles too," Faryn rambled.

"Baby, calm down. I've been a parent longer than you have. I know what I'm doing. Me and the boys can handle them by ourselves for a while. Just go enjoy yourself," Landon laughed.

Faryn tried to make everything easier for them before she left, but Landon didn't let her. Once she saw that he wasn't budging, Faryn got dressed and headed out to enjoy her day with her best friend. Akira wasn't going to get her hair done with them, but she wanted to join them at the nail salon and dinner when they were done.

"You know I hate driving, but I feel like I've been behind the wheel more than ever lately," Faryn complained when she picked Harley up from her house.

"Stop complaining with your spoiled ass. Your husband is your personal chauffer, so you never drive anyway. Hell, you don't even lift a figure when Landon is around," Harley replied.

"Shut up and enjoy this free ride," Faryn laughed as she drove them to the hair salon.

As soon as they got there, their stylists got right to work coloring Faryn's hair. They made small talk for a few hours, as she relaxed and trimmed Harley's hair as well. Once Faryn was done, she had to sit and wait while Harley got her hair curled.

"Bitch, I'm jealous. I want my hair that color. It's beautiful," Harley said as she admired the magenta colored hair that her friend was now sporting. Faryn's dark hair had to be lifted to display the color and it came out better than she thought it would. She couldn't wait until Landon saw it. She knew that he would love it as well.

"It's so pretty," April, their stylist, agreed.

"Thanks y'all." Faryn smiled.

"Faryn has a nice grain of hair. She doesn't get relaxers, so she can get color anytime," April noted.

"I guess I need to thank my daddy. Whoever he is," Faryn said, making them laugh.

"When are you gonna bring the babies, so I can meet them?" April asked.

"Girl, Landon ain't letting his babies come in here," Harley said.

"They're my babies too, bitch. But, um, she's right. My husband ain't having it," Faryn laughed.

"I'm trying to see how you dropped all that baby weight so fast. I'm still trying to shake back, and my daughter is almost two," April said.

"Slim Fast and water were my life," Faryn said as she got up and walked to the front sitting area.

The receptionist was sitting there with a cute little boy who must have been her son. She looked like a hot ghetto mess, but she was sweet and professional on the phone and to the customers who walked in. She answered the phones and took appointments for some of the barbers and stylists and she assisted with walk-in customers too.

"He is so handsome," Faryn said as she smiled at the cute little boy.

She couldn't wait until her babies were at the age that they could go places and walk on their own.

"Thank you," the woman said as she smiled back.

"Mama, I have to use the bathroom. I can't hold it no more," the little boy whined, right as the phone started ringing.

"Give me a second baby. These phone just won't quit ringing," she replied as she answered the call.

As soon as she was done with one call, the phone started lighting up again.

"I can take him for you, if you don't mind," Faryn offered.

"No, I don't mind. Thank you so much," the lady replied.

"Come on baby. Let me bring you to the bathroom," Faryn said as she grabbed his hand and led him to the back of the shop.

She took him into the women's bathroom and helped him undo his belt buckle and pants. He went into the stall alone, and Faryn fixed his clothes once he was done. She picked him up and helped him wash and dry his before they exited.

"I want something out of there," he said as he pointed to the vending machine.

"Okay, point to what you want," Faryn said as she lifted him up so that he could see.

"That," he said as he pointed to a bag of cookies.

Faryn put him down and took some money out of her purse to buy it. Once he had his snack, she grabbed his hand and led him back to the front. She wanted to turn right back around when she saw Kane standing there talking to the receptionist.

"Thank you so much. Come on Kane, your daddy is here to get you," the lady said, shocking Faryn with her revelation.

According to what she knew, Kane only had his daughter with Ava. Faryn knew that him and his wife were getting a divorce and his outside child was probably one of the reasons why. Now that she really looked at him, the little boy favored Kane a lot. It had to be a slap in Ava's face that he was named after him as well.

"The fuck is my son doing with this hoe, Shantel?" he spat while pointing at Faryn.

"Excuse you?" Shantel said while looking at him like he was crazy. She wasn't aware of Kane and

Faryn's history and she just thought that he was being rude.

"Don't worry about him girl. He's just mad because his son probably has a bigger dick than he does," Faryn said, making Shantel snicker.

She couldn't even dispute the other woman's claim because that was so true. Kane didn't have the biggest piece, but he knew how to use the little that he had.

"You're talking all that shit, but you kept my shit in your mouth," Kane said, loud enough for the entire shop to hear.

Harley had just finished getting her hair curled when she, April, and some of the barbers looked up front to see what was going on. She wasted no time going to stand next to her friend when she saw that she was arguing with Kane. Harley remembered him from Faryn's wedding. Landon beat him down to the ground and he was still trying to come for his wife.

"That lil shit wasn't much to suck on. I've had bigger lollipops," Faryn said, as the entire shop erupted in laughter.

She didn't know that people were watching, and she was instantly embarrassed when she saw that a crowd had formed. Kane felt played as he walked over to her in a fit of rage.

"Bitch," he spat as he grabbed Faryn by her shirt.

Faryn and Harley were ready to swing on him, but they didn't have a chance to. The men in the shop quickly sprang into action and immediately pushed Kane back.

"Nigga, you must not be from around here. You better get the fuck on before your people be reporting you missing," Jimmy, Roman and Chad's barber, bellowed.

"Give me his shit and let me get the fuck up out of here!" Kane yelled as he walked back over to Shantel.

"I don't want to go," her son said as he held on tight to her arm.

"Let's go boy!" Kane barked, making his son jump in fear.

"Oh, hell no, nigga. You ain't taking my baby nowhere with that attitude," Shantel said as she held her crying son.

"Fuck you too then, bitch. And don't call my people begging for nothing else. Take care of that lil nigga on your own," Kane spat as he stormed out of the building.

"I'm sorry everybody. That's my son's sperm donor because he's damn sure not a father," Shantel apologized.

"That nigga got the entire game fucked up. He must not know who shorty's brothers are," one of the barbers said, referring to Chad and Roman.

"Y'all be careful leaving out of here. I don't trust his ass," April said as she peeped out the front door.

"Let me know when y'all are ready. I'll walk y'all out," Jimmy offered.

"We're ready right now," Faryn replied.

She and Harley made their next appointment with April before Jimmy walked them out and made sure they got to their car safely.

**

"He didn't hit me. We just argued," Faryn said as she watched her husband pacing back and forth with the phone up to his ear.

He was on the phone with Ella, trying to get her to ask Ava about Kane's whereabouts. Faryn had barely made it out of the shop when her brothers started calling her to see what had happened between her and Kane. She tried to assure them that it was nothing, but they weren't having it. She picked Akira up and continued with her original plan for the day. By the time she made it home, her brothers were already there and had filled Landon in on what was going on. He was upset with her because she didn't call and tell him herself.

"That man don't give a fuck about that. His bitch ass needs to get dealt with," Roman said as he and Chad played the game on the big screen with the boys.

"Shut up you snitch," Faryn whispered.

"That's how you feel lil sis?" Roman asked with a smirk.

"You damn right. Y'all didn't have to tell him nothing. Trying to get my husband locked up and shit. I already told y'all that he got a bad ass temper," Faryn mumbled.

She got up and started the twins' swings up again, right as Landon hung up the phone.

"What did she say?" Chad asked.

"They don't know where that fuck boy lives at right now," Landon replied as he cast an angry glare at Faryn.

"I'm sorry baby. I should have told you, but I didn't think it was a big deal. Nothing really happened," Faryn said while apologizing to her husband again.

"I'll deal with you later," Landon said, making her brothers chuckle.

If it were anybody else, that statement about dealing with her would have been a problem. Since it was her husband, they had nothing to say about it. Landon was good to their sister, so they knew that he wasn't going to harm her. He was pissed, and he had every right to be.

"Don't trip brother-in-law. That nigga gon' get what's coming to him. That bitch Monica is on my radar too. I hope she don't think I forgot about that fight y'all had the other day," Chad smirked.

"What fight?" Landon asked as he turned to look at his wife once again.

"I got the snitching charge, so I might as well become a snitch," Chad said as he and Roman fell out laughing.

"Get out! I want both of y'all out and I'm blocking y'all numbers!" Faryn threatened angrily.

"Answer my question Faryn. What fight are they talking about?" Landon asked.

"It was nothing baby. Don't even stress yourself out over that," Faryn said while rolling her eyes at her brothers.

"It must be something if you keep trying to hide shit from me," Landon fussed.

"I think it's time for us to go. Y'all be good and we'll see y'all later," Roman said to Lance and Lennox.

"Okay," they both said as they continued to play the game.

"We'll get up with you later brother-in-law. And don't worry about nothing, we got this. You're a family man and you need to focus on your family," Chad said, as Landon walked them out the front door.

He shook both men's hands right before they got into the car and pulled off. When he went back inside, Faryn was sitting on the sofa scrolling through her phone.

"Come on, so we can give them a bath," Landon said as he picked his son up from his swing.

"You want us to help dad?" Lance asked him.

"No, y'all can finish playing the game. I need to talk to Faryn," Landon replied, right before he walked away.

Faryn grabbed her daughter from her swing and followed her husband upstairs. She and Landon never really argued, but there was a first time for everything. He was heated and Faryn knew that just by looking at him.

"Baby-" Faryn started before he cut her off.

"Tell me what happened and don't leave nothing out," he ordered.

"Okay," Faryn said as she ran the entire story down to him, leaving nothing out.

"Didn't I tell you when we first got together that we don't do secrets?" Landon questioned.

"Yes, but-" Faryn started.

"It ain't no buts, Faryn. You can't pick and choose what you want to tell me. That's not how this works. A lot of marriages fall apart for that same stupid shit," Landon argued.

"You're right and I'm sorry. I promise that it won't happen again," Faryn swore as she leaned over and kissed him.

"I like your hair," he complimented.

"Thanks. I was wondering when you were gonna say something." Faryn smiled.

"I was pissed, and I wasn't thinking about that at first," Landon admitted.

"I'll make it up to you later. I won't even get mad if you run your hands through it," Faryn smirked.

"Will you be on your knees while I'm running my hands through it?" Landon asked hopefully.

"Whatever you want baby." Faryn winked as she grabbed what the twins needed to take their baths.

"Hell yeah. Your fat ass better go to sleep early tonight," Landon said to his son, as the baby smiled in return.

Faryn laughed at his silliness, but she was happy that they could resolve their minor disagreement. Landon was always cool and calm, and Faryn wanted him to stay that way. It wasn't that she was trying to keep anything from him. She just didn't like to upset him. Even still, Landon was right. She couldn't pick and choose what she wanted to tell him. She had to share everything with her husband, no matter how it made him feel. Landon was a man in every sense of the word, so she knew that he would fix whatever the problem was.

Chapter 40

❝ I know that y'all are used to having your own rooms, but this is only temporary. The room is big enough for me to fit two twin beds and some more furniture. I'll get y'all a game and tv to put in here too. It'll take some time, but I just need y'all to be patient with me. I'll make good on my promises," Malia said as she looked at her sons.

With the help of her mother, Malia had just signed the lease on her new apartment. Cora co-signed for her and she even paid her rent up for three months. She was so proud of her daughter for taking steps in the right direction. Malia worked a full-time job and went to school. Aside from spending time with her sons, she stayed inside and hit the books. Cora was happy to do whatever she could to help, but Malia had to promise not to tell her sisters. They would have a fit if they knew that Cora had their younger sister living in an upscale apartment while they called the projects their home. Malia was different though. She wasn't as tough as her sisters were. She was fragile, and Cora knew that.

"Do y'all like it?" Malia asked after they had looked around for a while.

"Yeah," Lennox replied.

"Faryn used to live back here, right dad?" Lance asked while looking up at his father.

"Really?" Malia questioned while looking to Landon for an answer.

"Yeah, but she lived in another building," Landon replied.

When Malia told him that she had an apartment, he wanted to see where it was for himself. He had to make sure that his boys were in a decent neighborhood. Malia asked him to meet her at her new apartment with their kids, and Landon happily obliged. He was pleasantly surprised when she sent him the address to Faryn's old apartment complex. The area was nice, and the apartments were nicer. They had a gym, playground, and three swimming pools. He would definitely feel comfortable with his boys being over there.

"I have a living room and bedroom set already. Y'all can sleep in the bed and I'll get a blow-up mattress for when y'all visit," Malia said.

"Can we get bean bags like we have in our rooms at home?" Lance asked.

"Yeah, I'll get y'all some." Malia smiled.

"Come on Lennox. Let's go outside on the balcony," Lance said to his little brother.

"Look, I'll get whatever they need for their bedrooms when you move in. I'm not trying to have my kids sleeping on no floor," Landon said once they were gone.

"Seriously Landon? I'll sleep on the floor before I put my babies down there. I have a king-sized bed and it's all theirs whenever they come over," Malia replied.

"You don't have to do that Malia. I got whatever they need. When are you moving in?" Landon asked.

"Hopefully, next weekend," she replied.

"Cool, I'll get my wife to get them some furniture and stuff for their room. I'll buy their game and tv too," Landon offered.

"Thanks Landon. I appreciate everything that you do. You're raising them to be great men," Malia complimented.

"That's my job." He shrugged.

"How are your twins?" Malia asked.

"They're good," Landon replied.

"How old are they now?" she questioned.

"Three months old today," Landon answered.

"Wow, they're getting out the way fast. They look so much like you and their big brothers. Lennox and Lance are always showing me pictures. I'm surprised they're not with you now," Malia said.

"Nah, my wife is hanging with her brothers and sister and she took them with her," Landon replied.

It felt weird for Malia hearing him call somebody else his wife and talking about other kids besides their own. It was also weird now that she knew that Faryn's brothers were Roman and Chad. Her sons told her that they were always at the house and that was crazy to her. Landon embracing the man that she left him for was odd, in her opinion. He and Roman never did have any bad blood, so maybe he didn't see it that way. He was his brother-in-law now and they seemed to get along great. Malia was the one who looked like a fool, but she was trying to get herself together.

"I know that you probably don't care anymore, but I want to say it anyway. I'm sorry for how I left you and our kids. I was selfish, and I didn't think about anybody but myself. We were so young when we got married and had kids, and I just felt like something was missing. I regret a lot of decisions that I made and that was the biggest one," Malia confessed.

"That's water until the bridge now Malia. Everything happens for a reason and things were destined to happen the way they did." Landon shrugged.

"I agree, but I just felt the need to apologize for my actions. You were a great husband and father, Landon. I don't want you to think that it was something that you did wrong because it wasn't. You did all that you could to make me and our kids happy. If anyone deserves happiness, it's you and I'm happy that you found it," Malia said.

"Thanks Malia. I appreciate that." Landon smiled.

He really did appreciate what she said because he did feel that way when she first left. Landon kept trying to think back to anything that he could have done wrong as a husband, but he was coming up short. He was happy that Malia had matured enough to take full responsibility and clear up the confusion. Landon hated to admit it, but he'd carried over some of his insecurities from his first marriage into his second. Faryn always reminded him that she wasn't Malia, and she was right. His family's happiness was all that mattered to him, especially his wife.

"When are you moving mama?" Lennox asked when he and Lance walked back inside.

"I hope to have everything in place by next weekend. I'm gonna start moving some things in here throughout the week though. I have two days off this week," Malia replied.

"I'll have my wife to get on that other stuff as soon as possible. Hopefully, it can be in place by then too," Landon said.

"Okay, just let me know so I can make sure I'm here," Malia replied, as they all walked out together.

She saw Landon and her boys off before she left to go do some shopping for her new apartment. Malia had never had a place of her own without a man and she was excited about it. Cora was right when she said that she had to learn to be alone. She was loving the single life and it was definitely stress free. Men tried to talk to her all the time, but she wasn't interested. She had enough on her plate already and a relationship would only complicate things.

***

"I can't believe you moved in those high ass apartments. Can you even afford that?" Monica asked as she, her sisters, and her friend sat at the bar at one of her favorite clubs.

"I'm sure she wouldn't have moved there if she couldn't," Felicia replied with a frown.

"Do you ever have anything good to say Monica? Damn, be happy for somebody for once in your life," Malia snapped.

She was sick of Monica and her negative attitude. She was always hating on somebody for one reason or another. Felicia had recently gotten back with the father of her kids and she had something to say about that as well. He had been in and out of jail for a while, but he seemed to be trying to get himself together. He and Felicia both worked, and they were trying to get their family out of the projects. That was more than she could say about Monica though.

As soon as she walked into Malia's apartment, she started finding things wrong with it. Landon had kept his promise, like always, and purchased everything for his sons' room. Malia still had a little ways to go with making her house look like a home, but it was getting there. She needed a tv for her living room and a few decorations for her walls. Aside from that, her place was fully furnished and comfortable.

"I'm just saying," Monica shrugged uncaringly.

"Just so damn negative. I can see that I'll be leaving early. Even if I have to call a cab," Felicia said.

"Girl, is that Roman and Chad sad asses over there?" Monica said out loud as she looked at a group of people huddled in the corner across from them.

There were a group of half-naked women popping bottles and twerking on the men who were seated in the area. Monica clearly recognized Roman and Chad, but she couldn't make out who the other men were.

"I might be leaving right with you, Felicia. I'm not in the mood for the drama," Malia said as she discreetly looked over where the men were.

Monica was right. Chad, Roman, Aiden, and Raheem were all sitting over there with a bunch of thirsty bitches all vying for their attention. Raheem seemed to be trying to separate himself from the madness, while the other three men were eating it up. Malia cringed when she locked eyes with Roman and he raised his glass and winked at her.

"Bitch, he's coming over here," Monica said when Roman got up and headed in their direction.

Malia didn't care one way or the other and she didn't have anything to say to him. She didn't hate Roman because she allowed him to treat her like a door mat.

"What's up Malia?" Roman asked as he walked up a little too close for Malia's liking.

"Hey Roman," Malia spoke back.

"What's up with it? You trying to get a room with me tonight or what?" Roman smirked, already knowing that she wouldn't go for it.

"I don't think so boo. Go on back over there and finish entertaining your groupies. Let me enjoy my drink in peace," Malia replied.

"I can respect that," Roman said as he nodded his head.

Malia had matured a lot since the last time he saw her. She was being more active in her sons' lives and Faryn hadn't had any more problems out of her since she was pregnant with the twins.

"Nigga act like he got it like that or something," Monica spoke up, even though she had nothing to do with it.

"You got a lot of mouth for a bitch with dirty feet," Roman said while looking down at the wedge sandals that she had on.

"Your sister and her ugly ass kids got dirty feet," Monica said, as her friend laughed. She was with the same girl that she was in the mall with when she and Faryn fought not too long ago.

"Now, you're going too far Monica," Malia said, not wanting her to involve innocent kids. Her sons were crazy about their siblings and that wasn't cool at all.

"Don't tell her funky ass nothing. Keep talking and watch you get that ass spanked again," Roman threatened.

"Again? Nigga, you got me fucked up. That hoe wish she did spank me," Monica replied.

"Let's just go y'all. I did not prepare to spend my off day like this," Malia said, right before she downed the rest of her drink.

"I'm not going nowhere," Monica said defiantly.

"Well, I'm your ride home and I'm about to go," Malia informed her.

"My friend got a car. She'll bring me home," Monica said while pointing to her girl.

"I'm ready right now. You can bring me home Malia," Felica said as she stood to her feet.

"You really are as dumb as you look," Roman laughed.

"Fuck you, Roman. I'm not Malia. You can't snap your fingers and make me jump," Monica replied.

"Don't put me in this. Say what you have to say but leave me out of it. My life has been drama free and that's how I want it to stay," Malia snapped.

"We're cool Malia. We've moved on from our issues and we're all good. Your sister needs to learn how to keep her dick suckers closed though," Roman replied.

"Fuck you. Don't worry about these dick suckers if they're not sucking your dick," Monica spat.

"Let's go," Malia said as she tapped Felicia on the arm.

Roman watched until they walked out of the club, before he turned his gaze to Monica once again.

"Bye nigga! The fuck you still looking in my face for?" Monica yelled, as her friend continued to giggle.

Roman remembered her from the video as well. She was standing there watching as Faryn beat Monica like a dog.

"You got that love," Roman smirked as he walked away.

"Stupid ass," Monica said with a frown. She was happy to be out for a while, and Roman was not going to ruin her night. The music was on point and the club wasn't too crowded. That didn't happen very often, and Monica was enjoying herself.

"The fuck are they looking over here for? Stupid ass hoes," Monica's friend said.

Monica looked over and saw that just about all the groupies who were surrounding Roman and his entourage were looking over at them. She was about to point her middle finger up to them all, but she decided against it. She and her girl were outnumbered and that would have been a stupid move.

"Girl, fuck them," Monica said, waving them off.

"I think we should go Monica. That nigga might be telling them hoes something about us," her friend said nervously.

"Stop being so damn scary Reece. Look, they're about to go. Sit your nervous ass down and relax," Monica said as she observed Roman and his crew preparing to leave. A few of the women were leaving with them while the others stayed behind.

Everyone else headed for the exit, but Roman walked over to them instead. He ordered them both another Corona and paid the bartender.

"Y'all drink up and enjoy. It's the least I can do. Y'all have a good night, ladies," Roman said as he winked at them both and walked away.

Monica could no longer resist. She threw up her finger in the middle and kept it up until he was gone.

"What was that all about?" Reece asked her, as she immediately started sipping on the free drink.

"Hell if I know. He just saved me from buying another drink, so I don't care." Monica shrugged as she too sipped her drink.

That was her fourth one of the night and she was just getting started. Monica was like a fish in water when it came to alcohol. She never got drunk, no matter how much she consumed. The only problem was her bladder. The beer that she loved to drink kept her running every hour on the hour.

"Girl, I gotta go too," Reece said when she saw Monica getting off the stool to go to the bathroom.

She grabbed both her and Monica's purses and followed her friend to the bathroom. She was happy that only one stall was occupied because her and Reece ran to the others. Once she was done, Monica walked out and came face to face with one of the girls that was sitting there with Roman. She was at the sink washing her hands when Monica went and stood right next to her. The other woman was staring at Monica like she was crazy, and Monica stared right back.

"Fuck you looking at?" Monica asked when she got tired of the stare down.

"Not a thing boo," the other chick replied before she walked out of the bathroom.

"What's her problem?" Reece asked as she came out and washed her hands.

"Girl, I don't know and I don't care." Monica shrugged as she fluffed up her dry wig.

She and Reece made small talk before they walked out of the bathroom and prepared to go back to the bar. They both stopped when they saw the chick who had just walked out of the bathroom and all her friends standing there waiting.

"Roman wanted me to relay a message. Behind his sister, you better be lucky that he didn't put a bullet in your head. Consider yourself lucky," the woman said before she hit Monica so hard, her wig shifted and almost fell off her head.

She and Reece immediately started fighting back, but it was a waste of time. They were outnumbered, and they went down to the floor in a matter of seconds. Monica's entire body was on fire as she was kicked and punched in every visible part. Her family always said it and it was proving to be true. Monica's mouth had finally written a check that her ass couldn't cash. She was getting her ass beat down and there was nothing that she could do but take it. She had learned her lesson and Roman was the teacher.

Chapter 41

Kane sipped on his drink as he watched the dancer grind and twerk her ass all over his crotch. She had a bad ass shape with a cute face, but she moved her body like nothing that he'd ever seen before. Her hips seemed to have a mind of their own as she gyrated to the floor and back up again. Kane had become a regular there for the past two weeks and she had become his private dancer, just like Faryn was at one time. He tipped her well, but he didn't break bread with her like he used to do with the other woman. JB's was still closed and it didn't seem like they would be opening any time soon. One of Kane's frat brothers told him about another strip club out in New Orleans east and he'd been going there ever since.

"You want another drink handsome?" the topless bartender came over and asked.

"Yeah, bring me another one," Kane requested.

Drinking and sleeping seemed to be all that he did lately. He refused to be treated like a child, so he'd been calling a rented suite at the Marriott his home for over a month. His money was running low, but he wasn't worried about finding a job. One call to his mother and she would get him right if he needed her to. Kane was depressed and missing his family. He hadn't see Ava or his daughter in over a week and it was messing with him. Ava was always coming up with an excuse when he wanted to see Kylie and she was starting to piss him off. Either that or his daughter was with Ella and he wasn't going anywhere near that house.

"You feel that?" Kane asked, China, the dancer who was entertaining him.

He grabbed her petite hand and put it on his growing erection to let her see what he was talking about. China smiled, but more for the payout that was coming than anything else. Kane wasn't much for her to get excited about, but he was generous. He came fast as hell so that was another good thing about being with him. They'd only had sex twice and fifteen minutes was long when it came to him.

"What do you want me to do about that?" China asked seductively.

"Let's go to the private room," Kane suggested.

"We can't. The owners have cracked down on that. They installed cameras back there earlier. See," she replied as she pointed and showed him the sign saying that the private rooms were now under surveillance.

"Damn man. The fuck they do that for?" Kane asked angrily.

"They don't want to get shut down like a lot of these other clubs. They're getting strict with that shit," she replied.

"Y'all don't have no other duck off spots around here?" Kane inquired.

"Nope, not unless you're trying to take me home with you," she replied with a smirk.

"I don't have a home," Kane said as he gulped down the brown liquid that was in his glass.

He frowned as the potion burned his chest and settled in his stomach. He had never taken China to his room and he didn't want to start. Kane didn't want to make the same mistake twice and get too caught up with a dancer. He just needed to get his dick wet, and she was the perfect person to do it. He didn't care if she just gave him some head. Anything that made him bust a nut would suffice.

"Oh well, I guess you ain't getting no pussy tonight." China shrugged.

"Where do you live?" Kane asked her.

"I live wherever the night catches me. I don't ever call one place home for too long. I guess I'm considered a drifter," China replied.

"Man, I'm trying to drift up in you," Kane hissed as he pulled her closer to him.

"I'll think of something. My shift is just about over. I know a secluded spot close by that we can go to. Go wait in your car while I go change. You can follow me there," China suggested.

"Bet. Don't be all day either," Kane said excitedly as he stood to his feet.

"Okay," China winked as she walked away.

Kane had run a small tab at the bar, so he cashed out and went outside to his car. He took a chance and called Ava, hoping to speak to his daughter. Just like he'd predicted, Ava didn't answer the phone, but he decided to leave a message. Kane poured his heart out to his wife, letting her know how much he loved and missed her and their daughter. He knew that he'd done Ava wrong, but he wished she would give him another chance. People made mistakes and she needed to know that. Kane loved the company of other women, but he was in love with his wife. It sounded crazy, but that's just how it was.

The honking of a horn shook Kane away from his thoughts. He spotted China sitting behind the wheel of a white Benz, beckoning for him to follow her. He was excited about what was to come, so he wasted no time tailing her to wherever she was going. They only drove for about five minutes before China stopped at the perfect spot. It was a secluded parking lot that was once home to a grocery store. It was barley lit and no one was outside. China didn't know it yet, but that was going to be their new rendezvous spot. It was free and isolated, two perfect combinations. Once they parked, China got out of her car and walked over to his. Kane was already undoing his pants because he didn't want to waste any time. When he grabbed her hair and tried to force her head into his lap, she pulled away.

"No nigga, you know the routine. Run me my money first," China said as she held her hand out.

"I got you, man. You know I don't play with your money," Kane replied.

"Fuck all that. I need my money upfront just like always. If that's a problem, we can go our separate ways," China argued.

Kane wanted to slap fire from her ass, but he let her make it. He needed her, so he reached into his back pocket and pulled out his wallet. After counting off more than enough money, he handed it to her. Now, he needed her to work for it.

"Come on man. Handle your business," Kane snapped.

"Don't rush me, nigga. I'm not them other hoes," China replied.

"What other hoes? You're the only hoe that I'm fucking with right now," Kane chuckled.

"I guess I am, since Faryn got married on your ass," China said, making Kane pause.

"What?" he asked as he looked over at her.

"Did I stutter nigga?" China inquired.

"How the fuck do you know anything about me and Faryn?" Kane asked.

"I got my ways," China smirked.

"You know what? I'm not even feeling this shit no more. Give me my money back and get the fuck up out of my car," Kane ordered.

"Nah, ain't no refunds boo," China informed him.

"Bitch, you got me fucked up. I'll drag your hoe ass out of this car and stomp you behind mine. Think it's a game," Kane threatened.

"Your weak ass ain't gone do shit," China laughed.

"Bitch!" Kane snapped as he lunged at her.

He immediately froze in place when China produced a small hand gun and pointed it right at him.

"What were you saying Kane? Bitch what?" China taunted.

"Chill out China. You can keep the money man. Just get out and go on about your business," Kane said.

"Nigga, I'm paid. I don't need that lil chump change you threw at me," China informed him.

"Look, I have more. You can have it all. Just put the gun away. It's not even that serious," Kane said as he pulled out some more bills from his wallet.

"I just told you that I don't need your money and it's very serious," China noted.

"It can't be that real. I've only known you for about two weeks," Kane pointed out.

"Yeah, but I've been knowing you for two months," China replied.

"That's not possible," Kane said as his heart beat rapidly in his chest.

"I've never met one person who was hated by so many people. Your wife, your baby mama, you just don't give a fuck about nobody," China said, shaking her head.

"You don't know shit about me. You just had my dick in your mouth last night and you wanna talk," Kane bellowed.

"Nigga, that ain't no dick. You should call that lil shit a pecker. And I don't need to know anything about you. Roman feels like you're better off dead and I have to agree," China said as she pointed the gun at his head.

"No!" Kane yelled, but it was too late.

China let off two silenced shots and ended whatever words were about to come out of his mouth. She took the money that he gave her and threw it all over him, as well as the baggies of cocaine that she took from her purse. She took her handkerchief and wiped down everything that she touched, just to be on the safe side. Kane's lifeless body was slumped over his steering wheel when she got out of the car and raced back to her own. As soon as she got in, her phone rang, but she already knew who it was without having to look.

"Yes Roman," she answered as she pulled away.

"The fuck was that Jessica? You were supposed to go back to his room with him!" Roman barked.

"I know that Ro, but he was acting like he didn't want to take me there. I had to improvise, but I think this worked out better. They have cameras at hotels anyway, so I'm happy I didn't go there," Jessica replied.

"Yeah, you're right. Did you cover your tracks and do what I told you to do?" Roman asked.

"Yes, I did. Nobody saw me leaving the club or followed me, right?" Jessica asked.

"No, you're good," Roman assured.

"Okay boo. I hope you're still coming over tonight," Jessica purred.

"Yeah baby. I gotta handle something right quick and I'll be there," Roman replied before hanging up.

"Landon was right. Pussy really was the death of that nigga," Chad said, shaking his head.

"One less fuck boy that we have to worry about," Roman replied as he drove off and got on the bridge.

When he reunited with his sisters a few months ago, he had no idea what was going on in their lives. They were very forthcoming about everything that had taken place over the years. He learned all about Faryn's history with Kane and he wasn't feeling him from day one. Faryn was one of the sweetest people that someone could have the pleasure of meeting and she had been that way since she was a little girl. He was tired of people coming at her sideways. Malia seemed to get her mind right quick, but the same couldn't be said about her sister and Kane. He was sure that the two-night stay in the hospital got Monica right, but it was deeper with Kane. He was doing too much to too many people.

The last straw for Roman was when he got a call from his barber saying that Kane had tried to hit Faryn. He was already talking to Jessica about getting at him, but they hadn't officially come up with a plan.

It was like fate was on his side when Jessica told him that Kane had come into the strip club where she worked. She had seen Kane a few times when Roman pointed him out, so she knew how he looked. China Doll was Jessica's stage name and she caught Kane's eye the moment he saw her. Roman had her working to gain Kane's trust, but he never really let his guard down. The plan was for her to go to his hotel room, but things turned out even better. Jessica was a pro at what she did, so she knew how to handle herself. Roman didn't care how she did it, just as long as it was done. He wanted his sisters to live normal, drama free lives for once and he would stop at nothing to ensure that they did.

***

Ava replayed Kane's final voicemail to her over and over as the tears continued to cascade down her face. To an outsider, she appeared to be crying over her husband's death, but that wasn't entirely true. She was still angry for a lot of reasons, but she was hurt too. She and Kane were far from being civil with each other, but she still wouldn't have wished death on him. It had been almost two weeks since he was killed and buried, and no one knew what had happened. The media was calling it a drug deal gone wrong, but Ava wasn't buying it. Kane had kept a lot of things from her throughout their marriage, but she didn't think that selling drugs was one of them. They found money and drugs thrown around his car, so it was an open and shut case in their eyes. New Orleans had too many murders for them to focus all their attention on just one. Of course, Kane's case made the news, mostly because of who his parents were. They were both respected attorneys, so that was nothing new.

"What did they say Ava?" Ella asked when she walked into the living room.

She had been staying with her daughter since her husband was killed, in an attempt to comfort her and her granddaughter. Although Ava and Kane were separated, they were still legally married.

"The same thing. I thought it was a mistake, but it's accurate. I can't believe how stupid I was. He had me thinking that we were balling out of control and we were damn near broke," Ava said, her anger now overshadowing her pain.

The biggest mistake that she'd ever made in life was letting Kane have full control over their finances. Ava had a bank card, but she just swiped without a care in the world. When she went to the bank to check their balance, Ava thought that the representative had made a mistake. She had just called back and spoke to someone else and got the same answer. She and Kane didn't have nearly as much in their account as she thought. Ava was thankful for his insurance policy, but that wasn't enough for her to live on. She was happy that she had a job because she definitely needed it. Ava was crying for more reasons than one. Even in death, Kane was proving to be an asshole. She was learning things about her husband that she would have never imagined.

"I don't know why y'all young women do that. Let these men control all the money and don't check to see what's going on with your account. I used to be on your daddy's ass honey. He wasn't taking care of another bitch with none of that money. God rest his soul, but he was on his death bed and I was checking the bank balance," Ella noted.

Ella's feelings towards Kane had changed, but her heart went out to his parents. She remembered when Raheem's father was shot some years ago; she almost lost her mind thinking that her son was dead. She was so thankful when she got to the hospital and learned that he was only shot in the arm. That was a blessing too because some people didn't survive those either. No parent wanted to bury their child and she hated that they had to go through that.

"I know mama, but that's the way it's always been. He worked and he handled the finances," Ava replied.

"The dumbest mistake that you've ever made in your life," Ella said as she walked off to go finish cooking.

Ava couldn't even say anything because her mother was right. Kane pretended to be the perfect husband, but he had been doing her dirty all along. She had to sit on the front row in the church at her husband's funeral, while a baby mama that she didn't even know about for years sat a few rows behind her. Carmen and Kyle embraced Shantel and her son, but they still treated Ava like his wife. She wasn't mad at them for wanting to get to know their grandson. She also knew that her daughter would be happy to have a brother. Kane's parents had taken some time off from work and they had both his kids at their house with them. Ava and Shantel were cordial to each other at the house when they both showed up and she hoped that's the way it would always be. Ava wasn't about to have beef over a dead man. She wasn't going to have beef over Kane, even if he was alive.

"Is the food done?" Aiden asked when he walked into the house.

"I don't think so," Ava replied as the interruption broke her away from her thoughts.

"Where's Robin?" Aiden asked while taking a seat next to her.

"She's at work, but can I ask you a question?" Ava inquired.

"What's up?" Aiden questioned.

"Please be honest with me, Aiden. No matter what you say, my loyalty will always remain with you. I know how important family is and I'll never forget that again," Ava replied.

"You said all that to say what?" Aiden asked, wondering where the conversation was going.

"Did you have anything to do with Kane's murder?" Ava asked him.

That had been bothering her since she first learned of her husband's death. She'd wanted to ask her brother that question from day one, but she didn't know how to approach him. Aiden and Kane never did get along, so it wasn't impossible. She would go to her grave with his answer, but she just had to know.

"As much as I hated that nigga, I would never do that to you and Kylie. I thought about it a few times, but I didn't fuck with it. He got a pass on the strength of y'all," Aiden admitted.

"I didn't mean to offend you, Aiden, but I had to ask. I know that y'all didn't have the best relationship," Ava replied.

"Nah, for once in my life, I'm innocent," Aiden said as he got up and went to go see how long the food would be.

Ava felt good to know that her twin had nothing to do with her husband's murder, but she wondered who did. That was a mystery that would probably never be solved, seeing as how Kane rubbed so many people the wrong way. Knowing him, he'd probably done things that Ava didn't even know about. Obviously, something and someone from his past had finally caught up with him. Thanks to whomever it was, Ava had gone from being a divorced woman to being a widow.

Chapter 42

"Hey Landon, I'm at the gate," Malia said when she pulled up with their sons.

They had stayed the night with her and she was bringing them back home. They usually stayed all weekend, but Malia had a big test to study for. They didn't bother her, but she didn't want to keep them inside all weekend doing nothing.

"Okay, it should be open," Landon replied before he hung up.

Malia drove through the gates and pulled up in front of their house.

"Look at the twins!" Lennox shouted when he saw Faryn walking with her friend and pushing his siblings in their stroller.

She and Landon always took the babies for walks around the estates, just to get them out of the house for a while. Since Harley and Kyron had come to visit, she walked with her friend instead.

"I'll call y'all when I take a break from studying," Malia promised her sons.

"Okay ma, I love you," Lennox said as he leaned over from the back seat and kissed her.

"I love you too, baby, and I promise that we'll do something fun next weekend," Malia said when he got out of the car.

"Good luck on your test," Lance said with a smile.

"Thanks baby. I'll see you next weekend. I love you," Malia said while kissing his cheek.

"I love you too, ma," Lance said, bringing tears to her eyes.

That was his first time ever saying it back to her since they had started spending time together regularly. He reminded Malia so much of his father with his mannerisms and take-charge attitude. He was mature for his age and very smart. Malia knew that Faryn had a lot to do with that too and she appreciated her. She had prolonged the inevitable long enough and it was time for her to do the right thing. After getting out of the car, Malia walked over to Faryn and her friend.

"Hey, can I talk to you for a minute Faryn?" Malia requested.

"Yeah. What's up?" Faryn asked.

"Uh, y'all help me bring your brother and sister inside," Harley said to Lennox and Lance.

Malia recognized her as her sister Monica's friend, but she didn't think they talked anymore. Monica didn't really talk to anyone much anymore. Ever since she got jumped at the club that time, she mostly stayed to herself. She didn't go out at all anymore and she stayed inside a lot. They did her dirty and she was paranoid about every little thing now. After suffering a broken nose and multiple other injuries, she was like a new person. Cora said that she got some sense beat into her, and Malia believed her.

"Is everything okay with Lance and Lennox?" Faryn asked once they were alone.

"Yeah, they're fine. I just wanted to take a minute to say thank you for everything. I appreciate how you take care of my sons and how you love them. They love you just the same and that makes me feel good. I thought that a relationship with Lance would never happen, but even he's come around and I know that it's because of you. I'm happy that Landon found you, not only for himself, but for my boys too," Malia said, shocking Faryn with her kind and heartfelt words.

"No thanks needed Malia. I love them like my own and it's my pleasure." Faryn smiled.

"Okay, well, I won't hold you. I just wanted to say that," Malia said.

"Thanks Malia. That meant a lot to me," Faryn said as she walked away and watched as Malia did the same.

"What was that all about?" Landon asked as soon as Faryn got back inside.

"I should have known that your nosey ass was looking out the window," Faryn laughed.

"Hell yeah, I was looking. I thought we was gon' have to jump her ass," Landon joked.

"No, she was cool. We'll talk about it later," Faryn said, not wanting to talk in front of their guests.

"Now that that's settled, let's finish our discussion Faryn," Harley said as she and her husband sat down and held the babies.

"There is nothing to discuss Harley," Faryn replied.

"Come on Faryn, these babies are four months old now and you haven't done anything fun since before you were pregnant," Harley noted.

"I'm a wife and a mother. That's very fun to me," Faryn replied.

"You know what I'm saying Faryn," Harley fussed.

"I don't want to go clubbing nowhere Harley. You and Patrice don't need me to have fun," Faryn pointed out.

"Yes, we do. We're like the three musketeers. All for one and one for all," Harley said, making them laugh.

"Why can't y'all be the dynamic duo?" Faryn asked with a giggle.

"You always have to be difficult. Patrice is baby free all weekend and she wants to go out for a while. We'll go anywhere you want to go," Harley offered.

"Okay, well, y'all can come here. This is the only place that I want to be," Faryn replied.

"Help me out Landon. Don't you want your wife to go out and have fun?" Harley asked.

"Leave me out of that one," Landon replied as he watched his sons play the game.

He'd made that mistake before and he wasn't about to do it again. He encouraged Malia to go out once before and she ended up meeting another man and leaving him. If Faryn wanted to go out, he wouldn't stop her, but he was damn sure not going to suggest it. He had gone out with Aiden and Raheem a few weeks before, so he would never have a problem with it.

"Ugh, I give up. Don't get mad when you hear about all the fun we had either," Harley warned.

"I won't," Faryn said as she took a seat next to her husband.

Harley and Kyron stayed over for a little longer before they left to go home. She and Patrice were going club hopping later and she wanted to take a nap before they did. Faryn contemplated going with them, but she changed her mind. She would have much rather stay at home with her husband and kids instead.

"Makena said that my grandma cooked enough food to feed an army. You wanna go over there and eat?" Landon asked her.

"Hell yeah. No cooking for me today. I didn't feel like it anyway," Faryn replied.

Lance and Lennox made the babies some bottles, while Faryn and Lance got them dressed. A few minutes later, they were in Landon's truck in route to Ella's house. She was so happy to see them once they got there. She and Makena grabbed the babies while Landon, Faryn, and the boys ate.

"They are getting so big. I'm so happy y'all came over," Ella said as she smiled at her great-grandkids.

"We came over a few days ago, but you weren't here," Landon noted.

"Yeah, I've been going back and forth from here to Ava's house. That damn Kane was a no-good somebody, but that's what her ass gets. She tried to turn her back on her family for his cheating ass and look at where that got her," Ella replied.

"She makes me sick, but I feel sorry for her and Kylie. Thank God, she got a job to support herself," Makena spoke.

"Yeah because he barely left anything in the bank. She should have had a bigger insurance policy on his ass too. She could have been set for life," Ella added.

"She was a fool for letting Kane handle all the finances without having input," Makena said.

"Her and Robin are some dumb bitches. At least Ava had a ring and a policy. Robin don't have shit but an expensive wardrobe to show for all the years that she was with Leroy. His kids even sold the Cadillac that he just got before he died," Ella informed them.

"I'm sorry, but I don't feel bad for her," Makena said, right as the front door opened and Robin walked in.

She was still in her work uniform and she looked tired and beat down.

"Hey everybody," Robin greeted. Nobody but Ella and Faryn spoke back to her, but that was nothing new.

"I cooked a little bit of everything. Go fix yourself something to eat," Ella suggested.

"I'll fix it to go. I'm tired after working those twelve hours," Robin replied as she sat down.

She had been working a lot of long hours and she just wanted to see her mother before she went home. She was thankful that Ava let her borrow the car because catching the bus most days was hell. Both her kids were financially well off, but they wouldn't even buy her a skateboard if she asked.

"Fix something for Ava and Kylie too," Ella requested.

She hated the tension that existed between her family, but they were all adults. She couldn't make them have a relationship with each other, even though she wanted them to. Landon and Makena made it clear that they wanted nothing to do with Robin, and she had to respect that. They didn't really say much to Ava either. Ella was just happy that they could be in the same room without arguing and trying to fight.

"Can I hold her?" Robin asked as she stood over Makena and looked down at London. Makena looked to her brother for an answer before she did anything.

"Yeah, you can hold her," Landon replied, making his wife smile.

He and Makena made it very clear to their mother where they stood. There was no need to be petty and he wasn't trying to be.

"She's so pretty," Robin said as she smiled down at her only granddaughter.

It was bad enough that she didn't have a relationship with her kids, but she probably wasn't going to have one with her grandkids either. Robin took the blame for the role that she played in it all, but she honestly thought that Landon and Makena were being a little too harsh. They had a reason to not want her around and she understood that. She just wanted them to let her be a part of her grandkids lives. She wanted a chance to get it right, but they weren't having it.

"Thanks," Faryn replied to the compliment.

Robin stayed around a while longer before she fixed her food and left. Makena and Faryn put the food away and cleaned Ella's kitchen before they all left too. Once they got home, it was only a little after six. Landon gave the kids a bath one by one while Faryn folded some clothes. Both babies had a warm bottle and went right to sleep afterwards. The boys went to their rooms, and he and Faryn went downstairs and chilled on the sofa. Faryn was on the phone with Harley, who was still begging her to go out.

"Bye Harley. Bye Patrice. Y'all have fun," Faryn said before she hung up on them.

"What are they talking about now?" Landon asked as he laid on the sofa behind her and pulled her close. He had the baby monitor in his hand, just in case one of the twins woke up.

"The same thing. They're going to that new club that we've been talking about," Faryn replied as she flipped through the channels on the tv.

Landon felt bad as hell when she said that. Faryn and Harley had been talking about a new club that was having a grand opening for months. Now that the time had come, she wasn't even going. He knew that she was only staying home because she didn't want to leave him alone with four kids. Landon didn't understand her reasoning behind that because she stayed home with all four of them when he went out to celebrate Raheem's birthday. He felt like he was being selfish and that was nowhere in his character. Faryn was a great wife and mother and she deserved some time to herself.

"I think you should go," Landon said after a few minutes of silence.

"Why?" Faryn questioned.

"Because I know you want to. You and Harley have been talking about that club for a minute. I think you should go," Landon repeated.

"I did want to go at one point, but I'm good," Faryn replied.

"I know you're worried about leaving me with the kids, but I can handle it. You haven't done anything in a long time. Go out and enjoy yourself," Landon suggested.

"Are you sure baby?" Faryn asked as she turned around and looked at him.

"Yeah, call and put Harley out of her misery," Landon laughed.

"Thanks baby. Let me go find something to wear," Faryn said as she jumped up and ran upstairs.

Landon had a sinking feeling in the pit of his stomach, but he tried his best to ignore it. Clarence's words kept ringing in his ears and he knew that his stepfather was right. Faryn was nothing like Malia and he had to stop thinking the worse. His wife had never given him a reason to doubt her love or loyalty. He had to shake off the bad feeling that he was getting and trust that his wife was the same woman that he had married some months ago and nothing had changed.

Chapter 43

"Bitch, these niggas are thirsty as fuck. How you asking to eat somebody out in a crowded ass club? Stupid ass don't know if I wash my ass or not and he's trying to put his mouth on me," Patrice fussed when she walked back over to them.

"They don't care either. Nigga probably got a wife and kids at home too," Harley replied.

"After working in a strip club for four years, I've seen it all. Some of these men need to be single. And some of these women are dumb as fuck," Faryn noted.

"Yeah, like your auntie by marriage," Harley said, referring to Ava.

"Fuck that bitch. She be trying to talk to me on the slick, but I be ignoring her stupid ass. As long as Kane was alive, she was throwing me all kinds of shade. Now that somebody put him out of his misery, she wants to be my bestie," Faryn rambled.

"She sounds like Landon's mama. Didn't you say she be trying to be friendly with everybody too?" Harley asked.

"Yeah, but she doesn't bother me as much. I don't fuck with her too much on the strength of my husband, but she's never done anything to me," Faryn admitted.

"I'm sorry, but I don't blame Landon and his sister. I thank God for my daughter every single day. I couldn't imagine turning my back on her just to keep a man," Patrice spoke up.

"I feel the exact same way," Faryn agreed.

"But, on another note, they did a damn good job with promoting this grand opening. This bitch is packed," Harley said as she looked around.

They got lucky and found an area to sit in, but the place was jam packed to capacity. It was hard to see who all was in there because they were shoulder to shoulder. They walked around to see the entire club but, when they found a seat, they sat down and ordered some drinks.

"I'm just happy that we found a seat. I didn't realize how long it's been since I wore heels. I gotta get used to wearing them again," Faryn replied.

"Are you supposed to be drinking Faryn? Aren't you breastfeeding?" Patrice asked her.

"I pumped before I left, but I can drink. I would just have to wait about four to five hours before I fed them if I didn't. They drink formula too though," Faryn pointed out.

"I can't wait to have me a little bundle, so I can join in on the baby conversation," Harley smiled, right as a man walked over to them.

"Hey. Can I talk to you for a minute?" he asked while looking directly at Faryn.

"Sorry, but I'm married," Faryn answered politely as she flashed her ring.

"Can I buy you a drink?" he offered.

"I'm good, but thanks anyway." Faryn smiled.

"Come on ma. What's one drink? What your husband don't know won't hurt him," the man persisted.

"I know it won't hurt him, but it just might hurt you. No, you can't talk to me and I can buy my own drinks. Have a good night," Faryn said, dismissing him.

"Fuck you then, bitch!" he spat angrily.

"I wasn't a bitch just now when you were Keith Sweat begging!" Faryn yelled to his departing back.

"These niggas are a mess," Patrice said, laughing at Faryn's last comment.

"The fuck I want with chicken when I got a lobster waiting for me at home. Stupid ass is the same height as my stepson," Faryn fumed.

"Bitch stop, I almost spit out my drink," Harley laughed.

"Damn man. They act like every woman that comes to the club is looking for a man. Can a bitch just sip a few drinks and listen to some music?" Faryn questioned.

"Exactly. I'm surprised your brothers aren't in here Faryn," Harley said as she looked around.

"They're in Florida laid up with some rats. They called me on Facetime this morning," Faryn replied.

"How you know they're with some rats?" Patrice asked.

"I don't, but that's how they described them," Faryn laughed.

"They are true bachelors honey," Harley said.

"True male whores is more like it," Faryn laughed.

"How's Akira?" Harley asked.

"She's good. School is kicking her ass, so she doesn't hang out too much anymore. Her and Clarence are coming over for dinner tomorrow though," Faryn answered.

The three of them continued to sit around and make small talk until a popular song came on. Faryn hadn't danced in a while, but she was happy to see that she still had her moves. One song turned into several more as they occupied the dance floor with lots of other people. Faryn's feet was killing her, but she had a ball. Between dancing, drinking, and walking the club, she was worn out. She was happy that Landon had talked her into going, but she was happier when Patrice said that she was ready to go.

"Baby, this outing don't owe me nothing. And Kyron better put a baby up in my ass tonight as tipsy as I am," Harley slurred as they walked out to their cars.

Faryn had driven her Camaro and met them there, but Patrice was driving her to her ride. She had parked in the back lot, since she got there after them.

"I'm happy I'm driving. This drunk bitch ain't good for nothing," Patrice laughed as they helped Harley get into the car.

"I had fun. We have to do this again," Faryn said when they pulled up to her car.

"Yes, we do honey. My baby is getting bigger, so my mama is getting her more. I love my free time," Patrice replied.

"See you later boo," Faryn said when she got out of the car.

"Get in your car Faryn. I'm not pulling off until you do," Patrice noted.

She watched as Faryn got into her car and started it up before she pulled off. Faryn sent Landon a message letting him know that she was on her way. She was about to pull off until she remembered that she was still wearing her heels. She had her slippers in the trunk, so she got out to get them. Faryn felt instant relief when she kicked her heels off and replaced them with her Gucci slides. When she closed her trunk and tried to walk away, she was forcefully grabbed from behind.

"Ahhh!" Faryn screamed before a strong sweaty hand was clamped over her mouth.

"Shut the fuck up before I shoot your hoe ass," a male voice that she slightly recognized threatened.

Faryn felt like she was about to lose her bladder when she felt the hard steel of a gun being pressed into her back. She couldn't help the tears that welled up in her eyes and rolled down her cheeks even if she wanted to. Her babies, Lance, Lennox, and Landon came to mind when she turned around and locked eyes with Jo-Jo. He'd lost a little weight since the last time she saw him, but that was the only thing different about him.

"Jo-Jo, please don't do this. I have kids at home," Faryn pleaded as tears continued to fall from her eyes.

"Bitch, fuck you and those kids. You think I give a fuck about that," Jo-Jo snapped as he slapped her down to the ground. Faryn's bottom lip split and she tasted the blood inside her mouth.

Jo-Jo couldn't believe how good his luck was when he saw Faryn and her girls at the club. He had gone there with some of his boys when he spotted them walking around like they owned the place. Not too long after her punk ass man did him dirty in her apartment, Jo-Jo got arrested for being a felon in possession of a firearm. Before he got locked up, he went to Faryn's apartment one night, hoping to catch her off guard. He waited until well after dark and kicked in her front door. He was stupid to think that she still lived there, but he took a chance anyway. Not only had Faryn abandoned her apartment, but Kyron and his wife had moved as well. Kyron didn't want to tell him where he lived, but it was all good. It wasn't him who he was looking for anyway.

While locked up, Jo-Jo got in touch with Monica and she put him down on everything. Not only had Faryn married the nigga who had attacked him, she had twins for his punk ass too. Monica informed him that she didn't know where Harley and Kyron lived, since she had never been invited over. Once Jo-Jo got all that he needed from her, he didn't even bother trying to call her again. Monica wasn't his type and he didn't have time to pretend that she was. She sucked him up a few times and that was the extent of their relationship. She was a rat and he treated her as such.

"I'm so sorry Jo-Jo. Please," Faryn continued to cry and beg.

"Fuck your apology bitch. Because of you, I was laid up in the hospital with a broken jaw and fractured ribs. You thought I was gon' let you and that nigga get away with the shit that y'all pulled? Both of y'all got me fucked up. That nigga about to bury you and raise them kids by his damn self," he threatened as he pulled her up by her hair and pressed the gun to her temple.

Faryn closed her eyes and said a silent prayer, waiting for the bullet that was going to end it all. She would never get to celebrate her first year of marriage or see her babies take their first steps. She wouldn't witness Lennox and Lance's first dates or their high school graduations. She and Landon deserved happiness but, sadly, they would never get it. When the loud explosion came from the gun, Faryn braced herself for the pain that never came. She opened her eyes and saw Aiden standing there holding the smoking gun that he'd just shot Jo-Jo in the head with.

"Oh God, Aiden!" Faryn shrieked as she fell into his arms and cried. Her entire body shook as she thanked God for sparing her life.

"Let's go Faryn," Aiden demanded as he grabbed her arm.

Faryn was paralyzed with fear as she looked down at Jo-Jo's dead body. Memories of when she found her mother dead came back to her and, just like before, she felt no remorse.

"Move Faryn! Let's go before we both be going to jail," Aiden yelled, snapping her out of her trance. He shoved Faryn into her running car and jumped in on the driver's side.

Aiden was happy that he took Raheem up on his offer to check out the new club. He spotted Faryn and her girls the moment they walked in and he kept an eye on them all night. It wasn't long before Aiden noticed that he wasn't the only one who was watching. He saw Jo-Jo staring at Faryn all night, but he didn't know who the nigga was. Aiden asked one of his boys who he was, and he gave him an entire rundown. Realization kicked in the moment Aiden heard his name. He remembered Landon telling him about Faryn's childhood flame and how he had to beat him down in her house that time. Aiden also assumed that Jo-Jo was the one who had kicked Faryn's apartment door in, even though she no longer lived there. His first mind told him not to drink anything and be on high alert and he was happy that he'd listened. He had Raheem and his boys under the impression that he was leaving the club with a female, but he had followed Faryn and her girls out instead.

"Faryn, listen to me," Aiden said as he grabbed her shaking hand.

"Okay," she replied as she looked over at him.

"I know that you're scared, but you can't say shit about what just happened. Even if you hear people talking about it; act like you don't know nothing," Aiden ordered.

"I won't Aiden, I promise. I'll take this with me to my grave. If you wouldn't have come, he was going to kill me," Faryn sniffled.

"Exactly, but that nigga's mama needs a black dress now," Aiden said as he dialed a number on his phone.

"Who are you calling?" Faryn questioned.

"Your husband," Aiden answered.

"What! No! You can't talk about that over the phone," Faryn panicked.

"I didn't just become a criminal overnight Faryn. I know what I'm doing," Aiden said, right as Landon picked up the phone.

Chapter 44

"**W**hy can't you stay sleep and chill like your sister?" Landon asked his baby boy, as if he understood what he was saying.

The baby only laughed and cooed like it wasn't after two in the morning. Faryn had sent a text saying that she was on her way home, and Landon was happy. He was ready to have some alone time with his wife when he heard Junior start to cry over the baby monitor.

"Here dad, I warmed his bottle," Lance said when he walked into the room and handed his father his baby brother's bottle.

"Thanks, bruh. I'm sorry that he woke you up," Landon apologized.

"It's okay. I was going to the bathroom anyway," Lance replied.

"How many bottles do they have left?" Landon asked.

"London have more bottles than him. You eat too much Junior. You gon' be short and fat just like my grandma Cora," Lance said, making the baby and his father laugh.

"You better not let Cora hear you say that," Landon laughed.

"She would kill me. Good night dad," Lance said as he yawned.

"Good night," Landon replied.

"Good night fat boy," Lance said to his brother, right before walking out the bedroom.

As soon as he left, Landon's phone rang, displaying Aiden's number.

"The fuck you doing calling me at almost three in the morning," Landon said when he answered the phone. He sat down and started feeding his son.

"Man... Faryn... this nigga... she left," Aiden said, his phone cutting off after every other word.

"Wait, what?" Landon asked as his heart rate increased. The only thing he heard was Faryn left with some nigga.

"That nigga... Faryn... when she left," Aiden said, frustrating his nephew even more.

"Bruh, I can't hear shit that you're saying. Your phone is breaking up too bad," Landon snapped in aggravation.

Again, all he heard was Faryn left with some nigga. Landon knew that there was no way that could be true. He knew that God couldn't have possibly hated him that much. He wasn't perfect, but he wasn't that bad either. Maybe having a wife wasn't in the cards for him. Maybe Aiden was on to something by having multiple women and refusing to settle down. That wasn't Landon's style though. He loved being a family man because that was something that he never had while growing up.

"I'm on my way bruh," Aiden said before he disconnected the call.

Landon fed and changed his son before rocking him back to sleep. He checked on his daughter as well, before grabbing the baby monitor and going downstairs. He sipped on the drink that he'd fixed himself as he paced the living room floor and waited for his uncle. He didn't know what happened, but it had to be something serious for Aiden to be calling and coming to his house at that hour.

When Landon heard a car pull up, he disarmed the alarm and cracked the front door, granting Aiden access. When he looked up and saw his wife walk in first, he stopped pacing and studied her face.

"What happened?" Landon asked as he walked up to her.

Faryn's eyes were red and swollen and her lip looked to be busted. When she fell into Landon's arms and started crying, he was curious as to what had happened.

"Jo-Jo tried to kill me," Faryn said as she cried and shook just from the memory of it all.

"What!" Landon boomed.

"He followed me outside the club and grabbed me when I was getting something out of my trunk. He slapped me and then pulled a gun out on me," Faryn sobbed.

"The fuck! I want that nigga dead!" Landon fumed as he tried his best to comfort his wife.

"Done," Aiden said as he sat on the sofa and looked at his nephew.

"What?" Landon questioned.

"I saw that nigga watching Faryn all night and somebody put me down on who he was. Long story short, I followed him when he followed her and handled his ass. I just hope they didn't have no cameras or nothing out there. I wasn't even thinking to look for that shit. We were the only ones in the parking lot, so I know there were no witnesses," Aiden noted.

"Fuck! I'm so sorry baby. I shouldn't have told you to go out. I feel so fucked up about this shit," Landon said while hugging her close.

"It's not your fault Landon. We haven't seen Jo-Jo in over a year. There was no way you would have known that he would be there tonight," Faryn said, trying to ease his mind.

"Turn on the news," Aiden requested.

Landon did as he was asked, but there was nothing on any of the news channels. They sat around watching for over an hour and nothing had been reported. Aiden decided to stay the night in one of the guest bedrooms, and he and Landon were the first to get up later that morning. Faryn was too scared to sleep, so Landon gave her some over the counter sleep aids to help her get a little rest.

Finally, later that morning, the news outlets had started to report that there was a murder outside of a night club at their grand opening. That was a terrible rep for a new club to have, but people would forget about it eventually. Thankfully, for Aiden, the club had cameras, but the ones outside were not activated yet. He was able to relax for the first time since he'd pulled the trigger. There were no witnesses just like he'd assumed, and the loud music inside made it hard for anyone to hear the single gunshot. Jo-Jo still had the gun in his hand when they found him, and he had a warrant out for his arrest at the time of his murder.

"Come bring me home man. I need a shower and a bed," Aiden said to his nephew as he stood up.

"Take Faryn's Camaro. I'll bring her to pick it up later," Landon said while throwing him the keys.

He walked his uncle out and saw him off before going back inside. He checked on the kids first before going in the room to check on Faryn. Her eyes were open, but she was just lying there. Landon climbed into the bed behind her and pulled her close.

"I feel so bad Landon," Faryn mumbled as she melted into his embrace.

"I know baby, but you didn't do anything wrong. It was either him or you," Landon said as he tried his best to comfort her.

"No, that's not what I meant," Faryn replied.

"I don't understand. What do you feel bad about?" Landon asked.

"I know that what I'm about to say sounds harsh, but I'm happy about what happened to Jo-Jo... and Kane," Faryn admitted.

"Damn," Landon sighed, not knowing what else to say.

"I hate being afraid of anything Landon, and I was afraid of them and what they might do to one of us. Kane was unstable, and Jo-Jo was straight up crazy. I hate that I feel that way, but I can't help it.

Those were two people who would have never let us be happy."

"I just want you to be okay baby. That shit that you saw is traumatizing and I don't want that for you. You couldn't even sleep last night."

"I'll sleep better knowing that they're no longer a threat," Faryn replied as she snuggled up closer to him and closed her eyes.

***

Two months had passed since Jo-Jo's murder and the case was still unsolved. Honestly, Faryn doubted if anyone was even working on it to begin with. She'd had nightmares for the first few weeks, but they became less and less frequent until they just stopped altogether. Harley and Patrice had called her, shocked that someone had been killed at the very same club that they were at. Faryn pretended to be surprised and played dumb, just like Aiden told her to. When Harley and Kyron told her that it was Jo-Jo, she pretended to be equally as shocked as they were. Kyron suspected Jo-Jo's friend, since he had it out for him for messing with his daughter. There was lots of speculation, but no solid proof.

Faryn and Landon were in a happy place and she prayed that it stayed that way. Landon had finally opened his laundromats and his brother-in-law was doing a great job running them. He still had his job at NASA and he didn't have any plans to quit. It was easy money, as he called it, and he would have been a fool to let that go. The twins were now six months old, and he and Faryn were approaching their first-year anniversary. Landon was trying to convince her to go on a trip, but Faryn wasn't feeling it. Makena and Ella offered to stay at the house with the kids until they came back, but she was still undecided.

"Come on London. Come to me. Come on, so we can win London. Stop laughing and come to your big brother," Lance said, coaching his baby sister to crawl to him.

"Come on Junior. You can do it. Crawl to me. Come on fat boy and crawl to me," Lennox said, hoping to be the winner.

Both babies had just learned to crawl, but they weren't very good at it yet. They scooted more than anything, but they were getting around. Lennox and Lance had a blanket on the floor entertaining themselves at their siblings' expense.

"Didn't I tell y'all about trying to race them? They're not cars," Landon fussed.

"What are y'all betting for this time?" Faryn asked as she put the finishing touches on their Sunday dinner. She thought it was hilarious how the boys used the twins to compete against one another. The babies had fun and it was fun to watch.

"Five dollars," they both said, making her laugh.

"That's a damn shame. Using my babies to gamble," Landon chuckled.

Both Lance and Lennox were doing well in school and he was proud of them. They still spent time with Malia and they were building a stronger bond with her. She and Faryn were far from being friends, but they were cordial with each other for the sake of the kids. Malia had changed back into the person who Landon had first met and that was a good look, in his opinion. She was still in school and working as a teller at the bank. Being with Roman almost broke her, but she bounced back and got her mind right.

Roman and Chad were still the same as they'd always been. They clubbed all the time and had multiple women to choose from when they wanted to. It was crazy to Faryn how they weren't even thinking about settling down. She was the only one of them who wanted kids because Akira had decided that being a mother just wasn't for her. Clarence was fine with her decision, since he felt like he was too old to become a father. They wanted to spoil Faryn's kids and that was good enough for them.

"Come on London. Don't let his fat self beat you," Lance said when he saw that his brother was moving a little faster than his sister.

"Yes! I won! Give me my money. We won five dollars Junior," Lennox said as he picked his brother up and kissed his chubby cheek.

"I can't believe you let him win London. Don't smile at me," Lance said as he picked her up and kissed her.

"Y'all come put them in their high chairs, so we can eat," Faryn said, right as her phone started ringing.

"That's Harley calling," Landon said while handing his wife the phone.

"Hey friend. Can I call you back a little later? I was just about to feed my family," Faryn said when she answered.

"Fine. If my best friend doesn't care about what's going on in my life, I guess I'll just find somebody else to call," Harley said, being extra as usual.

"You are too damn dramatic. What's up with you girl?" Faryn asked as she started fixing everyone's plates.

"My baby did it bitch! I told you that he would," Harley yelled.

"He did what?" Faryn questioned.

"He knocked me up the same night that we went out. I'm eight weeks pregnant bitch!" Harley yelled.

"Yessss! Congrats friend!" Faryn yelled, scaring London and making her cry.

"Seriously Faryn?" Landon asked as he got up to get their daughter.

"I'm sorry baby. Kyron and Harley are having a baby." Faryn smiled.

"Tell them that I said congrats," Landon said as he rocked London to calm her down.

Faryn finished fixing their food before she took her phone conversation upstairs to the bedroom.

"I'm so happy for you, friend. I know Kyron is going crazy," Faryn assumed.

"You already know he is. His mama is too. You know this will be her first grandchild," Harley replied.

"Aww, that's so sweet," Faryn cooed.

"But, enough about that. Now, on to the real tea," Harley said.

"What tea?" Faryn asked.

"Bitch, I saw Monica at the pharmacy when I went to get my prenatal vitamins. Why she told me that Roman had some girls jump her at the club? She begged me not to tell you anything because she didn't want it to get back to him."

"I know this is wrong to say, but she gets no sympathy from me. This is the first I'm hearing of it, but she probably asked for it."

"I'm sure she did. But, baby, that ass whipping got her mind right. Ole girl said she don't do the clubs no more and she's working at the nursing home with her sister. Maybe that's what her ass needed all along," Harley chuckled.

"Her sister got her mind right too. I never had a problem with her though. She was the one who didn't like me," Faryn noted, speaking of Malia.

"She didn't want to lose that good ass man," Harley replied.

"Too late for that boo. This ring ain't coming off my finger until I'm dead and gone," Faryn swore.

"I know that's right. What's up with your crazy ass brothers?" Harley inquired.

"Same shit, different day. Clubs, women, and God knows what else. Aiden is their new best friend so that's a disaster waiting to happen," Faryn laughed.

"Yes, it is. What's up with his twin bitch... I mean sister?" Harley laughed.

"Nothing that I know of. Ms. Ella said she got a job and stuff. Landon's mama is still living with her too."

"What has she been up to?" Harley questioned.

"Girl, ask me why she tried to invite me and the kids out for lunch. She must not know about me. I'm loyal to my husband, if nothing else. He laughed when I told him but, of course, I turned her down," Faryn laughed.

"The nerve of her to act like it's all good after how she did her kids and grandkids," Harley said.

"She never did anything to me, but my husband's beef is my beef. Too bad for her that we can't be friends," Faryn replied.

"Alright Deborah Cox," Harley laughed, right as Landon yelled for Faryn.

"Girl, I gotta go, but we have to hook up and celebrate the good news. I'll see if Landon will grill for us next weekend by the pool," Faryn said.

"Yes, tell him to grill some more lobster tails. That shit was good," Harley replied.

"Okay, we'll talk more about it later," Faryn said before she hung up with her.

She had cooked steak, lobster tails, and baked potatoes for dinner, but she didn't tell Harley that. Landon didn't really like company over on Sundays. Any other day of the week was fine, but Sundays was considered family day. He wanted to enjoy his wife and kids with no added interruptions.

"Well damn, I guess you forgot what today was. Got me and my kids down here eating by ourselves while you talk on the phone," Landon said as he fed the twins some baby food.

"I'm sorry baby. I got caught up in all of Harley's gossip," Faryn replied as she kissed him.

"The food was good Faryn," Lennox said as he sat his plate in the sink.

"Thanks baby. We have lots more if you want it," Faryn noted.

She fixed herself a plate and ate before cleaning up the mess in the kitchen. Once she was done, they all retired to the living room to watch a movie. Faryn and Landon cuddled on the sofa while the twins were falling asleep in their swings. Lennox and Landon were on the floor stretched out on top of a blanket.

"This is what Sundays are all about," Landon whispered as he kissed the back of Faryn's neck.

"Back your nasty ass up. I feel you getting excited already," Faryn laughed.

"We need to be trying to work on the other baby that you promised me," he replied.

"Not right now Landon. Damn, can the twins make a year first?" Faryn asked.

"Alright, but I don't want to hear no excuses," he warned.

"I'm a woman of my word. We agreed on one more, but that's it," Faryn argued.

"That's all I want. I just pray that's it's only one this time."

"Aww shit. Maybe we need to rethink this. You got the daughter that you wanted, so you should be good."

"I want another one. I got her named picked out and everything," Landon noted.

"What is it?" Faryn asked.

"I'll tell you when the time comes," he replied.

"We might have another boy," Faryn noted.

"Nah, the way I plan to aim, it'll be another girl," Landon said seriously.

"You are crazy," Faryn laughed.

"Aye, let's go upstairs right fast. We can get in a quickie," Landon requested.

"What about the kids?" Faryn asked.

"Look," Landon said while pointing to Lennox and Lance, who were on the blanket knocked out. The twins were also asleep in their swings, giving the two of them a little free time to play.

"They got the itis," Faryn chuckled.

Landon jumped up and picked her up with him. Faryn squealed when he threw her over his shoulder and ran up the stairs. He threw her on the bed and rushed to remove her clothes. When he removed his own, Faryn stared in admiration. She was kicking herself for taking so long to give Landon a chance, but she was happy that she did. Her life wasn't perfect, but it was damn near close to it since he'd been a part of it. Landon showed her what it was to be a great husband, father, and just all around great man. He loved her and his kids unconditionally, and she loved him just the same. She hated that his kids had to be without a mother for over a year, but she was so thankful that God had blessed her with her husband. As selfish as it sounded, she was happy that Malia had left him. She was also happy as hell that Landon really didn't want her back.

Epilogue

"**C**ome on London and Junior, jump!" Lennox yelled to his brother and sister.

Two-year-old Junior was the first to run and jump in the pool, followed by his twin sister, London.

"Oh Lord, have mercy," Ella said as she held her chest.

"Calm down grandma. They've been taking swimming lessons for a year. They know what they're doing," Landon laughed as he cradled his newest addition in his arms.

Not long after the twins made a year old, he and Faryn tried for another one. They didn't have to try for long and their daughter, Lyric, was now three months old. Landon was happy that he had another daughter and they were done. He and Faryn both agreed that their family was big enough. Lyric was the last blessing that they wanted to receive in the form of children.

"I know, but I can never get used to that. They scare the hell out of me every time I see it," Ella replied.

"I think all parents should make sure their kids can swim, even if they don't have a pool," Makena spoke up.

It was her idea to send her son and her nephews to Mr. Fish's swimming school and she made sure that the twins went too. She and Landon had built-in pools, but his was way bigger than hers.

"I just signed my baby up too. We don't have a pool, but he'll be able to swim whenever we come over here," Harley spoke up.

Her son, KJ, was a year old and cute as could be. She and Kyron wanted another one, but they wanted to wait a while. They were enjoying the one that they had for now.

"He's gonna love it. The twins hate when they have to get out of the water," Faryn replied.

She and Landon had an impromptu barbecue and she invited her friend and her husband over. Harley loved when Landon put lobster tails on the grill and he had an ice chest full of them. Makena picked Ella up and she prepared all the sides to go with everything.

"Here baby, hold her while I start putting this food on the grill," Landon said while handing Faryn their daughter.

"Where are your brothers and sister, Faryn?" Ella asked her.

"My sister and Clarence are on a cruise and my brothers are supposed to be coming over. I'll just put them some food up because it'll probably be late when they do," Faryn replied.

"They better stop all that whoring around out there. These women ain't playing that mess no more. Two girls showed up to my house for Aiden, talking about they're his girlfriends. They were about to fight on my porch until I threatened to call the police. That's just why I put his ass out. I'm too old for that bullshit," Ella fussed.

"It's gon' be even worse now that he's in his own place. But, that's on him. As long as they don't bring the drama to your doorstep, I don't have nothing to say," Makena replied.

"I'm sorry that Robin moved her disgusting ass so close. I just want to be left alone sometimes. I don't need her coming over there every damn day. She got two kids and six grandkids and she's still alone. That's what she gets though. She thought she was big shit when she was living in Leroy's big house and driving his new Cadillac."

"Why didn't she just stay with Ava, so she wouldn't have to be by herself?" Faryn asked.

"Chile, Ava got her a new man now. She didn't want Robin there all the time no more," Ella noted.

"I feel bad for him already." Makena frowned.

"I don't like him. He reminds me too much of Kane. High yellow sneaky looking ass," Ella replied.

"You don't like nobody grandma," Landon said when he walked back over to them.

"Boy, please. I can spot a liar from a mile away. But, Ava is grown and that's all on her," Ella replied.

"You used to always tell me that Malia was sneaky too," Landon reminded her.

"And I was right on the money with her too. I'm happy that she got herself together now though. My babies said that she's about to be graduating from college soon," Ella said.

"Yeah, she is," Faryn confirmed.

"That's good. I'm just happy that she's doing right by my nephews," Makena said.

"That makes two of us," Landon replied.

Landon got up and started taking the food off the grill. Makena held her niece, while Faryn got the twins out of the pool to eat. Once the table was filled with the food, Landon said the grace and they all dug in soon after. Faryn sat in the chair next to husband and he pulled her closer.

"Baby number six," Harley joked when she saw them kissing.

"Nah, we're all done with babies," Landon replied as he and Faryn ate from the same plate.

Faryn giggled like a school girl every time he kissed her, as if it were their first time. She remembered thinking that they wouldn't make it to their first-year anniversary when Jo-Jo tried to kill her outside the club. Now, she was blessed that they were approaching year three.

Faryn looked around at all the love that surrounded her, and she couldn't help but smile. She didn't do bad for herself, being that she was an ex stripper born to a drug-addicted mother. For as long as she could remember, Faryn had always wanted a family. When she was younger, she dreamed of having a mother, father, and siblings under one roof, but things didn't work out that way. Faryn had a rough upbringing, but she refused to dwell on that. She'd learned a while ago that all families weren't traditional with mothers, fathers, and kids all under one roof. Looking around at everyone seated at the table, she found that to be true. Non-traditional families are what some people called it. She wasn't related to all of them by blood or through marriage, but they were her family nonetheless.

Made in the USA
San Bernardino, CA
15 November 2019

59941665R00242